Praise for FALLING AWAY

'In her description of this mundane life, and the drama bubbling beneath it, Crewe has achieved so extraordinary a leap of imagination, that even the effort of leaping is indiscernible ...The detail is wonderfully, painfully accurate'
THE SCOTSMAN

'There is much that is heartfelt in this novel and it has a passion and a fervour which are very appealing...it is at least alive with optimistic feeling'
THE LITERARY REVIEW

'Candida Crewe manages the difficult task of making ordinary lives seem fascinating and full of incident'
THE TIMES

'An interesting and unusual novel'
THE SUNDAY TELEGRAPH

'The novel engages subtly with the question of modern woman's emotional needs'
TIMES LITERARY SUPPLEMENT

'A touching novel of love in middle age'
THE GUARDIAN

FALLING AWAY

Candida Crewe

ARROW

Published by Arrow Books in 1997

1 3 5 7 9 10 8 6 4 2

Copyright © Candida Crewe 1996

The right of Candida Crewe to be identified as the author
of this work has been asserted by her in accordance
with the Copyright, Designs and Patents Act, 1988

Arrow Books Limited
20 Vauxhall Bridge Road, London SW1V 2SA

Random House Australia (Pty) Limited
16 Dalmore Drive, Scoresby, Victoria 3179, Australia

Random House New Zealand Limited
18 Poland Road, Glenfield
Auckland 10, New Zealand

Random House South Africa (Pty) Limited
Endulini, 5a Jubilee Road, Parktown 2193, South Africa

Random House UK Limited Reg. No. 954009

A CIP catalogue record for this book
is available from the British Library

Papers used by Random House UK Limited
are natural, recyclable products made from wood grown in
sustainable forests. The manufacturing processes conform to
the environmental regulations of the country of origin

ISBN 0 09 960591 0

Printed and bound in Great Britain by
Cox & Wyman Ltd, Reading, Berkshire

For Donovan

Author's Note

The establishment in this novel called Piccadilly Park is inspired by the Magdalene Laundries in Ireland, and similar institutions for 'wayward' girls in England and Scotland. Remarkably, a few of these places existed in Britain until the 1970s, perhaps even later. There are no new recruits to the Magdalenes in Ireland, but some 'girls', though no longer slave-labouring, still inhabit them and are growing old. Descriptions of the routines, rules, and punishments at Piccadilly, and details concerning living and working conditions there, are based on careful research, and telling testimonies by former inmates.

London, September 1995

Chapter One

When a blind man gains his sight after years of bleary darkness, he is startled by the look of an orange.

I was blinded, in a sense, for nearly a decade of my youth. Though I never lost my sight, I was sent to live in an institution which was a working laundry. I and my fellow 'moral defectives' had to labour every day, cleaning sheets, cleaning our bodies, cleansing our souls. Twenty-four years after having been released, I still marvel at the touch of simple things, such silly little simple things, like my own hot-water bottle.

It has a knitted cover because the warm wool feels more like human flesh than burning, bare rubber. It can't keep me warm all over as could a man, only my stomach, or my thighs, or my feet. But it's comforting enough. In my fifty-two years, I've only ever spent one night with a man. It's too long ago to remember whether or not his body was warm. Too many cold nights since.

At the laundry, hot-water bottles weren't allowed. They were a luxury, and luxuries were for sybarites. Funny, now, to think of such a practical object as immoral. Every morning when I empty it, I have to remind myself it wasn't a self-indulgent thing to have had it in my bed with me. The blowsy seaside wind denies a fug the opportunity to form in my seaside bedroom. A hot-water bottle, though I may ever wonder at its sinful feel, is common sense.

It's the early hours. My bleeper has just gone off, stab, stab, stabbing sleep. I'm feeling nausea-in-the-throat loneliness, even though I know that in under half an hour I'll be in the stifling strip-lit hospital, surrounded by colleagues, mind on the job. When one of my ladies is in labour, I'm all concentration, I have no sense of myself. It's the best of times.

I dress quickly in front of my bar-heater. Through my tights, the heat stings my shins. My gas blue uniform is inadequate against such cold. Outside, as I start the car, it groans in the dawn, and I think of Deborah, a lovely girl, and all that pain. I must hurry.

The twenty-minute journey, from my small town to the hospital in the larger town nearby, gives rise to the usual thoughts. The transformation from moral defective to midwife. Scum to saint. And in both guises, the cause the same. Babies.

Bun in the oven at nineteen, very much not the thing. I was from a respectable, church-going family. Our home was all crocheting and antimacassars and *South Pacific* songs on the upright piano. Sherry trifle was just a little bit risqué, because of the sherry. My father, the village ironmonger and haberdasher, wore a coat for work like a doctor's, only beige, not white. He was on the parish council. The sole purpose of women's existence, he believed, was to marry, and 'do' for men. Whenever my two sisters or I took a male friend home for tea, he would turn on the gramophone loudly to play the Wedding March.

When I more than 'did' for Alf Whittaker, things came to a not so pretty pass. I went quietly. The regulation grey blanket with its conspicuous red stitching – a haberdasher's daughter, I had learned to notice such things – was wrapped round me so tightly, it squeezed the womanly touch of flesh between the top of my arm and my breast so it hurt.

I was taken far away from my Staffordshire village, to the outskirts of Glasgow. It was a vast Victorian building, the same colour as the blanket, and its very façade chilled the heart. My ladies often comment on the grimness of the hospital where I now work, formerly an army barracks complex which was put up hastily and without love during the Second World War. The main structure is a red-brick maze of corridors, all on ground level, with a flat roof, and cold metal window frames. To accompany it are some Portakabins and corrugated iron igloos which house some of the less privileged departments. But compared to the laundry asylum, architecturally speaking at any rate, St Dominic's is a positive fun-fair.

Inside, though, the smell is the same, a sort of mottled mixture of geriatric incontinence and dinner-trolley meatballs. Some mornings when I hasten through the obliging automatic doors, and my usual thoughts of the past have given way to more immediate considerations, this can catch me off-guard, and I'm catapulted straight back to the asylum. They say dustmen become so used to the stench of rubbish that, after a while, they no longer smell it. My nostrils are less forgiving, but today I'm ready for the assault.

I hang my regulation coat which scratches my neck on my hook in the staff changing room, dash straight to the labour ward, and put on my see-through plastic apron which rustles as I move. I'm taking over from my colleague who has been at it for some hours. Deborah is already in Room 10, but for all the character of this purely functional space, it could just as well be 9 or 11. I had my baby in traumatic circumstances, but at least the birth was in a friend's house. I was glad of a real bedroom, with eiderdown, mantelpiece, and curtains with marigolds and buttercups. I pity my ladies all this sterility.

I squeeze Deborah's hand. Her husband, Ryan, is in a chunky-knit jersey and thick brown trousers. Highly inappropriate. Under the ruthless lights, sweat twinkles on his bald patch. He is stroking his wife's forehead. Helpless, that's what they all do, the men. Precious little good it does, too. Deborah is howling. I am so used to it, but it still haunts me, that sound.

'Is she all right?' he asks.

While going about my business, I nod efficiently and give him a smile. Ryan's a nice one. He seems to love his wife. Of course, you never can tell. The stories in this place. Many a time and oft my ladies have rung their partners to tell them they're in labour, and these people are in the throes of amorous couplings with their little bits on the side. When I first because aware of this particularly virulent form of infidelity, I wept. Now, after years of experience in this profession, I can sniff it out as clearly as I can the nasty chemical you swill down the toilet. Those amongst them who feel as much as guilt, mostly manage to extricate themselves in time – though I do remember one who scurried into the delivery room with his flies still undone. The others, thankfully only a sordid minority, don't even bother to try to interrupt their extra-marital excesses. It is at their leisure that they later visit the postnatal ward, first to compare the newborns' features favourably with their own; second, to give the mothers of their children the benefit of some excuse which has been carelessly concocted in the hospital car park and, as one of my younger colleagues frankly puts it, is every bit as flaccid as their post-coital penises. Luckily for all concerned, the wretched women are too out of their minds with exhaustion to question them.

The baby's head is showing. Deborah's face is so stretched and contorted with agony that lines of maturity, as yet minuscule and unobserved, are forming as she writhes, and will be with her for good. Ryan is saying, 'Shhh . . . shhh . . . shhh . . . my love . . . shhh.' Being a nice one, he is feeling guilty because he sees himself as the thing responsible for his beloved's present pain. Even in their generous guilt, men are thinking of themselves.

'Is she all right?' he asks again. Her legs are open fit to snap, like a wishbone.

When the baby is born, I do the necessary, the umbilical cord, the weighing, and so forth, including telling Deborah that he is beautiful. This is not a false sentiment, like that of the funeral director who expresses his sorrow to a bereaved family he's known for all of six minutes. A birth, even when you've seen hundreds, is always moving; no infant, whatever its lurid colour, and despite the gunge, is ugly. I still believe that.

Ryan has tears running down his cheeks. Some men are at their best at this moment, vulnerable and emotional as at no other time, as in no other place.

I leave the couple be and go to the rest room. A junior doctor and a student midwife are drinking cups of tea in front of the Technicolor cheer of breakfast television.

'Has Debs had hers?' the student, Jane, asks me.

'Yes, all very straightforward. A boy.'

'Ah, lovely. Bless him. Cup of tea?'

'Just a quick one, thanks,' I say. 'I've to be in Room 6 in a minute. Justine might have to have a Caesar. Rob's in with her now. Then, 9 o'clock, I'm down in the antenatal clinic.'

'It's all go this morning.'

I look at Jane and briefly wonder about her: the sweet platitudes, the neat bun, the milky hands. It's hard not to think of myself at her age. While she at nineteen has a good career ahead of her in midwifery, and a boyfriend called Peter who appears to all

4

intents and purposes to be adequately sentimental, I had just a few months to go before my sweet platitudes would turn to silence, my hands to scouring pads; and I wouldn't set eyes on a man – with the exception of the van-driver, the maintenance man, and the foot-high statue of Christ in the chapel – for nine years.

It was a man and a woman who came to take me up to Glasgow. He wore a black suit and a grey expression. Miss Montgomery had pebble glasses, marbles for eyes. Beth and Jessie and I were up in our attic bedroom when they arrived. My sisters were packing my trunk, both in tears. I breathed in the cold air hoping the searing sensation in my lungs would harden my body and mind and make me cold. I thought of the floor in my father's shop which has always been no-getting-away-from-it, gratuitously, concrete. I wanted to be like that.

In the parlour, the powdery skin round my mother's chin and neck was wanting to quiver, I can see it now, but her self-possession, not the tight pearl necklace, prevented it from doing so. She was pouring tea, into our best china, for our two guests, strangers who had come to fetch her daughter away indefinitely, whose duty it was to correct her moral aberration in the way they thought fit.

Jane hands me a thick mug. The sister on duty pops her head round the door.

'Sorry, Dorothy, Rob wants you in Room 6. Looks like Justine's going to theatre. Bit of an emergency, nothing to worry about. Baby's in a little distress. All right?'

I put the tea down and hurry along the corridor. My adrenalin doesn't pump any more unless there is real danger, but it is nonetheless on stand-by. My thoughts are entirely with Justine and child. I'm going to lose myself for a while.

Back at home, I feel shattered by the bloodied hours of my day. Working in the laundry broke your back and turned your brain cells to soap suds, but you weren't dealing with people's lives. You could be silent with a sheet. You didn't have to be nice. I tell you, being nice all the time, though I like to think it comes naturally, doesn't half take it out of you. Still, it brings a better class of exhaustion.

When I arrive home, it's always the same routine. First, I substitute my rubber-soled lace-ups for fleecy slippers – I start with the luxuries from the feet upwards. Next, I put special cream on my hands so they smell of geraniums. Then it's a strong cup of tea, milk one sugar, two digestive biscuits cream cheese on top, a Radox bath temperature just so, a good thriller with any luck on the television and, if not, a book – I like Dickens – or maybe a letter to Jessie or Beth.

I suppose I'm quite particular about my time, having lost so much.

Out of work, I spend most of it on my own. So odd to have unpopulated hours of the day after years of enforced accompaniment (I wouldn't call it companionship; most of our waking hours we weren't allowed to talk). For nine years, I longed for them, yet when they became possible at last, I feared them. Now, after twenty-four years of freedom, I have come to see the state of being alone as extremely two-faced. On one side you have solitude, and on the other side, loneliness. I think I've achieved a manageable balance between the positive and the negative. Currently it stands quite well in my favour.

It's the routines that account for this. Alone, you are entirely selfish. It's the one time when being selfish is permissible. I mean, it makes sense to organise things completely to suit yourself – the slippers, the hand cream, the tea, and so forth, in that order, are a good example. It would be foolish not to. I don't know, perhaps this doesn't count as selfishness? Can you be selfish for one? It's like paranoia – is it still paranoia if it's *true* nobody likes you?

In the periods of solitude, I think, I could be like this for ever, I don't want anyone interrupting or questioning my routines and my convenient, comfy little ways. Then, a queasy of loneliness comes to unsettle me, like this morning, and the rest of my life is suddenly measured out in front of me very graphically. I see row upon row upon row, stretching out of sight, of knitted hot-water bottles and fleecy slippers; and I can't help but weep for the warmth of a man.

Tonight, though, it's OK. At the weekend, I've arranged not to be on call. Jessie's coming to visit me to get away from Derek. She's loved it here since I moved in. The one thing I promised myself in the laundry was that, when I got out, I would live by the seaside, and I would have Jessie and Beth to stay, and any children they might have. I qualified at St Dominic's and found and rented this place soon after; been here ever since. I don't care that Stoneham-on-Sea's a bit run-down, a bit dilapidated, and that the cottage, overlooking the harbour, is so tiny. When Jessie comes, she sings back at the seagulls, licks luminous pink rock, and rolls on the beach even though it's all pebbles. You wouldn't guess she was nearly forty. She's a laugh, our Jessie. She shakes me up. We'll go out, have some fun. There's more life in my sister than in a pantomime.

The antenatal clinic is crowded, as always on a Friday. You begin to think the population is made up entirely of pregnant women and so have rather a distorted picture of the world. They sit heavily on low plastic chairs, their stomachs like a small galaxy of different-sized planets. They cast melancholy, happy, hesitant eyes over each other's shapes beneath T-shirts, leggings, dungarees, dresses, and they are forced to ponder the mundanity of miracles.

Some swallow pints of water from a plastic jug so their bladders will fill up and force the foetuses into view during their scans. Some turn the pages of the ageing mother and baby magazines on display. Some stare at the mosaic on the noticeboard of busybody leaflets – all anti-smoking warnings and pro pelvic-floor exercises.

They come with mums, with partners, with children, alone.

All my years as a midwife have not dimmed my enduring fascination with women in this context, and with the men who accompany them. You see couples in the street and you may vaguely wonder why they opted for those trousers, or what they ate for their breakfast, but in here, in this dreary little waiting-room, your imaginings go all over the place.

Men and women don't talk to each other in the antenatal clinic. They might whisper stray words, might even hold hands. Even in this near-silent, clinical setting, you would not be human if you did not think of the very moments which were the cause of their presence here in the first place. This room is all about sex in other rooms.

7

Sometimes you wonder how conception took place at all. Ill-suited cheeks, limbs, hands, ankles. An obese man with a petite wife; a woman with a gnarled frown, her companion with a sporting, noble forehead; a teenager of marbly beauty with a youth, all gawkiness and misplaced testosterone. And these are just the physical disparities. What of the intangible ones?

Yet they keep coming in. Although I had a baby, I was denied the right ever to be with her, so I can't equate my singular experience of sex with all this production. I fill out forms every day, I examine huge stomachs till I think there cannot *be* another variation on the female form. And all the time I marvel not at the goings on inside these stomachs, at the forming of lives, but that these lives ever got there in the first place.

I am seeing fifteen, maybe twenty, women this morning, with Rob, the senior registrar. Routine stuff: scans and general check-ups. I love it, I love being with women, whether here, in the classes, or on home visits. There's a lot of chatter and understanding, so it doesn't feel like work as I know it. The time will whiz by, I'll be home soon, and Jessie will be arriving.

Jessie and I, we're very close, we're like that, even though she was only six when I went to the laundry. She was a wicked little thing with knees as knobbly as a horse's, and had a provocative gait from the moment she could stand. Father called her the Sprat. She's been divorced four years, and lives in a village up north with the three kids. She's always wanted to be a hairdresser, and now runs a very successful salon in Stoke-on-Trent called Snips. Her boyfriend, Derek, has a business which makes mugs with people's names on in swirly writing. He wears expensive knee-length coats and she jokes that, if he could have sex with his company car, he probably would. As it is, he flirts with women every bit as vulgar – Sandras, and Sadies, and Susans – all of whom seem to favour fake leopardskin jackets and have crotchless-knicker morals to match.

She's had a bad time with men, our Jessie. She says, 'Look at me, Dotty, I'd be better off without.' Then she looks at me and I can see her thinking: perhaps not, better a bastard, even if he is less than nothing, than nothing at all. In my lonely times, I feel she has

8

a point. Then I find solitude again, and just about manage to regain my sense.

In my bedroom, I unclip my wide elasticated belt, step out of my uniform, and sniff my forearm. I'm sure I smell of hospital. It's a constant fear of mine. I spread my geranium cream up to my elbows, put on a skirt and go to make up Jessie's bed, which is not something I relish doing. Unlike almost everyone else in this world, I hate clean sheets. I've got a little phobia about them, as you can imagine.

Pushing the pillows into their newly laundered cases with haste and unease, I hear from downstairs the thud-knocks on the door and Jessie's voice outside – 'Dotty, Dotty, Dor-o-thy, it's me, me-ee!' She never was much of a one for patience. This is due less to a spoilt temperament than to a natural enthusiasm, exuberance, and desire to get on with the fun as quickly as possible.

I go down, open the door, and let in her extravagant embraces. I am enveloped in the silky sleeves of her mandarin shirt and a flourish of expensive, celebrity-endorsed perfume. We draw back apart, though arms still intact, to study each other's faces. She has an aubergine eye.

'Silly me, I bumped into a street lamp,' she explains, reading me even before I have time to gasp.

'Derek?'

'Granted, a street-lamp that wears grey lizard loafers and bears a passing resemblance to a bloke we know in the personalised mug business, but let's not talk about that. How are you, ducks? How's the baby business?'

'Oh, Jessie, what's he done to you this time?'

'Tell you what, Dotty,' she says, shimmying into the lounge, 'I could do with a drink, I fancy a wine, then I promise I'll gurn some. But first I want to hear about you.'

She sits down in the armchair and crosses her legs so the mid-blue jeans lose track of their well-ironed creases. She kicks off her high-heels to reveal pretty bare feet with frost-pink-painted toenails. Many a man has marvelled at the delicacy of those feet, said their owner should have been a ballerina. Pity such idle admiration amounts only to bed. I hand her a glass of white wine from a box, and she coos winningly with gratitude.

'I've brought you a present,' she says, reaching for her sugar pink leatherette overnight bag which has lots of useful zips and a logo on it saying HEAD. She takes a package from it. 'It's exactly twenty-four years next Wednesday you got out. I think we should celebrate. Bottle of champers. I thought we could have it tomorrow night.'

Jessie is determined never to let go of such anniversaries, and I appreciate that. While my parents and Beth don't talk about the past, let alone the laundry, she does so, doggedly. She took my imprisonment very badly. As a child she mourned my disappearance like a bereavement. All her hair fell out so she was bald from the ages of six to eight, a fact never mentioned in the family home at the time, or since. Only she does, occasionally. Trust me, eh, she says, bald two years, and all I want to be's a hairdresser. I don't think she will ever forgive my mother and father, now in their dotage, for what she terms their ultimate betrayal of their eldest daughter. Even now she carries the injustice of what happened to me as a burden far harder to endure than any venomous divorce she has experienced, any psychological cruelty by numerous past lovers, any amount of violent blows by the ex-amateur boxer with whom she now (misguidedly) shares her life.

She urges me to rant and rave, to hate, to seek revenge; to find my daughter. It is a curious response, especially when she treats injustices in her own life always with such mulled resignation.

The indigation I feel about what happened to me is less outwardly energetic. It never ends, it burns low throughout winter, throughout summer, like an Aga, but it never fires.

Often Jessie says, not joking: 'Why do you *speak* to Father after what he did, let alone love him? I would strangle him, slowly, with one of your beautifully ironed sheets.'

Often she says, also serious: 'Why don't you find Eliza, let her know who her real mum is after all these years, get to know your own daughter?'

Always I talk of letting bygones be bygones, but she doesn't hear. Perhaps she would if I told her what really made me angry; that the men in her life are the ones at whom I'd like to air my most violent inclinations.

'I will never forget the evening in November 1970,' Jessie is saying as she sips at her wine with the daintiness of a doily. 'You appearing at the door at home, just like that, out of the blue after all them years, still wearing that horrible uniform. For all your letters, I couldn't believe, and still can't, that such a place ever had the audacity to exist.' Even her severely bruised eye manages to narrow in disgust.

Such a place of which she talks existed for the containment of women – deaf women; dumb women; blind women; tumorous women; physically deformed women; ugly women; obese women; neurotic women; stultiloquent women; idiosyncratic women; abandoned women; alcoholic women; penniless women; thieving women; violent women; psychotic women; schizophrenic women; insane women; feeble-minded women; morally defective women; spinster women.

Piccadilly Park was an asylum established in the 1870s, built by priggish and cruel Victorians, as were many of its counterparts throughout the British Isles, as a means to rid society of its less amenable female members without actively killing them (though, of course, many did die while incarcerated, directly as a result of their treatment). Submission was achieved through hard labour, beatings, solitary confinement, starvation, straitjackets, and later, drugs and electric shock treatment and a combination of all of the above.

Those of us at Piccadilly who were in a fit state to work did so in the specially designed basement of the building which was a laundry. We worked down there, ate on the ground floor, slept on the first, and were kept separate from the obviously incapable or insane at the top so as not to catch and be corrupted by their indolent, useless ways. But, upstairs, downstairs, it didn't really make much odds. We were all treated with inhumane contempt.

Yet this was not in Victorian times, not in wartime, not even in Elvis Presley time. I arrived at Piccadilly Park in 1961, when Kennedy was walking about, as yet unassassinated, symbolising hope for a new and better world. This new and better world, if it had crossed the Atlantic in the form of liberating fashions, drugs, music, and hippie love and had begun to make London swing, had not yet come to the Black Country whence I was removed, nor had it made it to the suburbs of Glasgow, to the unloving, peaceless place to which I was taken.

Chapter Two

Jessie and I polished off the box of wine, no holds barred. When we're together we like to have a few wines. I don't drink much, except at the team midwives' Christmas party, and with my sister. Obviously, I never got into the swing of alcohol when I was younger, and my temperate habits have pretty well stuck. It's not that I don't like the effects of drink. I do, it's just that my palate's unused to it, like a child's, so I don't much care for the taste. This would seem one of the less significant legacies of the laundry. Some would even say I was lucky. But, oddly enough, though no one would guess, and I wouldn't tend to tell people because they'd think I was stupid, it remains one of the things which rankles badly. I feel, having been denied the chance in my youth to learn to appreciate alcohol, I have missed out on one of life's great pleasures.

Jessie likes a pub. Our house was as good as dry – my father thought it was 'inelegant' for women to drink more than a small sherry on Sundays after church. So, according to the letters she wrote me during her early teens, there she was, escaping to the local most evenings to get a few down her neck between homework and bedtime. Always vodka, so her breath wouldn't smell. Occasionally, when she threw caution to the wind, it would be gin, and whenever our father detected it on her, all hell would break loose. He once had a go at her with one of the mops from his blessed shop. Not a violent man, he didn't hit her with it. No, he just gently squeezed the spongy fronds into her face as if her face were a bucket.

Gin still smacks of the illicit for her. When she comes to stay, after we've had our meal, we usually go down to the Crown, and that's what she'll order. It's a sort of up yours to our dad, and I join her in that, I have one too.

The Crown is packed out tonight, which is just as Jessie likes it. She says she enjoys checking out the local talent – on my behalf, of course. I tell her Stoneham's hardly rich with bachelors on the prowl for lifelong commitment to a middle-aged midwife and, besides, I personally am past such girlish pursuits, so she needn't bother for me.

I've got a lot to learn, apparently. 'Look,' she says pragmatically, 'you have to start somewhere, and the Crown's as good a place as any. Remember, I met Derek in a pub.'

I give her the raised 'and-look-where-that-got-you' eyebrow.

'Ah, no,' she says, 'he can be a sweetheart. He's good with the kids.'

I was in on the births of her (and her ex-husband John's) kids – Samantha, Tim, and Natalie. As a midwife, you do get to know the mums on your caseload quite well. This means that of the hundreds of births you see, every one is joyous because each, after all, is a new life, and born to someone you know – and, more often than not, really like. But your sister's labours, well, they're a bit special. I'm ashamed to say that sometimes when you bump into mums in the street with the babies you delivered just a few months before, you can get muddled, not remember their names and occasionally not even the sex of the little ones. Yet you continue to love and care for your sister's children. (And you continue, thirty-three years later, to love and miss your own.)

We're sitting on the velour banquettes and the smoke is smarting inside my nostrils, but it's good being here in the pub with Jessie. When I ask after the children, she smiles that smile of soft motherliness which I can and can't smile. I envy her her knowledge of her children: their faces, their voices, their disappointments, their worries, their laughter. While I have knowledge of my daughter, that is all I have, knowledge of her existence, no more than that. I'm technically a mother, but I have none of the detailed love, the love close-up, so I wonder if I *really* am?

Jessie is squeezing my hand as she tells me about Samantha's first day at her new school. My sister knows I want to know all about it, but also knows it pains me somewhere deep within.

'She was so nervous,' Jessie is saying, 'she was literally sick before we left. In Sam's terms, her childhood worries are every bit as worrying to her as our adult ones are to us. I just wished I could have taken it all away so she didn't have to feel a thing. I'd rather have the pain myself.'

Such are the concerns of motherhood. I suppose I was a mother, of sorts, for three weeks. My child and I were hidden away in my parents' house, not allowed to go out for shame. Whichever room we were in, all curtains had to be closed. The last illegitimate child in our street, born just five years earlier than Eliza, had been put in a box and drowned by its mother in the river. Loose women, such as my unimaginably wretched predecessor and myself, had two choices really – that of 'correction' in an asylum, or of murdering our little bastards. I can only think my desperation cannot have matched hers, because at no point did I so much as consider that I could kill. I'd rather have suffered myself for eternity.

While waiting to go to the laundry, and while a couple was being found who could adopt my daughter, my parents dictated to me in every way. I was not allowed to pick Eliza up if she cried because, my mother decreed, it would spoil her – 'Babies must learn manners, and not to think only of themselves' – and it would ruin me – 'We can't have you getting sentimental.' But hearing the baby cry would dagger and twist my heart. No amount of ludicrous jurisdiction meted out by my parents could stop me loving her. It was unconditional.

The day before the grey Children's Welfare Officer and his secretary, Miss Montgomery, came to take me up to Scotland, an elderly couple and some similar kind of official came to collect Eliza. I was not hysterical. Part of me believes my mother was a wee bit disappointed I didn't go in for the histrionics she was expecting. She always enjoyed a drama. I sometimes think that that was the reason she colluded with my father in the plot to have me sent to the laundry. She cannot really have been convinced that her child had committed an abominable sin and that the only appropriate punishment was confinement and hard labour for nearly a decade.

My mother behaved with any visitors as if she were the hostess of a suburban cocktail party, whether they were coming to take away her grandchild (though Eliza was never acknowledged as such), or not. Smartly dressed sandwiches with parsley bow-ties, and home-made ginger cake as dark as shoe polish, were laid out two hours before the arrival (a performance which was to be repeated the following day).

Such compassion as Mother allowed to surface meant I was permitted, in my room and unaccompanied, to give three-week-old Eliza her last ever feed by her rightful mother. While doing so, I heard lowered voices at the front door. I looked out of my window and saw the threesome on the stoop waiting to be let in. She was wearing a yellow coat and matching handbag and, even though I was three floors up, I could see that her shoes were misshapen by bunions. Her hair was enhanced auburn. I couldn't see the face. The two men – which was to be Eliza's father? – both in their forties, looked undistinguished but decent types. One had the sort of hair which is a thin haze round the head, seemingly unsupported by underlying layers. The other had a face which appeared to smile even without his lips in a curve. I liked him. I thought, I hope he is the one.

Eliza and I had forty-seven minutes alone together. Three-quarters of an hour! What are you supposed to do with your child when you have your last forty-seven minutes with her ever? I mean, in the normal course of things, you cradle and feed and stroke and coo at your baby. But what can you do that's so different from the usual to mark the significance of terrible, crucifying, final moments? Parting lovers have the luxury of several options. At least both parties can exchange everlasting words and promises, can make love with all the exertion and passion fitting to the occasion, shed tears in each other's arms. But mothers are not supposed to be wrenched from their newborns, so there's no conventional behaviour set for them when this happens, and they are dogged by the limitations. I could have hugged Eliza tighter and tighter, but to hug her as tight as the urgency of the situation called for would have been to hurt her, to hug the life out of her. I could have told her how much I loved her, and that I would for ever, but she was far too young to understand any words. All I could do was to cradle on, to stroke, and to coo too, but to try to do so in a way so's I would never be able to forget what it felt like to have the weight of her wee body in my arms, to feel that flesh soft as junket against my cheek, to hear the quick new breaths. I wanted to store these sensations in me, so that in the future I could conjure them up as good as real whenever I wanted. I knew that as every day passed without her, even if I succeeded, she would be growing all the while, and my memories could never catch up. It was like when a child blows a soapy bubble though a little plastic hoop and tries to catch hold of it with his fingertips and keep it steady as long as possible, but all the while he knows any second it's going to pop.

I had nothing more tangible to cling to. Nevertheless, as the minutes ticked by, I tried to tattoo these soon-to-be-dated sensations on to my brain. I didn't know if I'd imprinted them securely enough when I heard my father's step untimely tapping up the lino stairs towards me. He knocked on the door, ever courteous, but then blew it by striding straight through, before I'd a chance to say my 'Come in.'

I was sitting on the bed. Her hand was gripping my thumb as if for dear life. I stroked her forehead with my lips, and kissed her. While old people smell all sickly of damp between the legs, decay and impending death, she smelt new and pink and young and full of life as strawberries and clouds.

Careful not to drop her, Father relieved my arms of Eliza as if taking a paint pot down from one of the shelves in his shop. Then out came, on cue, his usual, 'Right-io.' A thread of the baby's white shawl caught round one of the buttons on his jacket. His fingers, used to dealing in planks of wood, metal buckets, and rolls of sandpaper – my mother used to look after the haberdashery side – were not equipped to tend to such miniatures. I unhooked it.

My brain is like a pincushion, clustered, from those moments, with such pins of detail.

He looked at me, ever so fleetingly, ever so hesitantly, before he took her through the door, down and away. His lined complexion, closely shaven, was white, white but brimming bluish with dark bristles just beneath the surface. His eyes had a gluey quality, faintly troubled, I had a fancy.

Was it naughty of me? I smiled at him. A real corker of a smile, making sure that my eyes sparkled with it so it was an all-over smile. A much better way of making the guilt in him unbearable, I hoped, than if I had made to cry. I didn't want to cry. I was beyond that. I'd moved on to silence.

When he had gone out of the room with her, shut the door, I rolled over on my stomach, and I read a book. As the four of them left there was a flurry of goodbyes outside, but I didn't look out from my window again.

Jessie sets me off, thinking about such things, though never on purpose. What she's brilliant at is recognising the nature of my pensiveness and either quickly deflecting the mind, or talking about it straight up.

'Right,' she might say, 'are you thinking about the day they took Eliza away, or the day they took you away? So shall we talk about that, or about frivolous things?'

Tonight, in the pub, two or three gins down me, of course I say, 'Frivolous things.'

So that's what we do. Jessie should have been a stand-up comic. She cracks me up with her stories – tales of Derek's thwarted attempts at romance (a single red rose last Valentine's Day which somehow smelt of fish – 'Only Derek!'); her clients who come in with boot faces and cauliflower bottoms demanding, with the snip of a scissor, the whiff of a blow-dryer, to be transformed into fabulous film stars. I love it when our Jessie gets going. The fellahs watching the sports channel on the telly above the bar give us friendly looks of pleasure. They are enjoying our merriment. My face is blotchy with laughter.

We tipsy back home after last orders. Tomorrow, if we want, we can talk about serious things.

At breakfast, it's funny to hear the crunch of somebody else's toast and marmalade. I like it, it makes me feel alive.

'Can we walk round the town a bit and along the beach?' Jessie asks, sipping her coffee. 'The place looks as though it's changed a lot, even since I was last here.'

'We'll go by the front,' I say, 'so I can deliver some tins of beans to Miss Watson and Ted Tiffin.'

'God, are they still alive? They must be a hundred. I wonder if they'll remember me.'

'I expect so. They're sharp old dears.'

It's a blowsy old day. I put on my dark green duffle while Jessie takes down, from one of the hooks at the bottom of the stairs, something altogether more elegant, a pale mac with a yolk of pleats at the back and leather-trim collar and cuffs. She will cut a fancy figure in our high street. Stoneham-on-Sea is a dilapidated town geared to B&B bucket-and-spade holidaymakers, and the plethora of pensioners who live in the 1930s pebbledash bungalows at the back of the town or in the Edwardian buildings on the front. T-shirts or patterned jumpers and floral man-made fibres are the more usual fare.

We walk to the high street arm in arm. Jessie stops at souvenir shops and looks at postcards so garish their scenes are unfamiliar even to me. A booth is selling pale mint ice-cream, even though it's November, and we shiver at the thought. We pass White's, the department store, once a town glory, now innocent of quality goods, old-fashioned service, and customers.

'That's new,' says Jessie, pointing at Raffles, the wine bar which opened last month with its nice line, not in fish and chips, but in kidney bean salads and goat's cheese in filo parcels.

'We could go there later for lunch if you like.'

We wander down by the Countryside Centre which we visit when the children are here with Jessie. It has little grottoes with seaside scenes – mannequin fishermen pulling nets of papier mâché fish across painted floor waves, the recorded sounds of seagulls. This, Raffles, and Virtual Reality World by the roundabout, are all part of Stoneham's latest attempts to become a more modern resort now that the Chinese take-away family have been driven away by racist taunts, and the ageing mini-fairground by the little harbour no longer appeals.

We reach the front, which is all guest-houses, B&Bs, and old people's homes with façades flaking cream and pastel blue. Its green is decorated with municipal flowers, uniform pansies, in pastry-cut beds. To one side of them is a dog-fouling sand-pit which we skirt around. We approach the first house in the row which is where Priscilla Watson and Ted Tiffin live. Completely exposed to the wind on one side, its paintwork is cracking up even more than the others. It looks run-down. Though blessed with

19

Stoneham's loveliest view, is not the town's best old people's home by any stretch.

We ring on the doorbell, and a woman in a nurse's uniform answers. This inspires a certain confidence in the visitor which I know from coming here twice a week for some years is misplaced. The staff try, and their hearts are in the right places, but they are pretty incompetent. I like to come and do what I can for one or two of the old dears. It's the community spirit in me which sometimes I wish I didn't have. I spend my working hours doing my bit. Would that I could relax in my time off, guilt-free like other people, but no, I've got to be helping out. Call it what you will – a social conscience or whatever – it can be a right royal pain in the arse. I can't give it up, though.

The nurse, Maureen, says hello. 'Nice to see you, Dorothy. And this is?'

'Jessie Burford, my sister.'

'Come to see Ted and Priscilla, have you?' she asks her, giving a nursely smile. 'I think he's in the front lounge. She's in her room. She's feeling a bit poorly at the moment, Dorothy. Her nephew's up with her.' She lowers her voice to a whisper. 'Between you and me, I think we might have overdone the ice-cream dessert last night and our stomach's not really up to it. We've got a little pain, but it's nothing to worry about.'

I thank her and put my head round the door on the right. Ted Tiffin who is in his eighty-ninth year is sitting on a low armchair of an olive green and yellow rose print, very faded. He and four others, all in tartan cartoon slippers, are slacked in front of an enormous television, drinking tea which you can smell has been practically caramelised by milk and sugar. The exaggerated knobbles of their fingers make it difficult for them to hold their cups. They try to bend them but the handles prove too narrow to be got through, too spindly to clasp. Every time I come here I notice this sort of detailed struggle to which old age subjects them, and am moved to melancholy.

Ted, spotting me, makes to rise from his seat, but I indicate with my hand that he shouldn't. He's watching the football, one of the things which gives him great pleasure. I don't like to disturb him.

'I've brought you some beans today,' I mouth. 'I'll leave them

20

in your room.' Ted looks torn. I reassure him. 'Never you mind, I'll be back Monday, and then we'll have all the more to catch up on.'

He smiles with his crumpled face, relieved, and blows me a kiss. I am so used to dealing with new lives, it is levelling to tend to the old.

Jessie follows me upstairs to Priscilla Watson's room. The dreary corridors, papered with magnolia bobbles, are stinking warm.

'If I'd thought about it,' whispers Jessie as we walk along the swirling red and grey carpet, 'I'd have known we'd be coming here and would've brought her one of Derek's mugs with her name on, and birds and flowers and that. I feel bad arriving empty-handed.'

'Don't you worry, she's got enough mugs. What she likes is visitors.'

I knock on the mock wooden door. It is hollow and makes a great sound.

'It's only me,' I say through the keyhole, 'Dorothy, come with my sister Jessie.'

'Oh, come in, love.'

I open the door gently as if haste and noise will somehow further affect her troubled stomach. The pale pink room is small. It has a window overlooking the tarmac back yard, and a wooden wardrobe. A low dressing table made of white Formica has silver-inlaid handles on the little drawers. It reminds me of Sindy Doll furniture. In front of its three-sided mirror are a modest selection of make-up things which only old ladies have – Yardley talcum powder, for example, in a turquoise bottle with a gold top.

Priscilla is buffed up by pillows supported against a buttoned bed-head. Even beneath the candlewick counterpane, her legs look thin. She is in her late eighties. He face has little veins webbing her complexion like the legs of money spiders; her lips are purple glossy not with lipstick, but with spit, and remind me of a newborn's. She is wearing a white nightdress and a soft woollen bed-jacket of baby-girl pink. I have enormous affection for this woman who, though physically burdened, mentally speaking has all her marbles, and more besides. She is no relation, just a friend. Still, it'll have me in bits when she dies.

'Do you remember Jessie? She was here the last time she came to stay with me.'

'About eight months ago? I remember. Of course. How are you, dear? Last time you brought the children.'

'That's right,' says Jessie. 'Are you well, Miss Watson?'

'Priscilla to you, love, for goodness' sake. I'm a little bit poorly, but it's nothing. It comes of over-indulging in last night's sweet. Serve me right. An old lady like me shouldn't be eating ice-cream like a child! The system rebels.'

'We've brought you some beans.' I place the tins on her dressing table. 'I'll get Maureen to take them away for you and store them in the kitchen, so they'll be there whenever you want them.'

'Oh, thank you, that's kind. Did you see my nephew? He's brought me some flowers, gone to find a vase. I thought you might have caught him on the stairs.'

'Is that Mr Mills,' I ask.

'The very one.' Priscilla turns to Jessie. 'Harold works in the cake factory on the outside of town, in "quality control". That's a fancy way of saying he's the one who gets to taste them all day long. I tell you, they're gorgeous, lovely. They make all sorts – apple tarts, mince pies, the lot. He's a pet. He brings me all these jam tarts because he knows they're my favourite. I'm spoilt, I got six boxes of six today!'

'I always say she's going to turn into one if she's not careful. He brings her so many, honest, he's like Father Christmas.'

'How often does he visit?' Jessie asks.

'He comes here as often as he can,' Priscilla tells her. 'He only lives down the road, but it's sometimes difficult because he works odd shifts and he's got the dog to look after. He's a good lad. You've bumped into him once or twice, haven't you, Dorothy? It's funny you haven't met him more often, the amount you come here. Jessie, she looks after me well and proper, I assure you. I'm a lucky woman. There's some in here don't get as much attention from their own families as I do from Dorothy. Breaks your heart.'

We hear a knock on the door, and I let Mr Mills in. He looks a little younger than his fifty-nine years. I think it has something to do with the blooming pallor he has acquired from taking his beloved dog for so many walks, and his closely shaven chin. He has thick glasses which slightly distort but do not detract from the friendliness of his face. The collar of his Viyella shirt is worn, and the pattern of his tie is raining cats and dogs. He is holding a cut-glass vase of giant daisies.

'Miss Sheffield!' he says, putting it on the dressing table and taking my hand in both of his. 'What a nice surprise.'

I introduce Harold Mills to Jessie. He says, 'Call me Harold, for goodness' sake. Can I get either of you anything?' He seems slightly thwarted in his chivalry when we refuse tea, coffee, squash, biscuits, everything. 'A jam tart?' he asks in desperation. 'I'm sure Aunt Priscilla wouldn't mind.' He opens the wardrobe to reveal a little stash of the Technicolored boxes he has brought her. Jessie and I laugh at the amount.

Harold undoes a box, pulls out its red plastic tray. The jam in the real-life tarts doesn't much resemble that in the illustration which somehow manages to sparkle like fairy lights. Marketing man's licence.

Both Jessie and I decline politely.

'There's plenty here,' says Harold, before putting them back in the wardrobe. 'I keep telling her that she should keep them downstairs or she'll get mice, but she won't have it. She likes to have them near her for visitors and midnight feasts.'

'I like a mouse. Anyway, that Ted Tiffin would have the lot if I left them in the kitchen. Better to keep them here so at least I can ration him when he drops by my room.'

We talk on for half an hour or so, and then make to go off for our walk on the beach before lunch. Jessie asks Harold if he'd like to join us. He would like to join us, he says, very much, but unfortunately he has to get back to his dog.

'We're going to the new wine bar,' Jessie tells him 'Are you sure we can't persuade you?'

He is very courteous, and says no. A while later, on the beach, Jessie asks about Harold. All I know is that he's lived all his life in Stoneham-on-Sea. His father, Priscilla's brother, died within a year of his mother, about twenty years ago. He still talks about them both, shows photographs. Harold never married, never left home. He loves his dog called Jones, his job, and his car which is nearly thirty years old but remains as good as new because it barely ever ventures outside its garage.

'Priscilla says his car exists just to be cleaned,' I report. 'In winter he has a heater on in the garage to keep it warm!'

'I think he'd have liked to join us for lunch,' Jessie says, watching me. Then she runs ahead, footsteps crunching on the pebbles and, head thrown right back, starts singing at seagulls.

You hear some stories from the women. Women talking, telling their tales, is part of the job. Quite often their personal testimonies attest to such bleakness as it's hard to listen. You wonder at their resilience and dignity in the face of the untenable physical and emotional upheavals which assault them.

There's the woman has a ten-pounder inside her, and who in labour splits open like an over-ripe tomato. There's the woman who after five miscarriages finally gives birth to a healthy baby which three days later dies a cot death, no explanation. There's the woman who's giving birth without her husband present because he begged her for a baby, then got her and another woman pregnant at the same time, then begged his wife for an abortion, and then left her when she refused because he wants the other woman, and the other woman's baby. What impresses me is that they talk about all this with admirable equanimity, courage. It happened to them. So. Trials are in the nature of things.

I hear it close-to and feel glad to have opted out, not to be positioned for like trauma. I am not part of the shrill, metallic tingle of life, and what is left is bland, but calm.

Then, as in Raffles at lunchtime, Jessie gets going about her love, serious things, and because she's my sister I become aware of a sort of vicarious tingle, literally, around the string of my tongue. While I feel compassion and affection for the women I look after, with them I don't get quite this.

'Whenever I see Derek,' she says, 'my stomach flips over! Still. Even though it's been over three years we're together.'

Derek's got this extra woman called Carla at the moment.

Jessie's best friend is called Lulu. Carla is Lulu's sister, so he's arranged it nice and neat.

Jessie shows remarkable stoicism when she relates the circumstances. She sees them very clearly. She loves him: she will hold out for him.

'I know you don't much care for Derek,' she says, sipping a glass of red wine, 'but you only get to hear about the bad. The good is just life going on as normal, the everyday, the contentment I feel with him. It's hard to explain because it's so ordinary.'

Other people's arrangements, relationships, marriages, are always a puzzle. You only see into them through a keyhole. There are vast spaces which will always remain out of view. You can speculate as to what's in them, but you're invariably wrong and out of tune. Couples, perplexing enough to each other, are an impenetrable mystery to their family and friends, the rest of the world.

Through Jessie's and Derek's keyhole, I see infidelity, deceit, conflict. He beats her up, sometimes isn't even cunning enough to avoid her face, and I see the black eye. What I don't see are the little things – because they are unique to Jessie's vision of him, and stay private. But it is these which add up to the sum of her loving him. I wonder what they could be? I don't know. They're different for everyone. But if I loved a man, I know those things would be every bit as important as the big swathes, the full-on characteristics running through him. I can't say for sure, but for me they might be his attempt, when helping to make the bed, at a hospital corner; could be his enthusiastic recommendation of a book or film he knows I'd love; perhaps the unconsciously erotic tilt of his cigarette.

It's hard for an outsider to understand. Derek's got the looks, the car, the penis (that's one private part Jessie has chosen to make public). Perhaps, when brushing his teeth in the morning, when tying his pyjama cord, he has humanity. Perhaps she loves him because he stands for everything Father most abhorred, and even I am in love with him for that. He is vulgar and noisy and enjoys a bad joke. Admit it myself, I can't believe I'm saying this, he does have a sort of charm, a characteristic of which Mother and Father were always suspicious. To them, the first was necessarily fraudulent, the second invariably vain and self-seeking. Who's to say if that's the case with Derek? Jessie says he gives a lot of time to her children, reading to them, playing board games, showing them round the mug factory.

'They adore him,' she says. 'There's not many men would take on a divorced woman with three kids.'

Although it is bright outside, it is quite dark in the wine bar. It could almost be night time, which I suppose is the effect they're after. Jessie and I are sitting in the corner at one of the black tables. It's only 12.15 so not many people have yet arrived. The atmosphere seems to call for intimate conversation. We talk quietly.

'Christ, if I left him, who'd have me? No, I will not let that girl take him away from me.'

'You don't want to be on your own.'

'You know, Dotty, the other day I thought, "Right, Jessie, you gotta make a decision." So I took a piece of paper – you're going to think I'm mad – and at the top I wrote "Pros and Cons" and, beneath, two lists. Well, course, the Cons went right down to the bottom and it was serious case of Please Turn Over. Right big Cons they were too. He beats me up, he disappears for two or three days at a time without telling me, he sleeps with other women, he's not into marriage, you name it. As for the Pros, well, I admit, they didn't come to much, but the thing was, the Pros was the column that had, "I love him", in it, and, rightly or wrongly, those three little words wiped out every Con in the book. It may not be rational, but that's how it is.'

'I suppose it makes sense,' I say, because I think I understand. It's hard to imagine tolerating his behaviour. It would seem to negate the very point of being with someone. So intellectually I don't approve, but that vicarious little tingle, it's there, pulsing with a dim sort of life, and I find myself – hate myself – thinking that, however agonising, at least it's a *frisson*. And we all tolerate different things. In my time, I've had my fair share of things I've tolerated such as others wouldn't have dreamt of putting up with. Maybe Jessie, however hungry, would never have raided the bins for the leftover food from the staff quarters which was chucked out for the pigs. Maybe, had she been in my position, she would never have allowed herself to have been sent somewhere like Piccadilly Park in the first place. I think my character came to be more one of tacit resignation. I properly rebelled only after years of suffering, whereas she'd have done so at the very prospect of that suffering, and I admire her for that. Would that I could have taken a leaf out of her book, then my life might've been different. What she'd have done was to challenge our parents, to shame them out of their decision and, if that hadn't worked, she'd have fought them with all her might. One thing I do believe is Jessie would not have wound up in the laundry like me. So it's all the more puzzling her aberration when it comes to men.

'He's in a muddle,' she says. 'It's best not to interfere, then this thing with him and Carla will burn itself out. As long as he doesn't lie to me.'

'As long as he doesn't lie to you – what?' I ask.

Jessie pours herself a second glass of wine and smiles. 'I don't know, I'd prefer him to sort it out in his own time, I really don't know.'

'He does lie to you, but.'

'Yes, only till I find out, though, then he admits. At least, in the face of scorching evidence, he doesn't go on denying it like I was stupid. Some men would.'

'That's something.'

'Though, when I went round her house at one in the morning and caught him literally going down the drainpipe at the back, he did have the nerve to say he was just round doing a spot of DIY. Honest, I'm not joking you. The whole thing was such a bloody cliché. You can only laugh.'

'How did you know he was having an affair with her?'

'Well, Lulu hadn't come out with it outright, but she'd been giving me these kind of hints. She's on my side, not her sister's. Apparently Carla went right up to him at Lulu's party and offered, just like that, to model her torso for a new novelty mug she thought he might like to manufacture. Ruddy cheek. If I'd been anywhere near within hearing distance, I'd I've lynched her. I can't believe there are women like that, so brazen. I thought we were meant to be in this together, supporting each other. Whatever happened to sisterhood and all that? I suppose it's not surprising. Carla always was a right little slag, and he likes that. She was doing Mrs Braithwaite's husband when she was fourteen, and never has stopped screwing other women's property ever since. That's how she gets her kicks. Bitch.'

As Jessie speaks, she lights one of her long menthol cigarettes which has a shiny gold band round the filter. Her very puffs are indignant.

'She's the one should be getting the shiners, not me.'

'Why do you get them?'

'Agh, it's nothing to worry about. He just gets a bit pissed. The way I look at it, you can't have it all ways. It's the price I pay for good sex.'

'Quite a high one.'

'Oh, not really, what's a wee black eye every now and then? Of course, if he laid so much as a finger on any of the kids, that'd be a different story. The four of us would have him out of there before you could say knife.'

'So he hasn't yet?'

'No, and he won't neither, because he knows then there'd be trouble. Deep down in the mists of his drunkenness, some commonsense decency somehow prevails. He knows if he ever touches the kids, ever . . .'

Distress, like turpentine, thins her voice.

'It's a pity his commonsense decency doesn't somehow prevail when it comes to fidelity,' I observe.

Jessie bites her lip. 'You can be very unforgiving.'

'Yes.'

'Maybe if Alf Whittaker had been sent to an institution like you, you'd feel less resentful.'

'Possibly. I'm no good at hypotheticals. What's done's done.'

Alf Whittaker's fate was somewhat different from mine. While Jessie maintains that society's ways were to blame for the failure to punish him as I was punished, and while she gears all her resentment towards our parents, the fact that Alf got off spotless is something I can't quite budge from my mind. Everyone knew he was Eliza's father, but he remained free to stick with his job in the nearby Potteries, to wobble his bicycle round our village roads, to nip down the shops for a packet of custard, to chop wood for his fire with his beloved axe, to feel the ruffle of his choir uniform collar as he sang in church, to rub his white trousers with a red cricket ball during matches on the green, to know the comfort of his own bed, and the comfort of others'. He was just Alf, Alf who'd got a girl up the junction. For him there were no consequences.

A waitress with a pad tucked into her apron-string brings plates of salad and hard French bread to our table. For various reasons I don't wish to talk about Alf, but I can't tell Jessie that. As far as she's concerned there's nothing between us we can't discuss, and she's nearly right. Of all the things, I think Alf might rank as the exception. I can't talk to anyone about him, I haven't got the words for a soul. But I will not hurt her feelings. The food comes as a welcome diversion. We both sigh with pleasure as it's put in front of us, and I start to talk about easier things.

Chapter Three

People might think that by becoming a midwife I was rather rubbing my face in it, that by putting myself in the position of watching other mothers and babies every hour of the day and night, I was somehow wanting to bathe in my own distress. In fact, I'd started my nurse's training a good year before Eliza was conceived. As Jessie feebly jokes, I was a born midwife. Certainly, from a very young age, I knew I didn't want to go into the mops and buttons business. I always aspired to a profession. At grammar school we had a big red biology book with riveting diagrams of the inner workings of flowers and insects and men and women. One line illustration of a shapely woman showed a womb which prettily stretched and curled right across her stomach like an exotic, very relaxed sea creature. As I copied it into my exercise book and learned the function of the fallopian tubes, I thought I'd like to work with this curious organ. The teacher told me what I'd have to become – a gynaecologist or an obstetrician. The names seemed grand and out of reach. Then one day, when I was about thirteen, I was having tea round a friend's house and her mother told us about her life as a midwife. (It was six years later, in that very home, that that kindly woman delivered me of Eliza because my parents had refused to let me give birth at their's.) I'd never really understood what midwives actually did, but when she explained, I knew that it was the job for me. Well, it's hands-on, isn't it? You're there, you're dealing with the practical side of one of the most important things imaginable. I think of politicians so-called doing their bit, ruling the world from on high. In their gilded palaces, and with their photocopied sense of poverty and the way real people have to live, it's hardly grass-roots. The midwife's contribution is a modest one, but she's helping women cope with the fears and the pain, and sympathetically giving them the benefit of her knowledge and experience. So I'm not so sure that it is so modest. She's also easing the passage of a journey no more than a few inches long, but which – bugger mountains, bugger jungles, deserts, the moon – remains one of the most adventurous and hazardous ever undertaken by anyone. Eliza being wrenched away from me meant my vocation temporarily wobbled but, thank God, it never did manage to diminish my desire to play an active part in this process.

On a Monday morning after a rollicking weekend with Jessie, my bed feels like a fly-catcher, it's going to be actively painful to emerge from it. I'm here reminding myself what I'm all about, otherwise I haven't got a stowaway's hope in a laundry basket of getting out. (I find myself still slipping into expressions we used at Piccadilly. A few girls tried the laundry basket escape – myself included – but not one ever succeeded. They were discovered every time, brought back, and punished.)

I wonder if April Shaw had hers over the weekend? After my days off I'm always keen to know the news, and that's what usually forces the issue in the end, by which I mean, gets me out of bed. My curiosity keeps me going, you see. Perhaps one of the reasons I'm a midwife is because I'm just downright nosy. While carrying out my morning routine, I'm thinking of April. Is she OK? She's a lovely girl. On her own with a tale to tell. Her story isn't a parcel-bomb horror story of dispossession, abuse, and what have you. No, it's the tidy, contained little package, nothing out of the ordinary. Enclosed is everyday news of ordinary folk, it's so humble it's deadly. The jolly sailor blue and white stripes of her nightshirt belie the neat nugget of truth.

When I arrive at the hospital, I go straight to the midwives' office. I dump my bag and coat on one of the blue plastic chairs and ask after April's welfare. A colleague tells me she had a boy on Saturday night, Caesarean section, he was in the Special Care Baby Unit – or what we call Scbu – for a few hours, with a slight breathing problem, but he's out now and mother and baby are doing fine.

My shoes make squeak and-suck noises on the lino as I hasten to the postnatal ward to pay my visit. The ward is a long room, strip-light bright, with twelve beds made up of steel mechanisms, coarse sheets, and pillows so overblown they look like they harbour ambitions to be beanbags. Each bed is accompanied by a wood-look Formica bedside table. On them are cards with fluffy pink or blue drawings of coy elephants with bottles or long-lashed bunnies with bibs, all conveying their heartfelt greeting in language as sickly as formula milk, but no less sincere for that. Bottles of squash, riotous orange or ludicrous lime, tower between them. New plastic bags of disposable nappies are balanced there too, swamping half-eaten packets of milk chocolate digestives and obscuring the yellowing stems and hanging heads of the flowers all suffering from manic depression. One or two have thin wooden bowls, each with a grouping of fruit as politically correct as the next in its echnic variety. A banana, an orange, an apple, a bunch of grapes, will all swelter together inside their incubator of cellophane. These things are the permanent props on the hospital stage, as familiar to me as the actual tools of my trade – my weighing machine, my thermometer, the scanning equipment. There's not a woman without them. Even the mums with little else – no father for their child, no money, no swaddling clothes, no love – usually the teenage ones, but sometimes the older ones too – they too have these approved and telltale signs of cosy motherhood. It is not part of our brief but, we midwives, we do at least see to that.

The air has achieved the near-impossible for air, that is, airlessness. That's hospitals for you, or more specifically, maternity wards endeavouring to emulate wombs. Eleven mothers are sitting or lying on their beds in T-shirts and static nightdresses which are not long enough. The skin above their knees, live yoghurt white and curdled not with shivery but with nervy goose-pimples, are on show for all to see. At this stage in the game, the women, some only just down from the labour ward, don't give a monkey's, and who are we to judge? Visibility stretches well up the thigh in some cases. My eyes have seen it all. They no longer naturally stray as far as the padded triangle of white knicker which protects fragile, put-upon crotch. They used to, mind, when I first started. They'd be drawn in equal measure to this conspicuous cotton zone and to the baby in see-through cot. Even if I'd delivered that very child from that very woman, I still found it hard to make the link between the two: one so miraculous, the other so mundane and yet mysterious.

A few of the eleven are sleeping, their eyelids, shadowed with fatigue, heavy as breeze-blocks. Some have visitors – relations and friends – who ooh and aah with feminine softness, even the men, cowed as they are by the crêpey bundle they have come to scrutinise for beauty and brilliance, and to start to love. Their voices low with respect and awe, and it's a sound can make me weep.

The women I have known more or less one to one until now, suddenly, when I see them in the postnatal ward with their bedside families, for the first time have a world, a life, a future, quite apart from me. Up to this moment, I've called them my ladies, my mums, but here they are transformed into Jean, into Bernadette, into Felicity, and they are the wives and mothers of Toms, and Dicks and Harrys, and Tinas and Courtneys and Pollys; and in a few weeks' time, for those who have work, maternity leave will be over and they will go back to being cleaners and teachers, shop assistants and solicitors, farmers and dinner ladies. Agh, how can I any longer call them mine?

The one empty bed looks cardboard flat, unreal, forgotten, alone. It will have an occupier before the morning's out who will bring with her all the fruits of the neonatal experience. In the bed next to it I spot the reduced but familiar outline of April Shaw. She is by herself, staring into the mobile incubator beside her. It is filled with a blue light which is beaming all over the tiny figure within, doing its bit to eke away his jaundice. As I move closer I see the baby is on his stomach, his new and malleable hips enabling his legs to lie inhumanly flat open behind him, like a frog preparing to leap. A protective mask covers his eyes. As he breathes, the peach skin of his back moves like a conveyor belt over the cogs of his little spine.

For adults, it's only with the physical pain and pleasure, and with the tangible manifestations of emotion – tears, laughter – that they are confronted with the actuality of life. These are the news flashes which interrupt the scheduled programmes just rolling on throughout the day. Watching newborns is the same. The very sight of them in the delivery room sets you to musing, brings you to life as you speculate as to what lies ahead of them. It's not a case of once you've seen one baby, you've seen them all. Each one has a unique personality from the moment it's born, from before it is born. By the time you get to the postnatal ward, you're thinking about how it's going to transform the life of the family which has just shown up to welcome it. After that, in the calm which settles following the initial excitement, quickly you feel you're getting to know this person quite well, but its very size, and the conspicuous movements of its very breaths, prompts you to start to ponder your own life and, before you know it, you're thinking about life itself, and the whole damn caboodle.

'April, congratulations!' I say, and she looks up, wearily smiling, and thanks me. 'What's he called?'

'Gareth. I've known that all along. I knew he was a boy.'

'He's beautiful,' I tell her.

'I know,' she says, 'and he's all mine.'

April, who is twenty-three, is bereft of boyfriend, and father to her child. He is in Gibraltar. She was living there for two years and had a passionate affair with him. She's a photo she's shown me of him and her, standing together in front of some church. He's got a tanned arm round her, and black hairs nudging his Adam's apple, and they are smiling awkwardly at the stranger they have enlisted to take the snap. He's good-looking in that unremarkable, Latin sort of way. When she told him she was pregnant he was full of enthusiasm, forbade her even to think about having an abortion, and straight away named four godparents. Then, as her waist began to self-destruct and her stomach gradually to fill, he became repulsed by her. He began to disappear for two or three days at a time. His office was noncommittal, said he was away on business, but there was no doubt he was going with other women. A week after it was too late for her to have a termination, he left her. She scraped the money together to return home so as to have and bring up the baby alone. As I say, a normal enough sort of story, nothing grandiosely grim about it, just plain and boring, common or garden grim. But perishing upsetting just the same.

'I'm not going to ring and tell his dad, not yet anyway. I don't see he has a right to know, do you?'

'I think you should do as you think best,' I reply tactfully. The midwife's role is often mother, friend, adviser, therapist, counsellor, social worker, you name it. Our duties are never as straightforward as a few scans and internals before the event, and the odd breast-feeding and pelvic-floor tip after. Sometimes it's hard not to get involved with a woman you've cared for and grown fond of. But we have to be careful also not to interfere too much on matters not directly related to maternity. That's not really our place.

'Finally I've got a man to love me faithfully,' she says, eyes back on Gareth, fixed there. 'I reckon I can rely on about fifteen years before he finds another woman,' she adds, laughing.

'At least,' I tell her, laughing too, admiring her courage, and trying not to second-guess any problems ahead.

It's a happy and sad encounter. I have about ten of them in any working day.

Harold Mills is there at the old folks' home when I go to visit Ted and Priscilla after work. He is in her room with another delivery of jam tarts from the factory. It's odd to bump into him twice in three days. He greets me with his special warmth. I don't know why, I feel for him, by which I don't mean I pity him, I just feel very keenly that I don't want him to be unhappy. I barely know him! Sometimes, admittedly not often, particular men of a certain age do have this effect on me. It's their watery eyes, perhaps, does it, and their vulnerability. I don't know why, but I never seem to have this in the same way with elderly women. Women were always meant to be more soft and fragile than men, so I find the vulnerability in them as they grow older somehow less moving. In films, it's always the kindly old grandfather types who, when they're suffering or dying, have me crying my heart in two. In real life, it's the likes of Ted Turner and – though he's a good twenty years younger – Harold Mills. I find I want to look after them. Dear Ted, as far as he's concerned, I can't leave him alone, I'm always bringing him beans and things. I visit and do for Priscilla too, but that's a different, more simple story. She's a good friend, as is Ted, but I don't feel sorry for her in the same way.

'Dorothy, it was lovely to meet your sister,' Harold says.

'When she next comes with the children,' Priscilla tells him, 'you must bring them jam tarts too.'

Harold says but of course. His voice is imbued with sincerity. I think he's the sort who likes to give pleasure, and who couldn't give a fig about getting it for himself. He is sitting low on the white plastic dressing-table stool. He gave up the wooden and leather-ette armchair for me. I didn't want to take it from him, but I weighed things up, and I accepted. From my position beside the bed I am looking at him almost full-on, but can also see the reflection in the mirror of his back, his shoulders, his collar jutting out from beneath his thick-knit jersey. He is a big man with a pinkish neck, what's showing of it, and grey tufts of hair you want to leaf your hands through. On the wardrobe door handle hangs his jacket, nylon navy. A circular metal badge like a school prefect's is pinned to its lapel. Around the little picture of an Alsatian's profile it says THE NATIONAL CANINE CLUB.

'Harold's just been telling me about his bad day,' the old lady says. There is a knock on the door and the nursely Maureen drops off a tray with three cups of tea and a plate of biscuits – chocolate Bourbons, Nice, and custard creams. When she leaves the room, Harold passes them round and Priscilla continues. 'They've been laying people off left, right and centre, some that's been there for years. Out of the blue, just like that. In a job one day, out the next. No respect.'

'Gloomy news,' Harold says quietly, 'but I don't expect Dorothy wants to hear –'

'Why ever not?' Priscilla interrupts. 'It affects the whole town, something like that. There's enough of them's been sacked as to dampen everyone's mood. Fathers of young children! Poof! No job, no money! I have to say I think it's a scandal. Those men in Management are ruthless, ruthless. Haven't they hearts? All they think about is profit margins. They've no humanity, none whatsoever.'

'You're all right, though, Harold?' I ask.

'I should hope so,' his aunt replies. 'He's been doing that job nigh on twenty years.'

'That doesn't count for much these days,' he tells her. 'But for the time being, yes, I seem to be one of the lucky ones.'

'What will they do, those poor men?' As she speaks, Priscilla is wringing a sprig of sheet in her gnarled hands. 'There's no other jobs they're going to get. There's no other jobs full stop! Only despair. You ask yourself why on earth does this sort of thing have to happen?'

'We've been bought by a big, well-respected German company –'

'I should have guessed!'

'. . . and obviously they're wanting to fine-tune the place. We all thought everything was just so. All of us had our particular roles, did our bit, got on well, but they're coming in fresh, they want to put people on short-term contracts, and make all sorts of changes.'

'I suppose you understand that?'

'No, Aunt, I find it hard to, but they're businessmen.'

'Agh, business, business, my foot. In my book the whole lot's immoral. I don't care if they're German, it's all that woman's fault, it's all still in her spirit of each man for himself. Eleven years in power, and now everyone, down to the managers in the local cake-making factory, are treating their long-serving people like dirt. Still, even though she went long ago. It's just so's they can get more money for themselves. I hope to God they don't do you over, Harold, or else.'

'Except I rather wish they had laid me off, and not Michael. I may be the more experienced, but he works very, very well, and he's with a young family to support. I told them I was on my own, that I was nearing my retirement rightly enough anyway, and I suggested that I should go in his place, but they weren't having any of it.'

'You see, Dorothy, a heart of gold he has. Never looks out for himself. It's a wonder they didn't say yes, Harold. Thank goodness, or you would be out on your ear with the rest of them. You love your work. Whatever would you do? You wouldn't know where to put yourself?'

'Well,' he answers, clearly awkward that the conversation should so long have lingered upon matters related to himself.

'Just like Dot if she lost hers. You've heard even midwives are thinking of taking industrial action? It's come to that. Midwives! We used to call them and nurses angels, that's how we thought of them, and now with their piss-pot pay and poor security, even they're forced to act. And I don't blame them for one minute, sure I don't, it's about time they stood up and be counted.'

Harold and I must look alarmed at her outburst; not at its content, but its fervour. We're both sat there worrying about her heart. Anyway she obviously realises. 'All right, we'll close the subject,' she says, reading us, 'but I'll just say, I myself am not eating them jam tarts again, Harold. I'm boycotting them, that's my protest. You can take those ones you brought today and donate them to the local fête. That way they'll find a more grateful recipient than me.'

'They're your favourite, though,' I tell her, fearing her idiosyncratic gesture might hurt Harold, who had brought them specially. 'I'm not sure your boycott will do much to change things.'

'A protest's got to start somewhere. And, coming from someone who organised a full-scale riot, Dorothy, I'm not sure you've got much of a leg to stand on.'

As Priscilla makes this pronouncement, my eyes shoot to Harold. The expression on his face is one of utter incredulity. With the exaggerated surprise of a cartoon character, his jaw falls open and, simultaneously, his white eyebrows ping upwards so high they almost hit his widow's peak. He corrects his features quickly, but I fancy I can tell just what he's thinking. He's thinking, What, Dorothy a rioter? I may have met her just a handful of times, and always only in this room, but I know her, surely, to be one of those kindly, sensible sort of woman with that pillar-of-the-community spirit. She brings my aunt tinned pears and balls of pink wool, and looks after her with all the attentive care of a dutiful and loving daughter. He's thinking, in God's name, whatever sort of riot might she have started? He's thinking, Appropriate to her profession, she looks rounded and motherly. He's thinking, Yes, midwives ought to be shortish and plump; ought to wear flat, plastic lace-ups and a tidy lambswool cardigan in dark blue; they ought to have a touch of powder on a cotton-wool complexion; to have dark hair on the cusp of going grey; and to smell faintly of hand cream and geraniums. Everything's just as it should be; but Aunt's making out she's something of a revolutionary – *Dorothy*, nice, ordinary, good old Dorothy. Aunt must be having a turn.

Noticing her nephew's amazement and confusion, Priscilla glances at me and apologises.

'I'm sorry, that was very indiscreet of me,' she says.

She knows that only family, and close friends and a few colleagues, are aware of the fact I went to the laundry, and some of why, and of the things that happened to me while I was there. Most people I see know nothing of my past. All these years have gone by and, silly I know, I believe the stigma somehow still sticks to me. I'm frightened of people learning the truth. I may live in Somerset, about as far from Glasgow as it's possible to be, but I sometimes think my forehead is branded, that it says, 'Piccadilly Girl' for all to see. My incarceration's a subject I can only ever discuss with those I know very, very well, like Jessie and Priscilla, and one or two on our seven-strong team of midwives. I have told them the stories. They know the one about my helping to plan a mass-escape riot and they know that, to this day, though it was every bit justified, I still feel the criminal.

Of course, Harold is too tactful by half to start asking questions. But to my modest astonishment, I find I'm annoyed. I wish he would. Is it my imagination, or does he have a way with him such as makes you want to tell him things? Blow me down, when have I ever wanted to confide in a man before? I swear, Maureen must've put something in that tea.

'Will you have a Nice, Dorothy?' Harold asks, scattering the silence with his gentle voice. He is holding the plate towards me. I don't really want to eat.

'Thank you, I will.' The remaining biscuits are identical, but I am flurried by the choice. My hesitant fingers hover stupidly. As I take one, my sleeve strokes the tip of that sugar-mouse thumb of his which rests on the china. He blinks his deep smiling eyes at me, and I wish I was stable as a conker. I'm shaking like a leaf.

Harold and I, we take our leave together, he accompanies me downstairs and out the building. We stand on the stoop a moment adjusting to the dusk air which instantly stings the flesh with cold. Each of our private breaths becomes suddenly, unnervingly, as visible as hairspray. I tap my toes on the concrete step, one foot then the other, to keep them warm.

'I'm sorry about the situation at work,' I say, and immediately feel the clot.

'Well, fingers crossed,' he says. 'I've been lucky. I'm sorry about Aunt Priscilla's little outburst.'

'Please, not to worry at all. That's why I love her.'

'I mean me too,' Harold states quickly. 'Course, as I usually do, I agreed with every word she said, specially about midwives and their right to more financial respect, it's just she's so forceful. 'Cause of her age, I can't help worrying she might blow a fuse. Which way . . . ?'

'Oh, I'm headed home.' I nod in the direction.

'I've to go back and feed Jones. He'll be wanting his supper. Mind if I walk with you along the high street?'

Stoneham's streets at this time of the year, and at this time in the evening, are as good as deserted, eerie. Although I know them like the back of my hand, I tend to scamper back home after visiting the old people. Harold and I step on to the pavement and begin to stroll.

'It's kind of you to be concerned about my job,' he says. 'Perhaps I shouldn't have mentioned it to Aunt, she worries so. She says I'm married to my work and thinks I'll go to pieces if I'm put out of it. I have to admit it wouldn't be much fun, but I wouldn't go that far. I've a nice life outside it too. But she and my father were always the same, worriers the pair of them. I suppose, at my age, I'm a lucky man to have someone who cares enough to mind.'

'You don't have any children?' I ask, knowing damn well.

'Never did. Yourself?'

I shake my head. 'Not really.'

'I expect, being a midwife . . .' He stops short, checking his tact, and quickly looks down to do up another button on his coat.

'I see rather too much of them?' I laugh, hoping to put him at his ease. While I am touched by his caution, I don't want to him to feel uncomfortable. 'There is that, yes.' We are reaching Raffles wine bar and are nearly at the turning which leads to the harbour. As we do so, we slow down naturally and I wonder if Harold is thinking the same as me, that it might be nice to go in for a drink. A tomato juice would be nice. But he's already mentioned Jones, and I've said I'm going home. He's too dutiful to allow spontaneity a look-in, and I'm too socially ill-equipped to persuade him to throw caution to the wind and steer us inside, so we pass on.

'Another time,' he murmurs, to my surprise. I immediately echo his words inside my head to give me another chance to try and work out if I detect there a tone of regret.

We say goodbye, and I turn into a narrow back street. It has become dark very quickly. The brick of the small houses is made navy by the night. Dotted about it are some windows with curtains still open. Like an advent calendar, they reveal yellowy interior scenes of seemingly irresistible cosiness.

My cottage is in a row of six tiny ones by the harbour. As I come down the hill, I can see that most of my neighbours' lights are on, and feel strangely relieved. Although I'll be by myself, I don't want to be alone tonight. I like people the other side of my walls. Sometimes I can hear them padding about, taking a telephone call, making a cup of tea. There's a man to my right, Mr Hutchins, quiet chappie, in computers or some such. He likes a cuppa, trouble is, he's got a kettle that has a right whistle on her. Actually, it doesn't bother me. There used to be a young couple next door, the other side. Nights, their bed-head would bang against the back of mine, only a few bricks separating the two. One time Jessie was staying we were late-night chatting in my room before we went to bed, and we heard the woman groaning like a wounded woodland animal. Jessie said she couldn't stand it, how could I put up with listening to all that racket, other people making love? She was all ready to thump the walls to get them to shut up. I didn't mind it. They were a nice pair having a nice time. Who was I to spoil the fun?

But Jessie was indignant. 'All that caterwauling's completely unnecessary,' she said. 'It's just showing off. Why should we have to listen to this?'

I only just dissuaded her from knocking on the wall and shouting at them to pack it in. I think she was protecting my feelings, didn't like the idea of my having my nose rubbed in it.

Anyway, the couple had a baby – I delivered it, incidentally – and have left now, moved to Godalming, I believe, to a larger house. When I told Jessie, she said, 'Detached, with any luck, or I pity poor bloody Godalming.'

There's a rather mousy primary school teacher in there now. I don't hear a thing, but I can always tell when she's in for some reason. I can feel the presence of someone close by.

I reach the bottom of the hill and walk the curve of the ragged concrete harbour, past the post-office-cum-grocer's with its night-black window, towards the cottages. The smell of the sea is enhanced by the familiar stench of the green seaweed, slipperily jellified by the oily excrements of poorly boats. City people who visit the town wonder why the local council doesn't clear it away. It has neither the money, nor have the Stoneham people the inclination.

As always the water is pawing at the boats' bows, but tonight the sound is more reassuring than ever. I need stability of the tangible senses.

As I approach my cottage I can hear the telephone ringing inside. My fingers flurry in my handbag for the keys and I unlock my front door, the wood of which has been warped by the sea air. It needs a good shove to get it open. I don't like to miss a call, I don't get very many. Work's got my bleeper number so, with the telephone, chances are it's usually someone nice.

The front door opens down a stone step straight into the sitting-room. It's a low-ceilinged room with whitewashed walls, a squashy settee and armchair, and a knobbly grey brick fireplace which is like a miniature cave inside, and which has a huge solid beam surround. Because the room's so small and I know it so well, I can easily find the telephone on the coffee table in the pitch dark. I stretch to turn on the standard lamp as I lift the receiver.

'I wish you'd get an ansaphone, Dot, I've been holding on ages.'

Jessie.

'But I don't need one, I'm here.'

'No, but you weren't.'

'I just got in, so you've got me proper, isn't that better than some wretched machine?'

'I've been trying since lunchtime. I thought it might've been your day off. Where've you been?'

'Work and Priscilla's. Here, are you crying, Jess?'

'Not really. Well, sort of.'

'Ah, love, what is it?' I slough off my coat as I sit down on the settee cushions, and unhook my shoes with my toes so they fall to the floor. 'What's upsetting you? I hate to hear you like this.'

'I wouldn't mind so much if he was even halfway discreet about it. But what am I supposed to do when I dash back home unexpectedly at dinnertime to collect my wallet, I'd forgotten my wallet, see, and hear noises upstairs and go up to find him fucking her in our bed? I mean, am I mad or something? I mean, isn't that the lowest of the low, Dot? In the middle of the blinking day? In our bed, our sheets? Oh, my God! It was a nightmare. I saw his bum going up, down, up, down, into her, just like he does to me, same rhythm, same noises, everything. I couldn't stand it. I couldn't speak, I just stood there like a ruddy bargepole. And it just went on and on, like your worst nightmare, yeah? They didn't realise I was there. Then I puked on the carpet, I couldn't stop. It was like all me guts coming out. When he heard me, you should've seen, he moved out of her like a bat out of hell.'

'Oh, Jessie, Jessie,' I moan hopelessly. Down the line, in response to a sympathetic voice, I can now hear heaving sobs which bar speech. Meanwhile my throat contracts so words fail me too.

It's happened before, this vicarious misery, and almost always over Jessie and her men. It's a strange thing, she's the tower of strength when it comes to other disasters, like the time a few years back when her business nearly folded. You wouldn't have believed how she coped, anyone else would've gone to pieces under the pressure. But on the matter of her personal life, poor Jessie, all that strength, it just deserts her.

It was the same with Tony. Tony came before Derek. Jessie and he weren't living together, but were going out for some months. He was a sales manager for a glazier's company. He had a suspect all-year-round tan, his skin was the slightly jaundiced colour of a beeswax candle from a craft shop. I could just imagine him lying on a sun-bed, knees, ankles, and toes symmetrically apart the better to soak up evenly every possible blue ray. He and Jessie met in their local gym, puffing in unison on neighbouring running-machines. His opening line was something about Jessie not needing to burn up the calories, which for a woman congenitally worried about her weight, was always going to prove a winner. I think the first time they had sex, with all the haste of abandon, was in the men's changing-rooms. Jessie never was much of a one for restraint.

Tony was vain, rather prim, and sometimes a bit of a grump, which annoyed the children, but he and Jessie cruised along for five months or so happily enough. He liked to cook for them all, but wasn't one of those cooks who could stray so much as a pinch of cumin or drop of vanilla from any recipe. Sometimes she would encourage him to live a little, throw it all in, but no, everything had to be just so in the kitchen, just as on the sun-bed, and everywhere else for that matter.

One Easter, for the extended weekend, he went with a few friends on a long-planned barge break up the French canals. Jessie was not invited, but she didn't mind because she wanted to do a treasure hunt for the children. He came back, as arranged, after the Bank Holiday, in time for a late tea on the Tuesday. The children were at friends' houses.

When he arrived, Jessie was busy at the table puzzling the plug of a new kettle. He started on the small-talk, telling her all about the barge and all. He said the galley kitchen was a bit small for his purposes, how hard it had been to make the perfect soufflé à la goodness knows what in such confinement, but he'd managed it admirably all the same, and everyone had complimented him on it very highly. Then, a bit of a non sequitur, he'd started on about how he'd been thinking. What he'd been thinking about, it turned out, was Commitment, and he let her know this with a lot of woolly stuff about how he'd come to the conclusion that he and Commitment weren't entirely compatible, weren't the best of friends, how, sad to say, they'd never really made brilliant bedfellows; how, though this was the case now, he hoped it wouldn't always be like that between him and this Commitment thing, maybe one day they'd learn to hit it off, and then everything would be just dandy with the two of them, even if, right now, it seemed not to be that way, more was the pity for his relationship with her.

He'd been going on in this vein for about five minutes when Jessie said, no beating about the bush, 'Tony, what are you trying to say?' This was met with another tract of cowardly waffle. It only stopped when she was forced to interrupt and neatly interpret his words.

'You're saying it's over between us?'

The reply to this question was followed by a number of ums and ahs and I suppose if you want to put it like thats.

'Why?'

'Well, as I was saying, I have this trouble with commitment.'

'I see.'

'Also, well . . .'

'Well?'

'Jessie, you're the kind of person I have to be honest with, I mean, I feel I can be honest with you. I don't want to lie to you.'

'Fine. So?'

'I dunno, on the barge, well, there was this girl, all right? Nicola. And we really, really got on, kind of thing. OK, so she's got a boyfriend back here and everything, but the two of us, we really hit it off. She had this amazing bod on her, and, of course, this sense of humour. We laughed and laughed, I can tell you. I can't say for sure, but I think she fancies me. It's all a bit awkward, what with her boyfriend and that, but on the Saturday night, yes, it was Saturday because we'd all had a bit much that evening, she gave me this look which sort of said, I really fancy you. You know what I mean, Jess? I mean, you can sort of tell, can't you? And a bit later she ruffled my hair and said one or two really nice things, and well, you know. I don't know, you're a woman, what d'you think? Reckon she fancies me?'

Jessie said it was hard to say, but that, yes, it sounded as though she might.

'All I can say is I hope so, Jessie, I hope so. I mean, we're at this really critical stage. You know what it's like at the beginning – it could go this way, it could go that, it's like walking a tightrope. But I'd say the signs were very much stacked in my favour. Except for this boyfriend, that's a drawback, I'll admit, but I don't think it's too serious a one. I mean, you have to ask the question, why wasn't he there on the barge trip with her in the first place if everything was spot on between them? What do you think, Jessie? I value your opinion.'

Jessie at last put down the kettle's plug. Being Jessie, she smiled, but the irony of the smile was swallowed up in the quicksand of his self-absorption. She told him how she thought that, if he played his cards right, it could be he was in with a chance.

He beamed. 'I thought you'd say that. I'm glad, because you've confirmed what I was thinking too.' Tony flung out his yellow wrist and looked at his watch.

'I must be off. Mind if I nip upstairs? I think I left my sponge-bag there.'

'Help yourself.'

He went to fetch it and Jessie picked up the plug again to fiddle with its coloured veins. When Tony returned to the kitchen she glanced up at him. His smile was wide and pleased with itself, but the cheap sponge-bag in his hand, such pathetic luggage, appeared to diminish him.

'I'm sorry,' he said, sitting down opposite her. 'Can I help you with that?'

Jessie pushed the plug, the screwdriver, and the new kettle across the table towards him. He fixed it in a flash, then stood up to move to the door.

'I knew I could rely on you not to go in for the histrionics,' he said as he was leaving her life for good. 'Thank you, I'm glad we can remain friends. Tell you what, why don't you give me a ring in a couple of weeks, and I'll let you know how it's going with Nicola.'

'Dot, are you still there?'

'Pardon? Yes, of course.'

'What shall I do?' Jessie's asking. 'I can't throw him out. I know you and Derek have never seen eye to eye but, despite all this, I do still love him.'

'I know, but hasn't he pushed you too far this time?'

'Too right he has.'

'Perhaps you should be thinking in terms of making a break, no?'

46

'The pain, Dot, I don't know how to describe it, it's physical, unbelievable.'

'I don't want to encourage you to do something you don't want to do, but I have to say, my advice would be to make a break of it, love. It seems a hard thing to do, but I promise that when you've done it, it'll get better. The healing process can start then, see? Otherwise the pain could go on and on. What's to say he won't do it again?'

'He's full of remorse, Dot. He said he's going to change, he'll never do it again.'

'And do you believe him?'

'I dunno. I'd like to. No, I suppose you're right. A leopard and his ruddy spots and all that. I should tell him I never want to see him again. I should cut him out of our lives. For a start, it's not fair on the kids to see their mum in bits.'

'Will you think about it for me then, pet?'

'No, Dot, I know you're right. I shouldn't need to do any more thinking. I should just do it, yeah?'

'Yeah. And listen, if you want to come down for a few days, you know you can at the drop of a hat, with or without the kids.'

'Thanks. I suppose I've just got to do it tonight even, haven't I?'

'I suppose you have.'

'I feel sick. Will you wish me luck, and promise to scoop up the pieces after?'

'I promise. And ring me whenever.'

'I will. Look, I appreciate this. And don't be surprised if you get me ringing you at four in the morning, sobbing my lamps out.'

'I'll be here.'

Jessie says a tearful thank you and we do our goodbyes. When I put the phone down, I just sit in my not very light sitting-room, motionless. My eyes stare unblinking, so that in time my vision shifts just slightly and everything in sight is transformed into monochrome negative. All the better to think.

Tonight I think about women who apparently love to be treated badly by men, women who supposedly thrive on it. People have often said this of my sister, and I've heard it said of plenty of others besides. Frankly, it makes me mad. I've always thought it an ignorant assumption, whether made about Jessie or anyone else. Not only that, I've always thought it patronising too, and wholly lacking in compassion. I spring to Jessie's defence and I say to their faces, that's patent bloody nonsense. You don't have to work with women day in, day out, to know I'm right about that. What woman would choose to be treated cruelly if she had the choice? If she had the choice, she would want to be treated lovingly and with respect. Point is, some women don't have the choice. Their problem isn't that they are martyrs or masochists, but that they are vulnerable, and it is often the vulnerable who tend to be bad pickers. This means they often fall in love with – and prey to – men who exploit and take advantage of them.

I curse the person who says that what misery Jessie is feeling tonight is brought upon herself. So it's her fault she left her wallet behind and went home when he happened to be having sex with another woman? Silly fool for forgetting her wallet! Silly fool for going home during her own dinner hour! Yes, and, in case I ever forget it, I got pregnant all by myself!

I feel very, very strongly about this.

And yet, there's a part in me which begins to wobble in the face of all my strength of feeling. As I sit here, the indignant hen, all fired up, railing against that bastard, and all her other bastards, I disloyally wonder if she doesn't quite enjoy the drama of it all, the pain – unconsciously, of course. Otherwise why would the pattern always be the same?

I leap up, my eyes right themselves, and I can see colour again. I want to hit myself for having the very thoughts I've disputed so hard for so long. Nobody else to argue with, I sometimes do so with myself, and now find myself storming upstairs with all the gusto of a wronged spouse.

'How could you think that?' I roar in my bedroom, one part of me to another, furiously undoing my dress and throwing on my nightie.

As I get into bed, beneath the pale green eiderdown and between the waxy soft sheets, the row continues in my head. With all that racket. going on, it's a while before I detect a third voice reminding me that tonight I can have more enjoyable thoughts if I want them.

Hopes of my own are a rare luxury. I force myself not to let

Jessie's unhappiness obscure them, however faint they be. But it's hard to sleep. I'm too unsettled to read my novel, and sheep are no good. I must devise a new method.

I turn out the light. Counting biscuits on a plate seems as good a way as any.

Chapter Four

Sure enough the telephone does ring in the early hours. I think I'm dreaming so don't get out of bed for a minute. Then, as my mind makes a clearing through the glueyness of sleep, I realise the sound is real, and clatter downstairs at speed, the hem of my nightdress sliding up my legs and leaving a trail of goose-pimples behind it.

Jessie says she's been awake all night, she didn't want to wake me, but she couldn't help it, she's done the deed. She actually threw Derek out earlier this evening. I can't believe it. Perhaps I'm still asleep, this certainly doesn't feel real, but I know that it is in fact music.

Naturally, she doesn't sound too happy about it. A little tearful, poor love, but tending towards calm. She uses one of her favourite words – ape. Apparently that's what he went when she told him enough was enough – *Out!* I can see him now, dressed with all the carelessness of culpability – one shirt-tail hanging out, no socks, fly button fastened at the top but zip still undone – pleading his case like a petty thief in a magistrates' court, too pathetic even to have the wit to lie with style.

After Jessie had caught him red-handed at dinnertime, the woman had run for it, Derek had pulled on his clothes, shouted, ('Stupid bitch!' were the exact words he used; Jessie had assumed they were directed at her but wasn't absolutely certain), and left the house. He'd returned soon after our earlier phone call, and joined her in the bedroom. She says she wanted to scream at him, but managed to keep quite cool. Apparently he looked guilty as hell. I know Derek's guilty eyes, those of a dopey heifer with too much grass in its belly, rather appealing really, hard to resist. He certainly knows how to pull every trick in the book designed to make her crumble. Like he asked, if she made him leave, who would be the father to her kids? I won't insist that that was a low trick because I suppose there's a case to say he would be genuinely concerned about them losing a father figure. Still, he'd have known that that one would've pulled at her heartstrings. I'm proud of Jessie. She stood her ground. I hope such strength came from something more resilient than anger that was just flash-in-the-pan.

I tell her that although she's none too happy herself, I am happy for her. It's obvious she's done the right and most courageous thing.

I know, I know, she says, he's best out of my life for good, and right now I hate him but, Dot, he doesn't mean bad, you know, he's not a malicious person. I'm going to miss him. Of course you will, my love, I reply, but it's the initial shock, it will subside, it just will, always does. (I speak with the wisdom of one who has spent her life observing others. I myself have never missed somebody in that way. I've missed anybody, yes, but that's different, it's unspecific so it's more an abstract longing. Perverse as it may seem, I envy Jessie's being in a position to miss, for all its pain.)

I love him. I love him. I love him.

There, there, Jess, there, there.

I'm on early, so I don't bother to go back to bed. I feel all distracted anyway, by Jessie's news. Instead I sit in the semi-darkness of my sitting-room, shivering a bit but not minding. I've a nice cup of tea in my hands and the warmth from that goes up to my elbows. My thoughts are all at sixes and sevens. Eventually, when it's time, I stir myself and have a bath. I lie still for a while watching the soap clouding the water grey and, through the tiny bathroom window, the dawn diluting the thick blue of sky.

The hospital, bustling at this hour, prompts me automatically to adopt my routine efficiency. I'm covering for Shirley on the antenatal ward this morning. The ladies are having their breakfast when I arrive. I feel sorry for them having to eat at six. Their stomachs aren't themselves rightly enough as it is without having to cope with cereal and toast this early as well. But the administrators rule. It's cheaper to serve breakfast at six than at eight – though why on earth beats me – and, of course, cost-cutting in our Health Service must always triumph over the needs of a few women. Perhaps I'm soft, I feel sorry for these girls, too, because there's quite a lot of them who need constant monitoring so have to stay in here weeks, homesick, bored out their minds, and frustrated to bits. All the more important for us lot to be cheerful and caring when we're around them. The fact of Jessie's upset, and my concentration gone a bit awry for my own reasons, doesn't give me the right to look grim. Our private life's private, and stays outside the wards. While you make friends with your fellow midwives, when you bond with the pregnant ladies, it's like an emotional one-way street. You learn everything about them, but must try as much as possible to keep them at a professional distance from you. I could name one or two who have no problem with that, but I think the majority of my colleagues find it hard, as I do.

The ward is very full today, with many a familiar face. The ones who have already had kids are already chatting away, comparing experiences, competing for the most horrific birthing story. This is common among mothers. There's a sort of hierarchy between them depending on the amount of pain suffered. Certainly those who have had it easy are made to feel less fully rounded, small even. I've often wondered what this is about. I presume it's something very basic, like the worse the birth you went through, the more you are a proper mother, a real woman. Perhaps it's the female equivalent of that male thing, the more people you kill in battle the more you are a man.

I say hello to Grace, to Liz, to Julie, to Tina, to Ann, to Leila, most of whom I've got to know in here, or in my capacity as community midwife, when I've visited them at home earlier on in their pregnancies. Jackie in the corner had successful infertility treatment and is with triplets. A slight girl in her late twenties, her stomach is so huge it appears to be attached to her body but not a part of it. It reminds me of one of those tall saddles you see in postcards roped on to camels' backs. She has a good laugh against herself. She says she's always forgetting to open doors wide enough to get herself through.

A student midwife introduces me to Kelly, a girl of twenty-one who was admitted yesterday and is sitting on top of the bed next to Jackie's. She'd been out shopping with her boyfriend, had fainted and had a fit. The baby's fine, but she might have to stay in till she has it. It's her heartbeat they're keeping their tabs on. Under her T-shirt the monitor is taped to her skin.

'Mind if I take your blood pressure, love?'

'Please do. Go ahead.' Her voice is gravelly.

I sit on the bed beside her. She extends her arm towards me and pulls back the short sleeve over her shoulder.

'They told me it's not my brain,' she says, as I strap the Velcro belt tightly round above her elbow. 'It was good to learn I had one of those, I wasn't sure I did.'

I laugh. I've always enjoyed that self-deprecating sort of humour.

'I tell you I didn't get a wink last night. There were four in labour. They honestly shouldn't be left in here right up till the time they're ready to push. It's like listening to a bleeding orchestra of fog-horns. Frightens the life out of the poor first-time mothers. One went home terrified out her wits.'

'This isn't your first, is it?' I ask her. Kelly has skin that extra pale of milk of magnesia, and the whites of her eyes are as blue as a baby's. The soft brown hair is raggedly cropped. Her long, good legs are covered by grey leggings. I am often taken aback by the youthfulness of some of the mothers. I forget that I was once one myself.

'No, my third,' she replies chirpily. 'It's not right, Dorothy. Their other halves should be allowed in here to comfort them whatever time it is. The rest of us felt helpless. I wanted to soothe them, to rub their backs or something. I tell you, I'm going to have an epidural straight away.'

It's funny – how many hundreds of women must I meet a year, and get to know and like? – and yet I can be going about my normal business, during any old routine shift, and I encounter one who specially gets to me, who out of the blue delights me so I'm full of beans just to be in her company. Kelly is one such. I've known her for all of four minutes, but she's got something which has grabbed me. Call it spirit, I don't know, it's a rare, indefinable thing. Jessie has it, I think, and my best friend at the laundry certainly did. Bel was the one who kept me going when I was there. She was blessed with a natural happiness and humour and sheer enjoyment of life. She wasn't to be got down by such trifles as circumstances. Something drove her to rise above it. There aren't that many people like her about. Occasionally I've come across men who are the same. But it can get tricky: it's hard not to fall in love with them.

I think I must have been a bit in love with Bel. Still, that was because, if you were going to fall in love at Piccadilly Park, it was necessarily going to be with a girl because there were no men there – unless you count the horrible van driver who gave us the shivers; and Jack, the maintenance man, but he was about ninety and had a withered arm, poor soul. Neither was exactly ripe fodder for girlish infatuation.

If Kelly were a man, I might fall in love with her. She's instantly affecting. As it is, while I can admire a woman's looks and personality, and can see exactly why a man might fancy her, I've never myself been sexually attracted to another woman. I grew up with sisters, and I made friends quite easily at school, and during my year in nurse's training, then at the laundry, but they were always girls. I love women, but what with living with them, and them alone, for nine years, and after a sizeable stint in this line of work, they hold no real mystery for me. It may sound arrogant – of course we're all different, and there's obviously exceptions – but I do believe I understand women on the whole utterly, that there's little a woman can say when she voices her thoughts or feelings or fears or hopes or desires, that could ever surprise me. Quite often I feel the same way as they do, and identify strongly with them. Yet even when I don't, I am of their sex, I'm roughly acquainted with what they're about, so I can ninety-nine times out of a hundred sympathise with, or at least undertstand, their point of view.

How strange that one can know one's own sex so utterly, and the other sex so sketchily. I tend to go along with Jessie, who often says she'd like the chance to be a man for just one day. She thinks that that would give her more of an insight into how men's minds work than a whole lifetime as a woman living and sleeping and having children with them, and trying to figure them out. (Being her, of course, there'd be a stipulation – in the course of her day, she would have to get to sleep with a woman, maybe a few, because she's always maintained men's powers of description are less than adequate when it comes to explaining what sex is like for them. She longs to find out for herself.)

As a child I didn't know boys so I was frightened of them. Because of this I quickly grew to believe that they were superior to women, and more specifically, perhaps, to me. Their bodies intrigued me (still do, for that matter!). I knew girls' bodies, which, because they were an approximation of my own, seemed straightforward and unexciting. Today, I marvel at what the female body can withstand and achieve, but I have yet to be amazed at the way one looks because I've seen an unimaginable amount of them, in all their naked, open, and most contorted forms. It is the male mind and body which continue to fascinate. I am middle-aged, so should be past such thinking but, even so, I see men's minds and bodies as a challenge – a challenge for me to try to understand them, a challenge for me to try to attract them.

'I've had two already without,' Kelly is saying. 'This time I want the lot. Tens machine, gas, air, epidural, you name it. I can't be doing with all these first-timers' attitudes, saying they want it natural and all. I tell them, "You wait, sunshine, once you're in there it'll be, Bugger bloody natural, give me obliteration!" '

I laugh again and, releasing the tight strap, tell her her blood pressure's fine.

'Thanks, it didn't pinch as much when you did it. I normally hate those things.'

I am pleased at the little compliment because I pride myself on being as gentle as possible. Women are examined and poked at in here enough as it is. It's usually only the consultants doing the necessary, and as sensitively as possible, but my ladies don't need to be mauled about by midwives as well.

'Myself,' Kelly continues, 'when I'd been in labour with my second for three whole days, I was well past it. I had to have a ventouse, my legs in stirrups, that was a bit humiliating. But they could've wheeled me like that down the middle of the bloody high street, broad daylight, for all I cared. At that point, all I could think of was, "*Get it out of there.*" Later, when Steve asked me what it was like, I said, "Try passing a pumpkin down out yer nostril, get the picture, mate?" Got kids yerself, Dot?'

The mums, they love more than anything to talk about their own pregnancy and birth experiences – some are quite intense about it, some are very funny – but the one thing they all have in common is the desire to know the answer to this one sooner or later. I think they feel happier with a midwife who's been through it herself, more reassured. When I started midwifery, the question terrified me. I used always to say yes because, first, I wanted them to have full confidence in me and, second, I couldn't lie. Only, telling the truth upset me. Invariably, the next questions would be, Boy or girl? and, How old is she? I could answer them both all right, but then would come, She's thirty-three, so what does she do?

How could I not know? Her own mother? I do not know what she does.

At first I'd hedge my bets, manage, without exactly lying, to tinker with the truth. I'd say, She lives away from home, she's a busy girl.

Is she married?

I'd make it up. I'd rely on the law of averages, and say she was. To a lovely man, I'd add, because I hoped he was.

After that I'd try to change the subject, and became pretty expert at it. But sometimes the mums, naturally inquisitive, and very sweetly wanting to make friends with you, would still persist, and then I'd have to lie. I'd let one or two details about Eliza's life drop – about her little house, her well-paid job, my grandchildren, whatever – all of them pure fantasy, reflecting the hopes any mother might have for her daughter.

I couldn't keep it up. I learned quickly that refusing to lie a little meant I was then forced to lie a lot. The world I created for my daughter was not only false, it was also a self-indulgent flight of fancy on my part.

One day, after a particularly inquisitive lady had asked me to produce a photo of Eliza, I decided enough was enough. In future it would be better – and more in keeping morally – to use a single lie to avert having to resort to these bigger ones. I made a rule. From them on, to, 'Do you have children yourself, Dorothy?', though it broke my heart to deny my child's existence, I would say no. When you say no to a question like that, people tend not to pursue it. They know that the reason for childlessness, especially in a woman my age, is odds on a painful one. When I answer in the negative, the occasional teenage mum, not yet fashioned in the way of tact, will still ask, 'Why?' Then I say, 'That's a long story, dear, and we're here not to talk about me but to talk about you.'

'Do you, Dot, have any children?' Kelly repeats the question.

'Beg pardon?' I say, and without thinking I tell her. 'Yes, yes I do.'

What's come over me? For the first time in I don't know how many years, I've broken my golden rule. I don't know if Kelly caught me off guard, or if those very appealing qualities of hers made me need to tell her the truth. Whatever, I am at once taken aback and relieved.

Though I am not trying to change the subject, I ask if I might examine her stomach.

'It's all worth it though, isn't it?' she says, lying back against her pillows and pulling up her T-shirt. Because she has such pale skin, her rounded tummy looks like a smooth white ball straining in a thin silk net of veins. 'I love being a mum. It's the best job I can imagine. I wouldn't want to be anything else. Because I was seventeen when I had my first, people ask if I haven't wasted my life. It's quite the opposite. Me and Stevie – he's a brickie – we've been together three and a half years, our daughter's two now, and he and I are as happy as pig and pug. He's not Marcus's dad, but he's just as good a father to him as he is to our Topsy. I was married to his natural father for two years. I wish I'd never done it. That's my only ever regret.'

She jabbers away as I carefully knead her stomach to feel for the position of the baby.

'You're both all right there,' I inform her.

'That's good. D'you think I'll have to stay in? I'm already longing to go home. Bit of the business with Stevie might hurry things along a bit, get those contractions started.'

I smile. That a woman can be so intimate so soon in her acquaintance with another is not unusual. Here everyone talks about sex readily and openly, young and old alike. Kelly's joky about it, and you can but laugh.

'The consultant's starting his round at ten, I'm sure he'll let you know then.'

'Mine? Dr Walker? I hope so. He's a dish. Everyone in here fancies him.'

'They always do. Don't worry, he won't keep you in if it's not necessary. I'll be with him, so I'll see you later.'

I smile again, and move off to do more check-ups with the rest of the ward.

I'm a member of a team of seven midwives which serves two health centres in the area. We have about a hundred and fifty women on our caseload at any one time, and we see about double that number in a year. As community midwives we do home visits, but are based in the hospital so also do a lot of our work there, in the antenatal clinic, the wards and, of course, the delivery suites.

I prefer to be out on the road, visiting. After all these years, I still find that the wards remind me of the dormitories at Piccadilly. Granted, they are bright and full of flowers and joy, and their windows aren't fitted with wire meshing, but the rows of beds and the lino floors are the same. The only difference between the vast old-fashioned radiators, with their identical yellow-chipped paint, is that those at St Dominic's are on a permanent high, while the one at Piccadilly were never ever turned on at all. Their sole purpose, it seemed, was as a sort of morbidly mocking decoration.

Jessie often wonders why, following years of my living in a place like Piccadilly, I wanted directly to enter another establishment with rules and regulations. She suspects my nine years left me more institutionalised than I realised. I don't think that's true. What I love about my job is the getting out, the freedom of jumping in the car, venturing into people's homes, becoming part of so many different lives. I always knew my vocation, that strong since my schooldays, was going to lead me into a hospital some of the time. I was determined Piccadilly wasn't going to affect my desire to enter midwifery – either to put me off, or to propel me into it just because I craved the security of hospitalisation, albeit of another kind.

At nineteen, I was full of ambition. Certainly, that place did all in its power to crush my confidence.

As a child I was quite a lot like Jessie is now. We both had a bit of lip, a bit of spirit, a wish to do well for ourselves, a sense of survival. We got it from our mother. Mother was a curious creature: inconsistent, unpredictable, always her own woman, that is till she met our dad. One minute she'd be sitting at the piano and, for Beth's and my amusement, belting out 'My Very Good Friend the Milkman' with all the energy and drawl of a New York nightclub singer. The next, she'd be walloping one of us with a hairbrush for failing to wash our hands before the meal.

She was caught between two worlds. An only child, she'd been brought up by her father in Stoke-on-Trent. His wife, my grandmother, had died of tuberculosis when my mother was five. While he went off to work, his young daughter was farmed out to various aunts. With no abiding influence, she developed a more independent spirit than she might otherwise have done had her mother been alive. At seventeen, she defied her loving father's wishes, and went to work in Manchester as a maid in a big posh hotel. Although he condoned her earning her bread, he wanted her to do so in a bakery or a dairy, or domestic service – almost anything as long as it was close to home. He feared for her safety and moral welfare in the big city. She had rounded cheeks, vast eyes, and dark brown hair down to her waist. Grandfather knew that these attributes, coupled with her country-girl naivety, made her vulnerable. Before her first month was up, her beauty and her coquettish disposition had caught the attention of an American staying at the hotel. She was changing the sheets of his bed one morning when he returned to his room with a red rose, and invited her to go to New York with him! The very next week she was sailing the Atlantic. I once found a photograph in an old drawer of her against the white railings of the ship's deck, her hair released from its usual bun, standing beside a tall man with a square jawbone and a perfect valance of teeth draped beneath a broad smile. She remained in Manhattan for four years. Only three years into the war did she return home, aged twenty-one. She married my father a matter of weeks later, and I was born before her twenty-second birthday.

I still wonder why she married him. Father was of dour, Scottish Presbyterian stock, and very strict about religion. Church every day, that sort of thing. After her American, with his co-respondent shoes, his striped suits, his brown triby cocked at a jaunty angle, and his dandy air, it was a wonder she could stick such resolute strictness and severity.

For many years, I assumed the reason she married this upright ironmonger was because she was already pregnant with me, and I would otherwise have been born out of wedlock. I have since, with all the pedantic precision of a mathematician, worked out the dates, and found that it was impossible for the American – Joe, he was called – to have been my natural father. (The discovery was rather a disappointment, as a matter of fact. I liked the idea of being half American, and the daughter of an exotic man from abroad who gave women flowers and went on big ships. The nearest my real father had ever got to giving anyone a red rose was when he found a plastic one on the verge one day and jammed it into the rim of Mother's favourite hat, making a big hole in the straw; and the closest he ever got to sailing on a ship was a brief spell after he left school as a tea boy in the Glasgow shipyard.) Thus I remain puzzled as to her motives. I suspect she wanted, in the end, to fulfil my grandfather's wishes, having so blatantly disregarded them for so long. She had this respectable, religious streak in her, and I think it eventually must have triumphed over the spirited one.

Why Father married her is even more difficult to fathom. Her knock-out beauty was all-affecting, so much so that I can only imagine it must have moved even him, a man whose appreciation of the aesthetic for all the world appeared only to extend so far as the shine on a wheelbarrow, the curve of a tin pail, and the simple engineering of a Swiss Army knife. I like to think he could be swayed by such superficial things as a woman's looks, that would make him more human, but believe it was probably, more, that Mother's lively past served as an affront to his sense of decency, and he wished to set matters right and rise to the challenge of taming her.

Maidenwell was the name of our village. It was near Stoke where Mother had grown up, and Newscastle-under-Lyme. The house we lived in, above Father's shop, was in a street of that typical Staffordshire brick, the deep red colour of dried blood on tarmac. In the concrete back yard was an outside toilet behind a draughty wooden door (a bathroom was later fitted upstairs), and an iron and wooden mangle for squeezing clothes dry. Inside, it was plain but homely. My mother had painted the kitchen and parlour a warm yellow, and we had a three-piece suite (though Beth and Jessie and I weren't allowed to sit on it till we reached our teens).

Mother was an old-fashioned housewife. During her time in America I don't know what she was doing, but she hadn't forgotten how to bake and make jam, and zigzag her iron over piles of washing with extraordinary speed and expertise. I used to think she had magical powers to be able to do these things so quickly and so well, and would watch her for hours, longing to be able to do likewise. (My nine years at Piccadilly were soon to see to that. I learned there to be more efficient with an iron than she ever could have been.)

She would read bedtime stories to Beth and me, and later to Jessie too, when Jessie was old enough to understand them. On the whole those she picked were of the type my father would have approved – traditional morality tales warning against such sins as thumb-sucking and lying, with all their attendant consequences gruesomely detailed (thumbs cut off with giant scissors; slow death by fire, and so forth).

But just occasionally she'd throw caution to the wind, she'd cast aside the books, and she'd tell us stories of her own. We'd listen, stunned, to descriptions of streets and buildings in New York, including the Empire State Building, the tallest skyscraper in the world, which glimmered silver beneath the clouds and had a pointed aerial on top of it which, from the ground, looked no bigger than one of her darning needles. She told us of the apartment where she lived which overlooked a park so huge you could go there a hundred times and still could lose your way. She told us of the friendly people with voices like in the pictures, and though she'd never lost her Staffordshire accent, she'd imitate them with a husky but sugary whine so convincing we'd think she herself was a film star, and laugh with admiration and pride. She'd tell us what she ate: rolled mince in buns with cheese and ketchup they called hamburgers, and cherry pie with cream on top so high it nearly touched your nose. She told us about nickels and dimes, and the funny chirruping rings of American telephones. She told us of the vast baths with enamel sides so thick you could rest your soap on, and the fridges so large you could have a party inside. She mentioned the drink she once had in a hotel bar that was as red as a letterbox and tasted of boiled sweets made of spices. She spoke of the women with faces powdered white as flour, eyelashes thick as spiders' legs, and lips so painted they came off on the tips of their amber cigarette holders. The handsome men who drove vast cars with noisy, noisy horns, and drank whiskey with whole quarries of ice in their glasses.

We heard these things again and again but could never get enough of them. Sometimes we'd ask questions, and sometimes she'd fill us in, though only ever on the details. Other times she'd be evasive, on the bigger things, so we never were sure who she shared a flat with or why, or what she did for money, or where.

She never talked about America in front of Father. The only ever references to it came from him. We might be round at a friend's house and they'd offer her refreshment. If she asked for a gin or vodka, he'd say, 'We're not in Central Park West now, Sylvia, you'll have a cup of tea like the rest of us ordinary folks, thank you very much.' I didn't know exactly what Central Park West was, but I guessed it to be a posh area. Sometimes, if she ordered a few yards of material to make herself a new dress and he deemed it too fancy, or if she wore nylons which he felt were too fetching, he'd say, 'You don't need to dress for Madison Avenue any more, you know. No one's going to give fashion, let alone you, a second glance in Maidenwell's parade.'

Oh the whole, Mother toed the line. When she wasn't baking or ironing, or looking after us, she'd be putting in her hours in the haberdashery side of Father's shop, chatting politely with the customers, conscientiously selling them their cottons, their wools, and their buttons. Generally, she wore sober clothes, went to church like clockwork, and disciplined us three down to a tee.

Beth, born two years after me, was more like Father: quiet, serious, hard-working, and self-righteous. She looked like him, same high brow, same uneasy smile, and same earnest little frown, the troubles behind which more frivolous folk could only guess at. Of course, she was his favourite. I respected her, though couldn't like her enormously. There were times we got on, but she could never be said to have been much fun. At school she was teased on occasion for her studiousness. I must've cared about her a bit because, although she probably deserved it, I used to mind the taunts, and stick up for her whenever I could.

Beth would reward me for this when we got home with a game or two in our attic bedroom. She preferred to read on her own but felt duty-bound to do her sisterly bit. When Jessie came along, it was quite a different thing. From the moment she was born, when I was thirteen, we got on the pair of us, naturally, regardless of the age gap. Suddenly, home life with her about was less boring. Up until then it'd been Mother doing chores, Father working all the hours God gave, and Beth being only as merry as her piety would allow (which wasn't very). Quite often I'd get home from school, do my homework, and wonder how on earth I was going to fill my time before bed. Our evening meal was hardly the relief I was seeking.

We would sit the four of us, Mother, Father, Beth and I, at the wooden table in the parlour which was pulled back from the window and laid every time every day the family sat down to eat. Father would say grace and Mother would produce maybe fish, cod usually, which in his opinion, expressed without fail, was 'good for the brain'. Sometimes it would be steak and kidney.

Kidney made me heave. The sensation was of a ball of wool soaked in bile rising from my stomach and lodging in my throat so any more mouthfuls were out of the question.

'Dorothy, you will eat humble pie,' Father would declare whenever the dish was put in front of me, and he was right, I would, because he made me, even if it meant my sitting there from teatime to midnight.

'There are children like you starving in Africa.' Sometimes he said India, sometimes China. In fact, children seemed to be starving in every continent the world over, with the possible exception of Australia. I don't think he ever said Australia.

I could never understand why my inability to like kidney in Maidenwell was relevant to children starving thousands of miles away. Mother must have been equally puzzled because she used to tell him that it wasn't terribly important if I didn't eat it, and that not to enjoy the tastes of certain foods didn't constitute a sin. But he viewed making children do things they didn't want to as vital to their moral development. Such was his influence, that soon she learned not to step in when there was a battle of wills between Father and myself: her opinion was of such trifling importance to him as not even to comprise a matter for discussion.

So it was that, over time, her more imaginative and humane views became moulded into and overcast by his, like new clay being fashioned on to a half-made pot. Only occasionally did the join become visible and cracks begin to show. Once, for instance, Father ordered Beth and I out into a blizzard for a walk. 'It's good for you,' he said. Mother put in her bit; only quietly, mind. 'No,' she countered, 'I think it's better for them to stay warm by the fire.' He roared and, telling us we'd not be let in for an hour, dispatched us outside to catch streaming colds.

I do not believe he was a cruel man. He was just a bigot. This had its roots in an impossibly religious background which had him as a child going to church more often than we did. (We had to go at least once a week and that was bad enough.) He was from Glasgow, and his family was poor. He was brought up on a diet of potatoes and violence. We were lucky, he said, to get all we did: puddings with custard, and peace in the house. Such self-pity disgusted me. If there's any in me, it's he who I get it from.

Agh, he wasn't all bad. In some ways he was a good father. It's easy to condemn people for their failings when you forget their background. Often, in rare moments of contrition following an ourburst of temper, he would use his past as an excuse, which I found inexcusable, but nonetheless that past did exist and clearly accounted for some of his excesses.

Apart from trying to bulldoze my mother's own character right out of her, and replacing it with one he regarded as more appropriate to any wife of his, one that suited his own, he did make for a proper husband in many ways. He never failed to provide for his wife or family. There was always food in the larder, a well stitched pair of shoes on our feet, and coal in the grate of the parlour (even if it was only to be lit in extremes of cold, or in the company of visitors). Sloth was not a word my father knew the meaning of. He worked hard all his life. Often I think he was at his happiest in his beige overall behind the high wooden counter of his shop, full of knowledgeable authority, fingering his fuses, handling the latest type of light-bulbs (he the only stockist of them for miles around), and full of self-confident and jovial banter for his customers.

There were surprising elements to him. His appearance was one. You might expect a man of his temperament to have been stocky; rough-looking, even. Not a bit of it. Father was tall and elegant. His short black hair was always greased back from his forehead with a thin metal comb which left neat, minuscule furrows. His ears were prominent. Behind one he kept a cigarette (though it never seemed to graduate to his mouth; perhaps it made him feel secure – I don't think I ever did see him smoke anything other than his pipe). Behind the other he used to place a short orange pencil with a grubby pink rubber at the end. These were both removed without fail before he said grace, and replaced immediately at the end of every meal (even after Christmas dinner when he was still wearing a paper hat). His spectacles had thick black frames which might have lent him a sinister air but for the fact that his eyes had a permanent if improbable twinkle. Later in his life he developed a small paunch, but this was only discernible under his shirt if he leant backwards, otherwise it was unnoticeable and he remained for all the world a thin man. The skin of his neck had deep cracks running round it. Age saw wrinkles embed themselves in his face as if he were a fellow exposed for decades to all weathers, and his yellowing eyelids with their reddened rims begin to droop over his milky eyes.

There were various other things about him which somehow didn't seem to fit a man of his disposition. Such gruffness and severity, for example, you wouldn't naturally marry with immense generosity and hospitality, but immensely generous and hospitable he was (even though he was sometimes very suspicious of these two qualities in other people). He gave both his time, and imaginatively chosen gifts which were beyond his means, to family, to friends, to customers, even to strangers. Every single time our neighbour Mrs Gibbons came into the shop, he'd slip her a card of pearly buttons because she spent her life knitting babies' cardigans for others, and he knew she couldn't afford it. It was understood in the village that our home was open house for all. Once anybody crossed the threshold, it'd be Scottish shortbread all round, and whiskey or sherry for adult visitors even though he didn't approve of alcohol much himself.

Perhaps the oddest and most contrary thing about Father, was the fact that he was a pacifist. But he was also a hearty monarchist (his pin-up was the Queen Mother). I cannot for the life of me imagine, for a man of a background such as his, where on earth he developed either of these beliefs, let alone the two. Funny to say so, but holding such views, coming as he did from a Gorbals tenement, must have meant he was, after a fashion, a tearaway, a rebel even (the word certainly doesn't sit easily when applied to him, he the great upholder of convention and conservatism). Such fury as his own staunchly Scottish Nationalist parents must have felt at his betrayal can only be guessed at.

Anyway, when the war came and he, aged twenty-three, was called up, these two ideals wreaked havoc within him. After much soul-searching, the pacifist side of his nature won through, and he became a conscientious objector, and refused to join up. There are many charges I can make against my father, but physical cowardice isn't one of them. I do know for certain that his motives for not becoming a soldier were not white-feathered.

In 1939 he left Glasgow for Staffordshire so as to avoid National Service by working in a mine. Two years later, as a result of sheer strength of will, ambition, determination, and a spot of asthma which he managed to make out was more serious than it was, he had emerged from the pit, successfully dodged conscription a second time, and set up his own ironmonger's shop which he called Sheffield's. He'd had a passion for nails and hinges and all since he was a lad. He kept in contact with his family infrequently and never lost his Glaswegian accent, but he returned to Scotland only twice, once for his mother's funeral, once for his father's.

Starting a business, followed by marriage a year afterwards to my mother, in 1942, meant that at last people bestowed upon him the respect he had always felt his due. Up until that time, because of poverty back home, and because of his strongly held pacifist beliefs, this had always been denied him. By the time Jessie came along, he was a firmly established family figure in the community, and his was a highly opinionated voice on the parish council.

Jessie, who arrived eleven years after Beth, has always maintained she was a mistake. My parents were so meticulous about everything, that I find that hard to believe. The thought of my father suddenly being overwhelmed by a passion that precluded precaution is too comic to contemplate. His idea of letting go physically was walking round the house without shoes on his feet.

Accident or not, in my book Jessie was a positive asset to a household which was, most the time, grim. When I got into grammar school – unheard of in our village – my father celebrated the achievement by (and this really was a big treat) taking me to the dog races.

Mother and Beth and the baby were left behind, and Father drove me in his van to the stadium near one of the big towns not far from our village. I had never been on an outing such as this with Father before. He used to go to the dogs perhaps once a week. Mother rarely accompanied him, and my sisters and I never did. It wasn't, he said, the right environment for women or children. I don't know what changed his mind that evening.

When we arrived, we parked in the rain and he guided me expertly through a turnstile. As we emerged we found the place was jumping. It smelt of wet concrete, disinfectant, and stale sweat. In the sheltered area underneath the stands, men in cloth caps stood beneath unforgiving strip lights gossiping about the runners, and placing bets. The bookies, in sharp dogtooth suits, stood on boxes. Their pudgy hands, flapping and swooping, appeared to be playing seagulls. Every now and then they dropped any money proffered to them into outsized doctors' bags painted with funny names – Billy Bridgewater, Jack Postlethwaite, Peter Higginsbotham – and all the while they were either shouting an incomprehensible language or, heads thrown back, guffawing gruffly at the roofbeams to jokes I didn't catch or even hear being told.

Father pointed to a board chalked with six names and asked what dog I best liked the sound of. It was between Gypsy and Minty Boy, I told him. 'Try Gypsy,' he said, and gave me a coin which he indicated I should hand up the bookie nearest to where we were standing. The bookie gave me a clown-like smile and, doing so, took the precious coin that Father had given me, threw it in his bag, and passed me a pink piece of paper in return. I think I saw Father himself slip the man a note, but he did it so quickly and discreetly, I couldn't say for certain. Then he put his hand on my shoulder and guided me away, outside, towards the mesh surrounding the track. He pointed out where the dogs would be starting from, and then helped me up the steep steps of the terraces, past loads of people, to the warmth of the smoke-filled observation gallery. We sat on chairs with foam frothing out from the splits in their seats. I asked why we could come in here while others had to sit or stand in the open air.

Father replied, 'He's a friend,' and because he didn't say who, I was none the wiser.

Some minutes later a vast man slapped Father on the back, and laughed, and said in a Glaswegian accent as broad as Father's own, 'So, Iain, what'll it be?'

Father laughed back. 'Eck! Agh, why not a pint? Thanks there, Eck. And a bitter lemon for the lass, if you wouldn't mind.'

So this was my father's private, grown-up, manly world, where he knew people and did things he never did at home.

The punters in the crowd downstairs with the bookies and the men upstairs along the balcony didn't really notice me, but some of those who greeted my father tapped my head a couple of times so as to acknowledge my presence without having to say a word. While we were waiting for the Scottish man, Eck, to return from the bar, somebody did bend down to me and put his nose, which was like the strawberry at the bottom of the punnet, right close up to mine.

'Who are you then, ducks?' he asked, and two drops of his spittle landed on my upper lip. I pretended to scratch my chin so I could wipe them away.

My father held my hand tightly. 'This one's Dorothy, my oldest wee lass.' He sounded proprietorial almost. 'She's just got herself into grammar school,' he beamed. There was something about his tone I didn't recognise, except that it felt nice. I was still a bit damp and chilly, even shivering a little, from the cold we'd just left behind, but I was glowing well and good inside.

Eck returned and gave me this drink I'd never had before which was grey-green and cloudy and, when I drank it, stung the insides of my cheeks and went fizz high up my nose, but tasted delicious.

'Here, Eck, I was just telling Stanley, this one's just got herself into grammar school!'

'She's a clever lass, then, as well as bonnie,' he said, gazing down at me. 'Iain, you should be proud.'

I think my father said, 'Aye,' but I can't be too sure, because at that very moment a bell suddenly sounded to herald the fact that the first race was about to start, and there was the general commotion of anticipation. Father quickly held me up against the window overlooking the track, and advised me to cup my hands round my eyes against the glass to better to see.

'See, there, Dot, Gypsy's number four, you keep an eye out for number four.'

Suddenly I heard a loud swoosh of a metal missile hurling itself round the course like a wild thing, swiftly followed by a blur of white flashes and, a matter of seconds later, the sound of groans from the crowd, interspersed with a few cheers. I hadn't seen any dogs, let along my dog, Gypsy, number four.

'Whoa!' bellowed my father. 'Gypsy won! Clever lass, Dot, you won!'

He scooped me up and we hurried back outside and downstairs. 'You're a rich lassie now, I think we ought to collect your winnings.'

We reached our bookie, I gave him the pink slip, and he handed me some money in return. The coin Father had given me had turned into four coins. When I passed them to Father, he immediately pressed them back into my palm.

'They's all for thee, Lass, they's all for thee.'

I don't think I have ever since, not in two score years, experienced quite the soaring elation of that evening, of those words, of that moment.

After our night at the dogs, Father was back to his usual self again and, because I was a grammar school girl now, dictated all work and no play. Schoolfriends were no longer allowed round except on special occasions, and then only at the weekends. The only let-up from my studies were meals; helping the milkman with his round Saturday mornings (two free pints of gold-topped for the house and, if I was lucky, a bag of sweets for me, of my choice – usually sherbet lemons because their taste reminded me of the drink I'd had at the stadium); long hard walks on Sunday afternoons; and looking after the baby when Mother was in the shop.

I loved that best of anything because, despite my tender years, I already had maternal feelings. Our Jessie was my life. Cheeky monkey, she likes to think she still is.

She's probably got a point.

Chapter Five

The room is too small for this, and I apologise to my ladies. They are lying on mats all over the floor. The stockinged toes of the women in the back row are practically touching the hairstyles of those in the front. The window won't open and there is a right royal smell of female bodies – hot feet, spray deodorants, Pond's cream. There's no men in here. This is antenatal class number four out of a series of six. Partners tend to come to the first couple, then they're either too embarrassed and squeamish to attend any more because the women don't hold back when it comes to asking detailed questions, or the novelty wears off. Some's would say that's not very supportive of the boys, but you can't really blame them.

It's two weeks since I met Kelly in the hospital antenatal ward. Dr Walker did want to keep her in under observation, but I was there again this morning and he told her she was fine and could go home this afternoon. I imagine Stevie's probably picking her up right now. I've come on from a hectic morning of hospital comings and goings, to one of the two health centres to which our team is attached. It's a long bungalow basically, quite modern, with white fencing round. It's a lively, friendly place. There's always loads of kids in the waiting-room playing with toys.

I take the class with Tiffany, a young colleague in the team, and we show a video, and do exercises and relaxation. Most of the questions at the end are about the birth itself, because that's understandably all most of them can focus on. They feel like a train with its brakes not working heading in slow motion for a crash; the oncoming disaster of pain is inevitable, no turning back. It's the midwives' job to try to quell such fears. We inform them as best we can, using understanding.

There's lots of jokes, I won't tell you what about because they sound so silly, girls' stuff, you can imagine the sort. But it's important, laughter's almost as good as an epidural! I enjoy these classes even if I'm dog tired, say after a night shift, they're always good crack. When they're over, many of the women stay behind for a hot beverage, we do coffees and teas, and to have more chats. It makes you feel part of the whole plan, part of a cycle, part of a circle. I don't have so many friends of my own outside work. I've been a bit cautious since the laundry, a bit afraid of getting too close, because the closer you get, the more a friend wants to know and, as I say, I still feel the stigma. Certainly, my team colleagues are good friends, and Ted and Priscilla, though there's not really others. I'm not endowed with a best friend as such. I suppose Jessie, but she's family, so she's guaranteed. I don't know if that counts? A lot of the women I know say their husbands are their best friends.

We emerge from the class, jabber, jabber, jabber. Although it's late afternoon, the waiting-room is crowded, people come to see their GPs. I say goodbye to the ladies and go to the kiosk window of Reception to see if I've any messages. Becky is beginning to tell me them when I feel a gentle tap on my shoulder; one of my ladies, I assume.

'One sec, love,' I say without turning round, 'let me just get my messages and I'll be with you.' I am looking forward to going home, relaxing tonight, comforted by my routine of bath, telly, and early bed, these pleasures I've carved out for myself. It's been a long one. By this point I feel shagged out as an old beach donkey. I've got these aches, and am craving for my fix of Radox. I'm almost feverish in my longing to go home. I hope this lady won't be wanting to keep me long.

'Harold!' I say, turning at last and seeing it was. him at my shoulder. He is very smart in that navy jacket of his, the one with the National Canine Club badge on its lapel. 'What are you doing here? What a nice surprise.'

'I thought if my luck was in I might just catch you,' he replies. 'I've an appointment with Dr Raine. Aunt told me you were sometimes at this place.'

I scrape the hair and with it, with any luck, the look of exhaustion from my face. This is most unexpected. I've not seen Harold in here before.

'Excuse my appearance,' I say, 'I must be very dishevelled.' I know that in the course of my hectic day my hair has loosened away from its grip, and the clasp of my elasticated belt has inched to one side. The waist of my tights is on my hips and the gusset is making a bridge low across my thighs so I feel uncomfortable and restricted, and all I want to do is go somewhere private so I can jump and scissor my legs to get them up again. All day I haven't had the chance.

'Not at all,' he says, ever so gentlemanly.

'Been one of those days, haven't been off my feet.'

'Could you do with a drink? It would be a great pleasure to take you for a drink.'

'Goodness,' I say. My head can see my cosy evening plans and early night going out the window, but something else inside is putting out the bunting and juggling coloured balls and saying yes.

'Mr Mills,' calls Becky, 'Dr Raine's ready to see you now.'

Harold thanks her. 'Can you wait a few minutes?' he asks me. 'I shouldn't be long.'

'I'd love to have a drink, thank you,' I tell him.

'That's grand. You'll be here then?'

'I'll be here,' I say, and he smiles and moves off along the corridor.

So I have a moment at last to go to the Ladies and fix my hair, my belt, and my tights. In an ideal world I wouldn't be going out with Harold in my uniform, but needs must. I had been planning to go straight home, so I didn't bring my mufti. I feel a bit daffy sitting in the pub with all my work togs on. It's too easy for people to know what I am and, on those rare occasions when I do have a wine or some such, give looks as if to say, 'Someone in your profession shouldn't be drinking.' I was in the Crown with Jessie once, and a man I'd never seen before with a stomach as big as a woman's close to term, came up and actually said as much. He said, 'Nurses aren't supposed to take alcohol.' Can you credit it? I'll never forget it, Jessie turned to him and she smiled sweetly but then she indicated his beer gut, and she said, 'If that was a chat-up line, mister, you can fuck up, because frankly someone in your state shouldn't be drinking either.' Maybe that's part of why she has problems with men, language like that! I don't know, but what I do know is they don't like it in a woman, swearing and that.

I could've died. I felt myself going pitch red with embarrassment. I have to hand it to our Jess, though, I admire her guts. He deserved every word of it.

I'm standing at the mirror leaning over the basin with its Formica surround. All the fixtures and fittings, everything in here, is baby lotion pink, including the neon light-bulb. And it all comes together successfully to make me look like a dead person. I wash my hands in the matching liquid soap which comes out like that synthetic strawberry sauce they squeeze on to Mr Whippy ice-creams, but it doesn't make me feel as good. It leaves a surgical smell on my hands which is hardly appropriate, and I feel at odds and dissatisfied.

I feel all of a dither and excited, and I can't get myself looking right. I'm not a vain person – that was quickly drummed out of us at the laundry, so it was, no mirrors allowed, or anything like that. Nevertheless, there's times as I want to look right, I think that's only natural. I could never really look good. I'm the sort who, when people aren't relying on me, I'm quite easily invisible. I'm so ordinary, I sort of blend into the general scenery, the human equivalent of a soldier's camouflage in the forest, or a Nat West sign in any high street you care to mention, but I can sometimes look better than other times, times when people are moved to tell me I'm looking well. Only ever well mind, it never goes so far as pretty. I've a plain face, with a big nose. I got that from my mother. In her face it was OK, it complemented her huge eyes and Cupid-bow mouth, and the sum of them altogether made her beautiful. Unfortunately, my eyes are the unintended grey of a black garment that's been washed so many times it's faded to grey-green indistinction, and my lips are flat as runner beans. Cheekbones can't be said to be a feature I can lay claim to either. I've always had fat cheeks. In fact, I've always been tending to, if not exactly fat all over, then certainly plump and dumpy in parts (namely thighs, stomach, bottom). But I must add, I do have strong hands and a decent bust. There again, would you expect any less in a midwife?

Right now my complexion is misted with perspiration like condensation on a rear-view window, only I've no button like in my car to clear it, I've to make do with dabbing my face with a paper hankie, and it comes back as soon as I'm done. I apply a thin layer of black mascara to my eyelashes so they are at once thrust from blond obscurity into view. I take my little hairbrush from my handbag but my dead dull locks are as unresponsive as ever. Just as I'm on the point of despair, the door opens and Tiffany comes in. We talk about our class a moment, we agree it went well, and then she asks if I'm going out. I tell her, yes, for a drink, with a friend.

'That's nice,' she says. 'You look nice.'

'No I don't, Tiff, I look terrible.'

'Hang on, I'm busting to spend a penny.' She goes into one of the toilets. We continue to talk. 'Perhaps you could do with a spot of lippy?' she suggests. 'I've got some if you like.'

I've not worn lipstick for ages, I don't quite like the thought of the pigs' trotters it's made of so close to my tongue as I fancy I can taste them. Still, when Tiff emerges, she produces hers, a subtle shade of brown, not some startling scarlet which everyone seems to favour these days.

'Why not try some?' she suggests, and I'm quite tempted. I think, Why not indeed?

I lean to the mirror and soothe it over my lips. Tiff compliments me before she leaves, and I feel a whole lot better.

Get you, Dorothy Sheffield, I say to myself when she's gone, if you aren't pushing the boat out tonight! I emerge from the Ladies feeling quite the glamour puss. If only Jessie could see me now! Fair's to say she would be proud.

You have to go with a bit of small-talk to start with, don't you, before you move on to the autobiographicals?

Harold and I fairly do the small-talk.

I'm not saying we've got nothing better to talk about, because we have. Harold's an interesting man. He knows a lot.

We're in the wine bar, Raffles – gorgeous – each with a bevvy neat on our beer-mats, and we're discussing the weather, and things. Harold says he's a bit of an amateur meteorologist. There's not many can discuss the weather and keep me rapt like he can! It's none of your usual red sky at night, shepherd's delight for him. No, Harold can predict changes this way or that, rain or shine, by the way the birds are flying, their formations and direction, and that. He can explain such about clouds and winds as I've never even heard of. He not only knows the names of them, but their individual characters too. I'm rightly blown away.

He's good on nature as well. He takes Jones for walks, nights, and there's not a fact he doesn't know about nocturnal wildlife. If you're a midwife, all the technology's there so's you lose track of nature – natural childbirth's pretty much a thing of the past; it's a nice idea, but because the option of pain relief exists, the mums usually only get to a certain point, poor loves, before they're crying out for it. And I'm all in favour. Nonetheless, it soothes me to hear of natural nature, if you get my meaning, animals and all, away from the glare of operating theatre spotlights, going about their business, uncluttered, in the way God intended.

'I'm a bit of an owl man myself,' says Harold.

I think that's lovely.

He says there's a number live in Hayley Wood outside town, beautiful creatures. He goes to watch them sometimes, he and Jones have to be very quiet. Owls have got kindly eyes, he assures me, so much so you think they could be your friends.

I wonder if Harold's a lonely man.

It's hot in here, but he's kept his jacket on. Certainly, Harold's an old-fashioned man, stands on circumstance; he gives a woman respect. I suspect he thinks it wouldn't be right in my presence to sit here just in his shirt-sleeves. I am excruciated inside because I think he is perspiring, it's hard to tell in this low light. I want to take his jacket off of him, but I've not the social know-how to suggest it. I hate to see him uncomfortable on my account. Remember I said some elderly men have this effect on me, move me till I can feel the lump rising in my throat.

We spend a couple of hours together just, but we fit in a fair amount. As I say, he's an interesting man. He's interested too. Jessie says men's always talking about themselves. She's been on dates and it's been blah, blah, blah, me, me, me, they don't ask a single question, not even the most fundamental Where do you come from? What do you do? It beats me. Can't understand it. In fact, I'm fascinated by this. Not just men, it's anyone, there's plenty of women just as bad, who don't ask questions. I don't mean going so far as nosy, I mean, just being plain curious about one's fellow human beings. Perhaps it's because I'm in a world where questions are asked automatically. Like when you see a lady for the first time, she's a few weeks pregnant only, and you're doing what we call a booking, which we need for our records. It's a medical history, basically, with a bit of social thrown in, family background and so on. It takes about an hour; one question leads to another, but always a basic instinct takes over the mere professional interest. A curiosity to learn more about her life means, more often than not, you stray from the set questions on the form. It's join the dots. You're trying to get to know that lady, and make friends, and you hope she'll get to like and trust you too. It's not unlike dating, really, the point's not so far removed. You'd have thought that's what a man was aiming at when he takes a lady out. Yet these men Jessie's dated never seemed to have that. They never seemed to have even downright nosy. All they had was, 'I intend to get your knickers off you before the evening's out, so why don't I talk about nothing else but me, and bore them off you that way, seems as good a way as any.'

So I'm pleased that Harold asks away. They may be safe subjects he sticks with for starters – my work, my family, whatever – that's fine by me.

Of course, being me, I ask bits and bobs about him too. He's obviously not given to talking about himself, it doesn't come easy to him. He's about as far removed from one of these vain chappies, Jessie's used to as I am from being a can-can girl. I don't want to press him, poor soul, me and my inquisitiveness, but from what I can gather Harold's quite a fellow. He's had quite a time of it, you might say, quite a life.

So very different from mine. He speaks about his parents fondly, lovingly, you can tell there's no grudges there. They've been dead now, of course, twenty years or more. They'd been married sixty-odd. His mother had a stroke and died one week; his father held out the next one, then died exactly a fortnight after she did, on the Monday. Doctor said it was nothing but a broken heart. Harold says he still thinks about them every day, and takes flowers to their graves twice a week. My parents are still alive and I don't think about them as much as that, and I visit them on average once every two or three years if they're lucky.

The Millses were a real family, and stayed that way, strong bonds between them. Harold left school at fifteen and got his first job in soft furnishings in White's, our local department store, but he never left home. He still lives in the house where he was born. How far removed from my experiences! Being forcibly expelled from my home when still a teenager left me all over with grudges galore. As a child I was brought up a good Christian, but at the laundry I was forced to dump all that Christianity lark pretty damn quick. Almost as soon as I arrived I realised what religion meant there, how it gave the staff leave to taunt us with their singular strain of cruel piety. I'm glad I'm no longer a Christian. I'd have to forgive. There's a lot I don't want to forgive and anyway can't.

I think often, for example, of those actual moments of my expulsion from the house where I was born, and which for nineteen years had been my home. They were chillingly straightforward.

Mother and Father both gave me a kiss goodbye but, not given to larger displays of affection, neither of them could run to a hug. Jessie jumped up at me and locked her arms round my neck, her legs round my – from then on redundant – child–bearing hips. Clung to me like a koala bear, she did, and buried her head in my neck, crying, 'Don't go, don't go.'

'That's enough emotional carry-on,' Dad said, unclasping her limbs. 'Dorothy and these people have a long journey to make. Let her go, child.' Meanwhile I was wondering when I'd see my family again. I knew because I was going as far as Scotland – though I didn't know where in Scotland – that it would be some weeks, maybe months. It was never made clear, and I refused to give my parents the satisfaction of asking them. I would be miserable without Beth and Jessie for so long, and I was going to hate missing Staffordshire in the spring, our street, the cherry trees, Father's shop-front with its perennial arrangement of dustpans and brushes, striped aprons, tea towels, and his proud blooms of cotton reels with which he had filled his wheelbarrow, the centrepiece of his window display.

I blinked my eyes like a camera shutter to try and take a photograph with my mind of the parlour. The brass candlesticks on the wooden mantelpiece were shining vulgarly on as usual.

The upright piano was open, its yellowing keys for all to see. On its closed top, as ever, was the piece of lace which protected it from dust; the vase of dried flowers; and the picture of my beautiful mother on her wedding day, its sepia tones matching those of the walls unevenly stained by my father's pipe-smoke. I was born in the room above this little room which had remained just so all those years. I knew that when I returned, however long I was away, not a thing would have changed.

At the door, Mother handed me a cream tin with a pale green, scratched lid. I felt the weight of her special ginger-cake inside. Such motherly detail in the face of such unmotherly betrayal. Father thumbed one of his prized coins from his collection into my palm. To this day I am still puzzled by that gesture – was it for his guilt, or my bravery? When my mouth gaped to thank him, he held up his hand and said 'Hush' before my words had had the chance to splash out.

The grey man – the Children's Welfare Officer – his secretary Miss Montgomery, and I, all travelled to Scotland by train. I forget how many hours the journey took, but they did not speak to me, or to each other, the whole way – quite a feat by anyone's standards. I wondered if they had lost their teeth. She looked as cheerless and gnarled and unloved as someone who had lived all her life on a diet of dead wood, and had longed forever to get near enough a man to hear his heartbeat. She smelt of dry-rot spinsterhood.

I felt my round stomach and thighs beneath my coat for reassurance and, despite everything – the circumstances of my only brush with full sex, and the situation I was now in as a result – I blessed my youth, my plumpness, and my fertility.

We arrived at Glasgow Central, and the familiarity of that name, Glasgow, the place my father had so often mentioned in his memories and called home, gave me cause for hope. Perhaps I was being sent to stay with his family for a while. I'd never met my grandparents. I was suddenly, in all my misery, excited, wondering what they'd look like, and what kind of place they might have? I knew they'd be poor, but I imagined they'd be kind. Deportation from the bosom of my own family might turn out to be an enlightening experience after all.

My first sight of Piccadilly Park, up on a black hill, was not uplifting. It was the kind of place the very look of which was sufficient to deaden the soul.

There were no welcoming grandparents to greet me at the vast Gothic doors, or in the vast stone hall behind them. I don't know who to blame for the bitterness of that particular disappointment – perhaps my parents for not having the inclination or courage to warn me beforehand of my fate, or myself for being so foolish as to hope that where I was headed might be pleasant enough after all. Whoever, this is one of those things, little as it may seem, I cannot forget, and won't forg.ve.

'I've got no complaints,' Harold is saying. 'Since my mother and father died, I've had Jones to keep me company, and my fellow jam tarts, those of them that's not been given their marching orders.'

'There's been no more bad news since you were telling Priscilla and me about it?' I ask.

'Not any more redundancies in the last couple of weeks, no. Thank goodness. Rumour's there'll be more before Christmas. Oh dear, this is gloomy talk. Here, I ought to be getting back to Jones, but I'd like to get you another drink, will you have another with me?'

Harold's already persuaded me to have three wines, and I'm not really a drinker. It's feeling all warm and woolly inside my head, my brain feels like a sheepskin.

'Really I best be getting home myself,' I say reluctantly, picking up my handbag and clutching it to my bosom to convince myself I'm firm of purpose. 'I've an early start in the morning.'

'Are you sure not another little glass?' Harold asks, hospitable and generous.

I shake my head. 'Honestly, better not, but thank you. I've had a truly enjoyable evening.'

When we leave, some young people immediately sit at our table. It's nine o'clock and the place is crowded, but Harold and I are past late nights. We're a right old pair of early birds.

In the calm of outside, Harold offers to walk me home. Tonight I fancy a companion through the dark streets, and it's not far, so I accept. He unchains his lumbering bicycle with its battered basket from a nearby lamp-post. It's touching that he feels the need to lock it. It's so old-fashioned I doubt anybody in this town would even think to steal it. We stroll together towards the harbour, and I ask him about the factory.

'It's changed a lot in the forty years since I first went there,' Harold tells me. 'Then our cakes were near enough home-made. Not any more. It's all machines nowadays, doing every little thing – from squirting the jam into the pastry ponds to plopping each individual tart into its packaging. You should see it, Dorothy, it's a major operation as it is, but I expect these German fellows who've taken us over are going to modernise it even more.'

'But they'll always need a human palate to do your job.'

'I should hope so. I don't much fancy the idea of a machine in Quality Control. I don't expect any could ever be nearly discerning enough. The difference in taste between each different batch of pastry, for example, or jam, is so subtle. I like to think recognising that would always remain a human being's prerogative.'

'They'll never be able to replace you, Harold. Your tongue is like Shirley Maclaine's legs, you realise, must be worth a fortune.'

'I have to say, I've never thought of it quite like that,' he smiles, 'but now you mention it, it's a comforting thought. Perhaps I ought to get it insured?'

As we reach the harbour we are laughing. I haven't even noticed walking along the street with all the advent calendar scenes through the windows. Normally I can't resist looking into them as I pass.

It's not like getting home on an ordinary night.

'Perhaps you'd like me to take you on a tour of the factory one day?' says Harold as we reach my front door.

'I would indeed, very much, I'd like that a lot.'

'It's not really allowed, but we'll arrange it then. Something nice to look forward to.' He puts out his hand for me to shake. There are veins on it which protrude and move me. I thank him, and he cycles off on his own into the night.

As I go inside and make myself a bit to eat, I imagine him returning to one of those 1930s pebbledash bungalows which line the street where he lives at the back of the town. I imagine him lifting the latch of a wooden gate, picking his post up off the mat, putting a potato in the oven to bake, and being greeted by his beloved companion. I wonder what he talks about to his dog when they're together, what excuse he'll give him tonight for his belated homecoming?

Does Harold have an evening routine to keep himself occupied and happy? Does Harold lay the table for one, or eat supper on his knee in front of the television? Does he lock the door when he goes to the bathroom? Does he comb his hair, though nobody's there to see it? Does he slip every night into ironed pyjamas and a bed that's well made?

Does he, like me, arrange his solitude in such a way as all the better to stave off the onset of loneliness? Does he, like me, half relish the loneliness when it comes because it's so sad and there's a sort of tragedy in that which reminds him of the throb of life? At the same time, does he fear loneliness as he might a terminal cancer, and want to lop it off from his existence like a mastectomy?

Does he believe, as I do, that whatever any of us manages to make of solitude, people were not really meant to be alone?

Perhaps I should correct myself and say people were not really made to be unloved. I was never so lonely as the time when I was living with lots of others. The loneliness of more than twenty years by myself in my cottage is as nothing compared to what you had to endure at the laundry, knowing nobody loved you, even from afar. How could my parents love me and send me to such a place as this? Jessie probably did, but she was a child just and, as the years pass, children forget.

As for the girls loving each other, the laundry did its best to outlaw us from forming any sort of attachments. Although they failed, when love did prevail between us, it was never uninhibited.

Rule number one: you weren't allowed to speak (except for one hour a day most evenings). Of course we developed other means of communication, but they were limiting. Not legally being able to open your mouth to express yourself (odd occasions we did resort to covert whispering) takes its toll.

Times when I feel the silence at home too keenly, at least I've got the wireless or the television to talk to me. And I can talk out loud to myself. It started with a swear word when I'd stub my toe, graduated to, 'Oi, where did I leave you, scissors?', and now it's full-blown chatting, about my day, what I must remember to do tomorrow, and so on. First sign of madness, maybe, but comforting enough when there's nobody else to come by.

Imagine the frustration when there are plenty of people to come by, you're sleeping in the same dormitories, you're working and eating side by side, and you must all carry on as if rigor mortis has set into your tongues.

From the moment I passed through those imposing Gothic doors with iron studs, I was taken aback by the silence. There were young women, all in identical grey pinafores, kneeling on the floor and stairs below the most enormous painting I'd ever seen, of the angel Gabriel. I saw one girl pour some foul-smelling, nose-scrunching, black disinfectant from a bottle labelled Lysol into a pail of water. Instantly the liquid turned that diffuse white of a bride's wedding veils. The girls used hard brushes to scrub the lino and wood as if their lives depended on it, but they didn't breathe a word to each other while they worked.

The grey man and his companion handed me over to a woman called Miss Beveridge who held a huge bunch of keys and wore a long burgundy dress beneath a starched apron, and had black hair scraped so tightly into a bun that her eyes were as slits and her ears appeared to be farther round her head than was entirely normal. It was as if her hair and its attendant kirby-grips were alone responsible for holding her face together, and if someone cut off her bun her whole head might collapse and fall apart.

'Here goes. Here's where you're stopped now. Follow me, Dorothy Sheffield,' she said in an accent which was like my father's. As she walked along the corridor, the young women shifted themselves and their buckets out of her way so she could make a clear path through them and act as if they didn't exist. I followed her into a dank walk-in cupboard which was lined with identical pinafores. She gave me those nearest to her, and some grey socks and thick over-knickers.

'Get those on you, Dorothy Sheffield, and give me yours for burning. You'll not be needing them again, girl.'

That morning I had particularly chosen the woollen dress with cherries on that I'd worn the day before because privately it still smelt to me of Eliza, babyish and sweet. When I took it off and passed it to Miss Beveridge, she held it away from her body between her thumb and forefinger, and dropped it into a scrawny paper bag.

'Socks!' she demanded. Like everyone at the laundry, she was a woman of few words. 'Grey only. Blue not allowed.'

I peeled mine off and they too went into the bag.

'Brassière!'

I turned away from her as I undid the clasp.

'There's no use in modesty, Dorothy Sheffield. I need to assess you for a corset. Turn round.'

Slowly I did so, head high, not looking at her. My empurpled nipples were swollen with cold and the need to feed my no longer daughter.

'My, we don't have them *that* big. You'll have to make do.' She delved her hand into a large cardboard box full of greying corsets and hastily pulled one out, the first to hand, any old size.

'Knickers off first. Own knickers not allowed either.'

I remained facing her and staring at her slits for eyes. Very slowly I pulled down my pants, making sure she could see everything blatantly, have a real good look. Which she did. I stood completely still as if obediently awaiting her instructions, but it was really to test if I could shame her out of her intrusive stare.

The slits looked away. Miss Beveridge, silent, turned her back to me to pick out a pair of shoes. I struggled into the corset. It seemed to pinch my skin with malicious intent, to make a mockery of my breasts. Punishment for their enlarged state. Milk leaked.

The grey pinafore was too long and wide all round, and the brown lace-up shoes were warped into the shapes of how many former owners' feet I couldn't imagine, but they did not fit my own.

'These are too small,' I said.

'Girls are not allowed to speak.'

'But these are too small.'

84

'Too small, too bad; I said girls aren't allowed to speak. Put them back on.'

'They hurt.'

'Quiet! Now give me those,' she said, grabbing my own shoes from me though I had them clutched to my stomach. 'Bag.' It rustled as she put them in with my cherry dress and bra.

'You can't burn those!'

'Girls are not allowed to speak, I said, and they're not allowed belongings. I'll have your watch off you too, and any jewellery. Give!'

I undid the thin brown strap of the watch my mother and father had given me on my thirteenth birthday.

'That all?' she asked, pocketing it in her starched apron. 'You'll get it back when you leave. If.'

'If?'

'If you don't shut your mouth, Dorothy Sheffield, you'll be sent to the front.'

Being sent to the front, it (not much) later transpired, was the punishment meted out for almost everything. It involved being made to stand alone in the hall for hours, sometimes for an entire day, or two; no food. You were supposed to gaze at Gabriel without moving your eyes away from the picture for a single second, in order that a mite of his goodness might rub off your evil self. If you didn't, you were likely headed for everlasting damnation.

It was the inhuman silence of our days. I had never been especially talkative, but I was willing to risk being sent to the front, whatever it took, everlasting damnation, just for the luxury of breathing a word to the girl in the bed next to mine, or to the one working beside me all day in the laundry. When I did, which was often, I was punished. Usually this meant having to face Gabriel for hours on end, yet again. But there were other means of setting us to rights. Once my hair was cut right off. A staff perk was to sell our hair by the inch to the local wig factory. If a girl's grew long enough to be profitable, it wasn't ages before one member of staff or other found some spurious excuse to make an example of her and give her a crew cut to remember.

While the asylum existed only for the incarceration of the

insane, the aim of the laundry, you see, was a bit different. Those on the top floors were there for life, were never going to get out. And they were treated with all the lack of compassion which the powers that be believed no-hopers with mental illness deserved. Because us lot downstairs – about thirty in all – weren't in the raving mad category but in the fallen women or moral defectives one, we were living at Piccadilly, and working in the basement, specifically in order to be rescued (in the loose sense of the word) from a life of vice. Girls in danger of being led astray were there to be protected (again, loose term) from themselves. We could get out, but only at such time as we had shown evidence of reformation of character sufficient to guarantee that we would return to an honest and upright way of life. If we showed no signs of improvement there was a chance we might clean sheets for good, or even graduate up a floor or two for a spell of the insane treatment – a massive dose of incapacitating drugs here, a spot of electrocution there.

Such 'rescue' and 'protection' as the laundry provided took the form of prayers, hymns, work, silence. Piccadilly Park was neither run nor funded by the Church, but strong devotion and harsh puritanism were nonetheless top priority.

Our day started at 6.30, with the unforgiving sound of a bell. In the winter nights sheets of ice used to form on the inside of our dormitory windows, so much so that we couldn't see through the panes. Stepping out of bed onto lino with bare feet was like taking to a skating rink in nothing but nylons. Breakfast, like all meals, took place in the gloomy wood-panelled dining-room on the ground floor. It was porridge, and prayers, and hymns on the organ. From the moment you woke, your stomach ached. It didn't feel empty, as you'd imagine extreme hunger would feel, but was as if a sharp and heavy breeze-block was weighing in there so that when you moved it pressed against and dug into every corner of your middle body. Once swallowed, the porridge acted as a thin film round the breeze block, and smudged its edges, but only temporarily. An hour or so after the meal, the pain would once more be as sharp as ever. We never had enough food. What we were feeling was long-term hunger. The breeze-block never really shifted. You had to work and sleep with it, live with it, all those years.

Work started immediately after breakfast, at seven o'clock.

A few lucky ones got the kitchen. That was the cushiest job because they could steal pieces of bread. I was in the laundry itself.

The laundry took up most of the space in the basement and consisted of the wash-house, the drying and pressing room, and the packing room. There were stone floors throughout. A smell of damp and soap powder pervaded the whole place. (It was better than Lysol. Lysol was meant to be for sewers and drains. We had to use it on floors because vice, so they said, though invisible, came off our shoes in clods like dry mud, and needed everywhere to be exterminated.)

In the wash-house was a line-up of four washing-machines, dead old-fashioned. They had huge cast-iron barrels like prize draw drums which rotated all day long. You couldn't see inside, but water poured out of them so that you had to wear wellies if you worked in there. The wellies fitted better than the shoes. It was a right dirty job. The sheets were filthy. They came down from upstairs, and in from old peoples' homes on the outside. I don't need to spell it out; all's I'll say is that the stench was unimaginable. Some of the linen came from hotels. They sent sheets ravished by sex. Some of them had blood on, which was common enough on those from upstairs and the old peoples' homes as well, but the hotel ones had, also, less certain stains; and their smell was altogether saltier. The supervisor, Miss Read, after years in charge of the wash-house, was well acquainted with that smell but could not have recognised what it was. She was a right Tartar. She'd been in the Salvation Army. She was wee and dumpy, grey hair; she must be dead now.

I was in the drying room. My task was to work the callender machine which was a vast pressing contraption with two big rollers turned by a series of canvas belts. I fed the sheets in one end; someone else was at the other, responsible for taking them off. In the corner of the room were the irons – oh, they were heavy – for doing the shirts. Each iron was attached to a tube which emerged from the ceiling and which fed it the gas necessary for heating its flat bottom. It was ever so hot in there. Steam all about. I can tell you, we were sweating like pigs the lot of us, and gasping.

They used to have outside workers next door in the packing room. Girls weren't allowed in there because it was too near the door which led to the open yard where they loaded the van. You could see in there, though. It was full of wicker hampers, and piles of pale blue tissue paper for in between the clean folded sheets and tablecloths.

We hated the outside workers. We took our ten-minute elevenses break with them in the dingy corridor. They came with lunch boxes and had bottles of pop, and fruit, and sandwiches with mighty fillings – chunks of cold meat, corned beef, or spam, plus mayonnaise, cucumber, and that. We had one slice of bread, hard and curled, no butter, no jam; and nothing to drink because spending a penny was outlawed, it was a waste of precious working time. I remember once, I must've been at the laundry some months, one of them bitches sat on a bench opposite me and took an apple out of her little basket, and rubbed it up and down her chest very, very slowly, staring at me all the while with her fat, smug face. That green apple became shinier and shinier with every rub, so that the reflection of even the single dim bulb hanging from the ceiling began to gleam on its perfect surface. I could feel myself pulsating inside, blood rushing round me in sheer, violent fury. She took a bite trying to make the crunch as loud as possible. It cracked through the voiceless silence like an axe through a tree trunk. She had soft leather shoes; red they were. I wanted to hit her till I saw the red of her blood. Then she started to chew, her mouth all open so I could see the foamy flesh of that apple churn about her deep, purple mouth like the sheets in the washing-machines.

I leapt across the floor divide, tough shoes all ready to kick her hard as hell, but Bel, who was sitting beside me, pulled me back. She wanted to save me from graduation (the delicate term used for being sent up to the asylum). At that moment she became someone I could trust; my friend, the first and only real one I ever had at the laundry.

Bel's sin was her pretty face and slim figure. She was in the laundry because, still a spinster at twenty-five, she'd been considered a temptation the local men were unlikely to be able to resist, and a threat the local married women would be foolish to tolerate. Her whole village had voted to get her removed 'out of harm's way', and her family, ashamed she had opted for independence and refused to marry, consented. On the day of the apple incident, she had been in the laundry about two years, and had become a cunning survivor. It was not only for that reason she was a good and crucial ally.

That evening, during the talking hour, she told me secretly she had better schemes for getting back at that outsider bitch.

A friendship was well and truly forged that day. It was one which was not only to help ebb the flow of loneliness, but also to influence the views that I felt about, and wanted from, life itself.

Chapter Six

Jessie's on the line and I'm lost for words. I just don't know what to say to her.

It's my day off. I've been working solid the ten days since Harold's and my encounter at the health centre and our drink out. I'm shattered. I was in the middle of doing the usual – household chores, going through my accounts, that sort of thing. As usual when reading my bank statements and bills, I was worrying about money when the phone rang. That's one of the things I don't like about being alone, you've nobody to share your financial problems and anxieties with. I talk to Jessie about it, but it's not the same as confiding in a husband. You see, I earn rubbish. Even though I spend little, the figures just don't tally. There's this romantic idea with the public that us carers should be paid more than company directors for what we do, only the government don't seem to think so. They've got us over a barrel because they know we're not the types to strike, it's always been against our tradition. But recently, like Priscilla referred to in her outburst the other day, the Royal College of Midwives, for the first time in its history, has been forced to start planning a formal ballot on industrial action, for all our 30,000 members. I was horrified when I first heard: our abiding principles have always been with our ladies. Course, the team have talked about it plenty, and they're all for it, 100 per cent, but I couldn't think it was right. I found myself protesting on the phone about it to Jessie not so long ago, and she hit the roof. She was going on about rights and morals and inequality; and it's all very well for them £40,000-a-year fat cat politicians, but nurses and midwives are the backbone of our society and they're being shat on all over; how the hell are they supposed to survive on pigshit? it was about ruddy time we made a stand. She gave me what you might call a rather emotional lecture for, honest to God, fifteen minutes, but it did seem to make a lot of sense. I've thought about it long and hard since, and though it kills me inside, and I'll never abandon our ladies or put them in danger, if the Department of Health do ignore our case for a special pay and grading structure, I've no doubt in my mind where I'm going to be putting my X.

Ideally, I'd like to be able, each week, to set a little aside for a rainy day. At the moment I try, but more often than not it just isn't feasible. I don't know what's meant by rainy day, exactly. Is it that on a rainy day people are supposed to cheer themselves up by going out on a merry spree, blowing their savings on things they don't really need, but which give pleasure? But who likes to shop in the rain? Perhaps it's that on a rainy day the roof's supposed to leak, so it's sensible to have a little hidden extra to put towards this unexpected expenditure? I think that would be my interpretation: always be prepared for an emergency whenever possible. I never was much of a one for throw caution to the wind. I've never been one of those extravagant, exciting types.

Now, Jessie on the other hand, is the sort to throw caution, and God knows what else, anything that's going, to the wind. I can cite plenty examples.

She's taken Derek back, for one. That's what she's rung to tell me.

Well, who would have guessed it.

As I say, I'm lost for words. She's saying not to be angry with her. I can tell that what she's after is my approval. I'm not angry or disapproving, particularly. I don't know what I am.

'How did it happen?' I ask her. I am at my kitchen table, all my statements and bills laid out in front of me. As she speaks, I'm aimlessly pressing the buttons and making patterns on my calculator, 111222333444555 CLEAR.

'Oh, Dot, you sound so cross.'

'No, I'm not.'

'I suppose you've a right to be, only hear me out. Because we spoke since I threw him out, you already know that at first I don't hear a word so I begin to wonder what's happened to him. You agreed with me he's probably moved in with her, but I don't go trying to find out. Two weeks go by you realise – silence. I remember saying to you, good riddance to him; I'm full of these good intentions, see. Then, out the blue, he starts to come knocking at my door, nights, that's how it happens. Oh, Dot, I'm so good for the first couple. I did try and ring you to let you know just how good, but I kept missing you. I won't let him in, see. He says through the letterbox he's brought me flowers, a socking great bouquet to show me how sorry he is, and I tell him where he can shove it.'

'That's good.'

'Yeah, but the next night he comes with a whole new, bigger and better lot, and when I won't let him in, he starts down on his knees pushing them through the cat-flap. He manages to squeeze them in without hurting them, that's his gentle side coming out, see. And they're that beautiful, and smell that gorgeous. I still won't open the door, but. Then last night he comes knocking the third time running, more flowers and more remorse, and I can't keep it up any longer, Dot, and I can't do that to him. He's standing in the porch, all apologies and miserable as hell; and there's me, the other side of the front door, miserable as hell. You know the thick misted glass, well, I can see his shape through it. What else am I supposed to do? I love him, see. Tell me another woman as wouldn't have done the same in my position. If you know of one that tough and strong, introduce me to her, I'd have to see it to believe it.'

'Well that was easy for him, wasn't it? What was it, three bunches of flowers, and everything's rosy.' I shouldn't be saying it. I can't help myself.

'You don't understand, Dot. It's not like that.'

'What's it like, then?'

'Only time as he's ever given me flowers before, like I told you, was last Valentine's, the single red rose that smelt of fish. He's a changed man, I'm telling you.'

'Changed as a leopard.'

'No, I'm serious. I believe him and trust him now, I really do.'

'Are you sure about that? Even if you didn't believe and trust him, Jess, you'd still love him.' She starts to protest. 'OK, we won't dwell on that,' I tell her pompously. 'Just something to think about. Tell me, what happened when you let him in?'

'We talked about things. He made promises.'

'He's never going to see Carla or any other woman again?'

'That's it.'

'But Derek's made those selfsame promises in the past, am I right?'

'He has, too. Only this time I get the feeling it's different. It's over between them right enough.'

'We shall see.'

'Give him a chance, will you. You can be a hard woman, Dot, so you can. Hard on fellahs. They're harmless enough creatures, really. They just get a bit muddled, that's all.'

'Muddled, just?'

'Yes. Look, I have to forgive him.'

'He doesn't deserve you,' I tell her, trying to be gentler, less critical.

Jessie, my sister, I think she's a winner, you see, she's a special girl, and deserves better. It might seen an odd thing to say, what with her having had so many lovers and that, and being the survivor type, a fighter, but she's all innocence underneath. Jessie's car breaks down, and what happens? Some cowboy mechanic will chat her up, and charge her £350 to tweak the spark plugs. Jessie sees an ad in the paper for some new wonder slimming pills which boast magical powers, and what does she do? She sends off her cheque for £30 there and then. And, if she's lucky, six weeks later she'll receive half a dozen herbal tablets through the post which, surprise, surprise, are about as effective as rabbit droppings. She is no less trusting of the men who dwindle into her life on account of her pretty feet, her catching laugh, or her all-round sweetness of disposition. Her expectations of them are negligible. This means that if they go in for such rudimentary courtesies as a good morning at breakfast, or a by your leave when she places a lovingly cooked meat-and-two-veg meal on the dinner table, that constitutes a miracle of joy and love, to be mulled over and relished for a matter of weeks.

The one before sun-bed Tony was Craig, I remember. No one in their right mind would have trusted him as far as they could spit. Jessie trusted him to the end of the earth. I admire and envy her in a way, it's a great way to view the world, if rather a dangerous one. But, oh, was she let down.

I wouldn't have gone out of my way to choose for Jessie a man who was with someone else, but it has to be said Craig seemed every bit the mild-mannered sweetheart, he was a very personable fellow, you couldn't have helped but like him. He had a tremendous enthusiasm about life which was affecting, and was also talented at his job, which was as head chef at a country club. But there was something about him not quite right.

He'd been living with his girlfriend about two years round the time he met Jessie. Being a chef, he had time off in the afternoons. Every day he and Jessie met, or at least spoke. Often he'd bake her these gorgeous Black Forest gâteaux, and all the time he would tell her that he was going to be leaving Renee for her, he was going to be moving in with her, and how he looked forward to living happily ever after with her and her three kids. I have to say at moments even I was taken in, cynical old Dorothy. It didn't turn out quite like he promised, of course. In fact, he bungled eveything so totally that he managed, with record aplomb, to create the greatest amount of hurt, to the greatest amount of people (himself included), over a protracted period of time.

It started going awry when Craig was round at Jessie's one afternoon and his mobile phone rang, if you'll excuse the coarse detail, while they were in bed together. It was Renee. And Craig, undeflected from the pleasurable diversion being provided by my sister, managed to carry on a conversation with his girlfriend with all the nonchalant innocence of someone sitting in a crowded park making daisy chains. True story.

You have to hand it to him, I suppose. You have to marvel at that type of breezy deceit. It chilled Jessie.

Renee had a few wobblies when Craig tried, feebly, to leave her. She even threatened suicide, poor girl, she was that desperate. That would seem to me to be rather compromising the pride. I don't think that's a very honest way to go about keeping your man. Still, fair play to her, it worked. That was because he was a moral coward of untold proportions. She'd obviously bargained on that one. He carried on living with her, which was what she wanted. Naturally, he also carried on sleeping with Jessie, procrastinating to a devastating degree, managing to create the worst of all possible worlds. It wasn't long, thank God, before

Jessie found the strength finally to give him the boot. Enough was enough.

Russell was another one somewhere along the line. He was the only man apart from Craig to whom Jessie ever gave the old heave-ho. She should never have given him the come-hither in the first place. Perhaps it's bad taste to list my sister's former men in gruesome detail, but I think it's important. Says a lot about men, a lot about Jessie, and a bit about me too I suspect.

Of all of them, I suspect Russell was the worst. He wasn't like the usual run of her fellahs. She thought she'd hit upon something of a gentleman. He spoke awfully nicely. Posh, like. Perfectly chiselled vowels glistened in his speech. Pity it was so full of four-lettered Anglo-Saxon words. But he managed to make even them sound respectable. He'd been to a public school – not Eton or something, but one I'd not heard of, near Amersham – and was seeing an analyst. One of his brothers was in the army, the other worked in the City of London. Russell was the black sheep. He had an ex-wife and two unhappy teenage children, and was something in television. (Jessie met him while he was doing some programme in Stoke.) He smoked like a gangster's gun; and wore tight dark jeans, a leather jacket, trainers, and an adolescent smirk, even though he was in his early to mid-forties. (Russell used to lie about his age; so precious in a man.) Perhaps he was in children's TV. I remember Jessie was so excited when he invited her down for a weekend at his place in London. He lived in Shepherd's Bush. I can recall the name because Jessie said beforehand that perhaps he'd turn out to be her good shepherd.

He turned out to be a right real badun.

She became infatuated by him.

The six weeks their affair lasted she felt light-headed and sick all the time. She lost weight effortlessly for the first time in her life, and made jokes about marketing the R-Plan Diet and making millions; but I know Jessie, and I knew she wasn't happy.

If there are men who are physically violent, there are also men who are violent in subtler, more sophisticated ways. Russell was one of them. He was a menace to the female sex. He wanted to destroy any woman he slept with in a way a man with fists like Derek never could.

Didn't stop her.

Most of their time together was taken up in Stoke while he was working on his television programme. When filming was over and he returned home, he proved an all too inadequate communicator. Sometimes she would try to get hold of him of an evening. His telephone would be engaged and engaged and engaged, and then there'd be no answer through the night. For Jessie, the frustration and pain was akin to Chinese torture, but she couldn't admit it. She'd call me in the early hours, close to tears, both wanting to be reassured for herself, and offering excuses for him. I knew as well as she did that he was deliberately tormenting her; that he was more than likely going with other women and wanted her to know it in order to oil his own vacuous ego.

When she finally did reach him his voice lacked warmth, and he took his time issuing her with an invitation to visit him. Many hints later he finally managed it, and Jessie was a spinning-top of excitement. Poor love, the whole weekend was a disaster.

He lived in rented accommodation Jessie later admitted was unfit for a pig. There was a bucket on the kitchen table to catch drips from the ceiling; another one at the end of the bed; both looked as though they were there to stay. Things in the fridge were so out of date they'd taken on a life of their own, they were *heaving*. The bath was gritty as a sand-pit and had hairs curled over its surface, she said, like beach worms.

Instead of taking her out, Russell would send her off, alone, to fetch something from the local takeaway or corner shop. He was too busy on the phone to go with her, and too much the opportunist to reach into his pocket to pay for it. You might be amazed someone of Jessie's character would put up with it. She's said since that the behaviour was unacceptable, but so brazenly so that, at the time, she found herself questioning her own indignation; thinking, no one can behave this badly, perhaps it's normal and I'm the unreasonable one?

Even when she wasn't shopping for food, he'd make telephone calls for anything up to an hour. He would talk on and on, all the while watching her struggling not to listen to his conversation, struggling to appear interested in some age-old newspaper or magazine fading on the table. Sometimes he'd be speaking to women with an intimate tone designed to keep Jessie guessing. But more often than not it was to an actor friend called Lloyd who made laddish, explicit jokes about Jessie down the line, and asked after her performance in bed. Russell treated her to these and she was supposed to laugh. She didn't feel entirely comfortable about it, but feared she was perhaps being prudish. So, ever compliant, she humoured him, and laughed to convince herself they were funny.

I don't see sheer nasty as attractive. I'm lucky in that.

Fortunately for our Jess, Russell excelled himself, and sheer nasty at last lost its gleam when it sank to rusty cruelty.

I understand – as a midwife and as a sister to Jessie Burford you get used to hearing such things – that he wasn't a man to waste his time nurturing a woman's pleasure. Put it another way, or rather, Jessie's way, he was somewhat wanting in the foreplay department. When she told me this, she said, 'Let's face it, Dot, penetration's a bit tricksy when you're dry as a bone!' On the Sunday afternoon, they were trying to get down to the business and, if you'll forgive the crude detail, because he hadn't gone in for the build-up it wasn't really working out. Apparently he looked her straight in the eye and, I'm not making this up, he said in his ever so glinty voice, 'I've always wondered how rapists managed to overcome this problem. Truth is, rape must turn women on.'

Jessie let him finish off. She didn't say a word. There were no histrionics, that's not her way. She froze up inside, but. Just got dressed, announced she was leaving for an earlier train than planned, and went. He seemed vaguely surprised, if unmoved. Predictably, he didn't call her, she didn't hear from him again. If she'd still been under the influence of infatuation, she would have minded, minded very much. As it was, he could no longer get to her. Briefly she wondered, in the purely anthropological sense, that someone could have such a mind as his. But she soon forgot the phenomenon, and moved on to others that were less startling.

A year later Russell rang to apologise for not having rung. Jessie didn't recognise the voice at first. When she did, she cackled, as much like a witch as she could possibly cackle, and told him, ever so sweetly, that she hoped he was happy. That was sure to have screwed him up, because he was obviously so miserable.

They haven't spoken since.

'If you don't think Derek deserves me,' Jessie's saying, 'you should come and stay, come and see for yourself. We'd all love to see you anyway. When's your next weekend off? If you don't have one before Christmas, perhaps you'll come for Christmas itself?'

I was pleased for the invitation, less to see Derek's transformation (which, if real, would be something to behold) than to see Jessie and the kids.

'I shall have to look at the schedule,' I tell her. 'I'm not sure when I'm on and when not. I'll find out.'

People with families dread Christmas and bemoan its existence in the comfortable knowledge they'll probably enjoy it after all. People without families dread it more, but you won't hear them openly bemoan it. That luxury is denied them for their dread is justified. When is there a time more shaming than Christmas to be alone? I have family, but not my own family, not my own Eliza, and at Christmas more than ever, I feel the failure. I'm luckier than some: Jessie asks me up to hers every year. Except it's hard and poignant to spend it by someone else's hearth, with someone else's children, even if that hearth and those children are your beloved sister's. Sometimes I go; more often than not I opt to work instead. The hospital has tinsel; it has children, but it has no hearth. I find that easier. And, being on duty obscures the shame of being so essentially alone.

'Try and get Christmas off. You've worked the last three years. We'd love to have you.'

If I'm feeling strong, I'd love to go.

Other than hearing Jessie's news, it's a good day off I have. I'm glad of her invitation; and I finish my accounts and housework, I find them therapeutic. In the afternoon I have a two- or three-hour nap which goes some way to revive me. I wake up early evening. My curtains are open. It's dark outside, but the lights of the harbour dully orange my little bedroom. I lie still. Heavy as a rock. Waking at this time, in this light, I look at the clock yet the hour doesn't seem recognisable. I am disembodied from the familiar definition of my day. Late November six to seven is the sky getting inky; is enhanced artificial brightness in the wards; is the staffroom with Jaffa Cakes dipped in cups of tea; is that lift of home beckoning; is the dramatic strum of the evening news jingle. Late November six to seven is maroon; is headlights; is slate; and is Guinnesss, mittens, requiems, wood smoke, and brooding. Here, in only my knickers, tights and sweatshirt, beneath my thick eiderdown and disinclined to move, these are strange moments. I feel an obscure sense of aloneness, colour of amber, not lonely.

In the silence, I am wondering what Harold Mills and Jones do for their Christmas.

'With my first, Marcus, I was fine,' Kelly's telling me, 'but with Topsy, I tore to shreds, and they stitched me up crazy as a sock's darning, I swear to God. I had to sit myself on a blinking rubber ring for a month. Walking was like sliding in your altogether down a banister of razor blades.'

After my day off, I like to lower myself back into work gently. If I can, I usually start the morning with a home visit.

This is my third or fourth visit to Kelly's since I met her in the hospital. I feel I've got to know her very fast; perhaps because we get on, we can have a laugh. Also, she reminds me quite a lot of Jessie. In many ways they're similar.

Kelly lives on one of the better out-of-town estates, though it's by no means trouble- or poverty-free. There is dispossession here as everywhere else; just it's easier to spray paint on the inside of a lift in a tower block and remain unseen than it is to vandalise the façade of a house in a low-rise development. But that doesn't mean there's not problems here. As midwives, we see it all on the inside, we're not fooled. Having said that, at Kelly's what you see is what you get. Money is a struggle. Apart from that rather major consideration, things really are good. I'm not being fooled.

Kelly's house is honey brick, modern, nice. Her doorbell plays a rousing tune. The smell inside, though commonplace, is indefinable. Homes with children in them all smell the same, perhaps a combination of babies' dinners, toddlers' potties, dampened washing, and bargain household cleaner with a twist of chemical rose, or lemon, or alpine mist. The front room of Kelly's is square, white. The carpet is mossy coloured, mossy texture too. The two-piece suite is leather-look, dead comfy to sit on; squashy. Opposite it there is a black wooden unit. Stacked on its shelves are a bubbling fish tank – pebbly surface, green seaweed, blue water, couple of goldfish – highly coloured family photos in brown cardboard mounts with gold flourishes, a collection of videos – everything from *Aladdin* to *Terminator 2* – and a television with a screen practically the size of a shop-front. A breakfast programme is on, loudly, and a minor celebrity is extolling the virtues of exercise bicycles and holidays in five star hotels in the Seychelles.

Kelly and I are sipping tea from mugs that come free with brand-name chocolate Easter eggs. Her four-year-old, Marcus, is still in his lime green Biker Mice pyjamas and Pink Panther slippers, vulnerable white ankles sticking out between. He is on his mum's lap, dazzled by the autumnal fake flowers on the set of the TV show, and the daft celebrity with her hot wine lip-gloss and untimely gush.

'After Marcus, his dad and I were back at it in under a fortnight, no worries, 'cept he was useless in bed, hammering away with all the sensitivity of a Black and Decker, and we were rowing so anyway I weren't really bothered to be honest if we never did do it again. After Tops, though, it were different. Stevie and me were dying for a shag, but I had to say to him, "If you're after it with me, mate, you can hopscotch to Honolulu first 'cos, one thing's for sure, it'll take that time before I'm properly patched up and back in the action." '

It's Saturday, about a month since Kelly had her fit in the shopping mall. She's as chirpy as ever even though she's overdue and contractions don't seem to be forthcoming. The frustration of some of the women in these last phases can verge on the frantic. Fair enough. But Kelly's got enviable patience.

'When it comes, it comes,' she says, tapping her stomach, 'though I feel like a bleeding Space Hopper. My sister's dropping round every day now to see if there's any news. She's a traveller, New Age like. Fills her jerries with water. She had hers in the middle of fucking nowhere, in a bender. Midwife, poor thing, up to her knees in mud. It wasn't you was it, Dot?'

'I don't think so.'

'You'd remember. She invited everyone on the site in to watch, 'bout seventeen of them, all chanting peace songs or what have you, and staring up her jacksie. She's a laugh, our Leanne, except of course she calls herself Leaf, or Log, or some such now, I can never remember. She's got her problems, drugs and that, but I love my sister. I had her there when Marcus and Tops were born. She's wired to the moon, but I couldn't have done without her. She was massaging me and that. Helped a lot. She'll be there with this one too. You know, I bet secretly she's longing for a bath, only she'd say the soap would interfere with her karma or something. I think it's more a case of not wanting to let the side down.'

'She doesn't half leave a pong,' says Marcus.

'Agh, we don't mind, do we?' Kelly ruffles his hair.

I smile and undo my bag.

'Do you want my urine, Dot?'

'Please.' I unwrap the tester strip. It has shaded lines running along it, washed out yellows, browns, and orange. It reminds me of one of those souvenirs you buy at the seaside, glass test-tubes with pretty layers inside of different coloured sands.

Kelly passes me the sample phial. I unscrew the top and dunk in the strip.

'Course, Stevie and me, we've been at it like rabbits, every night, sometimes twice. It's meant to hurry things up a bit, isn't it? Hasn't done a blind bit of good, mind. Poor fellah, he's exhausted. All his mates at work are giving him a right ribbing. He's upstairs. He and Tops are sleeping. I'll wake him soon. I'd like you to meet him before the birth. Do you think you'll be on? I'd like it if it were you, Dot. Only I'm not supposed to say that, am I? Favouritism.'

'Doesn't matter. It's nice. I'd like to be there myself. I'll see what I can do.'

'Thanks. Tell you what, I'll go get Stevie up now. Why not?' She moves to the edge of the settee and Marcus, still looking at the telly, helps her up. 'You're a strong wee man,' she laughs. Despite the size of her tummy, her limbs are still elegant, slim. 'Scuse us a minute, Dot.'

When she has gone out of the room, Marcus backs on to my lap, eyes ever hooked to the screen. He settles himself comfortably there, nestling against me. His little body feels warm as milk, and he starts curling the locks of his fringe with the forefingers of both hands. I am always impressed when children have such a trusting nature. While some are pinned to their mothers' skirts and hide behind them to shield themselves from the world, others are happy to befriend people. I think it's a good sign. It must surely mean they are secure. For myself, it makes me feel well and truly motherly. I suddenly, momentarily, have a glimpse of what it might be like to be so uniquely dependable, so needed, so loved.

When Kelly returns some minutes later with Stevie, Marcus is chatting away to me about dinosaurs and radiators.

Kelly's partner, only a year or two older than her, is medium height and, though not handsome, has a nice face. His cheeks are round, with dimples; his brown eyes small but wide open and twinkly. Hair all at sixes and sevens, still with the imprint of his pillow. Topsy, their two-year-old, is sleepy in his arms. The sleeves of Stevie's tartan shirt are rolled back jauntily, and his grey tracksuit bottoms are too big for him. His socks are loose and both half off, so his feet look almost as elongated as a clown's. His hands are calloused by bricks, but the handshake is firm and sincere, the smile vast. You know how you can tell about a person instantly, almost impossible to say why, it's just an abstract feeling you get, that they are this way or that, good or bad. Well, Stevie is a good man. I have it on the authority of instinct.

'It's lovely to meet you, Dot. I hope this little fellah hasn't been bothering you.' He ruffles Marcus's hair. Marcus smiles, but still doesn't stray his gaze from the television. 'Mind if I sit beside you?' When Stevie's sitting back, Topsy's legs arranged over his lap, Kelly passes him a mug of tea. 'So when d'you think things might start happening, Dot? I'm worried about her. Specially after that fainting fit she had. She's brave, but I'm doing my nut here. I'm too excited to concentrate on anything.'

Kelly laughs. 'Dropped a brick on his toe at work yesterday.'

'Several. Bleedin' agony it was too.'

'I says to him, this rate we'll be taking you to the hospital before me.'

Kelly's like Jessie, a live wire, got a good sense of humour, only Kelly's happier. I watch her, and there's joy in her. There's joy in Jessie, too, but she's been clobbered by circumstance.

I'm not saying Kelly's had it easy. Having been filled in by my colleagues, and from what she's told me herself, I'm aware she had a miserable time of her marriage. Her husband, Rick, also seventeen when Marcus was born, was unemployed and volatile. Things were doomed from the start, even before she got pregnant. He'd knock her about pretty regularly. Soon as the baby appeared, the Social Services stepped in. When mother and son were still in hospital, Rick was barred from being alone with her and the little one in case he harmed them. Afterwards, he was only allowed to live with Kelly and Marcus if it was under her parents' roof. The marriage was well and truly over by the time Marcus was two months old. Shortly after they'd separated, Kelly met Stevie. They are skint, but have two lovely kids, and another due any minute. They are young, they are struggling against the odds, but they are making it work. You can just tell. They're living for the present, because they're happy there. It shows. It sounds a cliché, but her eyes gleam, her voice sings, and her skin glows. There's no hidden agenda.

Lot of homes you get the impression there might be. You go into them, and they're just like this one, same set-up, same décor even. Some are poorer (still the outsize TV, but maybe not the fish tank; instead, mildew on the walls ignored by an uncaring council, and the one bed for three kids suffering from asthma); and some are more middle class (a velvet-look three-piece suite and, by the fireplace, a brassy set of little brush, poker and tongs). The couples, the ones who aren't outwardly miserable with their lives, often look cheerful enough. The women are ambling along. Their husbands or partners don't beat them, after all, and few men are as psychopathic as Jessie's ex, Russell. As for the husbands, their wives aren't showing any signs of cheating on them. In any number of cases, she can be as chatty as all get-out, and the partner is genuinely friendly, interested. You ask yourself, how can you ever tell about other people? The exact nature of another couple's marriage or relationship is impossible to fathom or pin down. Yet you do somehow gather something of its truth, a fragment. I know with most the couples into whose lives I temporarily footstep, that it's not the same as Kelly and Stevie; whatever it is these two are blessed with (and those rare few I come across similar to them), it just isn't there for the majority. The difference between this pair, and others not so blessed, isn't necessarily so marked, so obvious, as that between true happiness and downright misery. It may just be wistfulness. Perhaps the man doesn't mind being out of a job, or enjoys the job that he's in, and is merely wondering what it would be like to have a life, same sort of life, not so far removed, only with another woman, like the pretty one with the ponytail who serves in the all-night garage, or the other who walks her collie and swings her hips on the green. Perhaps the woman loves him, and enjoys security, and is either simply wearied by familiarity (and vaguely has on her mind the allure of extra-marital adventure); or nervous she mightn't be able to keep his interest up for ever.

Sometimes I look at the women, and I see in their eyes such fear of desertion as I wonder, is it all worth it, isn't it better simply to be alone, than to be with someone and terrorised by the prospect of being alone? And always one of Jessie's fancies then springs to mind. She once said – when she first became aware of Derek's roving eye and unfaithful nature – she said, she wished she could be every woman at once. By that she didn't mean one woman who is the successful embodiment of wife, mother, and professional, like those beaming, unreal examples in magazines. No, she meant she'd like, magically, fleetingly, actually to be able to change into each girl or woman Derek – the man she loved – ever longingly glanced at in the street, so she could beat him at his boredom, and reign supreme over his frustration. 'He'd soon tire of his quest for novelty,' she said, 'tire of this string of different women; and he'd want me, the real Jessie, back with him for good.' (She said, 'I never did claim I'd make a good feminist. There again, maybe mine could be the ultimate feminist fantasy, as it would mean complete power over men, once and for all.') Sometimes, when I see certain of my ladies, I think there are others who have known these feelings such as Jessie's had, others who have had this same fantasy for themselves. Maybe it's not such an outlandish one as I at first thought.

I look at Kelly, there's none of that wishful thinking; as I say, she's dead happy with herself, her lot. I look at Kelly and can't help but think about what I might have been. If I had kept Eliza, hadn't gone to the laundry, and had had the chance to find a good man, I might have been at twenty-one, and thereafter, as Kelly is now and I hope will always be. I offer no apologies for making the comparison. I could have done with a front room littered with toys; I could have done with some happy snaps with brown and gold surrounds; done with a kindly fellah like her Stevie to be the father to Eliza, and to any other children we might have had, children I could call my own. If I sound sorry for myself, that's all wrong, that's not what's meant, what's meant is total admiration and respect when I say, I could have done with a heart like that, a heart like Kelly has.

I think back to twenty-one. I was two years at the laundry, no longer the completely unsuspecting novice. I didn't know it then, but I had another seven years to go. Had I known, they might as well have packed me upstairs there and then, because the thought of all that time cooped up, existence reduced to its lowest common denominator, would have instantly flogged me into insanity.

As it was, I always had the notion my parents couldn't be keeping me in much longer. I think to myself, I've done my time, paid my dues. It's a case, every night before I fall asleep, of, Tomorrow they'll come. When they don't for nine solid years, that doesn't leave me with much confidence in tomorrow. Hope and me, we're not comfortable bedfellows. The chemistry's as good as spent between us.

So there am I, at Kelly's age, two years into my sentence, all full of the thrill of tomorrow, and disappointment. For me at that time, to live as she does, in the present, is to feel the sting and ache of despair. It's to crawl naked through gorse. What's essential is to remove oneself from it as thoroughly as possible, to learn mind over matter, to believe the edge of the moor is nigh, or at least to imagine you're wearing clothing that is protective.

Bel was my protective clothing. From the beginning. I'll never forget her act of kindness in preventing me from kicking that bitch outside worker who chewed the apple, and how she bravely wreaked revenge on my behalf. Before break the following day, Bel took a great risk in slipping away from her post to hunt for the woman's lunchbox. When she found it, rather than stealing her sandwich – which would have led to big trouble – she unwrapped it, and cunningly rubbed soap powder into the meaty filling. Later, seeing the woman's face as she started eating it, oh, it was brilliant. Bel and I looked at each other, and inside ourselves we had the best laugh.

Bel taught me tricks of survival. Our friendship grew because of this, and because of the fact she was the only other girl there who was to my way of thinking. Whereas all the others might not have liked Piccadilly, and were saddened and aggrieved by the treatment, it seemed to be only Bel and myself who were moved to a true loathing of the place, and a sincere hatred of every one of those hard-faced bitches who made up the staff. The other girls accepted the bad submissively, and to a great extent so did I. We had no choice. Difference was, I had nothing but contempt for this submission, theirs or mine. Only Bel was brave enough to fight it. But if initially I lacked her courage for direct action, I was nonetheless her ardent follower and supporter. I alone seemed to share with her a resentment and hatred that burned so deep it was impossible to rise above it. The petty injustices of day to day were as insect bites to the psoriasis I was suffering – that of losing Eliza and being at Piccadilly in the first place. It was these small irritants which seasoned the wounds of my overall skin disease, and all the more made me itch and tremble with frustration and distress.

Father once told me that it is in the nature of all men (not women) to be violent. If there are men who don't physically hurt others, he said, then it is only because they are better able to control it, better able to draw on their vestiges of decency so as to hold back their violent urges. Until I went to the laundry, I had never experienced the wearisome chipping of an urge, and the need to restrain it. But there, I discovered one – that of wanting to make major mischief and small rebellions, all of the time. I saw it as my – female – equivalent to the male one of violence, about which Father had spoken so affectingly. It was probably bred of the same disease: anger, anger, and more anger.

The staff at Piccadilly, they taunted you with name-calling, and answering back was misbehaving. What amazed me: most the girls there could take it on the chin, but I could never. (To this day, I can't decide if that meant they were stronger than me, or more cowardly.) I couldn't keep my mouth shut. How can you when, just because you've mislaid the cheap pin for your apron bib, a member of staff addresses you, in a chilling whisper, as 'the daughter of the very devil himself'?

We all had these pins. Most people lost theirs at some point or other. I just seemed to more than anyone else. The first time I lost mine, soon after I arrived, Bel taught me that the thing to do was to steal another girl's. I thought that was awful. I ignored her advice. So I was labelled the Devil's daughter, and got a wooden spoon on the back of the hand. It happened again. I still did the honourable thing and didn't pass the buck by nicking someone else's. Wooden spoon. Third time I lost my pin, it was the cane. Fourth time, it was, 'If you do ever get out of here, Dorothy Sheffield, you'll be at it, whoring again, before the day is done.' I'm not a swearer, but I told her – it was Miss Beveridge – to fuck off. It just came out. By the look on her face, I thought I was going to be burnt slowly to death on a spit. In fact, they did away with my food for two days. I got off lightly. I don't think she knew what it meant.

Anyway, after that incident, I soon learned not to be so high-minded. I took to pinching other pins that were not my own, with impunity and without shame.

As I say, I think back to twenty-one. I remember, coming up to my twenty-second birthday, must have been about three years into my sentence, I lost my pin for the umpteenth time. I'd had enough trouble by then with bloody pins – losing them, being punished, starved, insulted; losing them, having to steal somebody else's. They were ruling my life, and I decided to end the tyranny of the apron pin. I had a plan. I told it to Bel and she was in on it.

That night when everyone was asleep, we risked our necks by creeping round the dormitories and silently stealing the pin off the apron of every single girl. Having gathered them up, we went into the bathroom. As always in there, it was as dank and smelly as a puppy's piddle, and we were only in our thin nightdresses, but we were too frightened and excited to feel the cold. I was aware of drips of tepid sweat under my arms as we pushed all the pins, including our own, down the square drain in the centre of the stone floor.

Next day, no one had a pin.

I owned up. I wouldn't let Bel do so with me; this was my scheme, and anyway I was repaying her for all the favours she'd done to me. My honesty resulted in the Isolation Room (solitary confinement; bread and water) for a week.

When I came out, I noticed two buttons had been sewn on to everyone's apron bibs, one fastened at each shoulder strap. (Bel informed me that the evening I'd been sent into Isolation, they had all been banned from doing their embroidery and ordered to sew on the buttons instead.)

So they had done away with the pins. I had my first real triumph over our cruel tormentors (I think that must have sown the seeds for greater rebellion later on.)

Now, it is unimaginable how a tiny apron pin could have been of such significance to my life. I think of Kelly, and of what is significant to her life – people, for God's sake, people she loves. If I allow myself to dwell on the comparison too long, it'd do my head in; I might become bitter, and that would never do.

So I stand up with my little bag of midwife's sundries, and smile at her and Stevie, Marcus and Topsy. 'It shouldn't be long now,' I assure them. 'Promise. My bet is you'll go into labour before the night's out.'

'You think so, Dot?' Stevie asks.

'Are you on duty?' Kelly pips in.

'I do think it'll be tonight, yes, I've got a feeling; and don't you worry, I'll make sure I'm there, whatever. It's important to me too. I wouldn't miss it for the world.'

My hunch is correct.

I'm back at the hospital. Early evening, about an hour or two ago, I was just finishing off some stuff in our office, tedious admin, and that, and gathering my things to go home, when Tiffany came in saying it's mayhem in the delivery suite, it's all go, four ladies have all just arrived at once, including Kelly Rushton, contractions going like pistons; any chance of a hand?

So I'm in Room 6 with Kelly and Stevie and Kelly's sister Leanne; and all's going smoothly. She's fully dilated but because she's had an epidural – the works this time – she's calm, relaxed, feeling no pain. The telly's on, some show like *Blind Date*. 'Aw, she better not pick number two,' she saying, 'he's a right wanker.' They're all having a laugh.

Leanne is sitting one side of the bed, close up. She has blonde dreadlocks, and fetching smears of earth or grime on her limbs and her face. She has these huge eyes, only the pupils are made small by heroin. Her legs are athletic thin and brown, and look all the more elegant for a flowing skirt which hangs above her sinewy knees and the big boyish boots covered in mud. Her hands are hidden by the thread-tufted sleeves of a black jersey but her knuckles and long fingers are visible. They can hardly bend for clumpy silver rings, yet she is rubbing aromatherapy oils into Kelly's sides and back, massaging her. The smell in here is all lavender, jojoba, and orange blossom. It's lovely. For once something's drowned the smell of hospital.

Stevie is up on the bed with Kelly, sitting behind her, propping her up. He is in a white T-shirt. His arms are round her holding her. Her hair is in a ponytail, and he's stroking her neck. There is something moving about seeing such roughened fingers, with nails bitten to the quick, adapting so readily to this gentle task. He's whispering encouragement in her ear. Occasionally she responds by smiling with pleasure at his private words. He's saying just the right things.

Kelly's pretty nightie – creamy satin-feel, with pink lace bodice – is improbably saucy for the labour ward. In our antenatal classes we advice women to put on old T-shirts or some such which don't matter if they get mucky. Kelly's ignored that, she feels comfortable in something better. And even though it's all hitched up, I have to say, she looks stylish as they come. She's a cool cookie, Kelly is, amazing. You wouldn't think she was in the throes of childbirth.

The head is showing. The heartbeat is fine. I'm here in my

polythene apron, monitoring everything, keeping a close eye, and judging how not to be too intrusive.

Suddenly, in a blabbering gush, the baby comes. Blood and matter spurt out after it all over the shop, and I hold it up, a girl, so she screams. Kelly and Stevie and Leanne are weeping buckets. Leanne's tears are making clear tracks through the smears on her cheeks; Stevie's mouth is open wide with silent wonder; and I'm going about my business with a lump in the throat size of a piece of coal.

'Ah, Dot,' Kelly's saying as she takes her from me, 'she's gorgeous.'

It may be predictable of me to say this, but she's beautiful. 'She's truly beautiful,' I murmur.

'Bless her,' her mother laughs, 'and, clever thing, she came out easy as a bleeding ping-pong ball.'

Chapter Seven

I think Priscilla is dying.

I say this because she's looking frailer tonight than I've ever seen her before. I've popped by the old people's home later than usual, what with staying in the hospital with Kelly and that lot till nearly ten. Priscilla sleeps little so I knew it wasn't too late, only the nurse told me on my way in that she didn't touch her food yesterday or today.

I am sitting on the chair beside her bed. It's very warm in here, the air so woolly I can hardly breathe. The radiator is alive, popping and creaking like an old man's bones. I smell tea, basic soap, elderly flesh. The small lamp on the dressing table is shedding a light not much less dim than a candle's. My friend's face glows blue-white in this semi-darkness. Her breaths are quick and short; her hand is weak in mine.

'All this fuss,' she whispers. 'I can't be doing with toad-in-the-hole, never could. I'm not hungry. Harold came round earlier with more of his blessed cakes. He thought because I'd said I'd never eat his jam tarts again I might like some almond or lemon slices instead. Stupid boy!'

'You don't want them? Perhaps we could give them to Ted, or I could take them to the hospital. It's always nice for the new mums to have something sweet to keep their strength up.'

'He says you've quite unsettled him.'

'Pardon?'

'Harold says you've quite unsettled him.'

'We're here to talk about you.'

'Who says? Dot, when you reach my age, I'll tell you this much, you're bored of you. I'd just as soon talk about something else.'

'Is your stomach playing up again, love?'

'He said no more than that. He's the quiet type, is Harold. Keeps himself to himself.'

I touch her forehead. It's warm but not boiling. She hasn't a temperature. 'You haven't had headaches or anything, have you?'

'He did seem unsettled, I have to say. All unrelaxed. Kept pacing about, and this room's not big enough for pacing. I told him to sit himself down. When he did, he was all of a fidget.'

'He was probably worrying about you, don't you think?'

'No, I don't at all. I've got to pop my clogs one of these days, I'm quite happy to too. I've had my time. And he knows that. No, his dithering about was all because of you.'

'That's very flattering, but I don't believe it for a moment,' I say, half standing up. 'Here, let me prop up your pillow. You look all slumped. You can't be comfy like that.'

'Do you think you could ever love him, Dot?'

'What kind of question is that?' I ask, holding her wee body forward, plumping the pillows behind her, and gently leaning her against them again. 'Now you save your breath.'

'A question between friends. Come on, could you?'

'You should be getting some rest.'

'Could you?'

'I don't see why not. He's a lovely man, a good man.'

'Only twice before I saw him unsettled by a woman. First time, he was about thirty, so it was a long time ago. He fell in love with Edith, Edith Carstairs, she ran the post office in those days. Do you know her? She married a bobby who did well for himself. Edith Mackenzie she became. They've got three kids, couple of grandchildren now, and these two carriage lamps on their front porch, all glass and brass, elegant like. Course, he's got a bit of a paunch now, her husband, so he does. A police sergeant. Her coffee cake, more than like. She was always a great baker, Edith Carstairs. Thick ankles.'

For all Priscilla's frailty, she can still talk. It's a breathless whisper.

'Name rings a bell. Perhaps I delivered her kids. I don't remember, to be honest.' I squeeze her arm gently to try to persuade her to stop talking, but she's having none of it.

'I think they had that in common, baking and what have you. He'd go round to the post office and buy stamps and the home-made cakes she used to set out for sale every morning on the counter. He must have spent a fortune out his wages on them cakes of hers. They made a change from his factory ones. Lord knows what he did with them all. Gave them to neighbours. He'd find and cut out recipes for her from the local paper, or magazines he'd get off his mother. She had this mole on her cheek. He called it a beauty spot when it was plain for all to see it was a mole. I think he took her to the pictures one time. I don't remember what they went to see. The Michael Caine one when the coach with all the gold balances over the edge of the cliff.'

'*The Italian Job*. It's famous. Lovely film.'

'Course, he didn't tell me any of this, but I knew.'

'How?'

'It was written all over his face for starters. To those of us who knew Harold – family, mainly – it was obvious like. And his dad told his mother and me of his suspicions, told me about the cakes and that. We were delighted. Thought he'd found himself a girl at last. Nothing came of it. She found her policeman, started going with him.'

'Poor Harold.'

'Poor Harold nothing! Truth is, he's so closed up she probably never knew they were meant to be courting. Though he never said as much, he was in bits over the policeman when he found out. But it was his own stupid fault. Edith Carstairs hadn't been led to believe there was anything more between them than friendship and a sweet tooth. It's no good being shy if it completely obscures your intentions. She was a lovely girl. Silly bugger.' Priscilla lets out a loud sigh.

'You're tiring yourself, love. It's getting late. You should get some sleep. Hush now, all right.' I am worried about her, worried as hell, but she won't stop.

'Then there was Christine. A few years later, perhaps five or six. Same thing. She was a receptionist at the Majesty. It were a beautiful hotel in them days. I knew her since she was a little girl because her dad was our milkman. She had to wear this maroon uniform with gold buttons, it was ever so smart. Her dad was that proud of her. Harold met her at the ballroom dancing classes. She was competition level, used to win all these trophies. Her dresses were absolutely gorgeous, every one made by her mum. All these sequins they had, sewn on by hand. Christine was a mousy girl, so she was, but when she stepped on that dance floor she were a princess. She could do the lot – tango, samba, cha cha cha.'

Priscilla stops to catch her inadequate breath. I urge her to finish telling me another time; all this talking's tiring her out. But there's an urgency in her voice. She's a determined old soul, she's going to carry on regardless.

'She liked Harold well enough. They used to have a few turns on the dance floor. She partnered him a few times and stole his heart. Same thing though as with Edith, I don't think she can ever have known. Harold was that reticent she probably thought they were just friends. She had a few fellahs after her. As I say she liked Harold, I don't know if in that way, but she might have done. Only he never seized the opportunity. He may have thought he did, but not so as she'd've noticed. Perhaps he said he liked her sequins or some such. A girl needs more encouragement than that! Next fellah that came along did the sensible thing, gave her flowers or what have you, took her out, made a proposal of marriage while the going was good. A sailor he was. He didn't have the time to hang about. If he'd dallied like Harold, he'd've been on the next ship before he could say sequins. Swept her off her feet.

'Harold comes to me one day soon after and asks if all women are fickle. He hasn't said a word to me about Christine up till then, though course I know about her. I try to encourage him to talk, I think maybe it'll make him feel better. So I says to him, "What makes you ask that?" He won't answer, mind. I tell him, some women are, some not. He says, "I'm glad they're not all as treacherous as some." He loved his mother, he loves me. He likes women in general, only now he thinks if he gets close to them, even if they're good and kind, they're going to betray him. It's up to whoever comes along, whoever she is, Dot, to do a lot of convincing. Perhaps anyway now he's too old, too set in his ways, past romancing.'

'Harold's not too old. He's not yet sixty.'

'He's happy to be alone, happy with his life. He's carved out one for himself, funny sort of life so it is, with that dog of his, Jones. Edith and Christine were the only women he ever loved. I

114

think it's a great shame he never married one of them. I tell him as much too, sure I do. He says he never wanted for a wife. Don't you believe it. No man ever doesn't want for a wife. They might have their reasons for saying as much but, whatever they say, believe you me, it's nonsense. They're full of rubbish the lot of them, full of rubbish, and Harold's no exception. Mark my words.'

Priscilla's eyes are beginning to flutter. As her words peter out, I still hold on to her hand.

Soon enough she is sleeping. I can hear the dull rattle and hum of her staggered breaths, a haunting sound. Reminds me, in its own more modest way, of the women's child-bearing howls. Same thing – fear and pain – only quieter.

She means a lot to me, Priscilla, so she does. She's my friend. Old as she may be, some's would say time up and all, I'll take it hard when she goes. She's got her own funny resilience and courage I admire. There's fight in her, always was. It's there yet. All that talking.

I stay holding her hand till the early hours, just being there, a presence. Through the night her breathing becomes less strained but I think to myself, I don't expect she has more than a few days. Behind her wrinkled face I fancy I can see her eighty-six years piled up, neat as dominoes, the last one in her quota about to topple over.

I'm that worried it might happen any minute that I don't leave her tonight, I don't go home. In the throbbing silence of the night, I ponder her reasons for telling me about Harold. She had a hard life, did Priscilla, dogged by money worries and family troubles, but she had a good marriage. Her husband died twenty or thirty years ago. She still thinks about him every day, even now. I think ever since the moment her Gilbert passed away she's wanted to die so she can be with him again. I think she wants me to have whatever it was that she had with a man, and it's with Harold she has glimpsed possibility.

Only in the early hours as she's beginning, falteringly, to awaken, do I softly let go of her hand and quietly slip from the room. I'm on early. I drive slowly to the hospital because of the mist scudding the dark air. My eyes are fixed on the crêpe road smudged with a patina of frost. All the while, my mind, in the inappropriate way minds work, is oddly hopscotching between thoughts of death and breakfast.

There's one or two I've got to visit in postnatal. Having just come along from a three-hour session in the delivery suite, I'm taking a five-minute breather in the little staff-room just off the ward. Two of my colleagues in the team, Tiff and Jan, both happen to be with me. We don't usually have time for elevenses, but it's a quiet morning, thank goodness. I'm always grateful for a bit of quiet when I've been up all night, as I have with Priscilla.

Jan is passing round a tin of biscuits which was given to us as a thank-you present from one of our ladies. It's nice to know we're appreciated, but this constant stream of goodies – choccies, biccies, what have you – plays havoc with the waistline. Still, I like a chat and a giggle over a custard cream or two. Right now we can hear Mrs Docherty next door giving her physio class to the girls as they lie on their beds.

I always forget she works Sundays. We can hear her through the doors. It's a rasping inflection she has. 'Stress incontinence is flavour of the month,' she is saying, same as she does every month. 'Come on girls, if you want to be old like me and still playing badminton without taking extra knickers, clench now, and hold, two, three. That's it. I promise you, girls, this is the most important exercise you can do, especially if you had a vaginal delivery. It reaches the parts your normal exercise programmes never reach, and it's easily done at the bus stop, anywere, with no one knowing.'

We can now hear one or two suppressed laughs coming from the beds, and we grin at each other. We know what's coming, we've heard it a million times before.

'Hold, four, five. Well done. You should be thinking in terms of doing pelvic floors at least ten times a day. Then, hey-ho, no more slackness! No more seepage when you sneeze! Extra purchase on your menfolk! Just think how much they'll appreciate all this added attention you're going to be lavishing on this special part of you. A whole new meaning to making love! Tra la!'

As per usual with the Tra la! the doors swing open, and a small woman emerges, briskly. She is wearing a white short-sleeved jacket of some medical importance, and navy slacks. She has grey hair and sturdy calves, and is clutching to her breast her most treasured possession – her spooky clay and Perspex model of the pelvic floor region. Some of the paint on the grey hip bone, pinkish muscles, and even the pale cervix, is chipped. If Mrs Docherty has any problems, you know that leakage or seepage, or whatever she calls it, is not one of them. I've seen her husband, Mr Docherty, nice man, fragile type, with a constant smile on his face. Whenever I look at that smile I try not to think too hard about where it's coming from. Whenever he bids me one of his cheerios, it takes all my strength not to sing Tra la!

We give Mrs Docherty – or Sinead to us – a wave as she passes the staff-room.

'I'll be seeing some of you, Wednesday, ladies,' she trills, half at us, half at her girls. Now that the ward is free, I plonk down my tea and go in to do my duties.

In the bed nearest to the door is a West Indian woman in her late thirties. Vernita. She is laughing such a merry laugh that she can't engage her baby's lips to her nipple. Her vast bosom is bouncing in time with her glee, a buoy in a rough sea. Some of the other girls are laughing with her, and I can't help it too, it's that infectious.

'I's gonna have this little one's daddy swinging from my new purchase,' she's saying, wiping away a laughter tear with the knuckle of her forefinger. 'Now on, I ain't never gonna let him go!'

I try to help the baby keep in touch with the nipple, but her mum is still laughing too hard.

'No more other ladies for you, man, no more, right?' She is addressing her partner, Curtis, who isn't here but who is about to come by to take her and their daughter home. 'When he arrives, girls, I'm gonna tell him, "From now on, man, you can quit messing around, going with others, 'cos I'm gonna have a gra . . . asp on your situation!" '

It's a good atmostphere in the ward this morning. Vernita's done away with the usual respectful hush and has encouraged in its place general chatting and interaction between the mums. It's always fun when someone like her is in. Livens the place up a bit.

She and her baby are thriving. She grabs my hand with both of hers and gives me an enormous smile. Then she thanks me (I delivered her daughter). Her thin white nightie is warm and smells of baby, and offers inadequate cover for her huge, smooth breasts. These squash against mine in an affectionate embrace. Moments like this, I am reminded why my job is so worthwhile.

As I'm telling her that I'll be round for a home visit, Jan pops her head through the ward door and beckons me over to her.

'I clean forgot to give you this, love,' she says. 'The message come for you earlier when you were up on Delivery. I think Maggie took it in our office.'

I thank her as she passes me a Post-it note. It's that inadequate yellow of those spreads that substitute for butter. On it our colleague Maggie has written in blue biro. Her letters, all exaggerated loops, and circles dotting the i's, are recognisably feminine.

'Mr Mills rang,' the note reads. 'Something about visiting Mrs Topley's Cakes. When's your next day off. Will you ring him on 662143.'

Oh, my goodness.

A little breath, and I slip it away, securely into the pocket of my dress, behind the straggly paper hankie that's long overdue for the waste-paper basket. I walk back over to Vernita and give her a kiss, I'm all contained, then I move on to the next bed: Honey Carpenter.

I've seen a lot of Honey since the beginning of her pregnancy, and she's a lovely girl, sure she is. I've got to know her well, like her a lot. And now she's got a beautiful baby boy beside her, asleep in his see-through cot. But she's had a troubled history, bless her. For starters, I suspect there was some abuse at home, she's hinted as much: certainly physical, probably sexual, probably her dad, an alcoholic. Then in her late teens she got involved in the squatter movement in Berlin, and started on the drugs. By her early twenties when she returned to England she was completely addicted to heroin. She moved into a squat in Lewisham, and had three kids by three different blokes, one of whom was in prison for assault and possession of a firearm. After the first child was born, evidence soon came to light from three neighbours that she was neglectful of him, that she had gone out, apparently to score, on more than one occasion, leaving him all alone in extreme distress, crying his head off. There is no doubt she was a drug addict, but there is also no doubt that she was a good mother who wouldn't have dreamt of leaving her baby unsupervised. The neighbours in question had a grudge against Honey, and were more than likely to have fabricated the story. But despite this fact, and although Honey passionately protested her innocence, little Liam was nonetheless taken into care. She gave up the drugs. But when the second child was born, she was taken away from her mother too. The reason? She'd told the authorities she was off the heroin but they didn't believe her. Not long before getting pregnant the second time, she had spent a couple of months travelling round India. To their way of thinking, the entire Indian subcontinent is one big syringe. So natually, Honey was lying, and she was likely to be as negligent with this child as she had proved to be with her first.

Honey is not a liar. After years as a midwife, you learn to be an accurate judge of character. There's them, not many mind, that are genuine troublemakers, and we can be firm with them. But Honey's got an honest face, open, and reliable. She has eyeliner smudged around her eyes, you get the impression it's been there a while, and a dusky complexion, raddled by hardship and misfortune, so she looks quite a deal older than her thirty years. Her long dark hair is matted so you think there might be any number of owls or wood-pigeons nesting in there.

She lost her way, but she's not a bad person. She was allowed to keep her third child, but he died at six months old of meningitis. Shortly afterwards, she went back on the drugs – crack this time – left London, and started travelling. Then, a year ago, when she was living on a site down here, she met Rashid. He works in a dry-cleaner's-cum-heel-bar in town. She moved in with him, into his council flat in a high-rise block on the Runnymede Estate. She told me he's the first man who's ever been kind to her, ever really loved her. If it wasn't for him, she says, she'd never have got off the drugs, and now she's off them for good. She says so, and I'm sure of it. They're planning to get married. I've met him. He's the gentlest person you could ever hope to know. He's the type you don't ever want to see hurt or unhappy.

'He's got the Ready-Brek glow, Dot,' Honey said to me once and, remembering those TV ads, I knew what she meant, I could recognise it in him straight away. 'Honest to God,' she told me, 'I've never seen it in a man before.' When she said that, I felt so sad.

She was dead frightened when she got pregnant with this little one, little Saad. She nearly had a miscarriage with the worry of what they might do this time. She was a bit aggressive to us at first, she's scared of a uniform, see. Don't blame her. In the past she's always been patronised and discriminated against by the medical profession, and whoever else besides. A story like hers, honestly it makes you think. Luckily we in the team took a little trouble, that's what we're here for. Jan and I attended her recent case conference which proved frustrating from our point of view. Although we argued against it, it was decided that when the child was born, he or she should be placed on the at-risk register. We all did our best to reassure Honey when the news was broken to her that this didn't mean the child would automatically be taken away from her. It took a bit of time, but we won her trust in the end. She realised we had been fighting her corner, and we weren't out to get her like all the rest, that we were on her side.

'All I wanted was for someone to listen to me,' she said, 'not just take one look at me and label me with all this hippie shit.'

Breaks your heart when you hear something like that.

'Eh, Dot,' she beams, as I sit down on her bed.

'How's our wee man today, eh?' I ask.

'Ah, he's a little miracle, he is. I'm in love all over again. Rashid better watch out for the competition!'

You watch her face, and you know you're seeing happiness. It's no longer an intangible thing, it's got a smell, a feel, a sound, you can almost hold it in your palms. It's frankincense; it's feathers; it's autumnal oak leaves gilded by a cold hard sun. It's that music which does something to you; makes you suddenly aware of the heart beating, suddenly detect its throbs resounding all round inside you, suddenly sense a sluggish blood lollop into life and shudder through the veins in bouts like dodgem cars.

I wonder if I can feel it.

The Post-it note's burning a hole in my pocket.

'You look like the cat that's got the cream, Dot. What's going on today?'

'Do I?' I am genuinely surprised. I'm good at covering up my feelings, keeping extremes of mood out of places they're not appropriate. It doesn't do to go round the ward with a face as long as tree trunk, or to dance about the place like a dolly bird on rum and Cokes. 'I've just had a nice invitation to go round Topley's some time in the next few days, see the cakes being made. I've always been interested how they produce them in those quantities.'

'Ah, come on, Dot, what's he like?'

'Eh, you're a sharp one all right, or am I so transparent these days? All right, love, you've caught me at an unguarded moment. All's I'll say —'

'At this stage —'

'OK, all's I'll say at this stage, is that he's got the Ready Brek glow you speak of, like Rashid. That's enough for you to be going on with. Now, my dearie, less of me. Are those nipples of yours still painful?'

'I'll get it out of you sooner or later, you'll see,' Honey says affectionately, like, bugger the age difference (I could be her mum an' all!), we're women together. She's like Priscilla, she's after my best interests, she wants for me what she's got. Pure generosity of spirit. She's a good girl, as I say. Luckily she doesn't press further, or I don't know what I might not reveal, it's all just hopping to come off my chest. 'Oor, yes, I can tell you,' she answers dutifully about the nipples. 'There's stuff about this business no one ever tells you. They're brown and cracked as bleedin' brazil nuts. Every time I feed him, he takes the scabs off, not his fault poor little mite. But it is disgusting.' Her tone seems to toss the pain off lightly, as if it's insubstantial and, in the face of such reward, really rather her due.

'I'll see if I can get some cream for you later, should clear things up a bit.'

On Honey's bedside table are framed photographs of her other kids, perhaps taken on occasions when she was allowed supervised access to them. The oldest boy has a formal parting and the top button of his shirt is done up. He looks very smart but he's got the expression of a lovable rascal. The little girl is mixed race. She's wearing this red jumper with a white Father Christmas motif round its chest. In her hair are these plaits and colourful bobbles. There's this incredible grin on her face, you just want to cuddle her, her legs to knot round your waist. The baby who passed away is lying on a spongy carpet in a romper suit, eyes dark and wide as a seal's; gummy smile perhaps waiting for the cocked knuckle of a mother's little finger. How does Honey look at these pictures and endure her childrens' absence? I don't have a photo of Eliza. It would jagger into my very flesh like twine.

Honey catches my glance.

'This is going to be the best Christmas I've ever had. First one with one of my kids. I'll be missing three, but I'll have the one. I don't think I could do another Christmas without one of them, that's what it's all about, innit? I mean, I couldn't actually live through another one on me own, you know, Dot. Does my head in just thinking about it. But my luck's changed, see. I've done my innings, paid my dues, what have you. Him up there's decided it's my turn at last.' She laughs. ' 'Bout ruddy time, eh? All I need now is to get these nipples cleared up, and I'm good as new, right?'

'I'll be thinking of you, I promise.'

'What about you, Dot, looking forward to it, Christmas?'

'Oh, I think so,' I say because I don't expect she wants to hear anyone who's less than enthusiastic about it. Still, as I take my leave, I do detect a little something there, a warm draught coming in me, I'm not sure from where.

Harold's got this car, it's a 1970 red Ford Cortina with chrome on the front. Inside there are black seats, and the white plastic above your head is patterned with tiny black dots that make your eyes go funny. He's that proud of his car that he keeps it as shiny as a patent-leather party shoe. For the most part the car stays under the protection of the garage beside his bungalow and his lovingly wielded chamois cloth. When it does venture out, it is never strained above 30 m.p.h., and at the first hint of rain it scampers anxiously homeward like a lady out with a new hairdo and no fold-out polythene hood to save it.

Harold goes to work on his bicycle, but today he's off to the factory in the Cortina. I am sitting beside him in the passenger seat, smiling round the new roundabout.

I've been looking forward to this day ever since last Sunday. Course, I rang Harold as soon as I got home, and we made this plan. I haven't a whole day off for a while, but today, Friday, I've got till 1.15, so we seized our opportunity.

'There's all this security now, not like in the old days,' Harold's telling me. 'They don't let visitors round the factory any more. Industrial sabotage it's called. Has cost companies millions, luckily we haven't been targeted. But there have been these pests who've been putting broken glass in baby food, and cleaning fluid in fizzy drinks, stuff like that.'

I notice Harold uses pests, whereas I'd have a much more colourful word for them. Partly it's because he can't bring himself to use stronger language. But I think it's more to do with the fact he can't hate, however much he disapproves. Harold's the sort to give every human being the benefit of the doubt.

'It's unbelievable to think there are people with minds to do something like that,' he comments.

'How do they get away with it?'

'Well, they don't any more. We all have to have these special passes with our photos to get us through the front door, and even if personnel like me have been in practically every day for the last century, we can't get in without them. And no visitors allowed. I think you'll find every factory's like that now.'

'So how come I'm going to be let in?'

'Ah, well, I went to see my supervisor, see. I've not asked anyone in before. He said as a special favour.' Harold, not someone who would think himself entitled to special favours, is visibly delighted he was able to make an exception for me, and I am touched. 'I had to sign these forms to vouch for you. He trusts me. We've worked many years together. He said, "Any friend of yours, Harold." He's good, young Mr Dawson.'

A five-minute drive outside Stoneham gets us to the factory

gates. I've often driven past them, seen the vast plant from the road, but never been through them. I've known quite a few that's worked there, it's the main industry of the area. I've delivered several of their lady workers' babies. We stop. A security man in olive green steps out of a wooden hut with a closed-circuit television and a kettle inside, greets Harold in a friendly fashion, and looks at me, intrigued, through the driver's window. He ticks my name off on a clipboard. 'It's only on special days that Mr Mills brings the car, isn't it, Harold?'

'Yes, indeed,' he replies jovially, as his colleague waves us through, and we pull up at the car park, a large patch of new black tarmac with bright white markings.

The main block with the offices, board-rooms, and refectory, is Victorian, red brick. Behind it is a maze of modern buildings all interconnected by narrow paths of neat paving stones. It is not unlike St Dominic's with its odd bits added on here and there at different times, all haphazard.

Harold takes me to the huge metal hangar which houses the main body of the production line. We step into a reception room with photos on the wall of Mrs Topley's Cakes in days gone by, and in the present – some old sepia ones, some glossy Technicolour and new. There's one, dated 1899, of Mrs Topley outside her original shop in a long dark dress and white apron. She looks like she was a right old harridan; same boot-faced expression as Miss Beveridge at the laundry. I'm glad Harold isn't having to work for her, I don't think he would be nearly so happy if she were his employer.

'Apparently she was a complete cow,' he says.

'Harold!' I can't believe it. Him saying something like that. So unexpected. We laugh. 'Just what I was thinking.'

Ever solicitous and attentive, he then introduces me to Suzi behind the reception desk which is like a high bar. I can only see her blue-black hair. She looks up and smiles like a girl in an advertisement, all mouth. Her eyes, behind loud royal blue eyeliner and matching mascara, don't appear to be taking part. She seems pleased enough to see Harold, though, and has a pleasantry or two for him. I can tell he's a popular man round these parts, is Harold.

He opens the door for me into a side room. We put on white coats, and hats that accommodate all your hair. I have to take off my watch and stud earrings, Harold explains with a chuckle, 'just in case they fall into any of the mixtures and cause a customer to choke or lose a tooth.' We wash our hands in blue jelly disinfectant, then pass through the swing doors to the red-tiled, highly polished factory floor. There is a loud din and bellow of machinery in heavy-duty motion but you don't have to shout above it, just raise your voice. I gasp at the scale of it all. I can't see the end of the production line for all the steel machines, and the sheer length of the place. Harold tells me amazing things like how they make 720 chocolate mini-rolls every minute. 'We could watch jam tarts or almond slices, whatever, but I think we should follow the progress of the humble mince pie,' he suggests, 'seeing as it's the festive season, but only if that's what you would like?'

I nod, and, as he takes me round, he explains it all so simply I understand everything. I wonder at his enthusiasm, still intact after all these years. He's really passionate for what he does. He's a little boy in here. It's like all this, these machines and everything, belong to him, not in a proprietorial way, but in a modest way which just simply says he loves them.

'We do all sorts,' he tells me proudly. 'Battenberg cakes; fondant fancies – they're my favourite: sponge cake with a blob of butter and cream with fondant icing. I can resist them all but those. It's a miracle I'm not a very fat fellow.' He taps his tum. 'I shall have to watch out.'

'We make our own mincemeat, 2,000 tonnes a year, I think I'm correct in saying,' he tells me: '75 million individual pies altogether. That's about one and a half mince pies for every man, woman, and child in this country.'

'That means I'm depriving a good many of their share,' I say. 'I could eat at least a dozen and a half myself.' All around there is a hot syrupy smell of spices such as to tingle the insides of your nostrils, you can almost see it, and you can certainly feel its thickness envelop you. I am intoxicated by it. I compare it with the smell of hospital which I still have never managed to get used to. This is a treat.

We stand before a computer-controlled machine that rises high above us and has a network of copper-coloured pipes over and around it like a spaghetti junction.

'It's specially programmed with the mincemeat recipe so the operator can put in exactly the right amount of cherries, apple purée and so forth.' As Harold speaks, he waves at a man in a blue overall and short rubber boots who is poised over the outsize cauldron and pouring in some currants, all the while keeping an eye on certain dials. 'There's all these meters, see, checking the temperature, colour, and weight and what have you. Gerry here is doing all these technical tests along the way – checking the instruments which monitor the acidity, or seeing that there's the right amount of liquids to solids. It involves a lot of auditing, and paperwork. I've been here pretty well since I was a lad. Then we learned our craft by putting our hands in and feeling. But I'm an old man now,' he laughs.

I deny this.

'Oh, but I am Dorothy. See, my title's quality control supervisor, but I'm way out of date, we don't really exist any more. Now we've got things called quality assurance technicians who all have full degrees in food science. Nice fellows all of them, but very trendy, not like me. You won't be catching them with their fingers in the pies!'

Harold laughs again. He must be worried about job security, I know he must be, but it's not in his nature for him to spell it out. He'd think he was burdening me with his troubles. We move on to the next section. It could be this heady atmosphere is making my eyes ever so slightly water.

'This is the good bit – the mixture's got the brandy, sherry, and port in now. Can you smell the liquor? I never drink the stuff myself, but here I can feel it in my bones, and very nice too. Can you feel it as well? It's been cooled down and filled into these tanks where it stays maturing for forty-eight hours. Lovely.'

When we reach the next stage – with the huge machine that forms, stamps, fills, and tops the raw pastry cases – we have to put on ear protection. So now Harold has to shout into my face to make himself heard, but he manages to do so in a way that's not violent, not like a youth in a nightclub clumsily trying to chat up a girl above the music. I can detect his breath – only just, through this gorgeous muffler of hot spice – and it is golden syrup. Perhaps he had treacle on his porridge for breakfast? I can't help trying to imagine his life, these seemingly unimportant details. I can see him over an old-fashioned cream-coloured hob, stirring a wooden spoon round a saucepan with a wobbly handle. Then him sitting alone at his table, Jones at his feet. Him being warmed by the rich, milky porridge, just as he likes it best, with Lyle's golden syrup which reminds him of his mother, of himself as a boy. He's setting himself up for the chilly ride to the factory on his old-fashioned bicycle, and for the hard day's work ahead.

When I can't hear his words, he gestures with his hands for me, and in his long white coat and funny hat he looks like a vaudeville player, and we laugh and look about to see if anyone on the production line has seen us and thinks Harold uncommon lively.

He never touches me, puts his hand to my elbow to guide me, or cups his fingers on my shoulder. It would be natural enough if he was to, but he's not so indelicate, so intrusive. Still, I can feel him all about me and, in the face of all this shrill steel and hard machinery, I want to put out my hand to his to feel the reassuring softness of his palm.

At the conveyor belt where the pies are marched through the oven section for ten minutes, before being given twenty to cool off, it is quieter. Harold reaches up to help me off with my ear-protector. He holds the dense sponges, clasping each ear so delicately as if they were meringues, and manages to pull them apart and away from my head without touching my hat or disturbing my hair beneath it. All the while he is looking into my eyes, and his closeness makes me feel quite the girl again.

We are standing by the mince pies whilst they are being given their decorative sprinkling of sugar, so Harold says, 'to make them sparkle, like in the picture on their packaging, ho, ho'. I laugh. There's ladies all along with beady eyes ready to expel those rebels which don't conform to rigid convention, toss them into the blue plastic buckets rubbing up against tired calves. I know just how they feel, them pies, I felt like one of them when I was thrown away into the laundry, not up to scratch, not good enough to be part of society, a reject. I watch, amazed, as the women work with such deftness and skill. With all these pies coming at and jiggling past them at such a speed, nearly 800 a minute, how, I ask Harold, do they possibly notice such detailed faults, imperceptible to the untrained eye – an ever so slightly smudged motif here, a few too many sparkles of sugar there?

'It's the hours of standing here,' he says. 'Soon enough the eye gets tuned in to its very particular task. It's incredible what we can learn to do, isn't it, how we can train the mind to focus in on and become almost inhumanly efficient at something so specific? You hone your skills down, right down. I love that; it makes the human being so special. I've been lucky to have the opportunity here to do that, to get my palate down to a tee. All the people along the production line, they're wonderful at the checking, and they swap about on to different bits of it so they can all do the various tasks with equal genius.'

'I suppose it's a bit like at the laundry, how I got to master the shirt collars and cuffs with a cumbersome old iron. It's day in day out, year after year practice, you get to be perfect at the job in hand.'

'That's it. Did you work in a laundry? I didn't know. Remiss of me not to have asked. I suppose I imagined you'd trained in midwifery from the beginning.'

'Not remiss at all. I don't really talk about it.'

Harold apologises, embarrassed.

'Oh, no, I didn't mean that,' I immediately reassure him. 'I can talk about it to you. I worked nine years in a laundry outside Glasgow. I can't say I enjoyed myself, in fact I bloody hated it.' I regret that bloody, it's not right with Harold, not that he's disapproving in the least, bloody's mild after all. No, it's me, it just sounds clumsy in front of him. But it's strength of feeling, I just come out with it. I try to cover it up with a laugh. 'Still, I'm a dab hand with an iron; I can wield an iron like almost no other woman can!' I smile.

'So you were in Scotland a good while then. Beautiful place. Would that explain the very faint trace of an accent? Sometimes I hear it in one or two words.'

'You're clever to spot it in amongst my Staffordshire–Somerset jumble. My father was from Glasgow.'

As we talk we're walking slowly alongside those pies which

have made the grade – the majority – as they continue on their way, are laid to rest in red plastic trays, course up and down big-dipper-like tracks, and are finally packaged in their boxes, ready for their journey to shelves in supermarkets or corner shops nationwide.

'That's why you were living in Scotland then, your father's connections there?'

'In a roundabout sort of way, I suppose, yes.'

'You don't mind my asking? I wouldn't like to pry.'

'Not at all, Harold! Not you.' I'm not concentrating on the pies' progress so much any more. I'm distracted. There's a warming sensation in my stomach, like the spicy smell laced with liquor has seeped down inside me and is there to stay. I don't want to leave the factory and for it to go away. 'I was sent when I was nineteen. Circumstances. In fact, I was forced up there.'

'You didn't want to go?'

'No, I was in a county hospital in Cheshire doing my nurses's training so I could become a midwife – you couldn't do direct entry in those days. Anyway I was interrupted in my second year. I wasn't planning on cleaning sheets, but that's what happened.'

We're now standing at the end of the production line, and Harold's quite forgot the tour for listening to me. He seems to have lost his enthusiasm for it. 'I'm interrupting,' I say.

'No, no, not at all.'

'We'll talk about it some other time.'

'I suppose it's not a very comfortable place to hold a conversation, but I'd like to hear more. Would you like me briefly to show you round the Quality Control room, which is where I do most my work? Or we can go to the cafeteria straight away, sit down, have a quiet coffee. We can talk there. We're all right for time.'

We do see the QCR because I want to. I want to get a picture of where he spends his time, an idea of how, and to see the faces of the two colleagues who sit alongside him at the workbench. I had a picture in my mind already, like I always do of somewhere I've not yet been but I've heard a bit about. This one was more vivid because I'd thought about it longer and harder, and felt the desire to conjure up more detail. As I walk into the room, already my mental picture is being obscured by the real thing. It's like when you see a television dramatisation of a classic novel, and however hard you try not to, you lose sight of your own fictional faces, you want them back again, but they are gone for good, replaced by the rouge-cheeked actors. But I'm glad now to get the real picture of where Harold spends so many waking hours; you don't feel nostalgic for mental pictures of places like you do for your faces of characters in books. I do remember there was a window in my picture of Harold's room, which there isn't here, and I feel sorry for him not having any daylight to work by. And the men in my mind wore blue coats, not white. I was wrong about some things, right about others. Harold's seat is a wooden stool, as in a science lab; and there are lots of cake packets all around, on shelves, in cupboards, atop the workbench.

I am introduced to Michael – the one who's been made redundant so not here for much longer – and Pete, both younger than Harold. Michael is taking some mince pies out of the oven. 'We've heard a lot about you,' he says, offering me one. As I thank him and put it to my lips, I squeeze it a bit hard and one or two crumbs scamper down inside my sleeve. 'We take random samples off the production line every hour and test them. We call Harold the Master Palate because he's the best. No one has a tongue to match his for tasting.'

'I wouldn't mind this job,' I tell them, biting into the pastry. 'Quite often the mums give us these round Christmas time. They've always been my favourite.'

'I tell you, you can get sick of them,' Harold assures me, 'good though they are. You taste the smallest amount necessary, and spit it out, and use lime juice to clean your palate. You don't feel nauseous, but when you're not put off your lunch you do long for something savoury.'

'Harold often gets such a craving for Scotch eggs,' Michael says. 'He's just like a pregnant woman.'

'It'll be coal next,' Harold says.

'I know all about that,' I tell them. 'One of our ladies had a craving for wool. One day her husband found her eating his socks!' They all laugh. I'm enjoying joining in. It's jolly banter, at someone else's workplace not my own, and it makes me feel welcome, accepted.

'Harold said you were a very special midwife,' Michael says, 'because all the mums love you and lots keep in touch long after they've had their babies.'

I swallow hard my last bite of mince pie and blink. 'I don't know where he got that from!' I say looking at Harold. I don't expect I can conceal the smile, but don't want to embarrass him into an answer, so change the subject. 'Why do you have to test so many samples so often?' I ask.

'There can be mistakes made, can't there, Harold?' says Michael. Together the three of them remember a time someone picked up the wrong container and put a whole load of lemon flavouring into the fondant fancy mixture instead of vanilla.

'And I can remember, before your time,' Harold says, 'there was less security in those days, when some joker put this blue food dye in the plain Battenberg mixture, and red in the pink and, what with the white criss-cross of buttercream, they all came out looking more like Union Jacks than cakes! The MD at the time, Mr Ellis, he went mad, I can tell you.' As he tells it, we all fall about. I love the way that even though he takes his job so seriously, Harold can still always be relied on to see the funny side.

'We can have a good laugh about it now, but at the time, oh dear!' he says, taking a handkerchief out of his pocket to wipe his eye. 'Production had to be stopped, every machine cleaned out. It wasn't funny when it happened.' Shaking his head, he bursts out laughing again. 'You should have seen Mr Ellis's face. He himself went all the colours of the Union Jack.'

In the cafeteria in the old block, we choose one of the wood-look Formica tables by a window overlooking the hangar we've just come from. It's just past midday; the morning's flown by in a flash. There are already people in here on their break, tucking into shepherd's pie and chips. Harold asks me what I'd like, offers more than coffee: lunch. I settle on a plastic chair. He goes to fetch it from the self-service hot and cold food bar and brings back a tray with a couple of sandwiches and some bright fruit. The plates, just out of the washing-up machine, are warm and with a drip of water in their curved dip, and the coffee looks a bit thin.

'It's not the Majesty Hotel, I'm afraid,' he says apologetically.

'I don't mind at all,' I tell him, and I mean it. I'm a bit nervous I notice suddenly. When I pick up my glass, my fruit juice ripples.

Perhaps to cover up my nerves, I find myself telling Harold about the laundry, things I don't usually offer up. I don't tell him about Eliza. I say, 'It was unfortunate circumstances that had me up there. I was very happy in my nurse's training, only had one more year to go, then I could move on to specialist midwifery training. I didn't want to leave. My parents took me away.'

'I'm sorry to hear that.' Harold, opposite me, is no longer in his white coat: we both took them and our hats off on our way out of the hangar. He's got a thick Aran jersey on, all cosy, but still he wears a serious expression, almost sad, I wonder if that's on my account.

'I wasn't even living under their roof at that point. I was in nurses' accommodation near to the hospital, some miles from Stoke. Still, they brought me home and soon after sent me on my way.'

'You didn't have any choice in the matter?'

'No, no choice. People were funny in those days, their attitudes. Apparently I'd done wrong, so I needed to pay for it. The laundry was a sort of punishment.'

'Why did they need to send you so far away? If they felt they had to send you to a laundry, why not one closer to home?'

'Shame, partly. Also, this one near Glasgow was a special sort. We lived as well as worked there. It was a corrective place as well as a laundry, a place to see young women right.'

Harold nods. I think I've probably made things clear enough without actually spelling it out. I watch Harold's kindly face: smoothly shaven; round cheeks; generous eyebrows; a double chin, though hardly.

You can tell, can't you? I think you can.

I stare down at my sandwich, and though it's delicious I can't finish it. I'm always peckish; appetite's clean gone. Maybe too much mince pie earlier.

You can tell very quickly. About a person, I mean. Whether it's the girl in the supermarket, same overall as all the others in the checkouts but she's got something you warm to, even if you don't exchange a word. Or it's someone like Kelly you talk to and get to know, and the more you get to know her, the more you have the opportunity to discover just how right your initial instincts were.

I've all that with Harold. Very quickly it's a certainty one's aware of. There's no faffing. They say that when you know, you know, and that's all there is to it. All's that left is to get on with it. First time I met Harold, I recognised a goodness. Now he's getting up to fetch me another coffee, and I watch his homely back view, shoulderblade moving beneath the wool to lean forward and hand the lady at the till some change. And I think, now there's a man about as far removed from Jessie's Derek as an elephant's arse from its ivory tusk. I'm not being smug in my comparision just because Derek's a safe distance from me and Harold's my friend. It's simple plain fact. He's shuffling back now with his eyes on the milky surface of the coffee, his lips in a little O of concentration. When he brushes past me he spills a bit on the table, a few tiny drops on the sleeve of my jacket. All of a spin, he takes a paper serviette, and dabs them up. The sugar-mouse thumb that touched my sleeve at Priscilla's over the biscuits, now skims my wrist. The skim's gone in not quite an instant, but I can still hold the trace of it there before it fades, like I learned to hold in my arms the weight and softness of my baby after she had been taken away from me. I want to clench my eyes for darkness so I can concentrate on keeping it there as long as possible, the touch of Harold's flesh against mine.

Then when he drops me home so I can change before going in for the afternoon shift, he stops the car outside my cottage, gets out himself. The harbour smells of seaweed and salt and damp, and the sun is nowhere to be seen; it's a sky like an old drying-up cloth. Harold steps round the car and stands by the little step at my front door while I put the key in the lock. I open it ajar, turn to say goodbye.

Suddenly he puts his arms round my coat-padded waist, and the physical of it I've not had before. It's more than I could possibly have hoped for; far, far more than I ever expected. My stomach seems to have disappeared somewhere quite else, lost track completely.

This is the icing on the cake, so to speak, if you'll forgive the pastry reference. I'm only used to elation in moments. I don't think I've had in my whole life so many hours, one after the other, almost no let-up, so happy as I have had this morning with Harold.

Chapter Eight

There's a feeling in my body this afternoon. Silvery feeling.

Tiff's on leave and I'm in our office and out with the timetable sheets and the Tippex, jiggling our shifts around so everyone's happy. A more boring task you couldn't imagine. I've been at it over an hour. A bit of a contrast to my exciting morning with the mince pies. Yet I'm not minding. I'll be finished soon enough now. Jan comes in to collect her coat and bag, in a hurry as usual. She says she's looking forward to our annual party on Monday night. Once a year at Christmas time, all seven of us have a get-together in one of our houses, pull a few crackers, down a few drinks, eat a great meal – usually Tiff's gorgeous beef stew with prunes, and Maggie's mum's moist plum pudding. It's a riot always, something to look forward to.

'How d'it go?' she asks. 'This morning? At Topley's? Blimey I nearly forgot to ask you.'

I have mentioned to Jan about Harold. I had to after his note, she was that intrigued after she'd given it me, fair enough. I get on with all my colleagues in the team, but Jan's perhaps the one I'm closest to. She's in her late thirties, so nearest to me in age because I'm the oldest. Married to Colin, an accountant; they've two children. Jan's a kind soul. She's very quiet, shy, but she can be a lot of fun when we all get her going. She wears one of those clasps in her hair, a wooden spillikin through a piece of branded leather, it holds her long tresses in a bun but little bits are always escaping. She's got a pretty face, no make-up, pink cheeks, dark eyes, innocent-looking. You can tell Jan things.

'It went really well,' I say. 'Ever so interesting. I've not seen things being made like that before. The scale! All these machines.'

'My sister-in-law worked there a while. I went once or twice, before all these new regulations about visitors. It is incredible. So is Harold Mills incredible too?'

I smile. 'Oh, Jan.'

'Oh, God, he is.' The notes of her voice are rising. I do appreciate that about good friends, the excitement they feel on your behalf if something goes right for you. 'You need say no more.'

'I'll be telling you soon enough. Tiff knows I was having a drink with a friend, she saw me getting ready at the clinic the other day; and then Maggie took his message. They'll wangle it out of me to be sure, probably when we're all together on Monday night and I've had a few, and all my reservations have gone out the window.' The funny thing is, I can hear my voice but it doesn't sound like me. This is familiar talk, but it is the talk of other women.

'Never you worry. I won't let you tell anyone more than you wish.'

'At this stage there's precious little solid to tell. It's all in the mind, but that's nice enough. Good enough for me. Hope.'

'Ah, lovely,' Jan sighs as she puts on her gloves. 'I best be off then.' She picks up her bag from the desk, and spots all my spreadsheets. 'Oh, poor you, Dot, landed with this lot. If you're still at them when I get back from Kelly's I'll give you a hand. She's the only home visit I've got this afternoon so I shouldn't be long.'

'Don't you worry there. I'll be finished, and then I've got a nice afternoon on postnatal. I expect we'll be letting Honey home today, won't we, she's doing so well?'

There is a pause. Jan sucks in her lips.

'Is Saad all right? He hasn't had to go into Scbu, has he, little fellah?'

'No, but he and Honey have been moved out of postnatal into a single. I think there might be something afoot.' Jan pauses. 'Fresh evidence about the little boy that died of meningitis has appeared. They're needing to clear up some concerns.'

Suddenly I feel sick. 'You're joking me, Jan. They're not . . .?'

'It's all up in the air, nothing's settled yet. It's rumoured there might be a possibility of their going to court for an Emergency Protection Order –'

'Jan, not if I have anything to do with it they won't. What evidence, is what I'd like to know?'

'It's to do with Honey not going to the doctor when the baby was poorly. They said she should have realised something was seriously wrong, what with his very high temperature.'

'Look, she's not a doctor, and even doctors often miss the signs of meningitis. She did everything she possibly could for him. Everything. Tending to him non-stop.'

'I know, Dot, but they're saying it's her fault he died because she didn't take him to the doctor straight away; but for her negligence his death could've been prevented.'

'Well it doesn't take much imagination to realise Honey's been done over that often by the authorities in the past, it was hardly like she was going to rush into their arms at the first sign of trouble. Would anybody in her position, seriously, Jan? I don't believe this.'

'Listen, it may not come to an EPO. And Honey doesn't know a thing. I'm sure it'll all be worked out and she'll be home with Saad later today or tomorrow. What we said at the case conference has got to hold some weight. With any luck she won't even hear anything about it, and that'll be the end of the matter.'

I am aware of anger clutching my gorge. I might be going to vomit. 'What room is she in?' I ask, standing up briskly. Jan mentions the number, almost guiltily when she sees my reaction. This is the problem. We care about our ladies. Of course you get close. It is an intimate relationship, and not just because periodically you have your fingers up inside feeling about for their cervix. The consultants do that too, but there's something more between a woman and her midwife. If we have any humanity at all – and I can safely say each one of my colleagues on the team has more than her fair share – you mind what happens to them; in your heart you mind, bugger unprofessional. Jan knows I'm really fond of Honey, particularly concerned about her circumstances. She knows just what I feel about the possibility of Saad being taken from her, and she's got the look as if to say she wished she hadn't been the one to tell me of it. It's not her fault. Anyway, I would have found out soon enough. 'Thanks, love,' I say. 'I'll catch you later. I'm going to see her right away.'

I abandon the shift sheets and race from the office, down the lino corridor, and head straight for one of the four single rooms reserved for the mothers who have had an especially hard labour, or who need to be away from the public wards for whatever reason. I knock and rudely walk straight in, impatience getting the better of me. The little room is calming pink, though it doesn't calm me, and there are spring flowers on the skimpy thin curtains. What I see is one of those family scenes, so simple it moves me as does the nativity scene with its yoghurt-pot crib and plastic figures which one of the local schools makes every year for hospital Reception.

Here is Honey sitting up in bed against a puff of white pillows; baby snuffling at her purple expanded nipple, giving himself up wholly to trust. The father of the child, Rashid, is right by their side, his finger in the grip of his son's. He's talking to them both, lowing with encouragement and devotion. You can't see the radiance of emotion as such, but if the feel of it is filling any room, then it is filling this one.

Like some poor wretch of inarticulacy, I can only go, 'Ah.'

'Look who's here, Saad, it's Dorothy,' Honey says in a loving voice. 'Nice to see you, Dot. Everything all right?'

Rashid moves to greet me, puts out his free hand. 'Forgive me for not standing up,' he says, 'I am rather hemmed in here. How are you, Dorothy?'

I am choked. 'Oh, me, I'm fine.' I nod, as if trying to convince.

'Would you like some orange squash? A biscuit?' Honey asks. I shake my head and thank her. 'You were visiting Topley's this week, weren't you?'

'That's right, love, this morning.'

'Big day today, then. Did it go well? I think there was more of an attraction there than just cakes, am I right, Dot?'

'Goodness me,' I laugh. 'You might have a point.'

'You devil. Come on, you can tell us.'

'I will, too, if anything comes of it, I promise.' I want to say some things, but this is not the moment. 'How's it all going? The little one feeding OK and that?'

'No problem,' they both answer at once. There is a pause for a moment while I smile at the child, but it's not an awkward silence.

'Julia was round this morning,' Honey comments slowly.

Mention of the dirty word is like the entry of the serpent into the garden of Eden.

I say this, not because I dislike social workers: we work with them a lot, and they're fine. Let's just say there's one or two. Namely Julia Gibbons, who's in charge of Honey now. Oh, she's all right, she means well and does her best, but she's that overloaded with work she can't be expected to get to know those on her caseload as well as we know our ladies, and this does sometimes make for misguided decisions about them. We in the team like and respect her well enough, but it's hard not to resent some of the choices she's made. It was mainly she in the case conference who secured Honey's kid on to the at-risk register.

'She's a fucking bitch, she is,' Honey says, jutting the bottom of her jaw in disgust at the very thought of her. 'I fucking hate her, Dot. She was sniffing round us this morning like a vulture, asking all these questions, personal like, none of her effing business. What does it mean? What the hell did she think she was playing at? Who she think she is anyway?'

'She'll be trying,' I say uselessly, 'to do what she thinks best.'

'She frightens me, you know,' Rashid admits.

'She'd frighten bloody anybody,' Honey says. 'I tell you, I hate her guts.'

'You can't tell what she's thinking,' he comments, 'yet the fate of our family is in her hands.'

'She's got no right, snooping. She really upset Rashid with it this morning, and me besides. So what happens? Yeah, Saad gets the vibe and can't stop crying his little eyes out. I don't care what she does to me, she can't touch me no more, but she's not going to hurt these two. They ain't done nothing wrong.'

'Don't you worry now,' I say gently. 'She'd only have to look at the three of you here now to be convinced everything's all right, and Saad's in more than safe hands.'

'She ain't taking him away from me. No one's taking my baby away from me. Not this time. Never again.'

'I'm sure not, love, You calm yourself there. It'll be all right.' God, such platitudes in the face of such fear and love, and possible heartbreak. Sometimes I curse the midwife's patter. How inadequate! It's there to reassure; same old stuff comes out our mouths every time. Who's to say it makes the blindest bit of difference? 'Everything will be fine.' There I am, at it again. It's like a built-in mechanism, the fitting response for all emotional upsets within these walls, but all it is is a surgical swab temporarily to ebb the flow of blood. Sometimes I wonder if we can ever do any good in this job other than the merely physical? And the physical's not even the half of it. I feel so useless.

'We can talk about happier things,' Rashid says. 'His nan's coming in to see him tomorrow. First grandchild.'

I wonder if there will be a tomorrow, but stamp out the thought quick as I can, and say on cue, 'How lovely.'

'Oh,' Honey says, 'Rashid's mum, Dot, she's as proud as snow. She's coming round in the morning, and probably every day after that for weeks, help me out. I won't have to lift a finger.' Then she laughs because Saad has fallen asleep at her breast. 'He's a greedy little number is this one.' Her voice has gone softer. 'Knocked himself out with that binge. Good thing it wasn't lager.'

'Will I put him down for you?' I move towards the touching trio. With a thank you, Honey carefully lifts him away from her and into my arms. The eyes of his parents follow him as if reluctant to look away, they can't get enough of staring in wonder. I peep down at his face which is almost hidden amidst the wraps of his swaddling clothes. He has dark, dark eyelashes, and tiny milk spots on his wee nose. I rock him up and down, feeling the weight of him against me, barely heavier than a fairy cake.

As we talk, the serpent seems to have flounced out of the garden again, dismissed. When we don't discuss her, we can breathe sighs of relief, and believe. Instead it's the usual chat we go in for; comforting like. Me asking a few practical questions about Saad's bowel movements, sleeping patterns, all the routine stuff. Honey doesn't mind answering, doesn't think my questions too personal because she trusts me. I will not betray that trust. We have a few jokes and that along the way. For example, she has a funny anecdote about her cousin's baby – all mums have a story to tell about their families' and friend's children, and they tell them with such sincerity – and then when Saad awakens, Rashid gets teased as he's changing his nappy. For many of the dads this is the normal rite of passage, the more prosaic, hands-on introduction to fatherhood, and really one of the first since their initial contribution nine months back. Anyway Honey and I have a good laugh about it, Rashid's so muddled and sweet. 'Go on, Dot, you show him,' Honey laughs, 'and he'll soon get the hang of it.'

I'm in with Honey and Rashid a good while. When I think I have deflected their minds enough from their unfortunate session this morning – that's the least I can do for them at this stage – I head back into the office to finish off the shift sheets. It does make me mad to think of it though, the possibility of an EPO. 'The child's welfare is paramount,' they say. I know all about paramount.

I find I'm making silly little mistakes, Tippexing out the wrong box sort of thing, writing in Maggie's name instead of Jan's. I am so frustrated. When I do eventually finish, I check out the labour ward, and all's quiet, so I go back to Honey's room, I can't help myself. I don't honestly think anything is going to happen, because there's not a single just cause for anything other than the three of them go home today or tomorrow, end of story, happily ever after. But if things don't work out as they should – and I worry Julia hasn't had time to assemble all the facts at her fingertips, and on that basis she might do the wrong thing – I am going to be there for them.

I saunter in. It's already getting dark outside, Honey's got her bedside lamp on, the curtains are closed, and it's really cosy in here now. Rashid is reading to her, an article out of *Woman's Own*, while Saad sleeps. To judge by the way she looks, her clothes and the like, and from what you know of Honey, you'd have thought something more youthful and zany would have been her chosen reading matter. There again, I think of how houseproud and domestic and womanly she is underneath all that matted hair, and it just proves how wrong assumptions gleaned from appearances can be. You realise how a magazine as dependable and as homey as *Woman's Own* seems entirely fitting for her after all.

'Oh, Dot, he's reading me this great article, a true life story, about how this bloke who was adopted set about finding his real mum. We've just got to the bit where they're about to meet up for the first time in forty years. I've got this lump in my throat, honestly I have.'

Rashid closes the magazine. 'I best stop now we've got company again.'

'Promise you'll finish it later?'

'Promise. Maybe tonight at home, to keep you company when you're feeding him in the early hours. Shall I go get some tea for us all?'

I tell them I can't stay long, I have to continue on my rounds, I was just popping in to see if everything was all right.

'Aw, come on, just the one,' Honey says, and I am persuaded.

'A quick one then,' I tell Rashid, and he goes off down the corridor in search of the hot drinks machine.

'Dot, you don't know how I'm dying for my own room again,' Honey tells me when he's gone. 'Rashid said he's set up the cot at the end of our bed. And he's done a Christmas tree in there, too. Decorated it, he did, all himself. He said the bedroom's where he imagined we'd be spending most of our time from here on in, that's why he didn't put it in the lounge. Fairy lights and everything. Said he made the angel out of a finished loo-roll and cotton wool, bless him. I can just see him, little cherub, struggling with the Gloy gum and the gold glitter. He's all for celebrating Christmas with us, never mind his religion. So, see, it's all ready and waiting our little prince here, all we need now is the word so we can get out of this wretched place. You haven't heard when we can go, have you, Dot? Someone should've been round hours ago. We've been in suspense all afternoon. I'm that pissed off.'

' 'Fraid I haven't, but they shouldn't be long now. I'm sure anyway they'll be wanting you out as soon as possible, now you're ready, so they can free up the bed. If no one's come by the time we've finished our cup of tea, I'll go and check things out, see what's going on.'

I'm sitting on her bed, I've my back to the door, and I hear it open. I am parched, actually. I just fancy that cup of tea. It's that time of the afternoon.

Honey's chatting on with her excitement but suddenly it's as if her eyes have registered something nightmarish, and immediately her complexion pales, disinfectant diluting in water.

You have never known anyone swing round so quick as I do at this moment.

And what's this I see? Do my eyes deceive me? Here is Julia Gibbons, a colleague of hers – male – and another young woman from the Social Services, no older than my daughter. It is not a pretty sight, in the circumstances.

I have never heard a scream like it in an adult. In babies, yes, at their most distressed, but in an adult nothing, nothing like this. It's a scream like a cat fight. Honey has a set of lungs on her as props open the young woman's eyes so wide it's as if they, and not her mouth, are responding to the dentist's request to say ahhhh.

All's I can see is Julia's nicely mumsy body above unexpectedly bulbous calves, advancing towards Honey, her eyes on the cot where Saad is sleeping soundly. Honey moves so fast I don't see her in focus: throws back her sheet and blanket, and starts kicking Julia in the stomach. Honey's bare, very white legs are going with all the feverishness of a swimmer in an Olympic race she's worked all her life to win. Hair is smeared across her face, glued down with the sweat of fear.

'Come on, now,' I can hear Julia saying. She is protecting herself with her arms and rather bravely ignoring the kicks as much as she can, and sitting down on the bed. She is not moving towards the baby, but speaking with rational calm. 'Let me explain what's happening. We're not taking the baby away from you as such, but I'm afraid we're to keep him here in the hospital a little while, just till we go to court for the Emergency Protection Order. You can go home but will be allowed to come and visit him till the court case, I promise. You can have plenty of supervised access, and in the meantime he'll be really well looked after. An EPO doesn't necessarily mean Saad will be taken into care.'

'No, no, no, no, no!' Honey is shouting. She stops kicking, but leans right over Saad's cot, practically covering it, and holds on with all her might. 'You fucking bitch, right, I'm going to fucking kill you . . . You fucking . . . Help me, help me someone. I'm not going fucking anywhere without him; I'm never leaving him, right? He's coming home with me for Christmas.'

Julia's bearded colleague, in thick green corduroys, tartan shirt, and docksider shoes, judging there might be trouble, steps nearer to Julia and the cot. The young woman looks on helplessly.

Rashid rushes in with the tea, throws it down. All three

polystyrene cups spill open in a brown steaming lake on the shining lino floor. He leaps forward to pull the man and Julia away from the cot. The social worker pulls himself free and goes closer to the cot with the clear intention of removing it from Honey's clutches and wheeling it and Saad away. The young woman, obviously confused and reluctant, joins him, as does Julia. All hands on the cot.

My hands are covering my face as if I were watching a film of unparalleled horror. I am groaning and crying. Honey is shouting, shouting, shouting. We want to die.

'No you can't do this Julia,' I say loudly. 'Please leave her alone, leave off of them, the lot of you. Please. There's things you mightn't be aware of, really positive. She wasn't neglectful of her little boy, quite the opposite in fact. And, as me and Jan said in the conference, she's stable and secure now, she'll be a good mum, honest she will, she already is! I understand your reasons but, truly, you can't do this! No need for an EPO.' Ineffectual midwife's patter. I step towards the fray, I feel so weak, my head throbs with a sudden migraine, I am going to throw up but I clench my hand round Julia's elbow and unexpectedly yank as if I want to unhinge it from its socket, like tearing open the bones of a chicken wing to reach the inner meat. I apologise; I don't know what I'm doing. The vision in front of my streaming eyes is that through wrinkled clingfilm.

'Please, Dorothy, you must let us get on with this,' I think she says. 'I know it's a horrible business but, believe me, it is for the best. The child's welfare is paramount.'

Through the blur I can see the man gently but firmly manoeuvring Honey out of the way, so Julia can lift the baby from the cot. The wraps of his white blanket are becoming unravelled and falling away from his little body, so it's exposed for all to see, arched back, palms pushing up the burden of air above him. Beneath Honey's screams, I can hear his less powerful cries.

'You can't take him!' I shout suddenly, shaking, shaking, shaking to the very marrow of my bones, hysterics billowing up inside me. I don't know but I think Honey's still lashing out, now at the bearded man who's trying to hold her down with his foot, she's a piece of litter in the wind he wants to stamp on then throw away. 'Help me, help me, my Rashid, help me she cries.' I am still yanking at Julia's arm.

'Rashid, Rashid. Stop them, stop them! Give me my baby back. I'm having Christmas at home with my baby. You fucking bastards!'

'Look, Honey, we know this isn't nice, but it is honestly for the best. We're only taking him to the nursery along the corridor. You can go home and rest, get some sleep, and come and see him tomorrow. There's nothing to stop you coming to see him tomorrow. Let us take him now,' Julia's patient voice, trained in the art of gentle firmness, is saying, 'and the quicker this sad parting is over with, the quicker tomorrow will come. We want what's best for baby, and for you.'

'You're never taking him from me. If I let you, you'll keep him and never let me have him back, I know.'

'Not necessarily. We'll wait to hear what the court says, no? Nothing's definite.'

'I want to kill you, fucker, pig!'

It is clear Honey is not going to co-operate. She screams some more and rushes to try to relieve honey Julia of her tiny burden. Quick as a flash the man steps in, and Honey starts to pummel and kick him with the full force of her adrenalin. She won't let him or Julia go. Rashid also tries to help the mother of his child by preventing them from getting away from her. Out of the corner of my eye I glimpse Julia make a sign to the young social worker to ring the alarm.

How many moments pass I don't know, but now I can see white coats, like Harold and his colleagues in the factory, only white coats here means doctors. There's two, maybe three. They coax Honey to the bed. She's still trying to resist.

A syringe, in my eyes it's the biggest syringe I've ever seen, size of a power drill, is going for her bare buttock. Honey's pinned down on the bed, Rashid is trying to push them away but his arms are merely flailing against their official force. He is crying like I've never seen a man cry: like a woman. The syringe is getting nearer, it's the serpent's tail itself.

'All of you fuckers, you can fuck, fuck, fuck off, fuck your mothers, fuck. Curse the lot of you. Give me my baby back, give him back to me! Help me, Rashid, help, help me.'

Honey's mottled legs are open and kicking. Her vagina is pink and splayed, soft and hurt and raw and colour of an open dessert plum, and there for all to see, for everyone to get an eyeful of, get their twopenny's worth. They've ripped her of her dignity, and now they're sedating her so they can rip her of her baby so all hope and joy will be snuffed out of her for ever; and she'll be left with the dregs of a life, the husk of a life, the bargain basement of a life.

This could be upstairs at Piccadilly Park *circa* 1961; this is St Dominic's Hospital in civilised Somerset, 1990s.

My stomach is rumbling, the belly of a volcano; the spit inside my mouth turns thin and metallic. It's rising up, tractor noise, and suddenly it's coming out of me, all the bilge that's been festering. I'm sick, sick, sick, it just won't stop coming; my very guts it feels like. All over the room – drudge-coloured, it spatters in that tea on the floor; all round the walls, a challenge to that calming pink; some on the white coats; and in Julia's hair it goes too, a bit.

'Honey, Honey, I won't let this happen, no,' I call down a tunnel as I am falling to the floor.

Blank.

Chapter Nine

I awake around four in the afternoon to the sound of a doorbell. The sheets and blankets are heavy on me. My face in my pillow has muffled out the world. There's nothing like waking from a deep afternoon nap to disorientate you. The push and shove of life have quite passed you by for an hour or two. Then all of a sudden it's where am I? what's that noise? who's this? With some effort, I push the bedclothes aside to get up. I'm groggy as an ageing peach. Last thing I want is company, but it's no good pretending I'm out. They've all been visiting me since Friday and know full well I'm here.

I stumble about in my nightie, snap on my bedside lamp, pull on my towelling robe Jessie gave me a few Christmases ago. It's seen more glamorous days. Now it's what you might call well worn in. The white's not what it once was, it's lost its ardour. I've had my soft slippers that long my feet fit them perfectly; my heels and toes have each their own resting place in the imprinted sheepskin. I feel cosy, but it can't be said I look my best. My hair's all over the shop; I've not on a scrap of make-up. But the girls don't mind. I guess it might be Jan coming back to see if I'm recovered at all, bless her. She was with me all Friday evening but it was the others came yesterday and earlier today. They've all been so kind. 'Hang on there, pet,' I call on my way down the stairs. 'I'll be right with you.' The soles of my slippers are going click-flap against my heels and the steps. 'You shouldn't be using up your precious Sunday afternoon visiting me.'

I unlock the door. It's Harold standing there. He's wearing a huge blue overcoat and looks very big on my small doorstep.

'Goodness me, Harold,' I gasp. 'I wasn't expecting it to be you. How lovely.' I must look the picture of surprise. My fingers automatically go straight to my hair and pull it about to try to make it look neater.

'Am I disturbing you?' he asks.

Suddenly the idea of company, so unappealing a few moments ago, seems attractive. 'Not at all. Come in, come in quickly, or you'll catch your death.'

To pass through my door he has to bend his head else he'd bump it on the beam. This cottage isn't used to tall men. Any men, for that matter.

Harold hands me a brown paper bag bulging with fat green grapes. 'I thought you might have had enough of cakes and pies,' he explains.

I'm all of a dither. I thank him. As I take his heavy coat and hang it on the hook with the rest, my hands go ever so clumsy, seem to have grown big as baseball gloves.

We exchange small-talk. Please forgive my appearance, I thought it was Jan, I look a fright. Nonsense, you look just gorgeous. Sit yourself down, please, make yourself comfortable. Thank you, this is a lovely place you've got. Those grapes look absolutely delicious, that's very kind. I heard you weren't well, Maureen at the home rang me. It's good of you to come, I'm feeling a bit better now. You must take it easy though. Oh, I'm being well looked after, can I get you anything? Don't you trouble yourself; I mustn't keep you long. No, I'm fine really, I'd like you to, cup of tea? That would be nice I must say, thank you.

Sitting by the fire, cups of tea in hand and a plate of biscuits and grapes beside us, we graduate, slowly, to greater things. When we are not looking into the flames for refuge from diffidence, we are looking into each other's faces where there is concern and curiosity and respect and pleasure all together flickering pale orange across our complexions.

I start to tell Harold what happened. I've not seen many men with that kind of face similar to Jan's in that way you want to tell it things. I'll tell you whose it reminds me of – Rembrandt's. Some years ago, when a friend sent me a postcard of one of his self-portraits, I was completely taken by the painter's crumpled face, his funny sticking out hair. I'd heard of him but not seen any of his paintings before. He appeared such a special man, so kindly and good, I felt he was the sort who I'd like as a friend. I kept the postcard, I've still got it somewhere, take it out sometimes. In this half-light – you're going to think I'm silly comparing him to a man in a painting and long dead at that! – Harold reminds me so much of Rembrandt. It's not only the unkempt hair and watery eyes, it's the same aura they share.

First, of course, I tell Harold about Honey. I don't say her name because that's breaching confidence. I say one of our ladies I like very much is in this situation. I describe a bit about her past, then about her finding Rashid, and all that that entailed in terms of hope and love and new beginnings. Harold's got a good listening ear, so he has, and pensive eyes. As I relate things to him, he nods his head to confirm his interest in what I'm saying, and that encourages me to go on. Jessie says men are incapable of listening like that. All her dates, as I've said before, just want to gob on about themselves, that's how she puts it. A lot of the men at the hospital, I tell her, do listen to me. But that's different, she says, that's because you're telling them things that concern them, their babies. I've said I think she's being a little unfair. There again I haven't had her experience in terms of *romance*. It's in romantic settings that comes the real test. Then you know if a man can or wants to listen to you and, in turn, whether he can or really does love you. How can a man love you if he never hears what you say, who shuts off his ears when you open your mouth, who only wants to wallow in the smug hum of his own voice? He's just bouncing self-love off of you and back on to himself. Not Harold, but. Harold is the listening type. Here I am, droning on, verbal dam-busting, and he's all attention. Course, he's not just attention, he's compassion. He expresses horror, and says he can't believe that that was the outcome of what should have been a happy story.

I try to describe how they managed successfully to inject submission into Honey, literally, by means of that gross needle shoved in her wanton buttock; and how, with that done, they were temporarily, and perhaps permanently, to absolve her of her baby, that she might never again be 'neglectful'; and how the baby was not going to be spending Christmas at home after all, but was going to be the subject of an Emergency Protection Order. Who could tell what the outcome might be? I try to describe watching this excruciating scene, what it felt like to be there. These are hard things to get across. New mothers say there's a conspiracy, no one ever tells them childbirth's so painful. I don't agree. I think everyone talks about it all the time, only what no one's any good at is *description*. Emotional pain's just the same; impossible to convey in words. I don't know if I'm making a good job of it; all's I can see is Harold is all ears, and that winningly expressive face of his is pasted with melancholy.

'If there's no justice in this world,' I tell him, 'the court rules against her and she doesn't get him back very soon, perhaps the best she can hope for is forty years' time when, at seventy-odd, and withered more by misery than by years, she's reunited with him in the personal testimony pages of one of her favoured magazines.'

As I'm talking I'm thinking about the nature of guilt. Guilt is an edgy thing, taps away at you like a woodpecker having a go at some tree.

'I wasn't any good to her, so I wasn't. You know, I feel so ashamed, mortified. I failed that family totally.'

'There was nothing you could do. It was out of your hands.'

'But she was depending on me for support.'

'You did all you could, but that's the problem with team decisions, there's only so much say an individual can have.'

'Of course I believe in a democratic decision, and usually I feel we come to the right one. It's unreasonable of me, I know, but there are just some cases I wish I had more say. I can't tell you how frustrated Jan and I felt during Honey's case conference. To us, it felt like the others had this set idea of Honey, and we couldn't make them see she was a good person, really, and had managed to set her problems behind her.'

'It's a cruel business,' Harold says, nodding, 'when you of all people feel you are in the position to know someone better than the other professionals involved. You've a unique relationship with a woman, correct me if I'm wrong, which I'm sure even the best social workers, even health visitors, can rarely have. You and I know you should sometimes perhaps have more say in what happens to those in your care. Unfortunately –'

'– It doesn't work like that? I know, that's what I hate about this job sometimes: some say in these things, but not enough. Still, if only I hadn't fainted, Harold, I might have prevented the whole horrible outcome, the mother might have that baby with her at home on Christmas Day, and forever after. If I'd had my mind, I might have been able to take Julia aside and convince her. I'm not blaming Julia, I'm just saying maybe she'd misunderstood things; that, OK, maybe the baby could stay on the at-risk register, but that, truly, an EPO wasn't necessary. Fainting at that moment was unacceptable in every possible way.'

'I don't think so. A lot of people might've reacted the same if they'd had to witness such a scene. It's amazing those of you in the medical world can be so contained every day in the face of such tragic incidents. The rest of us admire that in you, you know. I couldn't cope with the half of what you cope with.'

'You mean that? Only this time I didn't cope. Apparently I fell to the floor, went out like a light. That's not good enough, that's not behaviour becoming to a professional midwife. Jan had to be fetched to bring me home.'

'Well, I think it's no wonder it upset you so much, made you unwell,' he says.

'Oh, I was a disaster,' I say, thinking back with horror. I don't remember anything of being helped from Honey's room, though I can see in my mind Julia's surprise at my conduct, and hear her words, 'What on earth's come over poor Dorothy? Is she all right? Not hurt? Help her up, someone, and see she's OK, we really must try to settle our business without further ado.' Then on the journey, I felt drowsy and still a little sick, and remember thanking Jan again and again for her kindness to me. Tears all the while still running down my cheeks. I couldn't stop crying, I remember that. I hitched a lift with her up my stairs, one of my arms round her neck, the other gripping the banisters like an invalid. She helped put me to bed, fetched me my woollen-covered hot-water bottle and a cup of tea with lemon, no milk, to settle the stomach. By the time I was leaning against my pillows with it in my hands, Jan on the chair beside me, I felt a bit better I must say, though I was worried about my ladies. And then I suddenly remembered about Priscilla and sat bolt upright. Up until then, I hadn't had a moment to think straight. Oh, I thought, this is awful.

'I've got to get up, Jan,' I said. 'Priscilla! She's not at all well.'

'No, you rest there. We can ring the home, see if she's all right, and tell her you can visit in a day or two.'

'But she may not have a day or two. I really ought to go to her now.'

'You mustn't, Dot. You've had a turn yourself. You can go soon but not today. Harold can visit her in the meantime.'

'But he doesn't know that I can't. And I don't want to go bothering him.'

'Calm yourself. I can see to it. As I say, I'll ring the home and have them tell Priscilla and Harold you're not able to go for a little while.'

'She won't understand why I've abandoned her, now of all times, when she needs me most.'

'Of course she will, don't be daft. I want you to be a bit selfish for once. Enjoy your cup of tea, get some rest, OK? And leave everything to me.'

Defeated by her kindness, I sank back against my pillows.

'No need to keep apologising, love,' she said. 'It's all right. Everything's going to be just fine. And I'm with you for as long as you like.

All comforting stuff, and I was grateful to her, really I was, but I couldn't believe that there I was, the other side of the fence so to speak. I wasn't doing the looking after for once, the caring. I was the one being cared for. It didn't feel right, and it still doesn't. My colleagues have been bringing me food and flowers all weekend, full of compassion and attention, and sweetness, and I am truly grateful. I've been told the hospital has said I needn't return to work till after Christmas and the New Year, that I should get some rest. Oh yes? What good am I to anyone lying here like an over-cooked leek? I'll be straight back to work tomorrow; Monday morning up with the lark as per usual, and I've told them so. Fact is, they're worried about me.

It occurs to me that none of my colleagues really understand why I reacted as I did to Honey's predicament. After all, we've all of us seen babies being taken away from their mothers' arms, thankfully not that often, but often enough. And we see tragedies in the hospital frequently, especially on Scbu, with the ill or premature babies who cling on awhile, encouraging faith and hope, but who fail to make it in the end. We see such despair in the mothers and fathers as surely can match that of Honey and Rashid on Friday. Even if it mightn't surface in quite the same way, it's no less intense and deeply felt for that. And us lot, of course we all feel emotional and upset to witness such things, but we control it, we keep it in check, we carry on. That is our job. We each of us has mums we are close to, and we don't flip when they are dealt the crueller blows of fortune. So, they must be wondering, why did Dot flip at this one? What exactly was it set her off – calm, dependable Dot, known to be stable and professional to the last? There again, my colleagues are a tactful lot. In the last forty-eight hours, bless them, not one of them's asked that question – Why, Dot, did you lose it this time? What's with this time, Dot, that's so different from the others? It's the one thing I don't feel up to answering.

'You were never a disaster, Dorothy,' Harold is saying. His words muzzle and blunt the woodpecker's beak as if with a bandage so the stabs of guilt seem less sharp.

'They'll have me six feet under,' I say, 'and I'll yet be bristling and twitching and retching from the injustice of what they did to her, and my inability to stop them.' I jab at the fire with the short brass poker. Harold and I sit in silence. For some moments we do. He is watching me, tactfully making way for me to say more if I wish to. His very presence is a comfort. I stare at the newly fledged flames, feeling his gaze on me like the unexpected warmth of an English summer afternoon. I thought silences were always awkward outside of solitary silences. It's a novelty for me this easy silence. What is it they say, angels are passing over. Or is that only at table? I don't care. We must be sitting some good five minutes before it is broken. Time for plenty of angels.

'I've got my own reasons for feeling this strongly,' I say slowly, eyes turned now away from the fire and regarding his reaction all the while. His face doesn't change. He's not going to press me. I drop my slippers off on the floor, tuck my feet under my behind, and nestle more into the settee. Harold, a few inches from me, is sitting more upright, but not stiff. His lace-up shoes are tied loosely and his arm is draped over the arm-rest. He looks comfortable.

'I hope you don't mind me going on about this?' I say. 'Only her case was not so far removed from something that happened to me such as I can't get it out of my head.'

Harold nods, but this time he smiles as well as if to say he's prepared to hear anything I'm prepared to tell him, and to offer untold measures of sympathy. That smile along with the nod's what does it. That does me in. I tell him everything – my parents, Jessie, Eliza, the adoption, the laundry, the lot. Only thing I don't mention is Alf Whittaker, but Alf Whittaker's another matter altogether. I don't tell anyone about him, not even Harold. For the time being, at any rate.

It's a long time we're on that settee. I attend to the logs in the fire from time to time. Not looking at my watch, I can tell the hours are passing by the progress of the embers. I shed a tear or two – nothing hysterical like on Friday. These ones are squeezed out by the frog in my throat when I'm describing my last days with Eliza and her removal from me for good. I'm doing all the talking, but Harold asks questions along the way. His tone seems to suggest that if I don't want to answer a single one I don't have to, and to excuse him for thinking of asking. His interest and concern urges me on, it's irresistible, and he's that sensitive I don't mind answering the lot of them.

'Have you ever thought about finding her after all these years?'

'I have, yes, because Jessie mentions it often. She says if she were me she'd have no hesitation in stopping at nothing to track her down. But Jessie's not me, Harold, to be sure, and I'm not her. Of course, I think about it on and off, fantasise sometimes even, I'll admit, but I'll never do it. Let the past rest in peace, that's what I say.'

'Don't you think Eliza herself might be pleased to meet you?'

'I think she might, if she knows of my existence. I don't even know if she's aware she's adopted. But even if she does and pines to know her real mother, I'm not sure it's a good thing. It's dangerous to dabble, to try to right the wrongs of years back. She might not imagine it, but the emotional upheaval would be so traumatic. She has a mother, to all intents and purposes a real mother, who brought her up and loved her. What can a young woman be doing all of a sudden with two? Family life is fraught with complexities enough as it is. Who am I to decide to thrust upon her more? As for myself, to see her actually in the flesh, so young, so beautiful, to be able to touch and hold her again, would be to be confronted up front with everything I've missed these past thirty-three years. The regret and sadness would become tangible. I don't think I could bear that. You mustn't think me a hard woman, because many in my position would make it their life's work to find a lost child. You see them all over in newspapers and on the telly. But I'm all for restraint, letting bygones be bygones. And if it may look that way, it isn't hardness in me, or callousness, honest. It's thinking of her, mainly, and partly too of myself. There's not a day gone by, though, when I've not felt her mother, and I will always be her mother in thought, even if I never can in word and deed. Do you understand that?'

Harold understands.

Later, 'What did you do when you eventually got out of the laundry?' he asks.

'Well, I made it to Stoke, but I'd no intention of staying there. I arrived home unannounced. Mother embraced me; her smell had remained exactly the same, unaltered by the years. I felt her rounded stomach against mine and, unfair of me I know, I found myself aware of a sort of disgust; misplaced fertility – I mean, what kind of mother was she? – gone to sterile, superfluous fat. She said I had changed, that now I was a woman, I hear those words in my head with contempt, how dare she? And, sure as clockwork, she put out a cake on the table as if my maturity from girl to fully-fledged woman, and my homecoming, were a celebration.

'My father had wilted, but was still as sandpapery as ever, still in his perennial beige overall. He greeted me not quite like the prodigal daughter, but he was evidently pleased I'd come home. So I told them I had come to see Beth and Jessie, and that I was leaving as soon as I could, I had no wish to stay.

'Consternation all round, of course. "How can you leave again, you only just got here? Where are you going anyway? What are you going to do?" Can you believe it, Harold? Offence that I wanted out so quickly. I sometimes wonder at other people, you know, my own blood relatives not excepted. What's honestly going through their minds? Is it just me, or is it true to say people are odd? I mean, what on earth can they have been thinking that day? Did they expect me to stay? To carry on as if I'd just come back from popping out to the corner shop for a tin of Ambrosia?'

'Perhaps it never occurred to them they'd done wrong or, because you'd been in a religious establishment for so long, they took your forgiveness for granted?'

'They were in for a sorry shock, then. I was off down here within the month.' I find myself laughing. I shift position on the settee. I've got a dead leg, serves me right, I've been gabbing on for so long. 'Goodness, Harold, you've had enough of my talking for a year! And you probably have to be up at five for the early shift.' I look at my watch. 'It's half-past eight.'

'It's not late. Jones'll be fine. It's been a very interesting evening. I only worry I'm keeping you up when you're poorly.'

'I've been sleeping all afternoon. And I'm feeling much better. My only worry is Priscilla. I am desperately anxious to see her. Is she all right?'

Up until this moment I've been avoiding the subject of our mutual friend – I've an appalling admission – purposefully. Partly because I didn't want to hear the worst, although I assumed because Harold didn't mention her there was no really dreadful news. But also, mainly, I cannot deny, because of selfishness. Pure, unadulterated selfishness. Harold arriving at the cottage out of the blue – when I'm there thinking it's Jan, it didn't even occur to me it might be him – was such an unexpected bonus and pleasure I couldn't help thinking that the evening, from the outset so peaceful and intimate, was our evening, no one else's. I wanted it to stay that way, for it to remain just about us, and to savour it just so, for a little while at least. I have an inkling Harold felt the same, or else he might have mentioned her earlier.

'I popped round to see her just before coming here. She's not well, but she's stable for the moment. She asked after you.'

'She's a fighter, she's holding on, but she's not got long, Harold.'

'I know. If you're feeling up to it, perhaps we should visit her together tomorrow? She'd like that.'

'That she would. I'm at work most the day. How's about we pop in late afternoon?'

Picking up the empty plate between us on the sofa, Harold agrees. 'Now I must let a woman get her beauty sleep,' he says, rising and heading for the kitchen.

'Let me have that off you,' I say, taking the plate and putting it aside. 'I feel awful, I haven't given you anything to eat.'

'Those biscuits were just the ticket.'

'No, but I mean a hot meal.'

'I've been having too interesting a time to feel hungry.'

'Promise?'

'Promise.'

'Another time, then, soon. I'll fetch your coat for you.'

I stand behind him and help him put it on, big heavy thing. I compliment him on it.

'It's very warm,' he says, then chuckles at himself. 'Funny thing, isn't it, coats are always warm. You'd never get someone admitting their coat was cold. Same with shoes. If you ever tell anyone you like their shoes, the stock response is always how comfortable they are.'

We laugh. He turns round to face me. We're standing by the little table behind the settee, near the door. He's that close up to me I can smell that treacly breath again. This time it's not competing with hot spices and liquor. Forget the taste, even just the smell of treacle makes the underside of your tongue tingle gloriously. Harold holds out his arms, and clasps them round me. He kisses me on one cheek.

This is going to sound silly, but there's not many men I'm on these terms with. The only men who kiss me on the cheeks, hug me, are the fathers of the children I've just delivered. It's a strange kind of intimacy I have with them, based on my intimacy with their wives or girlfriends, and on the immediacy of their joy. It's nice, pleasing, but it's not the intimacy of long-term familiarity and close friendship. As I've said before, my only deep-down friends are women, and we're kissing each other greetings, congratulations, what have you, all the time. A kiss on the cheek from a manfriend I can call my own and arising from mutual respect and pleasure in each other's company, that for me is true novelty.

His lips feel soft as a raspberry warmed by the sun. Please let them remain there a little while longer.

'Tomorrow then,' he says, 'at Priscilla's.'

'I'll be there.'

When he's gone, the cottage, normally so unused to people, feels suddenly bereft.

I'm in the office on the phone all morning ringing round any mums who might be able to donate a pram to a young one of seventeen who's just given birth and who has nothing. She needs one desperately, poor love, and the allowance she gets from the Social doesn't begin to cover half such essentials. There's a lot of women happy to help with anything they can, to give some babygrows and that, but few round here can afford to spare a pram. It's a dispiriting task, but eventually, by about noon, it reaps its rewards.

I am not remotely wobbly this morning. It's life as usual. If anything, I'm feeling rather well. I'm especially pleased because Jessie managed to get through at one point earlier, and we had a good chat. Derek appears to be behaving himself so their Christmas in a few days' time might be as Christmas should be, that is, a merry family occasion, no upsets. I told Jessie about my turn.

'But you sound great,' she said.

That was nice.

'There's nothing like having a turn to have people rallying round, you should try it.'

'You hate for people to make a fuss of you.'

'Some people,' I giggle. 'With others it's OK.'

'Oh yes? I think it's time we met.'

'Well, I've decided I will come at Christmas.' As I said that I didn't know when I'd decided, it just popped into my head. 'I think I'll be able to come up on Christmas Eve.'

This afternoon my good mood appears to be holding out as I drive to Kelly's for a home visit. It's getting dark and colder, but inside her house it's warm and bright and welcoming. There's a Christmas tree beside the fish tank. It's one of those out of a box, all white like it's been snowed on, and hanging from its branches are silvery threads and plastic gold stars which reflect the pink and yellow fairy lights, and glitter with the high-contrast colours of the television's late-afternoon American talk-show. Under it, on the squashy green carpet, there are a few presents wrapped in paper covered in hundreds of Santas. There are red and blue and green and yellow toys dotted all over the floor like babyish, innocent personnel mines which, if you were to step on one of them, would have no more evil intent than a funny squeak or ping.

Kelly is sitting on the settee, pink sweatshirt ruffled up around her chest, bosom emerging beneath it, a vast and beautiful marshmallow with the nipple a spill of blackcurrant jam. You wonder how, with the baby sucking at it so ravenously, her slender body can hold it there, that it doesn't detach itself and come away from her. She is smiling at Marcus who is gulping thin Ribena from a see-through plastic mug patterned with cartoon transfers and fitted with a lid and lip to stop the drink from spilling. He's going at it like a man in a pub, first pint of the evening in hand; when he takes it from his lips he has to gasp for air in order to get his breath back. He has a faint purple moustache. Topsy is lying beside her mother on her back, head resting on her lap, kicking her legs in the air, white knickers showing. It could remind me of Honey, same kicks, almost same exposure, only so different. She is wearing white lacy socks with clocks on them that are pink roses, and she is singing with tuneless abandon between sucks on a Curly Wurly.

When I planned an escape from the laundry it was with all this in mind. I never wanted for more. It wasn't much to ask; in fact it's all most women would ask. It may be reactionary of me, I'm sticking my neck out a bit here, but I've seen plenty of career girls have a change of heart once they become mothers. Their resolve falters; their ambition dissolves as wool in acid. You don't know how many women have talked to me all through their pregnancies about going back to work, 'when my maternity leave's over' what have you, but when the time comes they're in bits. The wealthier ones, the ones that have a choice, often decide never to return. I remember one woman, a highly successful solicitor, who'd told me in no uncertain terms she intended to be back at her desk two weeks after the birth; she was very happy to be having a child but it was in no way going to change her life, to compromise her ambition and potential. Two days after the birth she told her husband she was giving up the law for life in order to devote herself to that child and any more they might have in the future. And she did. Fact was, till it happened, she hadn't bargained for the urgency of the maternal instinct. It grabs you from behind, knocks you off your perch. I remember one mum saying it was that startling, that violent, it was like being mugged, only nice. As for those that have to return to work for financial reasons, no choice, they frequently do so with enormous reluctance, grief, and emotional pain. There's many would bite my head off for saying this, it's an unfashionable observation, but I've witnessed it close-to and all's a lot of them want, see, is here, what Kelly's got – home life with the kids and a man who really loves them.

Certainly, that's all I dreamed about in the laundry. Course, I still liked the idea of being a midwife, but that wasn't the overriding pull. The overriding fantasy was for family life, simple domesticity. I used to envisage myself dressing the kids for school in their little uniforms, packing their lunchboxes, and cooking my husband's breakfast, all at the same time. I even used to have arguments with these imaginary figures I loved so much. 'I can't do everything at once,' I'd protest. 'You keep an eye on your eggs, I've got to get these kids' shoes on, I'll be with you in a minute.' I wanted to be the put-upon wife-and-mum who everyone relied upon for everything. I wanted to have piles of washing-up on my own draining-board, all the hoovering to do, and the opportunity to moan on about such chores whenever the next-door neighbour, Mrs So-and-So dropped by for a coffee. I wanted to have little creatures about me to whom I could say, 'Keep your grubby little fingers off the paintwork'; a husband who might be too tired to make love, but who in bed couched his naked limbs round mine and fell asleep, maddeningly snoring, perhaps a little the worse for wear, but warmer than any hottie I could ever find.

What I'm saying is that my fantasies weren't all rosy-coloured and perfect like some of the other girls' at the laundry. They seemed to view life as one of the chivalrous and chastely romantic short stories in any of the (contraband) magazines they could lay their hands on. I thought that to want the downs as well as the ups was more realistic and so, in its way, more pleasurable. It was with these thoughts and longings in mind that I decided to try and escape; it was these that prompted such rashness. I was gibbering with the injustice, you see, of being denied the chance of just such a life as I see before me now.

I suppose I must have been at the laundry some seven or eight years when it happened. I can't put too accurate a date on it because there the years were not containable quantities of time with edges and borders and measurable depths, but seemed to merge and sink and stagnate together like the layers of old make-up on the skin of an aged actor who no longer has the inclination to make the best of himself. I was twenty-six, or thereabouts. In the room where I worked, we were watched over by a woman who was strict but more humane than the rest of the staff. Occasionally she'd slip you a bar of sugar. Miss Porter, she was called. Sometimes I think she quite liked us. One day she and I were talking about some matter concerning the callender machine, when quite out of the blue she suddenly let her guard down. 'That door in the packing room,' she said, 'is always open for loading, don't you ever feel like going for a walk?' I was astonished. In fact, to this day, I marvel at that uncharacteristic remark. People never fail in their capacity to surprise, I learned that that day for sure. The way she spoke, it was almost, in suggesting a way of escape, as if she were on our side. I was too wary to react positively, she would surely recognise her madness and suddenly turn. But, remember, stuffed as I was to the brim as someone three times my age with a sense of loss, and waste, and regret, and fury, I was open to suggestion. I carefully said nothing to Miss Porter, gave nothing away of my feelings, but over the next few days I became obsessed by her mention of that open door.

It was Bel was my partner in mood and crime. Our plot was simple. We would slip undetected into two packing baskets during break one morning when most of the outside workers were filling their faces with sandwiches, and the other girls could be relied upon to be either too hungry or too tired to notice our absence and squeal. We'd have about five minutes to find, climb into, and secure two empty laundry baskets. Bel had a way of closing them from the inside. She could twine her little fingers through the two holes to do up the leather buckles. But my fingers were plumper and less agile. I knew it was the mundane detail of doing up the buckles that was going to prove the most troublesome, and I was right; it nearly foiled us.

Stealing away from the dark corridor where everyone congregated during break was easy enough; still frightening, though. Every aspect of this escape was frightening. No girl had ever been known to succeed this way, but it was virtually the only option open to us. Others were even more risky.

The packing room was empty. Unlike in the pictures, there was no sadistic prison guard we had to strangle first with a torn pillowcase. There were no members of staff to watch over the packing room because the outside workers were considered to be on their side; it was guaranteed they'd tell if they saw anything suspicious or untoward. It seems incredible now, though at the time relief overcame any incredulity. Looking back, I think the reason there was no one during break keeping watch by the door to freedom and the outside, was Bel's and my plan was so presumptuous and far-fetched in the face of all past failures that no proper precaution had been taken to prevent it.

We put a couple of baskets near those lined up ready and waiting for collection by the van driver. We did the fingers crossed sign to one another, and climbed inside our separate baskets hoping our weights would roughly match that of a pile of sheets and tablecloths. Inside was dark with eyelets of light. Within seconds of being in there, the weave of the unforgiving wicker was knitting a pattern into the surface of my bare thighs and knees. I've never since been so close to empathy with a hen.

As I'd feared, I could barely squeeze my fingers out of the small holes through which the buckles looped, and those buckles had to be fastened, so I bloody well pushed. The hard wicker scraped the skin of my knuckles raw pink. Even when I did manage to get my fingers fully out, I just couldn't get the strap far enough round to fit the metal spike into its hole. Panic made me breathless. The more I tried, the more clumsy and painful my fingers became. I

kept thinking of great escapes in films and books, where men are
toiling underground, picking at whole tunnels with home-made
razor blades, and using ingenious methods to put together fake
passports – official stamps achieved with carved soap and ink
manufactured from powdered grit mixed with water; canvas
covers made of patches of torn pyjama bottoms dyed in tea. And
here I am, I thought, trying to get a wretched spike into a
wretched hole in a wretched leather strap. It's so trivial and banal,
there's about as much romance and glamour about my escape as
there is about an upset stomach.

'I can't do it, Bel,' I shout-whispered. 'Have you done yours?'

'Shhh. Yes. Hurry, Dot, we've only a few minutes.'

'I can't.'

'Try.'

'What do you think I'm doing?' That was uncalled for. Bel was
only trying to help. I apologised to her for it later.

'Do you want me to get out and do it?'

'We've no time, they'll be back any minute.'

'Really tug at it, right. Don't let it beat you.'

Tongue jutting out over lower lip – I always do that when I'm
really concentrating – I try a while longer. I'm so nearly there,
spike only a few millimetres away from the hole now, I can't see it
but I can feel it. Get in there, you bastard, I shout in my head. I can
hear voices nearing the room. The outside workers are allowed to
talk and they're coming back in. I tug my fingers back inside the
basket, buckle so nearly done, but not quite. That's it, I think,
they'll spot something amiss, I'm done for now; it's upstairs for
me, they'll make a few crucial nicks in my brain, take a few bits out
here and there, size and consistency of the parson's nose, and
that'll be me, a cauliflower of a person. I won't even be a famous
martyr. I won't be famous because nobody outside the laundry
will know, and nor will many inside, and anyway no one will
much care; and I won't be a martyr because, though I'll be as good
as dead, I won't be as dead as dead is.

As it happened, my fears weren't realised. I heard an outside
worker approach my basket and simply do up the buckle, no big
deal. I realise now that, if such a boring matter had entered her
head in the first place, all's she would have been thinking was that

someone, one of her colleagues, just hadn't managed or had forgotten to fasten it properly, that's all. So it wasn't the great detection I'd been fearing, but I can't say it was an anticlimax. My brain was safe, for the time being at least.

After an hour or so of silent waiting, crouched away so it felt like our very organs had been folded tightly in Tupperware boxes for storage, the driver lifted us into the back of his van. He was as strong as a hippo, and had been in the job for ever. I was convinced he would detect that our bodies weren't the same dead weight as piles of neatly packed linen. I can only say he can't have been concentrating, or just wasn't interested enough to investigate. Our luck was in – he never even hesitated as he loaded us on. It was the next stage was going to be tougher.

Perhaps this was the bit I was most dreading. When Bel and I had laid our plans we'd been stumped about how we were going to get out of the basket without anyone seeing us. Were the van driver to deliver us to the basement of some big hotel or hospital, we hadn't a hope of not being spotted. There'd be all manner of personnel going about their business. Our uniform was familiar to everyone in the area. It spelt Castaway in flashing neon letters; there'd be busybodies aplenty to turn us in in no time. Our only hope was to bribe the van driver. What with, but? We had nothing, less than nothing, just ourselves.

Ourselves.

Bel was pretty (that had been her downfall after all, why she was in the laundry in the first place). I was quite plain: indelicate features, tired limbs, stiff hair, but at least I was young, had nice skin, and my teeth were gleaming. (You could always tell a Piccadilly girl, even if she was just in her birthday suit, by her teeth. We were made to clean them three times a day with salt only. Toothpaste has nothing on salt for rendering teeth white as ice blocks, but salt makes you retch. I've not used it since, and twenty-four years later my lot haven't yet yellowed.) The van driver was in his forties, a village idiot type who wouldn't be able to resist the two of us offering kisses and giving up our breasts for his clumsy caresses. We knew that for certain, only could we stomach his heel-hard hands stumbling over our private flesh like rats in the dark? Those rudely awakened lips with that raw egg-white spit quavering wetly over ours?

You have to do what you have to do. Means to an end.

We came to our first stop, probably one of the big hotels. We heard the van's doors opening and the driver take out a few baskets. The plan was, once he started to move either of ours we would start to speak. Turned out he didn't touch us till our third port of call, and then he took hold of Bel's first. I heard the rasp of wicker across metal as he began sliding it towards the door so as to lift it out. I couldn't be too sure it was hers till I heard her voice, firm and clear.

'Stop that. Unfasten the buckle.'

There was a loud gasp. I'd've done anything to have seen the shock on his face. I was picturing it in my head like in character in a cartoon.

'Hurry up. Get me out of here. I've got to speak to you.'

'What's going on?' The man's voice was muffled. 'Who's that?'

'Never you mind. Just open up, will you.'

'Who are you?'

'If you open up and don't say anything, I'll make it worth your while.'

'Are you from up at the park?'

'What do you think? Now, come on, open the basket, keep your trap well and truly shut, and it'll be your lucky day.'

The small sounds of the buckle being loosened, a metal tinkle, was a joy to hear, as was the wickery creak of the lid being opened.

Bel forgot to thank him. The first thing she said when she stepped out was, 'Dot, which one's yours?'

'I'm over here. Here.'

'Look, what's going on?' the driver asked, a frantic note in his voice as if this situation was beyond him. 'You shouldn't be here. How many more of you in there?'

As Bel was freeing me, she was talking to him, calming him. 'Listen, didn't I say it'd be worth your while to keep your mouth shut?'

'Look, lass, I'm finishing my rounds and taking you right back to that Miss Beveridge.'

'You'd be a silly fool, then, wouldn't you? There's two pretty girls in your van today, it's not every day, Sunshine, you should be so lucky.'

My first sight as I emerged from my container, eyes adjusting to the light, was that of the driver standing at the van's doors facing inwards with a clown-like expression, and my friend rubbing her hands up and down the sides of his arms and his neck all the while kissing him round and about his chin. It was a scintillating act to behold. I knew Bel was clever, but not this clever.

'Come on, lover boy, give us a ride.'

The driver made a noise that can only be described as a pleasured moan, like Bel there doing these things to him was a dream come true, and to feel at last the treasure of female flesh was something he'd been fantasising about all his idiot life.

I watched on as Bel cajoled him and singlehandedly carried out the most crucial part of our plot. I was motionless with admiration that she could be doing it at all, let alone so convincingly. Her performance was like the manifestation of our desperation. Only I was cowardly too. I wanted to help out, but I was terrified. I had tears pushing each other down my cheeks. I couldn't bear to see my friend being touched and licked and sullied by that goofy man with his jerky movements, and his opportune hands under her clothes roving urgently, smugly, and closing in on her very own breasts.

I was inching forward to take over, do my fair share. 'Here, it's my turn,' I whispered. As I did so, Bel pulled away from the man, and I braced myself.

'That's it,' she said to him suddenly. 'Enough.' She gave him an address on the outskirts of the city. 'You know the estate? It's in Thornliebank. So take us there now.'

The address was her aunt's flat. Bel's old Aunt Mary had done all she could to try to dissuade her brother and sister-in-law from sending Bel to Piccadilly. At the time she had lobbied on Bel's behalf, but in vain. So it was we agreed that she was the best person to run to, she'd be on our side, she'd help and protect us. We had thought of my grandparents in the Gorbals, but dismissed the idea. They had never visited me in that seven or eight years because they disapproved, or because they had no idea I was at Piccadilly in the first place. Either way, it was unlikely they would welcome me if we were to visit them. Aunt Mary was altogether the safer bet.

'I've to finish my round,' the driver protested.

'You'll finish your round when you've dropped us off,' she informed him. 'How's about you take us straight there, and when we arrive I'll give you some more kisses, right?' Her smile was all pouting and suggestive, you almost believed she was wearing lipstick bright scarlet.

'All right, lass.'

'We'll stay in the back, then. You get a move on, mister.' Bel spoke firmly, even rudely, I think because she was scared but couldn't afford to show it. 'Hurry up, will you, we haven't got all day.'

The driver buttoned up his shirt, he looked punch-drunk, and closed the van doors. Bel and I sat on the baskets. In the darkness we heard the engine start up, and gave each other a hug.

'We've nearly made it,' Bel said. 'Just twenty minutes or so and we'll be free.'

'How do we know he won't take us straight back to Piccadilly?'

'Oh, we know. Because he wants those kisses too bad. What he doesn't know is he ain't going to be getting them, dirty bastard. Minute we arrive, we're out of here. It's hardly as if he's going to tell on us. What's he going to say? We didn't stick to our part of the bargain? We didn't give him the extra kisses we'd promised? No, he's going to be keeping his mouth well and truly shut.'

'But you didn't let me do my share,' Bel.'

'No.'

'Why?'

'Because.'

'Come on, Bel.'

'You didn't need it.'

'Nor did you.'

'No, but better one of us, and it's easier for me.'

'What makes you say that? I hated to see him mauling you.'

'I've learned to cut myself off from some things like they aren't really happening to me. I go through the motions but I don't feel them, so they're not so bad. I learned from my dad.'

'What did he teach you?'

'He didn't teach me nothing. It was in his hands I learned things, put it that way.'

I didn't understand what she meant, but I was grateful to her for what she'd done for me. Now I do understand. My poor Bel, to think what she must have gone through before she ever got to Piccadilly! All the more, her little act of kindness, when I can bear to think about it, it brings tears to my eyes, honest it does, all these years down the line. That's what I call true friendship.

Turned out Bel was right, and the driver did what he was told, stopped the van right outside Aunt Mary's block of flats. When we clambered out we gaped at the low-rise tenement blocks. They were ordinary, some would say depressing that day; their façades dank pebbledash, colour of wintry tree bark. But they were homes; families in them. They were lovely. In my dreams I could see myself in one, with a kettle and mugs all of my own, a settee even, and upstairs a lovely Formica wardrobe all white and clean, inside it a dress, all nice like my woolly one with cherries, maybe two, and a pair of comfortable slip-ons, even a pair of party shoes besides.

'Oi,' said the driver and asked for his tip in a thick voice which acted as a rude awakening.

Bel refused. 'You got your lot,' she told him. 'Now get on out of here. Piss off on your round.'

I bit my lip waiting for a nasty scene, for him to erupt, but the man wasn't up to it. I don't think he knew what'd hit him that morning, if he was dreaming or what. Anyway, he stepped up into his cab without a fuss. At the time I think I thought, Quite right too. Looking back, I thank God he was the simple type or Bel and I might have been in for it. He might have beaten us up. Instead he just drove away.

We had to watch till he had completely gone from view to make sure he wasn't coming back. When he disappeared round a corner, the two of us felt suddenly exposed, naked in the cold. It's hard to describe what it's like being out in the air when you've been indoors, literally, mind, never even a turn round the garden, nothing, for nigh on eight years. It's the first time you can see the sky, not neatly framed into an artificial square by the limitations of a window, but all over, an infinite expanse of it. It wasn't a magnificent turquoise or anything that day, only common or garden oppressive and grey, quietly whingeing drizzle, but even so the effect was terrifying. I cocked my head right back the better to get the fullest view of it, and standing on the tarmac there, in the middle of this housing estate in the middle of I had no idea where, I felt dizzy and exhilarated and frightened and about to fall over backwards. I was a child again on a swing being pushed hard, harder, too hard.

'Oh, my God,' said Bel. 'Oh, my God, Dot, I could stay out here for ever.'

We must have looked right daft the pair of us, taking whooping deep breaths, bending down to run our fingers through the wet grass of the verge, picking up in our palms clutches of autumn leaves, and throwing them over each other. We were grown-ups. Any neighbours twitching behind their net curtains, to have spied us acting like that, they wouldn't have known it. We didn't care. We ran along the kerb just for the sake of it. Running was out at Piccadilly, forbidden. We wanted to have our legs move fast. To discover anew they had a function besides walking and kneeling. And perhaps we were afraid to ring on Aunt Mary's bell, scared to go in, putting off the moment. For whatever her reception, that would be our fate.

We could have been an hour there in her street feeling up the outside. I couldn't say how long it was before we went to ring her bell.

Aunt Mary's door was on the second floor, up a stone staircase that smelt coldly of drunk men's urine, and along a concrete passage overlooking the road. We stood in front of it, out of breath – a novel sensation – and giggled for whatever reason. Neither of us wanted to press the bell. Instead Bel's fist bunched itself a few inches from the upper panel and prepared to knock, then withdrew.

'I'll do it,' I said, and stepped forward to make an impressive rat-a-tat-tat. We jumped at the sound. Bel, more courageous now, lifted the letterbox flap to listen out for movement inside.

'I can hear the radio on,' she whispered. 'She's definitely in. Oh, God, I think she's coming now.'

I thought I could detect that shuffle I remembered from years ago of broken-heeled slipper on carpet. 'Who is it?'

'Aunt Mary, it's Bel, and a friend of mine.'

'Bel?' The door was unlocked and opened. Aunt Mary, was a huge round woman with yellow-grey hair and a complexion to match. She was wearing a thin cotton apron, all orange and yellow splashes and swirls, with beneath a baby-pink knitted dress run through with a silver fleck. Pale blue varicose veins spread on the surface of her bare calves like the old lead on a well-used telephone, the curls malformed and kinked.

The look of surprise on her face was a picture. She threw open the door, pulled Bel on to the mat and enveloped her in an embrace.

'You're so bloody thin,' she rasped. Her breathing was loud and difficult. 'Come in, lasses, come in.'

The small flat was decked out in red carpet which must once have been fluffy but by then had been flattened and depressed with age. In some places the criss-cross strings of its weave were visible. Others would have dismissed it as well due for replacement, but to Bel and me it wasn't lino so it was sumptuous as down.

That smell of old lady lingered about the whole place so humid that to walk through to the lounge was like pushing our noses and faces through a thick hanging of damp nylon eiderdowns. Such warmth, such homely warmth, though far from fresh, was nevertheless something to savour. In all our years at Piccadilly, the only warmth we could possibly get close to was that in the laundry itself, and there we had such a dank, sweaty warmth, and it was so infused with the unyielding odour of washing powder that it remained ever sharp in the nostrils and stinging.

The lounge was small, and the three of us sat closely together by the hearth made of cream-coloured tiles that had a subtle, pretty mother-of-pearl finish. Aunt Mary shovelled a few coal droppings on to the fire, and we began to explain to her how we'd got out and what we were doing.

She listened intently, and the expression on her face was one of sympathy mixed with regret that our young lives had been wasted in such circumstances. She couldn't believe the stories we told her of what went on at the laundry and how we were treated, and I knew she felt sorry that she hadn't been able to prevent Bel's incarceration all those years before. Yet I detected an unease about her. I don't know if, too gleeful at our freedom to notice the signs of someone else's misgivings, I didn't recognise this unease at the time, or whether it is only with hindsight that I now see it. Aunt Mary, welcoming and kindly as she was that day, was uncomfortable all the same.

She cooked us this incredible hot meal at record speed like she just couldn't wait to feed our underweight bodies, to convex our concave stomachs. When you've lived off mangy stews as long as we had, and apple pie with apple sludge the consistency and colour of new snow piddled on by a dog, you lose sight of the fact that food can have tastes, and textures, and smells that are actually good, so good you think you're going to burst with pleasure. I will never forget what she gave us that day. We had chops, and peas, and mashed potato gloopy with gravy, and she rustled up what Bel called Aunt Mary's Best-Ever Trifle. Food never tasted so good before or since. I can still feel the moist sponge, creamy custard, and the sweet green jelly on my tongue, the pink and white hundreds and thousands melting in the grooves of my teeth. And I can hear Bel's and my girlish exclamations of unadulterated joy. We had no room for the home-made shortcake. Our stomachs were so distended afterwards we groaned and bent double with pain, but we were full and, my God, were we happy.

I don't think we'd thought much further than the escape itself. I suppose we just kind of assumed Aunt Mary would take us in, and magically shield us from Piccadilly and the world till such time as we got ourselves sorted. Sorted meaning a husband, of course, if we could get one; and/or possibly a job. If you've been cooped up in an institution you can be over the moon to be free, delirious even. But, perversely, that freedom which has been the focus of your imaginative existence for so long, when you attain it, brings with it its own fears and troubles and pain. For all the horrors of imprisonment and communal life under duress, it's hard to adapt to a life innocent of structure and constraints and the rude inevitability of punishment. Aunt Mary's home would be the perfect halfway house.

Or so we thought. Whereas kindness and trifle were generously forthcoming, we hadn't bargained for practicality, or for the full force of Aunt Mary's conscience. There was no room in her tiny flat for two young women; or, more to the point (to stay under her roof we would have readily bedded down on the very carpet of her lounge, whatever it took), there was no room in the old lady's conscience for subterfuge. She was a good and proper law-abiding citizen.

Thus it was our chink of freedom was short-lived. Three hours, to be precise.

'I'm going to have to turn you in, I'm afraid.' Those were her words. She had tears careering down her cheeks. 'It's not right.'

'But Aunt, it's not right what they're doing to us!' protested Bel.

'I know, dear, I know. But they'll find you. We'll all of us get into trouble.'.

'How? Nobody will know.'

'They'll come looking, you mark my words. You hiding here, see, it's against the law.'

Bel and me, we were reclining on the settee, it felt ever so soft after our big dinner. It was about two o'clock. We were that stuffed to bursting, even our indignation couldn't get us to sit bolt upright. We were arguing lying down. I remember, my head on a brown furry cushion with a button in the middle, thinking it was the most comfortable place any head could ever hope for on which to rest; thinking about what Aunt Mary had just said. It's against the law, she said. *It's against the law.* But that was exactly the thing. It *wasn't*. Piccadilly existed not as part of a wider, recognised state system of institutions, like the prisons, where people were put away through means of the courts, locked up as a result of the workings of British justice. No, it was an institution established by an individual, one Thomas Greenwood, a Victorian gentleman (if he could be referred to as such) with a personal and over-zealous quest to rid the community of all those 'wastrels and degenerates' within it who ruffled his sensibilities and his purist picture of humanity. This was perhaps the most painful point about Piccadilly and our part in it – I don't know if I've yet laboured this truth enough: there was nothing about it that could be described

171

as legal in the proper sense of the word. What I mean is that, though it wasn't *illegal* as such, and was allowed to exist undisturbed for nearly a hundred years, it only did so because society seemed to condone Greenwood's vision, and deemed Piccadilly to be a Good Thing.

The tragedy of that day is that officially our escape was entirely within the bounds of the law; officially we had every right to be at Aunt Mary's place, or anywhere we liked for that matter; officially we were, and always had been, free citizens; officially it was not at any point a criminal offence for us to walk out of Piccadilly's door.

Aunt Mary had her thoughts in order – she didn't believe we, or anybody else, should ever have been sent to such a place, or that such a place should ever have been established in the beginning. But society had made her scared, made her conform to those dictates which went against her very nature.

'I'll have to send you back,' she said. 'I have no choice.'

We were desolate. We pleaded, but in the end we had to accept the inevitable. Later that afternoon she accompanied us on the bus back across town. It dropped us about a mile from the front gates. Aunt Mary embraced us, said she was sorry, sorry, sorry, would we ever forgive her? Of course we would, because, although we had rebelled, we knew in the end, as we probably had all along, that submission to the set pattern was our only option. We watched Aunt Mary board her bus back to Thornliebank, in tears, her whole big face buried in an old handkerchief. I felt sorrier for her than I did for us. Then, in silence, and both with the same thoughts, Bel and I voluntarily, though not willingly, walked the rest of the way back to our prison, hideous punishment looming closer with every step. We conformed. We had nowhere else to go. We believed that we must be bad; maybe we deserved to be at a place like Piccadilly after all. Women like us, that was our fate.

Women like what? We were women just like the lovely woman in whose front room I am sitting right now.

Kelly is giggling and whispering something to me as I place her baby on my weighing machine.

'Sorry, love,' I say. 'I was miles away there for a second.'

'S'all right, you must get a bit tired doing this every day.'

'No, I love every minute of it, really, I just had a rather full weekend, that's all.'

'Out raving, were you Dot?'

'Not exactly, but I was having a lovely time.'

'Good on you, gal. No,' her voice lowers to a whisper again, 'what I was saying was, Stevie and me, we did it last night, first time, like, since you know who.' She gazes down at the person in question, who's naked and crying on the cold plastic slab of weighing machine. 'Ah,' she says, 'it's OK, sweetheart, don't cry. Dot won't be a second, shhh, nearly done now.'

I pick the baby up, and quickly dress her again.

'There,' says Kelly soothingly as I put her back in her arms. 'It's all right now, isn't it?' the baby stops crying. 'That's better. Warm again now.' Kelly grins up at me. 'Oh, Dot, it were brilliant, only it were probably a bit soon, I reckon. I'd be offering you a cup of tea, love, so I would, but my fanny's that done in. Now I'm sat here I'm not sure I could make it to the kitchen. I could barely get myself down the stairs this morning. Stevie thought it were hilarious.' Throaty laugh. 'I don't suppose you fancy a fag? I know I shouldn't in front of the baby, but I could just do with one.'

I shake my head. 'No thanks,' I say looking at her; never disapprovingly, mind. She looks so happy.

Just the same as Kelly, we were, I think to myself. Good girls. Only different times, different fates.

Chapter Ten

To look at, I'm not a very prepossessing person but I can make the best of myself. There's not many occasions call for it. Our annual Christmas party is one of them. I pull out all the stops. Tonight's the night.

After visiting Kelly, I drop in on Priscilla on my way home to get ready and change. In the hall Maureen is full of how she has improved in the last few days I've not been able to visit. She tells me there's colour in Priscilla's cheeks. I doubt it somehow. But I suppose that that's the sort of platitude the nurse in an old people's home has to give out sometimes, equivalent to us lot saying every baby's beautiful. Only difference is we believe it when we say it. If I sound impatient with Maureen it's not meant, it's just the idea of a woman, age of Priscilla and poorly as she is, with colour in her cheeks. You have to admit it's faintly far-fetched.

Course, upstairs, I find my friend as pale as ever, her complexion the colour and texture of a peeled chestnut, but I cannot deny an improvement in her general demeanour since I last saw her. She's sitting more upright and smiles when she sees me. Though impending death has never stopped her talking, her speech is less breathy.

'You visited the factory then?' That's her first question, before I'm even sat down. No one could accuse Priscilla of losing her faculties. Determined old bird.

'I did.' I hang my coat on the handle of the wardrobe. There's that familiar heat in here, stifling. Radiators with an overwhelming sense of duty, but ever since those in the laundry with none at all, I'm not complaining. I smooth the thin material of my midwife's dress over my bottom as I lower myself onto the chair beside her bed.

'Harold told me.'

'I gathered as much. How are you feeling?'

'You enjoyed it then?'

'Very nice too.'

'He liked your cottage. You don't often get Harold enthusing about much other than dogs and cars, the odd cake at times. Said your cottage was lovely, cosy inside, nice atmosphere. He dropped by this morning to tell me.'

He didn't waste much time, I'm thinking, not without pleasure. 'Harold's not a man given to wanton displays of enthusiasm,' I say. 'Too much of it can smack of the insincere, don't you think? He's not short of interests, but.'

'You said it, love, not me,' Priscilla says with good humour. 'I'm staring one of them right in the face. Thank goodness. First sensible enthusiasm he's had in a long while.' She pats my full knee with her liver-spotted hand and I'm glad. 'There are some's would disagree with me,' she adds, 'but in my book a dog's no substitute for a person. If it's the last thing I do, I'm going to let him know – '

'Ah, now you settle down. Look, I've brought you some more baked beans, keep your strength up, and a couple of tins of steamed pudding with custard. Your favourite.'

She thanks me as if my modest offering were a rare delicacy. She's that appreciative. 'You'll make a fat woman of me yet, Dorothy Sheffield,' she jokes. We laugh.

'That'll be the day!' I say. 'Look at me.'

'You're all right. Nothing to worry about.'

'Stomach.'

'Pah, don't be daft. Doesn't seem to have put Harold off. He spoke so well of you, you know. What was the word? Illuminating. That was what he used to describe the evening with you last night. It was very singular coming from him. I've never heard Harold so poetic.'

'How are you feeling, love?' I ask again, now smoothing my dress over my knees.

'As good as can be expected. I'm all right. Not as achy as I was.'

'Keeping your food down?'

'Oh, yes.'

'I'm glad to hear that. You're looking better. Very pretty.' She seems pleased at that. I mean it, too. She's got these appealing eyes, no lashes left, but real blue and heavy hooded. Her white hair, she would have had it permed not so long ago, has soft curls, it's not all stiff and unmanageable like mine. Jessie says when she's old, she's going to let her hair go; she's never going to wear a dab of make-up; she's only going to go about in comfy sweat pants and bungy slippers; she's going to eat that many doughnuts and Dime bars till they're coming out her ears so's to make up for all those she's ever resisted: she's no longer going to give a damn about her appearance. I'll believe it when I see it. Even when a woman's Priscilla's age she likes to look nice. To tell any woman she looks pretty, however old, makes her happy.

I apologise to Priscilla that I can't stay long, that I've to go and get ready for the team's little Christmas party. I don't want to leave just yet, I tell her, but I fear I'm going to be late.

'You enjoy yourself, girl. I want you to do just that, promise me. You deserve it. We've our own Christmas party tomorrow, it's downstairs in the lounge, but I'll not be going. So I can think about you at yours instead. That'll be much better.'

'Why not go? Yours might be fun.'

'A load of wrinkled incontinents playing at being six again? All dribbling into their sherries and choking on the charms in the Christmas pud? Unable to pull a cracker for their arthritis?' She raises a thin eyebrow that's been pencilled on crooked, bless her. 'Not my idea of fun.'

She's a laugh, this one. It's good to see she's got her spirits still. I stand up and put my coat on.

'You watch that Harold,' she says as I do so. 'His idea of wooing a woman is to bombard her with jam tarts.'

'That's as good a way as any.'

'Next time I see you, Dot, mark my words, you'll have turned into one.'

'It was grapes he brought me yesterday, and very tasty they were too,' I say, leaning down to kiss her on her forehead. Her skin feels like crumpled wax-paper, but it's normal temperature, not raging hot. 'Now you take care of yourself, young lady.'

'Oh, he's graduated to grapes, has he?' she says, ignoring my appeal. 'He's coming on well then.' She smiles at me and me at her. 'Bless him,' she adds in a more serious tone. 'He's a good fellow.'

As I leave her, I feel more optimistic than I did. I think to myself on my way downstairs, we've got her for a little while yet. As she says, I can enjoy myself tonight. I'm going to get myself all togged up; have a good laugh with some friends.

This year, we're having the party in Tiff's house which is on a new estate the other side of Stoneham. Her husband Paulie's doing well in computers, and last year they bought the show house. She fell in love with it: furniture, carpets, curtains, dried flowers, the lot. It even had photo frames on the tables either end of the settee with pictures in of a pretend family. She and Paulie bought them too. So when they moved in, that was all they had to do really: substitute their own real family photos for the fakes. I thought it was a bit spooky, having all someone else's décor down to the peach-coloured toilet paper to co-ordinate with the bathroom walls and suite, and new teddys already there on the beds in the kids' rooms. Apparently there's women with the job of fitting out show houses on new developments so the insides seem just like a real-life family's living in them. I think that would be a very funny job. After I came round to Tiff's the first time, I told Jessie all about it on the phone, and said it seemed to me like there were a hell of a lot of potential buyers out there with no imaginations of their own, but she thought it was brilliant. None of the bleeding hassle, she said. 'Moving's second only to divorce in terms of stress,' she said. 'I'd give my right arm for a show house. I bet people wish someone could devise a way to make divorce so trouble-free!'

I must say, it is lovely. The girl with the task of making this place homely certainly made a good job of it. There's yellow wallpaper in the lounge that's a rag-rolled paint effect, makes it nice and warm, and yellow and blue chintz curtains, all glazed swags and billows, and paper borders round the ceiling to match. You could be in one of those plush coffins, all quilted and sumptuous, favoured by the Sicilian Mafia. No, that doesn't sound quite right, what I mean is, all the décor in here makes you feel that pampered It's very cosy, especially at night, just right for our girls get-together. You feel you can relax in a place like this; it's conducive to talking. The kitchen where we're going to eat our party dinner is like your dream kitchen. The units are this special hard-wearing material but made up to look like real wood, and the drawers slide in and out easy as skates on ice. I think Tiff had to provide her own egg whisk and food blender and what have you, but some of the crockery, cutlery and glassware was already here; even the chintz cushions on the white wooden dining chairs were tied on round the legs with perfect bows. Jessie almost fainted with excitement when I told her that.

We're not going to be talking about serious subjects this evening, like our current obsession with industrial action, which we've all talked about non-stop for weeks, and which we're all agreed upon: we'll go on strike if that's what it takes to achieve a halfway fair annual wage. Tiff's banished Paulie for the evening. Men not welcome, which doesn't mean they won't be coming up in conversation. When I arrive, there's Maggie and Jan already sitting on the settee each with a sherry. I do like this, seeing my colleagues enjoying a drink, letting their hair down – literally in Jan's case, you never see her without her leather-and-stick clasp, but tonight she's not got her usual bun, her beautiful long hair is well down over her shoulders, and she suddenly looks like one of those lovely Victorian ladies you see in old photos. It's really something special to see everyone in mufti. You get a bit bored of our uniform and, ever since the laundry, I in particular haven't been too fond of uniforms. I remember seeing Bel for the first time in normal clothes, not all dowdy in the regulation wear of Piccadilly, and she looked so different. Bright colours and her individual style served to enhance her beauty and personality. I see the importance of uniform, course I do, in the right context, like for schoolchildren and us lot in the medical profession. Only sometimes, in places like Piccadilly, it can be used as a dehumanising thing. I've never quite lost sight of that, so it gives me pleasure whenever I see my team-mates as themselves.

I compliment Jan on her dress, Maggie on her top. Me, I have myself up something special too. Bit of blue eye make-up, bit of blusher. It's true what they say about women dressing up for other women. Jessie says there's not many men as notice so much as a paper bag full over your head, whereas women clock everything about you down to the shade of your tights. In that sense it's quite a relief to have a uniform, you can't be judged as such. So anyway, this evening, for the girls, I'm wearing my white silky blouse, feels lovely against my skin, with a bow round the neck which Jessie says is a bit eighties, a bit Mrs Thatcher, but I'm not the fashion-conscious type, I don't care, I like my shirt very well, thank you. It's casual but smart, specially if you dress it up a bit with a nice brooch. Tonight I've chosen my Wedgewood – it's pale blue with a silhouette in white relief of a Georgian lady's profile, and a little gold pin, though you can't see that. Jessie gave it me, some years ago now, for Christmas, the Wedgwood factory's near where we come from. I've got on a silky skirt too, almost ankle length, paisley-type pattern. We set to talking about clothes. I'm sat on one of the armchairs, lulled into the cushions – and my sherry – by a sense of well-being.

Chantal and Penny arrive together, thick as thieves, soon after me. They're the two youngest in the team, and they're a laugh and a half. Chantal's all tanned, recently back from honeymoon in the Cayman Islands. Her husband's the deputy manager of a huge supermarket outside town. When she broke the news to us last year of her engagement, she said she was only marrying him for the 10 per cent discount on her groceries. For a minute we believed her, we held our breaths, she sounded that serious. But that's her sense of humour. Then she burst out laughing, she was having us on. We know she's mad about him. Her best mate, Penny, born the year I came out of Piccadilly, is less lucky in love. She's the opposite of down-to-earth, stable Chantal. Penn has more than her fair share of man problems. She doesn't half get herself into scrapes, that one. Quite often she'll come into work in tears, but she's always so funny about her misfortunes we're all laughing before you know it, and she's back to her usual self in no time. Each of us is forever giving her the benefit of our advice. Needless to say, it's dutifully ignored. Even so, I've infinite respect for Penn. Young as she is, and with problems such as she always seems to be up against, she's a good midwife, she never lets things get in the way of her duties.

Tiff's in her element. Her apron all frills, a match for the curtains, rustles as she sits Chantal and Penn down and hands them drinks and little eats. She goes to check on her special stew.

We're missing Dolores, she's not much of a one for time-keeping, but we're all of us jabbering away ten to the dozen.

We're already on the subject of some of our ladies and their partners. At their annual get-together, you can bet funeral directors have a few laughs about eccentric widows, grabby relatives, and mix-ups with bodies; so we can occasionally make harmless jokes at our ladies' expense. Let's face it, there's one or two rightly peculiar. Between us we've our fair share of funny stories and reminiscences.

Dolores appears eventually, full of traffic news and apologies. She's Northern Irish, got a wonderful accent and way of putting things, you forgive her anything. We go into the kitchen, and Tiff dims the lights. It's ever so pretty. There's holly and crackers and candles on the table to get us in the Christmas mood. At the meal, we lay into bottles of red wine and, while tucking into the dumplings in Tiff's stew, we discuss the diets we're going to go on just as soon as the festive season's over.

'Apparently, you can eat what the hell you like,' counsels Maggie. 'Mars bars, cheesecake, chips, the lot, long as you make sure you eat half what you'd normally eat.'

'So if I cut down to just four slices of cheesecake and two Mars bars at one sitting, I'll get thin?' Chantal asks.

We laugh.

As the evening moves on and the wine takes its toll, we ourselves move on to more intimate subjects. Penn fairly gets us going with a story of one of the blokes she was seeing a few years back. Apparently they were in bed together for the first time, naked and all, 'just about to get down to the serious business,' as she puts it. Then he asks her, 'Shall I get dressed now?' 'And there's me,' she's saying, 'feeling a bit short-changed, if you get my meaning, when I realise he's grabbling with the Durex box. Get *dressed*? It's his way of asking if it's time to put the condom on!'

Shrieks of laughter. It's not that funny, but it is, if you know what I mean.

'Last time I slept with him,' she says, 'I can tell you. I can't be doing with them type of euphemisms.'

Chantal and Dolores are wiping the tears from their eyes for laughing; they're clutching their stomachs. When they calm down, it's not long before the attention turns to me and I'm being grilled about the gentleman they know I've been seeing a bit recently. With the people you know so well, especially your women friends, subtlety's not exactly top of the list. There's no beating around the bush as far as Chantal and Penn are concerned. Their questions are quick-fire and straightforward and, with my rounded behind blended comfortably into the little bowed cushion, low lights to shade my blushes, the pleasant heaviness of the dumplings inside me and a sherry lightness in my head and veins, I find I am surprisingly willing to answer youth's impertinence. The others, for whom youth isn't quite so keen, are naturally more reticent but nonetheless spurred on by Chantal's and Penn's enthusiasm and the thrillingly unlikely news of my little turn-up for the books. Any involvement I might have with a man, I myself am overwhelmed enough as it is, but the novelty of it for those around me is total knock-out. They regard me as your prototype maiden aunt, see, one of life's entrenched spinsters. Dot Sheffield and men just don't go. No wonder it's questions, questions, questions.

It's our annual party, and I tell them things. Things as go down a real treat, just like Maggie's mum's plum pudding and Jan's brandy sauce. I relate the circumstances of all my meetings with Harold. They don't want to be spared any the details. Penn wants to know what I was wearing on each occasion, and almost all there is to know about him, practically his inside leg measurement! And there's me, I'm rather enjoying all this attention, can you credit it? I've never really understood that female tendency to reveal to friends and strangers, practically anyone, everything about every-thing. It's not just in the wards in the hospital. You can understand that – women collectively experiencing physical, emotional, almost every kind of upheaval. I see there it's only natural to want to share the enormity of feeling. But it also goes on in other places, in trains, in hairdressers – you should hear Jessie's customers, what they have to say to each other, fairly rumbles the imagination. I'm the opposite. As I've said before, I'm one to err on the side of discretion. I'm not saying I think that's necessarily a good thing, some's would call it bottling it all up. Whatever. Keeps herself to herself does Dorothy. But perhaps that's because she's not had such nice things to tell till today.

And this thing, no doubt about it, is a wonderful thing. So why haven't I spoke about it before now? You'd have thought the agitation of joy would have been a challenging enough opponent for lifelong discretion. Only I've not really had the chance to speak of Harold with Jessie – she's enough turmoils of her own – and, though Priscilla's said a lot to me, I've been unforthcoming even with her. Sort of shy, see. Untested in these waters. I've not had the words, for one. But also I've seen all this as a sort of lunacy on my part. Woman my age, and such a solitary soul at that. I've asked myself, can it really be true, in a dopey old cart-horse like myself, such strength of feeling? And, if so, can my middle years really withstand the ruffles of such things? Belated love has already been playing havoc with this ageing constitution. Can the body cope, let alone the mind? What is each hoping to gain?

But as I talk about Harold tonight, to my team-mates, my tongue let loose like the proverbial cat out the bag, I'm feeling the milky comfort of not holding back. The very fact of my unburdening, their intent listening and approval, makes something which these past few weeks has throbbed alone in me, seem real. Talking's not been such a relief since I got out the laundry and became accustomed to the fact I could open my mouth without fear of my lips being snared with parcel tape. To talk about it is to relive it, though it only happened a short time ago, but as I'm talking, acknowledging it out loud, I'm falling in love with him again, all over again.

Well, that's a Christmas party I won't be forgetting, you can say that again. While the others over the years have merged in the memory like moss, this one, whatever happens between Harold and myself, will stand out on its own.

Apart from anything else, it's three o'clock in the morning that I'm letting myself into the cottage. Goodness knows how many toasts we did – to midwives' industrial action, to Chantal's new marital status, even to Harold and myself, if you please. Jessie and Kelly would be proud of me: Dot out on a right royal rave, they'd say, good on her.

There is one message on the answering machine I acquired a few days ago (at Jessie's insistence). I'm so whacked, I think about leaving it till morning, going straight to bed. I'm halfway up the stairs, already undoing the buttons of my blouse to save a few precious seconds, when it occurs to me it might be Harold. Probably not but, blouse billowing open, I'm back down those stairs all the same. As the tape rewinds, I kick off my shoes, suddenly all excited by the possibility.

It is him. A melancholy voice he has.

He says he is sorry to have to break the news on the machine, he tried me at the hospital and at home various times throughout the evening. His message is that Priscilla died tonight at a quarter to midnight, but that he wants me to know she was at peace, and happy. That I mustn't hesitate to call him any time in the night if I need someone to talk to.

Need someone to talk to.

Anybody else apart from our Jessie I wouldn't dream of disturbing so late, but Harold's different because he hasn't invited me to phone him at all hours out of politeness just. I know he means what he says.

Five rings and he comes to the phone. I bless him for his reliability, for not sleeping through the rings when he's said he'd be there for me.

Sadness as I know it is always accompanied, compounded, by loneliness. For once, in the cottage, awake in the dead of night, not a soul in sight, and sad, I know I am not alone.

There's only a few turn up to Priscilla's funeral Friday morning. Harold, of course. He and I come together. Then one or two from the home who can make the trip, such as Ted Turner, accompanied by Maureen. And a couple of relatives who in Priscilla's lifetime proved less dutiful.

The brief service, under a quarter of an hour, is in the modern church next to the local cemetery. Its brick is perfect yellow and the treated wood has a smell, not a proper churchy smell but one that's still new and chemical itchy inside the nostrils. It obliterates the lilies.

Us lot in the congregation number seven or eight, not a lot for a life. Just as thirteen minutes is not very much time for eighty-nine years. We are old, dotted about the mainly empty pews as lone, random weeds in a garden. The 1970s artefacts – the wrought-iron altar rail; the stained-glass window with cubic patterns; the orange, yellow, and beige wool and hessian rug on the wall – they don't speak to us of any Christian symbols of worship as we know them. We hold scarlet hymn-books and rustling prayer sheets containing progressive words. I look about me, and utter Amen to prayers that aren't familiar. Feel a curious indignation.

The vicar is sparky political, you get the impression, and perhaps enjoys his Technicolor dreamcoat robe more than his sublime duties. His face is eager but his eyes are bored.

The occasion is beautiful, dismal. The vicar says nice, insincere things about Priscilla, and when he talks I don't recognise her. These aren't the circumstances in which I wish to remember.

Harold, beside me in his big coat and a black tie, holds my elbow. I am grateful for his hand there, welcome the press of it through the cloth of my jacket, silently issuing comfort and sorrow. He has a tear. But I can't grieve here. I will later alone, and with him, in private.

When the coffin disappears beyond the maroon midget curtains like the ones the Queen opens over a plaque in a new building, you can't help thinking of the fire, but afterwards that's not something you say.

When the ceremony ends, some of us go back to Harold's for food provided by a kind neighbour – Scotch eggs; stodgy, rose pink sausage rolls; and vol-au-vents with cold insides.

I've not been to Harold's place before. If only it were happier circumstances. It's ironic Priscilla's passing away is what's got me here for the first time. She'd have seen the humour in that for sure. I can hear her now, having a giggle, telling me how his bachelor pad could do with a bit of the feminine touch, that might I perhaps like to bring to bear on it some of my curtain-making and flower-arranging skills? Ever the matchmaker she.

It is a nice place because it's a family home, it's full of history, it's got love all right, but there's no doubting it could do with a bit of motherly affection. While the front gate is newly painted and the tiling round the bathroom sink recently re-grouted, the kitchen cupboards are likely in need of a clear-out, and the living-room carpet could probably do with a good going over to rid it of dog hairs, fluff it up a little.

We gather in the formal front room. You get the impression it is not much used, that Harold mightn't have sat in it for ages. It is tiny, and although the make-believe coals of the electric heater in the fireplace glow, the air feels unlived in and obstinately chilly, as if resentful that we've disturbed it. A tray's been put on the table by the windowsill. There's small sherry glasses, brought out from the cabinet, laid in rows. They've gold rims at the top and intricate engravings round them of foxes and pheasants and hounds. It feels special sipping from one of them because they're beautiful, you know they're used only for best.

There are five of us gathered in here, all standing with poise, ignoring the settee and speaking in hushed voices fitting to the occasion. Harold, topping up the drinks, holds himself tall and moves with dignity. He offers round the nibbles, but presses them on no one: gently hospitable even in his grief. When someone says, 'What, Harold, no jam tarts?', he smiles; when another observes that Priscilla would be cross to be missing out on the sherry, he laughs. As he does so, some crumbs fall from the half-eaten sausage roll he's holding near his lips, and scamper down his mourning tie.

They don't stay long, these relatives who say the right things but likely as not don't feel them. Conversation is not forthcoming in times such as these, especially after we've all commented more than once that she went the way she would have liked, that she was peaceful at the end, and we've all agreed we'll miss her (though some more sincerely than others). Politeness dispensed with, there's not much to keep them here. I put my coat on along with them; Harold should be left alone.

He sees them to the front door. I hold back 'cos although I know I must go, I want to be the last to leave. We all stand in the hall corridor by the shelf with the old-fashioned dial phone and the Yellow Pages, and we say our subdued and relieved goodbyes. They walk along the path, footsteps on the deep gravel like topsy-turvy fishing boats in a swilling sea. Then they wave as they reach the pavement, before getting into their cars. I think Harold will be secretly pleased now they've gone. He and I watch briefly from the concrete porch, then I smile at him a smile which says I best too be off, thank you, and I'm ever so sorry, all at once. I'm a foot or so in front of him, half turned away, my gaze towards the gate. I'm thinking of my friend that's gone, how I'm going to miss her madly, it sends me in bits just to think about it; and I'm thinking of Harold after I've left, smart shirt-sleeves rolled back, washing up the best glasses in safe warm water over his thick cream sink, and, in a grieving quandary, wondering what best to do with the left-over vol-au-vent, asking himself, is it too rich for his beloved Jones? And I can feel my smile quiver and wobble, then collapse like a soufflé in the open.

'Come dancing with me tonight,' he says suddenly, his voice quiet behind me but hopeful. If there was a strain about it a few moments ago, in the company of others, it has gone.

I swivel so sharply my sensible skirt makes a sound like a ballgown. That Rembrandt face, and a sausage roll crumb still on his tie. Jones is standing beside him at the open door blinking his ink jelly eyes.

'See, there's a bit of a do on tonight in the ballroom at the Majestic, being Christmas.'

'Dancing?'

'It was my idea, but she wanted us to go. I mentioned it when I went round to see her the morning after our evening at the cottage. I told her I'd like to take you some time. It's a hobby of mine is dancing.'

'Harold – '

'Then the evening she dies she says, had I forgotten I was going to take you dancing? I say, no, course not, Auntie, would I forget such a thing? "Then take her the day of my funeral," she says. "Harold, do that for me." Those are her words. "That night you'll both be in need of some forgetting." So please, Dorothy, will you come dancing tonight?'

Dancing, I scarce remember dancing. It was that long ago.

There's not been much call for it in my fifty-two years. I might have gone once when I was doing nurse's training, before I was sent to the laundry, I don't recall. Dancing such as I ever knew it were the dances at Piccadilly which took place twice a year. They were desultory treats.

Treats we had there were few and far between. Highland toffee was one. We had it on Sundays, a small square each, size of a stock cube. It's honestly pathetic now to think of it, but you lived the whole week dreaming of that transient taste, and when at last you got the toffee in your mouth, you damn well kept it there as long as humanly possible, doing everything to prevent natural erosion by warmth and saliva. It was the highlight of our week. We made an art out of eking out the pleasure. Bel was champion. She would stick out her tongue so the toffee would only melt from the bottom up. Others, including myself, tried to copy her, but the force to suck was too strong. After a minute, I'd have to pull my tongue back in so the sugary sensation would burst on to the top of my mouth as well, and in the back of my throat, and I could swallow it. Bel's record was seventeen minutes. Liquid toffee and spit would have to be running down her chin and neck before she'd eventually give up and rein in her tongue.

Once every three months we'd have Saturday afternoon off for a picture. Because it was usually a holy one, the treat was more in the time off work than the film itself. We all of us would crowd into the assembly hall. The flimsy curtains were inadequate at holding the light at bay, so it was a dulled view we'd have of the screen – black and white was more grey and greyer; Technicolor muted. But we weren't complaining, for sometimes we got a proper film. Then, up on the screen there'd be our dreams playing out. You could hear our sighs of rapture above the projector's whirring. Who didn't want to be a Garbo or Bacall?

Course when the kisses came, the projectionist's – usually Miss Beveridge's – hand would eclipse and blank the screen and a groan would rise up of frustration and disappointment such as I can still hear to this day, it stays with me.

They were good though, some of them pictures, even as they were, innocent of kisses. The dances were more dismal affairs. No boys, we'd be quickstepping or foxtrotting round with each other. Apron against apron. So dancing was wanting in the thrill normal people associate it with. And in our ever-painful shoes it was a bunion-making business. I've bunions today stick out my feet like gobstoppers. It was standing all those years at the callender machine, and never helped by soulless dances with clumsy girls in clumpy shoes.

When I came out of the laundry I was twenty-eight, I felt dancing, like almost everything else, had passed me by. Even if the other midwives I came to train and work with asked me to accompany them to parties, I couldn't go. There might have been men at them with nimbler steps and romantic intentions, but still I'd've been asked along by women, and for me the allure remained elusive. I'd have been dancing with dragging feet, foxtrotting with clumsy memories, quickstepping with little joy and much regret.

'Come dancing with me tonight?' says Harold, and the words make me hear the scratched records of yesteryear; the heavy, unfeminine thuds of Piccadilly girls with stiff uniforms and uneasy rhythm, not concentrating, their minds too full of other sorts of dances.

What Harold's asking me to now is another sort of dance, and I picture the type in the films I've seen since, with girls in white dresses, men in black ties, and kisses too.

'I've two left feet,' I say.

'Not possible!' he insists. 'Anyway, nothing would give me more pleasure than to teach you some steps.'

'I'd love to come,' I assure him.

In all my years living in Stoneham, I've not been to the ballroom at the Majestic for a dancing evening. In all my years full stop I've not been dancing with a man.

I've not got the shoes for it like the ladies in here. Theirs are so glamorous, in pastel-coloured patent and with two-inch heels and strappy T-bars like sandals; proper dancing shoes. And their dresses! Lemon yellow and lime green, colour of squash, only brightened with sequins. These are Jessie's colours. She'd go mad in here for them.

Harold and I, we arrived about an hour ago, and I'm still gawping round me in wonder, taking it all in like I was released out of Piccadilly and into the world only yesterday. It feels like that, truly it does.

After he asked me on the porch and I said yes, we went back into his house a little while. I helped him clear the glasses into the kitchen, but he let me do no more than that. He insisted I sat down and had a cup of tea and a jam tart and I was happy to comply. Time was marching on, it was getting dark when I drove home. I had a bath and changed. I hadn't a clue what to wear. I put on my smartest – what I wore to the Christmas party, the paisley skirt and white blouse. I thought something flowing would be appropriate for dancing. Harold returned at seven to take me for a bite to eat at the new wine bar. He looked rather dashing in pale grey trousers and a dark blue jacket. Same white shirt as earlier at the funeral, but the mourning tie had gone, been replaced by a plain navy one with the Canine Club motif at the bottom in red.

It was merry in Raffles, I must say, all the customers in the Christmas party mood. Harold and I didn't want to talk about Priscilla because she wouldn't have wanted us to. We had some sweet wine and a beautiful meal and he said I looked lovely. Said it in a way would have lifted her heart.

'I'm a bit nervous about the dancing,' I told him as I ate my chicken breast Provençal, potatoes Dauphinoise, and French beans. 'I'm not exactly Ginger Rogers.'

'What a relief! I couldn't keep up if you were.'

We talked about dancing. It turns out Harold's a keen fan of ballroom, he watches all the competitions on the telly. He's been going to classes since he was a young man.

'It's one evening a fortnight,' he said. 'I'm not a very gregarious fellow, so it gets me out of the house, I see some friendly faces.'

Sometimes you feel sorry for people who live on their own. Perhaps you shouldn't, because it's making assumptions, but there are occasions, I know, when I can't help it. You look at some people and you agonise about the fact that if they fancy company of an evening, they're forced to leave their homes, go out and find it; that they have no one with whom to share the details of their lives, no one to tell if some clumsy fool trod on their toe in the bus. Their loneliness is ingrained in them like coal dust into a miner's flesh, only you know loneliness can't be showered off at the end of the day. I've had some mums like that, no family nearby them; more importantly, no man. I suppose there are those that look at me and think, poor Dot, no husband, no kids (the irony of that assumption!), who's she got to talk to at the end of the day? Fact is, if they think that, I don't mind really: they'd be right. I don't have anyone, unless I pick up the phone. What I want to say is, I reckon they don't think it with Harold. He's got a face as could make you cry, but he doesn't have the air of someone who'd move folks to say, poor fellow, all alone. Could be because he's a man, and men are seen as bachelors through choice, while women are still seen as spinsters through default and desperation. But — and I was thinking this during the meal as he was enthusing about dancing — I reckon it's 'cos Harold's happy is the reason people don't pity him. People, even strangers, can tell. Knowing him a bit, though, I wouldn't say it was the kind of happiness we all aspire to, that which you get with another person, with love I suppose, like with Kelly and Stevie. I expect Harold's is the type of shadowy happiness which arises just from the satisfaction of knowing he's coping on his own, of managing to organise the solitary life for himself in such a way as it's not a daily tribulation. If a person's denied the secure throb of companionship and love, just to avert despair is a triumph, let alone to achieve, as he has, a level of contentment.

'You've never been dancing here?' he asked the moment I was thinking he must be lonely despite it all.

When I admitted I hadn't, he said how curious it was we'd lived in the same place for so long and not come across each other years ago.

'There's worlds within worlds only sometimes meet,' he said. 'While you've never been to dancing classes and I've never visited the maternity unit, perhaps you've delivered the baby of a lady I've partnered on the dance floor? That'd be possible.'

'Very possible.'

He asked me about the twenty-four years I'd spent since the laundry; where I'd been.

'There's not much to tell,' I told him. 'I came down south to this area very soon after I left Piccadilly. It took some getting used to, being on the outside, even after I qualified, when I moved into a small town like this. I remember going into shops and thinking everyone was looking at me. It was as if I was branded like a cow. I was sure they all *knew*. It was hard to adapt to the fact I wasn't the very Devil's daughter herself; hard to adapt even to the simplest things.

'Oh, I must tell you, one of the first things I did immediately I got out, at Glasgow Central. I bought a Mars bar – can you credit it, my priority was my stomach? I couldn't believe the size. Took me three sittings to finish it all. The next thing I did, on the train home, was ceremoniously to throw away the underwear we were forced to wear – these huge knickers which went all the way down from your chest to your knee. I undressed in the toilet, flung them out the window into a passing field. They were that ungainly, they didn't travel more than a few feet. I remember thinking how nice lacy ones would have flown, and laughing when I thought about the farmer who might've found them, wondering how on earth they got there. Soon after I arrived in Stafford, I visited Marks and went mad for nice wee briefs. I think I bought four pairs.'

Harold smiled when I said that. 'How did you find your way from Stafford to Stoneham?'

'Well, I always knew I had to be far from home. Though we were able to receive as many letters at the laundry as came, we were only allowed to send one a month. Mine would be to Jessie just, and I always told her that when I got out I'd live by the sea, and she could come and visit me whenever she wanted. I don't know why the sea, maybe the freedom. But I was determined in my mind.'

'So how did you choose here?'

'Luck, really. I contacted an old friend who I'd done nurse's training with in Cheshire before I ever went to Piccadilly. She'd gone south and become a midwife at St Dominic's. It was her suggested I finish my training there, said she'd set me up. I was away from home quick as a flash, on practically the very next train down south.'

'Where did you live?'

'In nurse's accommodation first, in town, but I visited Stoneham one weekend soon after I qualified. Walking by the harbour I spotted the cottage, it had a To Let notice outside it, and I moved in straight away. I suppose you could say I've devoted these past years since then to my work. I'm not a very sociable person. I see plenty of people all day, and I do enjoy that though it can be gruelling. When I get home it's feet up, and supper in front of the box.'

'Sounds familiar,' Harold says, with a smile.

'You too? It's good though, isn't it? It sounds corny, I know, but it's the little things in life you appreciate after something like the laundry. Your hot-water bottle. Don't laugh: boiled egg and toast with soldiers.' I think I must've sounded embarrassed admitting about the soldiers because Harold reassured me. He said there was no question of laughing: a boiled egg's not a boiled egg without the soldiers. I thought that splendid. I thought, maybe that's one of those private reasons why Jessie loves Derek, because he still has soldiers with his boiled eggs? 'The purple of a crocus,' I continued, I was glowing. 'I never saw a flower, not in nine years! It's barely possible to believe. Now I'm fierce for the changing of the seasons.'

I could've said just *colour* altogether, not just a crocus or an autumn leaf. You cannot imagine the dinginess of everything at the laundry, everything the same grey as washing-up water. I read an article in the paper, a few years ago, a description by a traveller of his first visit to Russia back in the 1970s when Brezhnev was still alive. He wrote that it was all so grey, not only the skies, the buildings, the uniforms, but the grass was grey too, and the bread they ate, even the faces of the people. I thought, nobody's going to believe in the colourless world he depicts, but I did, I knew what he meant, I'd been a Piccadilly girl. And when he returned to England, he said, he was dazzled by the red of a letterbox. Tonight here with Harold, all these swirling dresses, I'm being dazzled still.

We're sitting at a small table for two in the sidelines, on red velour chairs with gold frames, just watching. The room is vast with a paraquet floor of little squares, some with the grain going this way, some going that. The music is loud and rousing, but I can still hear the glamorous tingle of ice-cubes in my drink. I can smell above the smoke of cigarettes, sweet perfumes struggling with sour perspiration and heated shoe-leather.

And all the people! There must be two or three hundred in here, come from miles around. The dance floor is well and truly taken up with professional-looking pairs who are an inspiration to the rest of us. Plenty, even just standing and sitting about, are swinging their shoulders, nodding to the beat. There's one or two familiar faces, local people, including a woman I'm sure I looked after some years ago, now with a man I'm sure wasn't the one I met, the father of her child. I bet the child I delivered would be about fifteen now. Since the laundry, time's taken on a new character, the years flip by like magazine pages through the fingers of an impatient browser. It's freedom makes them speed, not maturity as most seem to think.

I catch a glimpse of Harold's look. He's staring at the band up on the stage; has got a smile on him that's rightly beaming. Silver dapples from the swirling mirrored ball above float over his face, cherry blossom petals moving on a breeze. His head is one of them that's nodding with the lively beat. Even my old toes are tapping.

The stage is wide and low and surrounded by a valance of dark green velvet. The small cluster of a band numbers about six or seven men, all in dusty tuxedos. The wings of their bow-ties are big and blooming and tickle their low-hanging chins. These fellows are not in the peak of youth, but the music they're playing is dreamy, music that sets the blood fairly racing, even in my enfeebled veins. Times like this, like seeing babies being born, you feel properly alive. I saw a science programme the other night about the sensations in the body. It said when you sit on a chair you very quickly lose track of the feeling of the seat against your thighs. There are some sensations we take for granted, but others – which actively give pain or pleasure – we properly acknowledge in our brains: the bitchy prick of an injection in our arm, the sumptuous taste of a chocolate on our tongue. In the same way, it's easy not to notice life till it bestows immense unhappiness or pleasure. It's only the ups and downs that wake you from the snooze of day to day. I'm luckier than some inasmuch as my experience of incarceration makes me enjoy some of the petty things such as might easily pass others by. But still, I sometimes find that hours have flickered on, and though I've lived them, I've not readily taken them in, been aware of myself in them, and other people and things; I've not properly been alive with every sensation there is. To my mind that's just cause for regret.

Night like this, I'm wide awake, but. I'm drinking in every sensation on offer.

A tune ends and some of the magnificent ladies and their partners leave the floor to rest. When the next number strikes up, Harold stands, holds out his hand to mine.

We take to the floor for a plain but jaunty waltz. We're among other couples who aren't so practised as the skilled men and their partners in lime who've just come off, who can smooth over the floor like slick mops. I move about with Harold tentatively at first while I'm getting myself into the swing. He guides me this way and that with his reassuring arms and his steady steps. Once or twice I make a bit of a wrong move, so we pull slightly apart by mistake and he has to right us again, but we are doing well considering the years since I last did this. At last I think I've found something to be grateful to Piccadilly for – I can do the steps required, granted not with any ability verging on what you might call elegant, but at least without treading on Harold's shiny shoes at every move.

I wonder if people see us as the courting couple, or the couple as has been together many years and couldn't be apart? To me, it feels like both in a way. I'm not so well acquainted with human contact as others but to see me now I don't think you'd know it. His hand on my shoulder is warm and comfortable there as a cat on an armchair. Yet we dance for I don't know how long, I'm having heightened fancies, like the mirrored ball above us is the moon, it's just he and I below it, alone, and I feel all the headiness of a foolish but carefree young girl being wooed for the first and last time.

It's just after midnight the music stops, but Harold and I, we're there till the last.

At the cloakroom he helps me on with my coat and walks me home. It's cold but I don't notice. My bunions are throbbing but I don't care.

At my front door he kisses me. Kisses like I've not had kisses before.

Chapter Eleven

Christmas Eve. I do my morning shift in a good mood. A more than usually good mood. I'm thinking about last night.

I'm humming in the team office, could be a carol. Chantal says, 'Something's certainly given you the Christmas spirit, Dot.'

I wonder if she can tell I've been kissed, if it shows.

We have a bit of a chin-wag for a few minutes. Then I tell her I'm off this afternoon.

'Somewhere nice?'

'My sister's, and her kids.'

I had to get up earlier than usual this morning to pack to go to Jessie's. I'd planned to do it last night, but then came the invitation to go dancing and I let spontaneity get the better of me. When I got in, I was far too overcome to think sensibly about how many pairs of knickers to take, and which skirt I might like to wear on Christmas Day. I flopped straight on my bed, with this huge big stupid smile on my face. I stayed awake a good hour just staring up at the ceiling. The familiar noise of the sea outside my little window had changed to music, or maybe the evening's music was still pulsating in my ears. My room looked different, like a room you recognise in a dream but, though you can't tell why, you know is not quite the same.

I don't think I got much sleep, but I'm bright as a button today. I do some paperwork and have a quick go round the wards till lunchtime. The time passes quickly enough.

When I bump into Dolores in the corridor on my way to see a lady in the antenatal ward, I even have the strength to ask after Honey Carpenter. Immediately following the traumatising incident with Saad, the team wrote to Julia Gibbons at the Social Services to put our point of view, hoping it might influence things a bit, try and persuade them to lift the EPO. Chantal told me earlier Dolores got a nice reply this morning. It comes as little surprise that Saad is not back with his mum, and there is still to be a court hearing (which, being Christmas time, has been delayed). But at least she and Rashid are going to be allowed time (supervised, of course) with him on Christmas Day, and for as long as the case takes to be resolved, which should be any day now. It's not much, but it's something. Julia wrote that in the light of the new evidence against Honey concerning the death of her third child, she could make no promises. We hope, she wrote, that Honey will, as you in the team believe, be deemed a fit mother for Saad. He may or may not be taken into care, depending on what happens in court, but the views of the midwives will, naturally, be taken into consideration.

'I think that's good news,' says Dolores. 'Dot, don't you?'

We are wandering past the big automatic Coke machine. 'What'll you have?' I ask her, taking some coins from my belt.

'Oh, Girl Coke, please.'

'What's that, Diet?'

'Well, have you ever seen a boy drink it?'

I laugh. I feed in the coins and the cold can rumbles out on to the narrow shelf at the bottom. I hand it to her. 'I think I'll stick to the normal, Boy Coke, yes?'

Dolores nods, amused to watch me being educated in these matters. 'Thanks,' she says, and snaps back the ring-pull. The mouth of the can gasps like a football fan watching a goal. 'So it's good about Honey anyway? Let's hope, eh? All is not lost.'

'All is not lost, no,' I agree. The hope I feel is rather like a snail's trail, jelly-delicate, but just about visible all the same.

I begin to make my way to the antenatal ward. There's a girl in there, Colette, who's been here a month with complications, and I stay with her a while because she's frightened now the moment's finally approaching to give birth. She says she thinks she might pop tomorrow, and I think she might be right. I tell her it'll be nice to have a Christmas baby.

Colette's from the roughest estate in the area, and she was a right handful at first. Still can be at times, effing and blinding at the consultants for not inducing her, and I mean effing and blinding something shocking. She and I, we've had our screaming matches once or twice over the past few weeks, and there's not much as can make Dot go in for screaming, so there isn't. One was when she told me she was intending, when the baby was born, to breast-feed, and I told her that she would be well advised for the duration to get rid of the gold ring in her nipple, that it mightn't be hygienic. Ooh, she went bananas. She can be a right little madam. But it's not all her fault. I happen to know she was interfered with by her stepdad from the ripe old age of ten, and went on the game in her dotage, at fourteen. There was dreadful rumours going round the hospital that it was her stepdad's kid she was pregnant with, but they were totally unfounded, and I put a stop to them pretty quick. I've met her boyfriend. He's come in with her sometimes to antenatal clinic, and has visited her a few times here in the ward. OK, he's somewhat older, forty or thereabouts, but he's no relation. He's an easygoing enough bloke, smokes a lot of dope but nothing more; out of work, but out of trouble too. Colette's got this thin little mouth, red lipstick, which would seem mean were it not for her flawless complexion and the youthful set of her face. Her legs are bright white as wouldn't shame a paint ad, but mottled purple and blue like a schoolgirl's. She's not much more than a schoolgirl. Sixteen she is, and by all accounts a nightmare sixteen years she's been subjected to at that. But she's a good girl at heart, so I believe.

'Will you be here, Dot?' she asks, which is a nice little turn-up for the books, so it is, considering some weeks ago she called me a fucking, wanking, fucking bitch, I think was how she put it.

'I wish I could be, lovey, only I've got the day off tomorrow,' I tell her. She looks so sad I feel it's my Christmas duty to come just as soon as I can. We've got quite close despite our differences. 'Jan's on call tomorrow, I expect she'll be here to look after you. But, tell you what, I'm back late tomorrow night because I'm on duty early on Boxing Day morning. If I'm not too tired I'll drop in. The hospital's on my way home. Happy Christmas, ducks, and good luck.' She looks so grateful, it's as if what I've said is like I've just given her the biggest box of chocolates she's ever seen.

Shift over, duties done, and having said my goodbyes and Happy Christmases to the rest of the girls and my colleagues, I dash to the canteen. There I grab an egg and cress sandwich with clingfilm wrapped round it so tight it looks like it's huddling in a plastic mac from the rain. Even when I open it out on the dashboard as I drive through town on the start of my journey to Staffordshire, it looks squashed and uninviting. To think last night I was eating chicken Provençal. It's a bit of a comedown. But I'm not bothered. I can't say I'm very hungry.

It's a long way to Jessie's but I'm enjoying the drive. Everything's in order – Christmas presents piled in the back, all nicely gift-wrapped. I'm listening to the radio. It's 'I'm Dreaming of a White Christmas', surprise, surprise, and 'Jingle Bells' done by a cathedral choir. Those boys' voices fairly set me off, tears pricking here and there. I must be coming over all sentimental. I manage to prevent them running down my cheeks, I don't want to arrive at Jessie's all bleary-eyed, and with my face pink and blotchy as strawberry yogurt.

It's a grey day and drizzly. The wipers are making their rubbery way back and forth across the watery windscreen. There's something satisfactory about watching the efficient manner they smooth away the raindrops, again and again. If it were me I'd give up in a right huff, like the way I sometimes do with the dusting. When you start thinking that way you can admire the even temper and persistence of a wiper.

The wet makes the motorway and the houses that fly by my vision look black, but my mood is more than holding out. I look at the roofs and windows and wonder about all the Christmases inside. If I were to let myself become fanciful I might suppose that Eliza was in one of them. I don't let myself become fanciful.

I'm looking forward to seeing Jessie and the children. I'm up to a family Christmas. Stronger than at other times. Even when we go and pay the obligatory visit on my own parents – a spot of Christmas cake on Christmas Day – I'm sure I'll rise to the occasion. It'll be nice to see Beth. She's staying at Mother's and Father's with her two, and her husband Malcolm. I've not seen her and her family for eighteen months or so.

I drive in the slow lane so as to avoid those smug men in flash cars, cars with streamlined noses and wide-apart eyes whose sneering faces snoop right up your rear. Jessie's like me, she can't stand them. She says they really know how to make women hate men; it's like the man's telling you, 'Out my way you poor sad bitch in a Mini Metro,' and his headlights, joining in, are going,

'Fuck off, fuck off, fuck off.' Honestly, I find it as intimidating and unacceptable as if a stranger were to pull up my skirt in the street. When people do it to Jessie, she stays in the fast lane, slows down, and refuses to budge for a good few minutes. I believe you can have a nicer ride if you stick to the slow lane. More civilised. Her way serves them right, she says. Although I'm not altogether sure Derek's not one of those types, when he's on his own in his company car, to shove out his path every little lady that comes in his way.

But I'm being unkind. Jessie assures me he's a changed man. I'm excited to see this phenomenon, but I don't put my foot down. I stay at 65. I can wait.

What with my slow pace and the holiday traffic, it takes several hours to reach the suburbs of Stoke-on-Trent where Jessie lives. The home she moved into with John soon after they married, and has stayed in ever since, is in a close of twelve houses. They were built in the late seventies. Six are of a pale grey brick, six of pale sand brick, and a few have weather-boarding going from the roof to halfway down their façades. All of them have a modern, functional look. Like houses in a child's drawing, they are completely square with two windows up, two down, an attached garage, a short gravel drive, and a neat square few feet of lawn.

The marks of individuality show in the different shrubs in the gardens, and the different styles of the front doors. Each inhabitant has made their place their home. You always know Jessie's. There's a kiddie's bicycle on her patch of grass (I'm not sure you could call hers a lawn), and decaying pieces of garden furniture – a white plastic chair and a table – which is still out even though it's December, and which no one has chosen to steal. Her front door has a frame in wood, of a spicy caremelised orange colour, but it's mainly thick glass with an abstract pattern of mist and raindrops. You can sort of see through it, though it does make people either side of it look as tantalisingly shadowy and shapeless as ghosts. The letter slot is in the part of the frame right at the bottom by the cat-flap so you can't help imagining the postman bending down each morning and being bitten on the behind by some officious dog, or thinking about Derek having to kneel when shoving desperate bouquets through its hole.

I park by the pavement at the bottom of the drive, unload a few of the parcels, and go to ring the bell which plays a long and corny tune which you'd have thought might have driven Jessie crazy by now except you know it's her favourite.

There are shrieks amidst the mist. 'It's Auntie Dot, it's Auntie Dot.' The door is opened by all four of them – Jessie, Samantha, Natalie, and Tim. There's that homey smell seeps out on to the porch, of baked beans and oven-ready chips, of damp washing, of cat litter, new carpet, and of Jessie's sensuous perfume called Nin.

I give them all hugs, and the kids take the gifts off of me and distribute them under the tree by the window in the front room.

'Derek's out picking up the turkey,' Jessie says, as she and I follow them in there. 'He'll be back in a minute.'

I decline to think about what else he might be picking up. It's Christmas after all, the season of goodwill. 'The house is looking lovely,' I tell her.

'New carpet. I came home one day, couple of weeks ago, and here it was. Derek's doing. I'm mad for it. The colour, Dot, isn't it brilliant? They call it Old Rose.'

It's a dense, thick pile the carpet's got, the type which, unlike my worn effort at home, if you've bare feet, tries to squash up between your toes. Smashing cosy. And in this lovely dusky pink. 'It goes perfectly with the paper and the suite,' I say.

'He's good like that, so he is. He's got an eye.'

'Really suits this room well.' I love Jessie's front room, especially now with the tree. It's small but comfortable, and it's so her. The walls are this beautiful paper, pale and dark pink stripes, with this burgundy border round them at waist level with a cream flower print. When she had it put up a couple of years ago, I remember she rang me specially to tell me all about it. 'It's all the rage,' she said. At the time I thought, only Jessie would have pink in her front room as opposed to a nice pale yellow or green. I said I thought it sounded like a bedroom paper more. But when I first saw it, I changed my mind. She'd put framed portrait photos of the kids high up either side of the fireplace, so they smile down at you as you sit on the velour settee. I think that's a nice touch. They were taken by the same guy in the high street who took pictures of us when we were children. He's got more sophisticated with his soft focus effect since our day. And she'd placed two little baskets with ready-made arrangements of dried flowers and lace on the tiled mantelpiece. She knows how to make things nice, our Jessie. For all her experiments with men, underneath, she's your ordinary, down-to-earth type who gets excited by a new carpet, just wants to make a nice home. Maybe I've undermined Derek, and in him she's found someone willing to partake and share in making it possible after all.

We swap news. The children tell me theirs. It's affecting having them crowd round me on the settee, showing me drawings, new shoes, baseball caps, what have you, all attention, except for when their eyes stray every now and again to the vast black telly on in the corner. I'm amazed how they've grown. I suppose if you're a mother, you see them all the time so you're denied this amazement. But that doesn't for me rank as consolation. I'd prefer not to be amazed any day.

'Right you lot, it's my turn,' Jessie says after a while. 'I'm going to help Dot take her things upstairs, then she and me are going to have a nice quiet cup of tea in the kitchen before Dad comes home.

Derek's Dad now.

They look disappointed, but turn to the telly all the same.

'It's just easier,' Jessie explains, leading me up the narrow staircase. I must have made a look, which is bad, but I don't know I'm doing it. 'John's got his new family now and doesn't have so much time for his old one. Sure he loves them and that, and when he does see them he's very nice and all. But Derek's around, being more like a dad, so it's better they see him that way. You're in Sam's room; she's on the floor in Nat and Tim's. All right?'

The room is tiny. I've grown fond of it from staying here in the past. It has a wardrobe fit for a little girl, short and painted a primrose yellow. The bed is narrow with a red wooden bed-head. There are numerous miniature china and glass ornaments on the windowsill; a pile of teddies and dollies in one corner; and on a small desk by the wall, some crayons and a shocking-pink nylon satchel the kind they all have now but which is still alien to my notion of a satchel. What's new since I was last here are the posters on the wall of a young man called Damon from the pop group Blur. I know about him because various of the teenage mums have mentioned him, they fancy him as a bit of a heart-throb, and Kelly once said he was a real dish.

'She's growing up,' I say, looking at his pretty face above the teddy bears. I wonder how long it'll be before she dispenses entirely with the latter to concentrate completely on boys.

'Yeah, only eleven,' Jessie agrees, 'and she fancies him as much as I do an' all!' She grins. 'It seems only yesterday she were still a baby.'

'That will never change. Even when she's thirty, it'll seem like only yesterday. I can't believe it's thirty-three years since Eliza came along.'

'Jesus, Dot, is it that long? I suppose it is.'

'Yep,' I say, sitting down on the bed. I don't know why, the mention of Eliza in this room for some reason upsets me. My throat's beginning to constrict a bit like it's being gently squeezed like a lemon, and I can feel the citrus sting of tears gathering in my eyes and nose. 'Oh, Jess, I'm sorry. Times like this, her birthdays and Christmas, they're still hard, you know?'

She sits on the bed beside me. Puts her arm round my shoulder. 'I know, I know,' she says soothingly. 'I understand. But it's OK, Dotty, it's OK, everything's going to be all right.'

'Oh, I know, silly of me. It's just some things set me off. All Sam's things.' I glance around the room, sniff a bit, and she rubs her hand up and down my arm. 'Can't help feeling sorry for myself, thinking what I've missed. It's ridiculous really.'

'Beg pardon? It's not in the least, pet, honest. It's only natural. I don't know if I can properly imagine what it feels like, and I do try.' She pauses. 'But I can tell you something, all them little ornaments on the windowsill there, they're a right royal pain in the hole to dust.'

I break into a smile and laugh, and she does too. That's so typically Jessie, that is, to make a joke of it like that, that's why I love her.

'There's no hankies about, why not wipe your eyes on this?' She holds up the corner of the duvet towards my face, and I take her up on her offer. 'Clean sheets, I'm afraid,' she says, tapping the blue cover patterned with fluffy clouds. We laugh again.

'I can manage,' I say.

'You can sleep in another room if you'd prefer? Tim and Nat wouldn't mind being put out of theirs.'

'No, no, goodness me, no. I like it in here, honest. Silly turn just.'

Jessie gives me a hug. When she kisses you on your cheek quite close to your ear, it's a huge high-pitched sound of enthusiasm she makes, and it tickles your eardrum. I've seen Sam and Natalie try to imitate Jessie's kisses, but there's no one can get near them. 'It's so good to see you,' she says. 'Come on down to the kitchen, the kettle's boiled.'

She's wearing the ironed jeans she always wears, and these baby-pink mule slippers with a feather powder-puff on the top of each one. Our dad wouldn't have approved of such frivolous footwear. Which is probably just why she likes them. And partly why I do too. The heels make her wiggle her bum on her way down the stairs.

The kitchen at the back of the house is wood-look like Tiff's, only Swiss cottage-style, and not quite as sophisticated. Jessie ordered it from a catalogue when she and John were newly-weds, only she was disappointed it didn't have quite the appeal it did in the photo. These days it's looking nicely lived in, to my way of thinking, with the kids' pasta and paint collages on the fridge door and a chip here and there on the units, though I know Jessie thinks it's about time for a new one. I like it in here myself. There's a sliding door on to the patio out the back where they have barbecues in the summer, but now it's got a thick curtain across which gives the place a homey feel.

Jessie makes two cups of tea, the water from the kettle with the poppy and wheat print at its base, the very same which marked the end of her life with Tony, the one who went on the barge and came home to find himself lacking in the Commitment department.

'Fig roll?' she asks. 'I know I shouldn't, but what the hell. If you can't at Christmas, whenever can you?'

We're settling down at the table with our personalised mugs of

tea, courtesy of Derek – I'm using Natalie's – and a plate of
biscuits, when the man himself appears with the turkey. The
children follow him in here, shrieking at the size of it.

'Blimey, Dad, he's a whopper,' Tim shouts, ramming his Biker
Mice into the dead bird's breast.

'Oi, oi, oi, matey, hang on a minute, let me give your auntie a
kiss.'

Derek leans down to do just that. His face is damp and cold
from the rain. He smells of the same strong aftershave some of the
dads wear in the delivery room. I always imagine they've taken the
precaution of putting it on because they want to drown the stench
of clotted female blood they're expecting to encounter, and
dreading. Or it could be a romantic thing, nice for their partners
that they've been seen to make a bit of an effort, to go some way to
complementing all the effort the little woman's going to be
putting in. I don't know why Derek's wearing it, maybe it's the
spiciness he's partial to. Maybe he knows that it's what Jessie likes.

Although he's holding the turkey away from me, it's still quite
close. Its disturbing porridgy flesh, and the horny old-toenail
yellow spikes where the feathers have been plucked, are nudging
into my line of vision. I must be making a bit of a face, because
Derek apologises, and clears a space for it in the fridge without
further ado. He offers me a drink. I decline, but he's very
persuasive, and I agree to a sweet white wine, just a small one.

'You'd never know I think of myself as a non-drinker, would
you?'

'Get it down your neck, love,' Jessie says as Derek passes me the
glass. 'It's Christmas, for God's sake, no holds barred. You're here
to enjoy yourself. Right, kids, it's fish fingers, baked beans and
chips for tea, right? Then you lot are going early to bed so me and
Derek can have a chat to Dot.

Tim's cries of 'Aw, unfair' are quelled when he's told Santa
doesn't visit kids that whine. Mothers' responses to young ones
aren't dissimilar to midwives' platitudes – automatic, predictable,
but effective in their way. Tim doesn't say another word.

We eat with the children, a raucous meal, but fun, I enjoy it.
They're over-excited about tomorrow. I help out with Natalie
and Tim at bathtime, and with putting them to bed. There's lots of

arguments and tussles. They kick and splash each other, pull each other's hair, and I am momentarily perturbed by the violence of it all. The funny thing is, although I'm around babies all the time, I rarely get to spend time with older children, only those I see on home visits or those that are brought in to the hospital to see their newborn brother or sister. It's nice to have the chance. They're playing up, mind. I know it's because they're excited. Jessie takes it in her stride. For all her own ups and downs, she's a spot-on mother in many ways. She knows how to play it, gets the balance just right between anger and indulgence. It's a difficult balance to strike. Who's to say if I could have managed it? I think it's partly Jessie's good judgement means the fights between the four of them turn quickly into cackling laughter and implicit forgiveness.

I've pulled myself together a bit now, since earlier in Samantha's bedroom. Maybe the wine's relaxed me, and I'm able to seize the pleasure of the moment without so much dwelling on all that I've been denied.

Downstairs in the front room Jessie and I sit on the floor and fill the old woollen socks with a few presents. Derek is on the settee, thighs in grey slacks wide apart, leaning down to do his bit. He is being unusually chatty and helpful. I could say over-solicitous, but that would be unkind. When he's done, shovelled four or five presents into Sam's stocking, he reaches for the plate on the fireplace behind Jessie's bum.

'Here, Dot, have some mince pies. Kids left it out for Santa. I think we qualify.'

I recognise it as a Mrs Topley's, but I don't say anything.

The evening passes off pleasantly enough. If I were to say Jessie's and my conversation isn't what it would be were Derek not with us, it would be to deny that his company had anything going for it. Fact is, it's quite good, his company, he makes a few jokes make us laugh. He's on about one or two of the customers at the salon who shall be nameless but who, let's just say, give Jessie a bit of a hard time. He's taking them off something rotten, their posh voices, it's always the posh ones give trouble. There's support for Jessie implicit in his mimicry, sympathy she has to put up with such people, that's nice I think. She's turned her back towards him and he's massaging her shoulder while he talks, he's got these big wide hands with a few dark hairs on the plump white fingers. Set into one finger is a gold ring that looks like it'd be good for delivering a black eye to remember. But it's gentle movements he's making on the exposed flesh of Jessie's delicate neck, like today he's scared of breaking her, he wants her to remain perfect.

It's these little things, these small indications, give an eagle-eyed sister like me pause to ponder that maybe he's not so bad really. Oh, I don't forget what he's done to her in the past, no, but perhaps he's turned a new leaf, and it's possible they've managed a good patch-up job despite my scepticism, despite all. I should be able to give him the benefit of the doubt. I can imagine them here together of an evening, after an exhausting day, kids finally tucked up, in his-and-her cosy tracksuit bottoms and floppy socks, and T-shirts, lounging on the settee, her leaning on his robust belly, him stroking her neck with those fingers which were made for sturdier things. I can see them together watching a good movie on the box, in a sort of comfy couch-potato harmony. It's a picture I like. And it's not impossible.

We talk about various problems at the salon – one of the staff fallen in love and now not pulling her weight as much: 'her head's up in the hairspray,' as Jessie says, and the expensive need to replace outdated and inefficient driers. Derek listens and puts on his masculine businessman's hat to make a few considered suggestions. Were I in a less charitable mood, I might think he was being patronising. As it is, I believe people are too quick to levy that criticism when the truth is someone's genuinely trying to be helpful. Later, when I ask him about the personalised mug business, he doesn't go sprawling off into some long description of turnover and profit shares. He's restrained in his answer, so I am honestly interested when I question him about his latest designs and proposals for expansion. Jessie's proud of him: she lets on he recently landed a big contract with one of the huge confectionery giants to do the mugs that go with their Easter eggs. Although he's clearly very excited about this, and pleased to answer my questions, that doesn't stop him asking about my work, life at the hospital. She must have got him well trained.

Later, when I get under Sam's cloudy duvet, I feel I can be more cautiously generous about Derek, even permit a little warmth towards him. I don't think it's imprudent to say I can afford some optimism about Jessie's situation. Reading between the lines.

We have stocking opening first thing, and then a flurry with the turkey, spuds, and sprouts to get them all ready by dinnertime. Course, the morning goes by just like that, and I don't have the chance really to think about any grandchildren I might have, in another house, with another family, faces as radiant as Sam's, and Natalie's, and Tim's. It's not till after the Christmas pud, when we have the crackers, that things really get poignant for me. I don't know why, I get this silly idea, I wonder if my other family, every bit as real-life as this one, yet nonexistent for me, are laughing as we are, even though the feeble jokes on flimsy slips round the rolled-up paper hats have been drained by every conceivable political correctness of every conceivable grain of humour. But, somehow, I manage to quash this thought after one or two dangerous minutes. I tell myself I am being foolish, and manage to find what passes for strength when it comes to putting it out of my mind.

Of course, in Derek's big car, as we make the short drive over to Maidenwell, to my parents', mid-afternoon, I worry that in their company my imagination and sense of bitterness and loss might suddenly overwhelm me, and I'll come all over queer there like I did with Honey and the baby. As I join in in a game of I-Spy, I think I could be headed for a panic attack. But when we arrive at the house, I discover myself to be unexpectedly calm.

I don't come back here often, I mean, as you can imagine, it's not the destination of my dreams. I suppose since I left voluntarily, by which I mean since I was released from Piccadilly and went to live down south and work at St Dominic's, I've been back, usually when staying with Jessie at Christmas, perhaps once every two to three years. Not much.

The funny thing about families: for all their tragedies, they retain a hold on their individual members such as would make barnacles and limpets seem wimpy. There's not many as can break away entirely. Even at the hospital, which is not in by any means a privileged catchment area, on the whole families seem to survive intact despite the stresses and strains hurled upon them – and there are a few of those, I can vouch. I've seen close relatives hate each other's guts, but still go back for more. What is it about families that have a pull on those who are a part of them, like a champion yo-yo? From my experience, it's only when one family member has done something really bad to another that the victim cuts the string entirely.

I came dead close.

So why didn't I? As we park on the street outside the shop – since Mother and Father retired, they still live upstairs, but Sheffield's has been bought by a couple who have turned it into Video Vicility – I wonder. It always gives me a cold feeling to come back, like I've swallowed an ice-cube whole before having the chance to melt it in my mouth. So then, what's it in aid of, my returning like this? You may well ask. Not for Jessie, because she believes I should have rejected Mother and Father for ever, she came close herself on my behalf. She wanted nothing to do with them. But I expect I come back for the same reason she does – for the sake of her children, who need grandparents, and family unity. If Auntie Jessie weren't to come for traditional tea and Christmas cake to Nan and Grandad's, it would unfairly inject into their canny but unconscious minds a sense of conflict within the family, and it wouldn't be right of me to draw shadows across their world. Perhaps another reason I visit, and I'm not proud of myself for this, is a morbid curiosity to see on my parents' faces the withering of regret, and to take an ignoble pleasure from that pathetic sight? Another could be a desire to be in the place I last set eyes on Eliza, an excuse to visit the room in the attic where I was a true mother once, if only ever so briefly. Or that going home, seeing it, seeing them, is the tangible act of wishing it had all been different?

Inside nothing's changed much. The lace over the piano in the parlour is there just the same as ever, only greyer. My mother's limbs have got fatter. She wears a thin, sulky green cardigan and beneath it the flesh of her upper arms hangs so it shivers as she moves. The two folds of her goose-pimply neck tremble like a gander's as I remember they did even in her younger days. One of these folds acts for her necklace as the velvet lining in a jewel-box, holding it in securely. The pearls attest to a beauty which was once there, but was extinguished long ago. Her and my father's faces break into soft smiles when they see me. They insist on kissing me, and seem momentarily to forget the others, like I am the prodigal son. Can I forgive them? My mother smells of that same old powder. Wisps of grey hair stroke her cheeks. Father has cartoon slippers similar to Ted Turner's. He is shrunken, woody, but struggles up from his chair to hug me as if the very effort will go some way to make amends. He's not the hugging type. The cracks in his neck have deepened as if his body has all its life suffered a drought of physical ecstasy or even pleasure. Perhaps this is just reward for marrying a woman he did not love much but who he challenged himself to change, to better, for his own self-satisfaction. He should have known a man can rarely fashion another out of all recognition. He could only achieve so much. I fancy she was like him when they sent me away, but she resents him now for making her like that. Only pride stands in the way of her giving out under the burden of her guilt, breaking down, begging salvation. Anyway, that's what I like to believe. I watch her dreary, dishwatery eyes for any signs. I don't say much in this room. I'm too busy watching.

The parlour is cramped. There's Mother and Father. There's Jessie and Derek, and their three, and Beth and Malcolm, and their two. It's a room not meant for more than two or three altogether. Tim and Natalie sit on the floor and keep their legs and arms to themselves in a manner which must be trying for their self-discipline. Beth, two years younger than me, I have to say looks four years older. Her teenage children, Gary and Michelle, smell of smoke and look about as cheerful as liver pâté. They are leaning against the door as if they'd like to push it off its hinges. Beth has the air of someone wearied by their existence. Her hair is what Jessie calls par-grey. She's got long thin legs after our dad, but a large middle covered today in a brave duster-coloured jersey. I'd guess from the colour it's a past gift from Jessie, and Beth's just being tactful because Beth's more a pastel person to be sure. If you were to look at Beth without knowing her, you'd think she was the type to wear her glasses round her neck on a string, and to have a telephone on the wall of her kitchen just by the oven (handy for when cooking), and a wipe-clean pad beside it with felt-tip attached, and you'd be just right. Malcolm and she are well suited, and I can say that even though I've not met Malcolm more than a handful of times. She's a dressmaker for a boutique, something which when she took it up didn't take many by surprise, she always did have a love of all things haberdashery, and would spend hours as a child in the shop tidying Mother's boxes containing the cards of buttons, hooks, and poppers, and what have you. At their Grimsby home she has a tape-measure, as well as the glasses, permanently round her neck. She works from home, and is very organised. He's also what I call exceptionally neat and what Jessie calls anal, and demands standards of efficiency in their home to a degree which suggests he's frustrated not to be actually running the company that employs him. He works in a modest capacity for a firm which exports steel meshing, the type they put round chicken coops. I asked once, and as a result know all about it.

It's good to see Beth. We're worlds apart, but she is my sister, after all, and somewhere in me there's a certain sentimentality about these things. I often speculate as to how she views Jessie's and my relationship, which is obviously so good and so close. I can't help but think she must be feeling she's missed out. To be honest, my belief is it's her fault. She was always a bit goody-goody and solemn which was never going to attract Jessie, and for me she was a bit too similar to my dad for my liking. Her greeting, though, is affecting. She's obviously pleased to see me. Hugs and kisses, though she's not the tactile type (unlike our youngest sister). You wouldn't know she and I were from the same planet, let alone the same family, and yet, and yet, something binds us. They always say blood, don't they, as an explanation. But that's poppycock to my mind. If I'm being literal, I could say I've as likely as not got an identical blood group to the man on the moon, whereas a completely different one to Beth altogether. The blood link is naught but a romantic notion. I think it's simply a shared past that binds us, nothing more.

Sam is settled on the couch, which must be making my father feel uncomfortable because she is under-age. Malcolm and Derek are sitting next to her, side by side, upright and unrelaxed, an inch or two apart, keen not to enjoy the warmth of each other's thighs. Men with nothing in common sure have nothing in common, while women, mere acquaintances or complete strangers, all have children, or diets, or men are bastards. While Malcolm throbs with his own sense of inadequacy and chippiness, Derek beams beside him with self-importance and the knowledge of a fat car nestling just the other side of the windowsill and all the masculine accomplishment which that represents. Mother and Father are in the two chairs with wooden arms. If they were a couple in our geriatric ward or at the old people's home I might think they looked rather sweet even though I know frailty and wrinkles don't a benign person make. Beth and Jessie and I are all in the upright dining chairs, grown women unconsciously abiding by the rule that the suite is too good for us. There's Mother's perennial ginger-cake, laid out on china decorated with corn-flowers at the table put up specially for the occasion by the window. Ginger-cake for family at Christmas, ginger-cake for those come to break up her family. Either way. It's a ceremony.

'There is Christmas Cake too, but I made this because I know it's Dorothy's favourite,' she says.

Of course in this room I am listening to family news and watching a pair of socks being opened here, a box of chocolates there, but I am thinking about Eliza. The panic attack hasn't materialised as perhaps it should by rights. For once I don't feel like the unmarried, tragic one who's only got her work for a life, and that I'm not quite like normal people, and I've only myself to blame. I may look that way for all to see, but I've got a strength this time enables me to rise above my father's sense of disappointment, and my sister Beth's little anxiety that I've never made it up the aisle, something which to her is not a failing exactly, but which is not quite nice.

I eat the old-fashioned ginger-cake with a certain distaste. I don't forget that tin of it Mother sent with me to the laundry. But for the first time I am also managing to enjoy it for what it is, that is rich, and moist, and heavy, and dark, and not wholly loathing it for what it's so long seemed to me, a sign of her rejection. It's typical she should get her wires so mixed she can actually delude herself it's my favourite. Time was when this stuff made me want to throw up.

I finish a cup of tea and excuse myself to go to the bathroom (put in a few years ago to replace the outside one out the back). Of course I go straight up to our old attic room and sit on the dusty bed awhile. I don't care who thinks I've got constipation, I'll sit here just as long as I need. My hands are limp on my lap without Eliza. There have been so many other babies in these arms since, I can't remember the weight of her I tried so hard that day to imprint into my memory and keep for ever. Naturally, I see an old book on the floor, the one which for all I know was the one I was reading when those two men and that woman in yellow with bunions spirited her away for good. The air in this room is oppressively dank and stale as could make a woman wheeze. It's this minute I could rightly wobble and weep for all that I have lost. Every time I come up here, that is every time I return to this house, I take it for granted that I'm going to have a good cry. Memories aside, it's as if the very walls, the air, the smell, the furniture, set me off, they've got something in them, same property as raw onions, that makes tears inevitable.

Only this time I don't cry. Usually when I come up here it's to think about the years between, and have a right old cry to make up for the one I didn't have on the day itself. Heaving, racking sobs. And then I spend as many minutes powdering my eyes so they don't look red and tearful when I go down to face them all in the parlour again. I never wanted to give Mother and Father the satisfaction. This time I sit on the bed waiting for it to happen, but it doesn't happen. It's like I don't need to any more. It's like I've found a courage, something else, not to replace a daughter, but to fill a gaping hole all the same.

Course, I go back down the stairs, and my sisters are probably expecting Dot to be in bits but putting on a brave face, and there's me going in like the cat that's got the cream. I look at Mother and Father. As per usual I'm trying to work out what was going on in those minds behind those faces when they did what they did, but not as per usual I don't really care if I can no longer find an adequate answer.

'I expect they'll be dead soon,' Jessie says later. 'They're that old. And that bitter and twisted, it's eating them alive.'

I've to drive home this evening because I'm on early tomorrow morning. The ordeal at our parents' is over, we've gone back to Jessie's, and she and I have left Derek and the kids in front of the box while we go out together for a quick breath of fresh air before I'm on my way.

We've walked out of the close where she lives, and are going along the verge of the main road headed away from Stoke. Behind the hedgerow there's fields of that red, red earth peculiar to this area. Even mud in Somerset is not as colourful as that in Staffordshire; there again, nor does it remind me of those miserable walks Father used to banish us on, come rain or shine. 'You think they really are bitter and twisted?' I ask.

'Fuck, aye. What they did to you. It's broken them, if that's any consolation.'

'Mother maybe. I don't think he has many regrets.'

Jessie stops in her tracks. We're standing on the grass verge by a puddle with rust-coloured water. 'You're wrong there, Dot. He thought he was doing right at the time, like, but deep down he now knows it was unforgivable. To let social stigma, and his Presbyterian side, dictate the fate of his own daughter? OK, because it was the dark ages and all that, he might've given you a bit of a bollocking and all, but to punish you to the extent of sending you to prison for nine fucking years? Any bloke what does that's got to be fucking psychotic, right? An' I reckon he realises that now, what's more I reckon from that day to this he's been haunted by the question of what possessed him then. Else why didn't he do the same to me when I got pregnant with Sam before I married John?'

'Because Piccadilly had been closed down by then?' I suggest. Jessie doesn't hear me. She's on a roll. We've not started walking again. We're still stopped here on the verge by that rusty puddle.

'And he dotes on her, right, always has, even more than he does on Natalie and Tim. You know why? 'Cos he's trying to make up for Eliza, that's why.'

'Possibly. But it's got to be worse for Mother. She has to live with hypocrisy as well as guilt. She may not have got pregnant, but she lived in sin, as they say, with a man in America, remember, and carried on loving him after she married Father. She was devastated by memories of Joe throughout our childhood, remained so, and

213

resented us because we weren't the children of the man she loved, the man she wanted children with.'

'How d'you know all this, then?'

'There's letters in the attic room I found and read last time I was dropped in on them, what, three or so years back. From her addressed to him, returned from America unopened. I opened them.'

'You never told me this,' Jessie says, scrabbling in her pocket for her cigarettes. 'I need a fag. What year?'

'1942. Year she married Father. One or two were '43. I suppose she gave up after that. Begging, sort of.'

'What did they say?'

'That she loved him. That she didn't love Father. She wanted to go back to America. That she wished her baby girl was his.'

'You're joking me. Why didn't she stay over there then?'

'It wasn't clear from the letters. My guess is Joe gave her the heave-ho. Explains a lot. Her suspicion of men; your exes, John, Derek. And why she agreed to have me sent away. I mean, it's not as if she's not a strong character and couldn't have prevented it if she'd really wanted to.'

'Why on earth'd she want to take it out on you?'

'For not being Joe's? I dunno. It's a theory of mine. I think when I got pregnant and Father mentioned my being sent to a corrective institution, she was open to suggestion. It's the best explanation I can come up with any rate. It was like a satisfying kick in the face to one of the people who was so much part of the life she'd never wanted.'

'If that's the case she's more of an effing bitch than I ever gave her credit for.'

'I think you have to feel sorry for her. Being so in love, and not being able to be with him.'

'I beg your pardon, Dot Sheffield, you're now telling me you feel sorry for her? Is that right? Well, I don't give a shit whatever happened to her, it's still no excuse.' Jessie starts walking again, striding. 'She should have resisted Father, so she should. They're both as bad as each other. I don't feel sorry for either of them. The day they sent you to Piccadilly, they dug their own graves. They may be the grandparents of my children, so I'll be polite to them, do the dutiful thing occasionally, visit and that, but I can never forgive them.'

'I've never wanted to forgive them.' I pause. 'Things change, though. I'll never like them, and I'll never forget, but I could see a way to forgiving them, maybe, some time.'

'Oh, yeah? What's brought this on, then? You've always said you can never forgive them.' Jessie lifts her arms beside her like wings and brings them down so they slap her thighs with something like exasperation. 'I'm more angry than you, you know. You should be angrier than me, and now you're talking 'bout this forgiveness crap. Has Harold Mills got anything to do with this?'

Now it's my turn to stop in my tracks. 'What makes you say that?'

'Well, you're in love with him, aren't you?' she asks 'Is that why you've come over all religious and Christian on me? You're in love.' She inhales her cigarette deeply as if it's going to keep her upright after all this revelation.

'I am?'

'I saw the way you took a bite out that mince pie last night. It was a Mrs Topley's, right?'

'Right. And how did I take a bite, then?'

'I dunno, you looked at it with a sort of reverence, and then gave this little sort of, you know, like, giveaway smile like there was this secret you had with it.'

'So? I've always been partial to a nice mince pie.'

'Aw, come off it, Dot, don't give me that bollocks, all right? I know you've a soft spot for that Harold.'

'And what would he have to do with my thinking about forgiving Mother and Father?'

'Love makes people go right weird. Look at some of the strange things I did in the past under the influence.'

We start walking again but there's silence between us. I notice the road markings are very white on the black tarmac. They must have been freshly painted, I think. 'I am in love with Harold,' I tell her eventually.

'Yeah, and it's obviously made you go right off your trolley,' she laughs. Then the information sinks in. She looks at me and narrows her eyes in silence. 'You what?'

Oh, God, what have I said? Suddenly she goes crazy. Here she is in her wellies and her glamour mac, the one with the leather trimmings, leaping up and down and whooping like a schoolgirl. Her bleached blonde hair going haywire with the wind and her excitement. She's asking why in God's name I didn't tell her before. Our parents and her anger of a few moments ago are quite forgot. That's what I love about our Jessie, her moods can turn one way to another quicker than she can change from one shocking coloured outfit to the next.

'Calm down, lass. I've not had the chance.'

'Dot, you've never admitted to being in love before.' Jessie's as good as skipping.

'Have I not?' I tease her. 'Well, it's not the sort of thing one goes round telling. And it doesn't happen very often. Once in a lifetime, if you're lucky.'

'You weren't in love with Alf Whittaker, then?'

'We'll not talk about him if you don't mind.' I notice the sky has gone that deep blue it goes before becoming black, before you can really see the stars. Jessie looks cold. Her face is white but even in this light I can still tell her nose is red. I'm a touch chilly myself. 'Shall we turn back?' I ask. 'I best be off soon else I won't be home before midnight.'

'You're not going nowhere before you tell me about Harold Mills,' she says in a tone which I know gives me no choice. 'I want from the beginning, Dot, all right, no details spared. We can turn back, but we're only to walk slowly, mind. You're to tell me everything. Is that clear?'

Just as she orders, I start to tell her everything, and it all comes tumbling out, like with my colleagues the night of the Christmas party. Only more so because she's my beloved sister.

Chapter Twelve

Though it's late, I've a promise to keep. I've to pop in on Colette to see if she did have the baby today, and to make sure she's all right. I've to be here early tomorrow, I'm feeling wretched tired after two long journeys to and from Jessie's yesterday and today, and I'm longing to get to my bed. But promises is promises. I'll make it a quick one just, and if she's asleep I won't wake her, instead I'll go to her first thing in the morning.

Though there's still activity, of course, what with mums coming in and being rushed to the delivery suites, there is always a hushed atmosphere at the hospital this time of night, round midnight. The sound of my soles on the lino, like wet fish being smacked together by bored fishermen, seems to resound around the place so you fear it's going to wake all the babies and give rise to a hundred cries. I find Jan in our office who tells me Colette had a girl yesterday lunchtime, and all's well. I tiptoe into the postnatal ward. It is dark except for a blue glowing light from one of the cots containing a baby with jaundice. One baby is crying. Though I am not in uniform, his mother recognises and beckons to me, rather desperate. I help her to lock him on to her nipple, doesn't take a moment, so then all is quiet. Colette is in the next bed, fast asleep. I write her a short note to say I'll be in to see her first thing.

I scurry out managing not to wake a soul and rapidly head for the main exit wondering how I'm going to keep my eyes open on the road home. I'm scared they might do that fluttering thing I so dread and which they only ever seem to do at the worst possible times, so I slap my cheeks to keep myself and them alert.

I've parked at the end of the car park which is near to the entrance to Casualty. As I'm unlocking my door, an ambulance draws up with its nagging siren at full pitch, its blue lights swirling like a drunk man's eyeballs. The two paramedics in their green overalls leap out and sprint to the back doors. Although I'm so tired my knees are about to buckle, there's something in me wants to see what comes out of that vehicle. If I were being kind to myself I'd say it was the nursely, caring instinct I have makes me feel I ought to hang around to see if there's anything I can do to help. Only that wouldn't be genuine. I know I'm not needed. There's nurses and medics in there aplenty to deal with every eventuality, whilst I'm only really good for one thing: maternity – in the midwife sense of the word, of course. What it is keeps me gawping here is the normal human being side of me, common to 99 per cent of the population, which is ghoulishly drawn to any accident or emergency. All my years in the medical profession, and so often being on the front line myself, curiosity more than satisfied, I'm still just like anyone else when I hear in the street the sound of a siren, or see in the labour ward the red light flash of alarm. I wanted to know what particular type of tragedy's on the menu tonight.

Frankly, I'd say that was a side of me as stinks.

I open my car door, disgusted with myself, and I'm all ready to get in and quickly drive away when I hear a deep-throated scream emanating from the ambulance which is like the childbirth scream of pain. It's a scream I recognise, only it's not coming from someone having labour complications. For starters, the ambulance wouldn't have brought her to this department, and second, the scream sounds of a pain even more obliterating than childbirth.

I don't move to get into my seat. That's someone I know making that scream, one of the mums. Debbie? April? Who is it? What is it? Cot death runs through my mind.

I rush over to the open ambulance. The paramedics are bringing out a stretcher and rushing it to the entrance. On it lies a man. His face slumped to one side, away from me. The young woman running beside him into reception is scantily dressed under a donkey jacket, looks like in nightclothes. Bare legs. Pink fleecy slippers. She's holding a baby in one arm, is clutching and clawing at the blankets with the other, and howling with horror in the extreme. There are two youngsters, one in pyjamas, the other in a T-shirt nightdress, dazed and wobbling along behind her.

'Stevie,' she's crying. 'Stevie.'

Kelly.

I slam my door and I run in after. It's all bright lights and commotion in here, very different from our department. I'm dazzled by the neon. The disgruntled groans of patients waiting to be seen – seems like hundreds of them – is like a harmonious hum, only interrupted by a man in his early fifties who'd had a bit too much, and has blood squashed all over his face. He's hollering and whining, and annoying everyone else, even frightening and disgusting some. I take all this in in a millisecond. My first concern is to grab hold of the two little ones who are not able to keep up with the progress of the stretcher and their mother. I step in front of them and say hello as calmly as I can, take their hands. 'Remember me, Marcus, love?'

'Yeah, you're Dot, the midwife. Dad's had an accident.'

'What happened?'

'Dunno, me and Topsy were asleep. Mum wasn't saying.'

'Well, let's go see what's happening, shall we, see that's he's all right?'

'I think he's dead.'

I take his hand, and his sister's and mutter something to the effect that I'm sure that that's not so. We chase after their mother and the stretcher, but they disappear behind two swing doors and I know it's best not to follow. In her distress, Kelly probably doesn't realise Marcus and Topsy aren't with her, but it occurs to me it won't be long before she looks round and notices. I weigh up her fright against the trauma of the children seeing their unconscious father surrounded by doctors in a flurry of anxious activity, Lord knowing what going on. I keep them with me on the chairs outside.

Five minutes later Kelly, who has tears but is no longer crying so scorchingly, is accompanied through the doors by a nurse who's holding the baby and telling her to wait here. Marcus and Topsy are playing with a crumpled magazine on the low-lying table beside them. Children have a remarkable capacity to appear oblivious to trauma, but you know it's only that, an appearance. It's all sinking in all right, it's just that while it is, they're not really aware of it, they can carry on playing regardless. I stand and reassure the nurse that I'm a friend of the family. I take the child from her arms and say I'll stay with them.

On hearing my voice, Kelly looks up, sees me for the first time. Her hands have been crowding her face with despair. Her face is red and wet all over, her eyelashes clumped together with tears.

'Oh, Dot,' she says, and gives me a hug, starts crying again. 'How're you here? He's not going to make it, you know, no he's not, I know he's not. They've got these clamps on him, and drips, and monitors, he's not my Stevie. He's not waking up, he's not waking up, he's never going to wake up.'

'Course he will, love, Stevie's a strong fellow and he's got so much to live for.' I take a breath. 'You, the kids, you're the world to him. He'll be in there fighting, believe you me, fighting, fighting.'

It's sounds I make just. Sounds. That's all it is.

'A fucking chair, right, Dot,' she whispers in my ear. 'Can you believe it, a fucking chair, I'm going to burn it, yeah, an' I'm going to kick down the wall an' all, so I am.'

I don't know what Kelly's talking about. We're still hugging, the baby cooing between us, blinking her eyes with the novelty of it all, all these lights, sounds, people.

The doors swing open again, and a man with a good face in a white coat comes out.

'Which one of you is Kelly?' he asks, looking at both of us. He knows the answer. It's procedure. He's got to be sure. Kelly's so frightened she can't speak, so I tell him. 'Could you step this way please,' he asks her. 'You're Kelly's friend? Can I prevail upon you to mind her children a moment? Very kind. Thank you. We won't be long.' There's nothing about his tone gives anything away. Stevie could be dead; he could be alive and out of immediate danger, even on the road to recovery.

The doctor takes Kelly into a little office a couple of doors down the corridor. Marcus, Topsy, the baby, and I, we wait. My head throbs like someone's inside it thrashing a squash ball around my skull, and the waistband of my slacks feels too tight following my big Christmas dinner, and Mother's ginger-cake.

'Dot, what's fire made of?' Marcus asks. 'Flames, right, but what are flames?'

It's not the perfect moment. Children, for all their canniness, are less good on timing. 'I'm not sure, love. Chemicals, gases and that.'

'Only you can put chemicals in a barrel, right, but you can't put flames.'

'That's right, pet.' The baby's beginning to whinge. Hungry. I sit down to jiggle her on my knee. 'Mummy's coming in a minute,' I tell her soothingly. I'm not equipped to feed her, so I'm no good, but I manage to quieten her down somehow, I think she feels secure in my practised arms. Nor am I capable of giving Marcus a chemistry lesson. I don't know the answer and, anyway, I'm not concentrating as I should, because I'm fixated by that door Kelly's gone in, and what's being said now behind it. There's no sounds, no loud crying. The news is good. Stevie's going to pull through.

'I'm not so good on flames,' I tell the lad. Then I feel unkind, like I'm palming him off, and the least he deserves is distraction. 'Ask me another, wee man.'

Suddenly, before he has the chance, our door opens, and the doctor and Kelly emerge, poised expressions on both their faces. He brings her to me.

'I'm afraid Mr Freely didn't make it,' he tells me softly. Kelly bows her head into my shoulder and clutches me as if for her own dear life. 'When he fell back off the chair,' the doctor's saying, 'his head hit the wall very heavily indeed. The impact meant that brain damage was very likely. He never regained consciousness, I'm afraid. We did our very best. I'm sorry.'

I manage to thank him. Then together, Kelly, the baby and I buckle on to the chairs. I'm not sure whether or not Marcus and Topsy heard the doctor's words, but they know the outcome as well as the rest of us. They look stunned enough just seeing their mother so apathetic with grief, winded with emotion, silent with agony, let alone what they must be feeling now Stevie's left them and gone up to Heaven (that's the line all children get about death). They come up to us, put their soft pink arms around her, and squeeze.

We're like a human igloo the five of us, packed tightly and turning in on ourselves against the severity of pain.

Not one of us breathes a word.

★

I feel tonight perhaps bitterer than in all my born years. And that's saying quite a lot, coming from Dorothy Sheffield.

There's a strong case for cynicism. Relationships are either rotten to the core or just plain bad, either way they're like cheap toys made in Taiwan: it's inevitable they're going to fall to bits. On the other hand, you can sometimes get good relationships and they stay intact – for a while, at least. Only they, too, though beautiful in themselves, even perfect in some cases, are doomed. Because the good and happy woman, though she doesn't know it yet, she's a living statistic, a one in twelve headed for breast cancer and discovery too late; or the good and happy man, who has a dangerous job and is lucky with the risks he takes from day to day, is going to misfire his behind on to his chair one night, to fall back, and to not get the little egg on his head he might expect, but a bump hard enough to kill himself on a malignant kitchen wall.

As with Stevie Freely. Stevie's down in the kitchen last night keeping Kelly company as she's breast-feeding their beautiful new baby; they've just made a cup of tea for themselves, are having a chat and a sleepy giggle – about bumping into one of his brickie colleagues in Mothercare – before going up to bed. He sits down at the table a minute to be beside her, and to put his finger out for his young one to clutch as she feeds from her mother's breast, a dutiful and loving fatherly contribution to the proceedings. Only he doesn't make it to his seat, does he. No, just off. By a couple of inches, that's all. With the consequence that within twenty-three minutes of impacting that wall, he's dead.

How very cruel is the banal.

And I should know.

I've driven Kelly home, put the chidren to bed, and am staying up the whole night with her, in the living room, talking, talking, talking, it's for the best. She's telling me in detail what it was that happened, and I'm not for stopping her. We've agreed not to ring anyone till morning, neither her mum or dad, nor his. I'm not going to persuade her against her wishes. She can't face the calamity of their emotions till dawn. She wants a few hours without; with just her own. We're going to call her parents at five, because she insists I mustn't miss my shift at six.

'Other mothers need you, Dot,' she says in such a way as could break a harder heart than mine.

'But you need me more, love, and I'm here.'

'My mum can come in the morning. The other mothers need you. I did.'

And I think of Colette, my promise and note, the frailty of her trust, and I know Kelly's right.

She's shivering and feeling sick. I've a warm flannel to her forehead, and a blanket round her. I'm tempted to say time heals, but of all the stupid sayings, that one's got to be the biggest load of baloney on offer. I'm not about to lie to her, but I'm also not about to tell her she'll be feeling the loss still in thirty-three years' time, and more besides. I'm tempted to tell her I lost someone I loved as much as she loved Stevie when I was near enough her age, and I'm still standing. But that's stupid, unhelpful. So what? I'm Dot, and that was back BC, and she's Kelly, and this is now she's lost Stevie.

Twenty-four years of professional care for women – being made redundant while on maternity leave, breaking up with partners, postnatal depression, losing babies, any bloody heart-break you care to imagine – I've come up against them all, yet I'm not up to this one. A good and special man, with a good and special woman, a good and special pair: him in the peak of health and happiness, losing his life to a bloody chair, and piece of fucking wall.

It happens all the time, doesn't it? These small insignificant things self-importantly puffing themselves up to play havoc with our lives. Who'd have thought it, for Kelly, a chair and a wall could give rise to a tragedy such as hers; for me, too, something as unnotable in its way, yet with consequences to ripple their way down the line of my all my years: a brief encounter with Alf Whittaker, an encounter, so it was, briefer than a stripper's G-string.

God give us strength.

The children are sleeping soundly, and the baby, though wakeful, is as good as gold. I tend to her without leaving her mother's side. Kelly vomits into a bowl, twice, and I tend to that too, clearing it away as well as trying not to leave her for more than a moment.

Calmly, Kelly tells me more and more about Stevie. How they met. His face bringing home his first wage packet having been on the dole for three years. The jokes they shared. Time they went rollerskating and he slipped on dog shit and went smack into a tree, how they laughed; time she beat him at darts in the pub and he poured half a pint over her, how they laughed; time she was breast-feeding Topsy in this pizza place, they'd spent twenty-three fucking quid in there, and this waitress had the bleeding nerve to tell her to put her boob away, how Stevie lost his wick and squirted mustard all over the manager, how they've never been back to that hole but how, at the time, they laughed. How after she had Topsy she had stretch marks on the backs of her legs, she was *fat*, but Stevie didn't use to mind, he used to kiss them, you guessed it, and how they laughed.

They were that kind of couple others want to be, with the kind of relationship individuals hold out for till the last minute, because they think there's still a chance they too might find this sort of simple but ever so elusive fantasy for real. Only it doesn't happen, so they're forced to compromise with someone kind of OK but they don't really love, even though they know as they're doing it they're condemning themselves to a lesser sort of life, of frustration and regret.

She's talking like he's still alive, and that is understandable. It's like it hasn't hit her yet, he's gone, and it won't for some while yet. It's hit me rightly enough. The lump's so big in my throat trying not to cry it's making my nose twitch. I can't swallow. Nor can I blink my eyes. If you're that close to tears and you blink your eyes, it's inevitable then, the whole edifice of your face, your features, and your self-control, they all come tumbling after. I'm trying to bring all my years of professional fortitude in times such as these to bear on my behaviour now. Kelly needs me strong. I cannot disintegrate now.

She talks on, and I listen, oh, I listen all right. We're nestling on the settee still, my arms round her, warm and comfortable together. There's crumpled tissues on the carpet all around us, and mugs with cold dregs of tea, a clean washing-up bowl just in case she needs to be sick again. We've not got the overhead light on, but the lamp on the floor quite close. The curtains are closed. It's pitch dark outside, no hint of dawn. Bang on five in the morning, Kelly looks at her watch.

'It's time to ring Mum,' she says, with the admirable conscientiousness of a career girl keeping a business appointment. 'Dot, I've got to let you go.'

'I'll go just as soon as your mum comes, not before. Would you like me to call her for you?'

'That's nice, Dot, but she might get a real fright a stranger's voice waking her this time in the morning. Perhaps it's best me.'

I pass her the phone. She dials. I can hear it takes four rings to answer. 'Dad, it's me. Can you and Mum come over?'

I can hear a man's voice asking what she's doing ringing at this hour. 'Are you all right, love?'

'Stevie's had an accident,' she replies in a whisper. She pulls in her lower lip, which trembles. 'He's dead. Can you come?' She sniffs, and puts down the receiver. 'They'll be here in ten minutes, he said.'

That's the last thing she says to me till her parents arrive. Her head is buried in my shoulder. She's silent. When the doorbell rings, I go and let them in. The couple standing on the doorstep look distraught. He is a short man, stout, in a felt hat, and with kindly eyes. Kelly's mum is a roly-poly woman with a rounded, pretty face, which now is coloured with concern.

'I'm Dorothy, Kelly's midwife,' I mutter. We're huddled in the tiny hall. 'I brought her and the children back from the hospital. Don't worry. I think she's all right. I've managed to calm her down. She needs you. She's in the living room.' I step aside, and they thank me for all I've done. As they go in, I see Kelly leaping up and rushing to her mum. She crumples into tears. I bite my lip.

In the commotion of questions and grief between them which follow, I slip away quietly, unnoticed, and drive to the hospital, my eyes fluttering all the way. Tears.

Chapter Thirteen

First port of call after dashing home to change into my uniform is Colette. When I get to the hospital I go straight to her, and find her slowly struggling with the ridiculously early hospital breakfast.

'You all right, Dot?' she asks. She's not a great one for noticing others, isn't Colette; it's nice of her to ask, but it must mean I look a right mess. I didn't have time to touch myself up in my bathroom mirror, and I'm obviously not doing a very good job of concealing my sorrow.

'I'm fine. How's you?'

'Bit tired, otherwise I'm brilliant. Do you want to look at her? She's sleeping at the moment.' Stiffly, she leans over to the Perspex cot beside her, and pulls back the blanket from her baby's chin.

'Beautiful,' I whisper. 'I'll come back to get to know her a bit when she's woken up. Only first tell me how it went. It was Penny was with you, is that right?'

'Yeah. Listen, are you OK? Honest?' she asks again. I nod. 'Look, Dot, it was really nice of you to come by last night. I know you weren't on duty, and you came specially. Thanks for the note.'

I manage a smile. Seems like motherhood has softened her already. I'm not saying it's the answer to everything, that it can perform miracles, but it's nice to see a troubled girl happy. Let's hope it lasts. For now, I'm refusing to think about any potential problems which might lie ahead. In my mind, not giving a thing away, she might think me presumptuous, I'm praying for her and her child.

Much of the rest of the day I spend in a daze. I go to the office and tell those of my colleagues who are there what's happened to Stevie. They are predictably shocked and horrified. Maggie speaks for me when, shaking her head with incomprehension, she says how 'it always happens to the really lovely ones, doesn't it, them who've got something really special?' Chantal immediately organises a whip-round so we can send Kelly a card and a present, and we all willingly put our contributions into the envelope even though each one of us feels silently angry at how inadequate is our token of support.

They offer to let me have the day off because I've been up all night having a traumatic time of it; they can easily call Jan who would be happy to come in and cover for me. It's touching, their concern; they know I have a particular soft spot for Kelly. Only I think I've got to press on as normal. In the usual course of things people can knock normality, criticise it, say it's dull and unexciting, but at times normality can really come into its own, can bloom, can be for the distressed mind as settling as Calpol for the distressed infant.

I do accept a cup of tea in the office, but, and a biscuit from a selection box given to all of us, 'with love and thanks from Colette'. Then Chantal's bleeper goes off, she's wanted in Delivery. A student midwife pops her head round to ask if one of us is free to go and say goodbye to a mum who's leaving to go home. Maggie willingly volunteers. So I have a few moments to be alone.

I'm hungry for the first time in twenty-four hours. I take another biscuit. It doesn't satisfy.

My colleagues have been very kind, so I'm now relatively calm at least (even when in Kelly's company and we were laughing together at her stories, I was tense with sadness and with the responsibility for her sanity). It's a moment of troubled peace I'm having, but peace all the same. First chance to think half straight since recognising Kelly's cry last night, and all I can think of or want is Harold. I feel this crucial need to hear his calming voice. And when he's comforted me with his special blend of common sense and hope, I know it's only him who'll be able to distract my mind with talk of those steadying subjects he favours, and so do I – of duck-flying formations, and the characters of clouds. I am moved by a sort of passionate intensity about as un-Dorothy-like as it's possible to get.

I pick up the telephone on the desk and press 9 for an outside line.

*

He's cooked me a lovely meal: chops, boiled potatoes, and butter beans, only I can't eat it all up, my stomach's squeezed tight with anguish.

'Don't worry, please, if you can't eat it all,' he says. 'I understand if you're not feeling hungry.'

I came here to Harold's place straight after work, and the relief of being with him is unbelievable. It's like I've come home.

His kitchen only just has room enough to accommodate the small table where we're sat. The yellow Formica surface with its black 1950s criss-cross pattern is almost completely covered with Perspex bowls for the veg, two glasses with some juice, two very flat pale green plates for our meal, and a bottle of HP sauce. Harold's tightly packed in with his back right up against the cream cooker, its red knobs probably sticking painfully into his back though he's not saying a word; he's left me as much space as possible by the wall. He's tall is Harold, so when he sat down he had to manoeuvre his legs this way and that, and it was a struggle to pull his seersucker serviette across his knees under the moulding beneath the table. He eats all his meal, slowly, and as he does so we talk about the accident and he tells me it's not always like that, like how I see it, tragedy only befalling the good. He adds he hopes I don't really believe that.

'Times like this it's hard not to,' I tell him. 'See, I'm not always so good at coping. The uniform's not a guarantee of coping. Now you're seeing me how it sometimes gets to me.'

'I'm glad it does, or you wouldn't be human. Occasionally you've got to let things get to you.'

'But this one specially. There was something about Kelly and Stevie. Perhaps I should be a hard woman and not care so much about my ladies, what happens to them, even the ones like Kelly I get close to.'

'Do you want to be like that?'

'No.' It was a stupid thing to say. I take a sip of my juice, embarrassed.

Harold puts his knife and fork together, takes a bit of bone from his plate and slips it to Jones under the table. All the while, he's not looking at what he's doing but at me and he's smiling that crumpled smile of his.

'Let's go and sit in comfort, shall we?' he says, standing and squeezing out from between the table and the cooker, his Aran sweater momentarily catching on one of the red knobs. He pulls the table away for me, and dismisses the washing-up. 'I'm going to leave all this for now. It's not often I have visitors. Settle yourself next door while I make some Nescafé.'

He directs me not to the lounge, but to the front room which he reserves for best. I am flattered. While he's in the kitchen preparing the coffee, I look at the framed photos on the mantelpiece of his mum and dad, very old, and what must be a relative, a niece or something, on her wedding day. I wonder if she and her husband are amongst his rare visitors, and I hope they are because Harold, though a solitary man, is one who sets a lot of store by family. I know this from how he looked after and attended to Priscilla in her ailing years, and how he talks of his late parents with such love and pride.

When he comes back with his coffee, he turns the electric fire on. 'Got to keep you nice and warm on a cold night such as this,' he says. Then we sit together on the settee, leaning back, all comfy, Jones at our feet, and suddenly I burst out crying.

Harold puts his hand on my knee.

'I'm so sorry,' I say. It's Harold's kind goodness, and thoughts of him, what he's lost, what he's never had; and thoughts of Kelly, what she's lost, and might never find again. 'I'm not such a good sort of visitor, am I, when you don't have them so often, all weepy like.'

'You're the best visitor I've ever had,' he says.

That's one of the nicest things anyone's ever said to me. The way he looks I know he means what he said, I know he does.

'Thank you, that's lovely. I know I shouldn't go on about Kelly and that. Only I can't stop thinking about it, Harold. I can't get out of my head that all it was was a chair, a plain, ordinary chair, and inch of wall. I saw the chair last night when I went in Kelly's kitchen to make us a cup of tea and that. It was on the floor on its side, it had metal legs, and a round plastic seat, a bit of greying yellow foam spilling out a split in the back. I mean, it hardly looked like it could kill a man. But I couldn't pick it up to put it right, I couldn't touch it, and I couldn't go near the wall. It's always the small things, isn't it, they don't seem harmful, but when you've got your head turned the other way, just for a second, they can do untold damage.' I stop, 'Oh, you must forgive me. Talking, talking!'

'I like you talking. There's been too many years in this house without. I want you to go on talking.'

'You do?' I ask, rising to go to the mantelpiece. 'Well, I've got plenty I can talk about, only I think it's probably best for now if I try and take my mind off things. Tell me, who's that pretty girl in the picture, in that gorgeous dress? I'm very nosy. She family?'

'That's my niece, Michaela,' he says, 'my sister's daughter. Lovely girl, very bubbly. She used to come and stay here when she was a child for holidays by the seaside; still visits sometimes with her husband. She's like a daughter to me. It was a couple of years ago now she and Alan were married. They live in Middlesex.'

'Very nice. What takes them there?'

'He comes from those parts and they've both got jobs there. She's a dental hygienist, and he's in computers. They've a baby on the way.'

'Ah, lovely.'

'It was a beautiful wedding they had, in Bristol. That's where Michaela was brought up, where my sister and brother-in-law still live as a matter of fact, have done for thirty-five years.'

'They're still together, then?'

'Oh yes, very much so, very happy. My sister was always going to make a good marriage. She's a great believer in the institution.'

'That's nice to hear. These days. Divorce and what have you.' I replace the photo and return to sit beside him on the settee. 'Can I ask you something, Harold? Rather personal.'

'You can ask me anything you like,' he replies, 'and I give you my guarantee I'll answer.'

'You never did get married, did you? I mean, I know that. I suppose I'm asking why. Is that very cheeky of me?'

'Not in the least. I think you have a right to know.'

I like that, him thinking I have a right to know. 'Only there's no reason you should be married – look at me, for goodness sake. It's just when someone's not, I suppose it's only natural folk begin to wonder. People don't often ask why I've not got children. I think they think that's going too far, 'cos it might be something wrong with my body, I might have defective insides, and that's gynaecological and embarrassing. But it doesn't stop them asking me about why I'm not married, and to my mind that's every bit as personal, even more so. Sometimes it annoys me quite a lot, actually. And now here I am asking you.'

'I'll answer you happily, not annoyed at all,' he says. 'I think I can say it's because the opportunity never arose, and I didn't want to force fate. There was an element, too, I suspect, of being spoilt by seeing a marriage like my parents', so good. It set such a perfect example, perhaps I was scared of failing. Parents can't win, can they?' He pauses. 'Truth is, there was once or twice I came close to marriage.'

'Yes,' I admit, 'I s'pose I sort of knew that. Not long before she died, Priscilla hinted to me that you might have had a disappointment or two.'

'Dear Priscilla, she was right of course. I never told her, but she was always perceptive. I think she knew about Edith from the start, and Christine.'

'I'm sorry things didn't work out.'

'Ah, they were lovely ladies, both of them,' he recalls. 'I loved them, and I was privileged for that opportunity alone. Only the moment just seemed to seep away somehow, and they went their ways.'

As he says this, Harold's hand barely perceptibly tightens on my knee, I don't think he's even noticed he's doing it.

'I used to tell myself the fault was theirs,' he continues, 'that they were not the types as were constant. Then as the years passed, I came to see my part in the blame. What I thought of as shyness and natural prudence in me was in fact just a cover for procrastination: foolish, misplaced procrastination as it turned out. Times in my life I've felt regret, but now I think age is beginning to wither even that.'

'Not age, surely not?' I smile.

'Oh, very possibly. But maybe also Aunt Priscilla's death. She was someone I loved and admired and who lived a long life, but she always maintained a scant regard for regret. Whatever the reason, I don't want to do any more regretting. I've chided myself too long for not seizing those moments.' He's shaking his head as he's talking to me. 'Next time such a moment comes, I'll not hang about needlessly, fatally dithering. I'm sixty-odd, I'm a wiser man, and I'll be ripe for the seizing.'

He stops a moment and offers to make me another coffee. I thank him and decline. I couldn't eat or drink a thing.

'I'm not too old, I hope,' he asks, 'for marriage?'

'Never,' I tell him.

'You never fancied marriage, I mean, yourself then?'

'Oh, it wasn't that I didn't fancy it,' I sigh. 'In some ways I fancied it every bit as much as other girls did. Hang on, spinsters aren't supposed to admit that, are they?'

'I don't see why not.'

'I think they're meant to make out it was through choice they stayed single, that they actively decided to strike out on their own, embrace independence. It's seen as humiliating or demeaning or something, that a man never asked them.'

'I don't believe a man never asked you.'

'They didn't,' I tell him. 'Honestly.'

'Eliza's father?'

'Ah, that was different.' I don't resent the question. 'A long story. My parents put the pressure on to make him marry me, but that wouldn't have worked at all. And, then, see, I was already twenty-eight when I finally got out the laundry. Even in 1970, twenty-eight and unmarried was almost as bad as in Jane Austen's day, old-maid-time. Didn't matter that you'd been locked away from men for nine years and hadn't had the opportunity. Also I was shy and frightened of men by then, they were such an unknown quantity. And they certainly seemed to give me a wide berth anyway. I just got on with my job.'

'You must have come across lots of men, though, in the course of your work?'

'Yes,' I answer. 'Other people's husbands. The fathers and doctors mainly. I came across lots of them for sure. It was like a crash course in men. I learned more about them in my first few weeks at St Dominic's than in my near enough thirty years. I can't say I was particularly enamoured about what I saw and, where I was coming from, I wasn't predisposed to like them very much anyway. I never did fall in love, and nor did any of them with me. Far as I know.'

'Jessie, you're very close to her, didn't she introduce you to some nice ones, encourage you to start courting?'

'Jessie? Oh God, Harold, her and men! Enough said. She encouraged me all right, she was always wanting to get me fixed up. But she was the worst advertisement herself. Just to witness her brushes with them was enough to make me blanch and run. What with one thing and another, I decided it was the solitary life for me. Though in theory, I suppose, I've never excluded the outside chance that one day someone would come along. In practice I tend not to give it much thought. A woman my age!' As I'm talking, I slip off my shoes and tuck my legs up beneath me. As I do so, Harold's hand falls from my knee, and once I'm settled again, more comfortable, he hesitates. When he replaces it, I put my hand on top to show that I'm glad he has. 'For a long time, though, I did very much want to get married.'

'Why was that?'

'I don't know, I often used to ask myself the same question. That enduring fantasy all girls have? Only in my line of work it didn't last long. Seeing couples in the raw, you might say, beneath the cries of joy, I came to realise rightly quick that the fragile fantasy, as a reality, was very rare, if not nonexistent. But even if I hadn't been exposed to warring spouses, I think the fantasy would've become dormant soon enough anyway.'

'What makes you say that?'

'Well,' I reply slowly, 'you soon learn to keep it in check when you realise your days for wearing long white dresses are over.'

Harold smiles. 'So did you try to think of other reasons why you might've wanted to get married?'

'I did, yes. For example, I would have liked more children and, after my experience with Eliza and that, I used to think it might be for their sake, no more children of mine were going to suffer insecurity, and the fate of being branded bastards. It was a real fear that to have them outside marriage was a sin, and they might somehow be taken away again. But even that didn't hold much water after illegitimacy stopped being a stigma. People started not to give a damn about it.'

'Thank goodness,' says Harold.

'Thank goodness for sure. Not much improves in this world, but that's one thing. But still I wanted to get married.'

'Could it have been social pressure?'

'Yes, social pressure was another one, worse for women, today just as much as then. But it's lost its power to touch me, thank God, now I'm older. Certainly there was a time, though, in my early thirties, when it was so strong I thought I might take any old body who'd have me just so people didn't think there was something wrong with me, like I was a leper or something. And I suppose I was also scared of growing old alone. But I held out, for some reason, something was stopping me from latching on to anybody for the sake of it.'

'What do you think that was, stopping you?'

'It began,' I reply, 'to dawn on me that if you're not particularly religious – it was the laundry knocked that out of me effectively enough – there's no reason in the world to marry at all, other than you love the person. It's that simple. I don't see there needs to be any other debate. What's the point of marriage today? Love.'

'I agree.'

'I have to say, I looked at Jessie with all her lovers and romantic activity, and a marriage under her belt. I'll not deny I envied her in some ways. Except I knew that, but for her three children, there was many a time when she was far lonelier than I was, even though I wasn't in love with anybody.'

'I'm sure that's true.'

'I know it, Harold. No, it was the solitary life for me. Fact is, solitude's served me quite well.'

'It suits me too,' he says, 'very well, and like you, I don't think I've been lonely. You adapt, don't you, and then you get to thinking that it's actually quite agreeable. You even begin to convince yourself you can't see it any other way. You're troubled by the idea of routines being disrupted, peculiar habits revealed, and you come to believe you couldn't ever adapt to living with someone, even someone you felt passionate about. Occasionally, you might speculate about life with someone else, how it would be different, but you don't let yourself hanker after it.'

I nod my head firmly in recognition and agreement.

'So,' he adds, 'you carve out this hermit-like existence for yourself, it's like a defence against the world. Nevertheless, to my mind, I think a person can be forever haunted by the fact they've not truly been loved by anyone, no?'

'Family excluded?' I ask.

'I think so, don't you? I mean, to have inspired it in someone quite else, someone completely unconnected. Not the kind of unconditional love of a parent. I mean, I'm not sure a person can live all their lives with the knowledge there's not been one person actually fall *in* love with them.'

'It's unlikely, though, a person would go through life without having anyone fall in love with them. Probability is, there's always someone.'

'True,' Harold agrees, 'but is it requited? I think that's the point. Man is very dismissive of the love of someone whom he himself does not love. He may be flattered, but in the end, because it doesn't benefit him, he regards it as a trifling irritant, like a sticky piece of chewing-gum on the sole of his shoe. It's got to be someone who he himself loves, otherwise for him it doesn't count. The idea of requited love never can quite lose its appeal, can it? It's too much part of the human condition, to love and be loved. As a single person, you try to suppress the thought of it, but you know really, for all the advantages of solitude, that in the end you are missing out on something greater. You know in your heart of hearts you'd be prepared to cast it all aside, the stringent habits and routines, and everything. They're only important precisely *because* you are alone. When you're not, when you're with someone you love, they probably assume an unimaginable insignificance. I think if a person too much allows himself to ponder what he's missed, allows the thought to get to him, he could drive himself insane.'

'I see what you mean.'

'You must've had people in love with you over the years –'

'Oh, I'm not so sure –'

Harold smiles. 'All right, *probability* is you have. Only, because you weren't in love with them it wasn't much good to you, you see what I'm saying.'

'And particularly if they never let me know about it!' I laugh, and he does too. 'I can't say I've been exactly burdened with declarations.'

'Oh no?' He pauses. 'Well you mightn't mind then, if I were to burden you with one?' As he asks this, Harold puts his free hand on top of mind which is on top of his other one on top of my knee, so that mine is now happily sandwiched. I have no idea what it is he's going to say to me.

He doesn't say anything for a while, and while I'm waiting, the only sound I'm aware of is that in my ears of my beating heart.

When it comes it's not such the burden as he's made out.

'I love you,' he says.

When I rang Harold this morning, jostling with the pain of Stevie's and Kelly's misfortune, I envisaged it was going to be the life cycle of the owl with which he was going to distract me.

Talk of love is not quite the type of steadying subject I was expecting.

There again, never before have I so relished an expectation so spectacularly unfulfilled.

Chapter Fourteen

When I was first in the laundry, I couldn't get used to the strangeness. I'd wake up every morning and not know where I was. Then the realisation would dawn on me, and an almost unbearable heaviness would weigh down my heart, like it was struggling to beat beneath a sackful of sand.

When I awoke this morning there was an unfamiliar light in the room, and the orange folds of a candlewick counterpane were startling to behold. But I never didn't know exactly where I was. There was a warmth beside me, kind of which I'd not felt for some time, and it was so very much warmer than ever it was last I felt it, over thirty years ago. The feeling inside me was far from heaviness.

Harold is spoiling me, he's cooking me a fry. Although we didn't go to sleep till past two o'clock, neither of us is tired. We're in his kitchen having a breakfast as lively as breakfasts don't come in real life, only in the ads. For a pair not used at this time in the morning to anything more than the sound of toast or cornflakes inside their own mouths, we are doing a fine job, so we are, of adapting to chatter and laughter.

I've always wondered why people with partners complain about doing the mundane things in life. If you've got company, even going to the supermarket, I imagine, isn't wanting appeal. I'm tempted to say to them, try going on your own, week in, week out, that's to complain about. They are spoilt. Satisfaction moves further and further out of reach, harder and harder to attain. Just choosing together a nice bit of bacon, or going on the bus with each other, doesn't suffice. It's bigger and better things they're after, it's got to be the purchase of a new hi-fi together, a flashier car, a holiday for two in Barbados, then a house, then another. For all the horrors of Piccadilly, and the absence of a soul-mate in my life, it means I can appreciate the little wonders of plain and simple company with the person I've eventually found who I love and who loves me. I don't think the spoilt couples would rate a mundane fry on a mundane Wednesday morning. But it never tasted so delicious, not even as good as the food I ate when I was first out the laundry. Partly to do with Harold's cooked it, but more because I'm here, and Harold's the one I'm eating it with.

I'm off today, but sadly Harold's to go into work, and I've got late shifts every night till the end of this week. We aren't going to be able to see each other till Saturday, but then we'll have a nice evening, he said, because Saturday's New Year's Eve.

At eight o'clock, after our breakfast, I drive home; it's only five minutes from Harold's house. I am feeling quite the different person, not the Dot Sheffield I know at all. It takes me a while to work it out.

When there's someone as loves you in your life, and you are on your own for a few minutes or hours, you are not alone. I've always admired those of my ladies whose partners are fishermen, or in the army or something, and working away from home for weeks or months on end. These ladies, even if their men miss the births of their children, stoically seem to maintain a strength and courage I've never really understood. But it's a peculiar thing, in my car, just me, it's as if Harold could be right beside me. I'm not saying there's an imaginary chat going on here, I'm saying I just feel that he's there in the passenger seat, and why we're not actually talking is we're just having one of those moments of ours, of easy silence. Perhaps it's this feeling that gets those women through.

I park the car outside the cottage in one of the few spaces along the harbour. It's going to be one of the most peaceful days off I've ever had, which isn't to say I haven't plenty to do, chores and that, it's peace of mind I'm talking about. Already it's beginning to dawn on me that I don't think I knew what I was missing all these years – what Harold was talking about last night – the need we all have for the knowledge that someone we love, loves us. When there's no one, you labour under the delusion you don't need any such thing – it's called coping. But that's all it is. And coping's hard work, you don't realise it at the time, but it's quite a strain stopping yourself from going crazy. It may be just a handful of hours since

Harold made his verbal and physical declarations, but already I know I've done enough coping for one life. Already I know I'm done with any more coping. Sounds corny, but even as I drive the short way from his house to home, I am absolutely certain that, starting from some unspecified hour last evening, and from now on, I'm going to start living.

I lean over to pick up my bag from the back seat, and am surprised by a knock on my window. I'm about to protest that where I've parked is fine, and turn round to see guess who standing there but Jessie! I quickly open the door and get out.

'What on earth – ?' I say. Her face is as round and yellow and battered as an ugli fruit. 'What in God's name?'

'Where've you been?' she asks accusingly. 'You weren't here. I went to the hospital, you weren't there.'

'When did you get here?'

' 'Bout five or six this morning. We've been waiting for you. I've brought the children.' Jessie nods her head in the direction of her car a few feet away. Through its windows I see three little figures, covered in blankets. Sam and Tim are asleep. Natalie has her nose pressed against a window, staring at us. Even with the shadows of the clouds darkening the glass, I can make out a big bruise on the child's cheek.

'What happened?' I gasp. 'To them too?'

'What do you think happened?' Jessie snaps. Then she collapses in tears, her arms around me. 'He started again, didn't he? Oh, God, it's agony to cry. He started on them too, so he did.'

'Listen, love, let's go inside, shall we, and you can tell me all about it? We'll get the kids, and I'll make you all a nice breakfast.'

'I've left him, Dot, right? I always said that once he started on the kids that that's it, finito, end of story, never going back. So here we are. I'm selling the house, selling the salon, giving it all up. I've decided to set up shop in Stoneham. I've already thought up the name. Permanent Waves, because we're by the sea, see? Good, innit?' She laughs. 'Ow, that hurt like hell,' she says, putting her hands up to her misshapen cheeks. 'Can't even fucking laugh. Bastard! We want to be near you, Dot. He can't get at us when we're near you.'

I take Jessie's arm.

'Me and the kids, we don't want no more "fathers". That's it now. We're going it alone, we're going to be doing it by ourselves.'

'All right, all right, calm down, pet.' I walk her over to the car. How, I wonder, over Christmas, could I have got it *so* wrong? How could I have so misjudged Derek's reformed character? And their idyllic, homey lifestyle together? Cynical old Dot, in love herself for once, was caught off guard, must've been.

We open Jessie's car doors and waken the kids. Tim's so tired he needs carried to the front door, and the girls walk floppily.

'Come on, little one,' Jessie's saying to him soothingly. 'We're at Auntie Dot's now. It's all going to be all right. We're safe now. I promise, I promise.'

'Don't worry about the stuff,' I tell Jessie as the five of us pile through the front door into my small living room. 'I'll fetch it all out later. Now let me get you all comfy and settled.'

'They've been awake most the night, Dot. Perhaps we could put them straight to bed now till dinnertime?'

We put Sam in my bed, and Natalie and Tim in the twins in the spare room. None of them resists. They all fall straight to sleep the minute their heads hit the pillows. I take Jessie to the bathroom and sit her on a stool while I clean up her face with cotton wool dipped in warm water. Even that stings her split-open cuts.

'Usually he avoids my face,' she says. ''Cept this time he'd lost it so bad, he forgot to do even that. He managed by some miracle not to cut the kids when he hit them, but they've already got bruises coming up on their faces as you saw, and their arms and legs. Oh, how can I have done this to them?'

'*You*? Jess, what have you done? It's him, all him. Worthless piece of –'

'It's all my fault.'

'Nonsense, put that silly talk away,' I tell her. 'It was no one's fault but his. You're not taking any of the blame, you're not, not as long as you're stayed put in this house, and not ever, am I clear?'

'Thank you, Dot.'

I help her up gently, and give her two strong headache pills. We wobble downstairs. I make some tea, and we sit on the settee.

'I'm so sorry,' she says, taking a cup from my hand.

'What for?'

'Well, landing on you like this. Only I had nowhere else. I wasn't going to be turning up at Mother's, not at four in the morning, or at any other time.'

'No, you did right. I wouldn't have expected you to do anything else.'

'What if he comes looking? He'll guess I'm here.'

'I don't expect he'll have the bottle,' I tell her, 'But if he does, he'll have Dot to contend with, won't he? And, if she doesn't kill him first, she will call the police. Simple. 999, no hesitation. You no longer need fear a thing. Dot'll look after you, protect you. Promise. All right? So then, what happened? D'you want to talk about it?'

'I can't believe it, sure I can't. He came over like a monster.' Jessie's shaking her head in disbelief for a few moments before she explains what happened. 'After you'd gone it was all going lovely, right, we had a good day, yesterday, Boxing Day, we all went for a walk together and Derek treated us all to a pub meal. Then last night I'd cooked him his evening meal and, after, he said he was going out drinking with some mates down the Lion. There was something about him, though, like he was full of anticipation, like you wouldn't be for just a few pints with the lads. He was jiggling up and down, like he was Tim or something before going to the fairground. I didn't like it, it felt wrong, but I thought I was just being stupid.'

'What did you think he was going off to do?'

'Well, Carla crossed my mind of course, I have to admit. But he'd been so long showing himself for the new person he was, it was like the old lack of trust come back to haunt me, and I told myself I was imagining it all, that I could trust him now. I thought, if he is still playing around, why would he've bought me that new carpet an' all? Why'd he have bothered if he wasn't for real with me? Cost him a packet.'

'Guilt perhaps?'

'Yeah, I guess I can see that now. But then I didn't want to believe it. It's amazing what your mind can do with convincing. It can trick you something rotten. I feel such a friggin' fool, sure I do, like I've got moss for brains.'

'You loved him.'

'Well, that's just proves it, an' all.'

'You mustn't torture yourself with all of this. It's already over, you can forget it. Past is past.'

'I can see now why you've always liked to put things well and truly behind you, Dot. That's a good thing that is. Never to dabble in it. I've always tried to get you to find Eliza, or to tell me about Alf Whittaker, but you were right never to. I'm not comparing having a lovely daughter to having a violent lover like Derek, but bad memories are best forgot, her being taken away, it's done, isn't it, there's no turning back. I swear me and the kids are never going to set eyes on that man, if you can call him a man, the rest of my days. Forgiveness out the question. I've done that forgiveness lark and where's it got me?' She pauses. 'I was right, of course, he had gone off fucking Carla again, hadn't he? Say what you will about female intuition, it's bingo every time. He didn't get home till two. I says, "What the fuck time you call this then? The pub closed two hours ago!" He was out of his skull, and he whacked me one on the stomach, kicked my shins, just for that. I stood up again, and he dragged me upstairs, shouting like, just so as to waken the kids up good and proper. Sam came out her room, and saw me being pulled by my hair into our bedroom. She started crying, and he whacked her a few for good measure, but was still holding on to me at arm's length, so I couldn't protect her, I couldn't protect her. "Get back to bed, John Burford's daughter," he's saying, "back to bed, you bitch." '

Jessie starts to cry again as she repeats his words to me, it's a real effort for her to get them out. I lean across to her and take her in my arms. She's weeping and sobbing into my shoulder. I stroke her hair.

'There, there it's all right. Hush now, my love.'

'Then Nat and Tim came out their rooms, crying their little hearts out, and he kicked them both, he fucking kicked them, in the legs, squeezed their arms, and slapped their little faces. I'll never forget the look on them, sheer terror. Never, never, never, it'll haunt me, Dot, the rest of my life.'

'Shhh. Shhh. You're here now.'

'Only can we stay, Dot, till we set ourselves up, find a place? Can we stay?'

'What do you think? Course you can. D'you think I'm going to let you go? You're not going anywhere.'

'But there isn't room for all of us, and we'll be disturbing you. I can't say how long it'll take us to get ourselves sorted, and you like your solitude, your peace and quiet.'

'I'm not so gone on solitude as I was, as it happens,' I admit quietly.

I'm not sure she's taken that in, it's enough just to hear reassuring noises. 'But there's not the beds,' she says, looking up at me. One of her eyes only opens so far.

'We can manage, sort something out, now relax your wee head just a minute, all right? So, do you want to tell me more, get it off your chest?'

'Where was I?' she says. 'Yeah, well, he slams our door closed, doesn't he, pulls his trousers down to his knees. I can still hear the kids wailing in the corridor, and I'm thinking I don't give a shit what he does to me, all I'm wanting is for him to get it over with, whatever it is, so's as I can get to them. I thought he loved them, that's the only reason I put up with him knocking me about a bit, I thought he was a good father to them, and that's the least they deserved. So, anyway, he's got me pinned down on the bed with one arm, right, and the full weight of the rest of his drunken body. With the other hand, he's pulling his Y-fronts halfway down his fat thigh, and trying to get it in me, but it won't go, it's all squashy. I know it's not the drink 'cos drink's not stopped him getting hard in the past. No, it's still soggy from her, that's what it is, like it's covered in snot. I'm sorry, Dot, but that's what I'm thinking as I'm lying there. And I want to throw up in that ugly bastard fat face of his. I'm telling him it's no good, it's as good as raspberry jelly, it never was much better than a choirboy's. I've never said this stuff to him before, I've not had the courage, but this time he got the children, so's I'm going to say anything I fucking well like, and he smashes me in the face. I spit in his eye, an' I call him oyster cock.'

'You didn't? Oh, Jess, sorry, but you've got to laugh.' I put my hand to my lips to suppress a smile.

'Yeah, I thought that was rather good myself. Course, he

doesn't care for it, not one bit, so before I know it, I've earned myself another smash, this eye this time I think.' Jessie stops and puts her forefinger to her left eye, the one that's most swollen. 'By now, as I'm struggling to get from under him – he's not managed to rape me and I know he's not going to, but he's still trying – all's I'm thinking is I want to get to the kids, they're still crying outside our door. Then it opens and out the corner of my eye I can see them standing there, huddled together watching us, and though I'm breathless with his weight on top of me, I'm whispering to them to wait outside, I'll be with them in a minute, Mum's OK, we've just had a bit of an argument, that's all. But Natalie steps forward, "Get off of our mum," she says, and Derek turns round and throws my Jackie Collins at her that's lying on the bedside table. It catches her on the side of the cheek, and little thing, she starts howling, and there's me saying, "It's all right, my poppet, it's all right, Mum's with you in a second", and I'm starting to struggle with all my might, lashing out at him like I wouldn't mind if I killed him in the process. I see Sam comforting her, and Tim approaching us on the bed. "No, no," I say to him, "he'll hurt you." Tim ignores me and starts thumping Derek but, against his bulk, his little fists are like small insects bumping into a windowpane, so they are. It's a sight makes tears as roll down my cheek. "Mum's all right, sweetheart," I say, "go back to your room now, an' I'll be with you in a minute." But he doesn't move, does he, so of course Derek shouts at him, "Do the fuck what your mother says, you little prick," and lashes out, like the worst of cowards. Timmy's only a little kid, so Derek's elbow gives a blow in his wee chest as to knock him sideways, but he rights himself, he doesn't move, he doesn't cry, he just stands there. "Get off of my mum," he says, "get off of her." His face is angry as a grown man's. I think Derek's going to lose his mind with fury, pummel Timmy to bits. He's silent and sneering for a minute, seems like ten, while he's thinking how best to kill him. You coulda cut the tension like butter. Then by some miracle, he slowly sits up. I catch my breath. "I don't want her anyway," he shouts. "She's a worthless whore and a crap fuck. You can have her for all I care." '

'I can't believe I'm hearing this.'

'I manage to escape, and sweep Tim up in my arms and out the room without another word. I daren't, because I don't want the children to hear what I've got to say, and I don't want Derek's reaction. I look back to see him flopped on his side in a stupor, completely out of it, he looks like one of those dead pigs you sometimes see inside open butchers' vans. I rush in to Sam and Natalie and help them to gather a few things, a few clothes, favourite teddy or toy, and that's it, we're off, no more messing. I grab as much as I can into a suitcase. He's already snoring but I'm still like shitting myself he's going to awaken any minute. The children are still whimpering. "Where we going, Mum?" they keep asking, and when I tell them Auntie Dot's, they all stop crying, just like that, it's like the pain's gone because they're so frightened and so excited. Course, I can't find the car keys, I'm searching high and low, but eventually I do, they're in the fruit bowl in the kitchen, and we're out that door and into the car before you can say knife. And on the way down here, I made up my mind never to go back, right, except to organise the sale of the house and the salon, and to collect our things, but apart from that, not ever. Start a new life completely. A new person. Never see him again.'

'It's for the best,' I say.

'Never to see any other men again for that matter.'

'Well, you don't have to think about that just yet.'

'No, Dot, I mean it, I've decided for good and all. I can do without the lot of the frigging bastards for good, that's it.' She laughs. 'Jessie's days of romancing are well and truly over. She's going to follow her sister Dot's example. She's going to be renouncing them from here on in, embracing the quiet no-nonsense life. She's going to become a nun. I've got myself three beautiful kids, what more can a woman want?'

'We'll see how it goes,' I tell her. 'When you're over Derek, and your circumstances have changed, you never know, someone nice might come along.'

'You don't believe me, do you?'

'Well, it's early days yet. You would be feeling like this on the very day you've come out of a long-term relationship. So unhappily at that.'

'Not unhappily, Dot, that's where you're wrong. Very happily. True as we're sat on this settee, I'm already over Derek. Course I will never forgive him for what he did to my kids, and there's nothing as can ever console me about that, and if it takes the rest of my life, I'm going to try to erase any scars it may have left on them. But it may be that there's one positive thing that's come out of all this. The moment he laid his hands on Sam, I stopped loving him. When he'd hit me in the past, it hadn't worked. As you know full well, I was always taken in by his contrition, and would go running back for more. But not when he hit my children, oh no, that's different. At that moment, love for him flipped over to hate, just like that, easy as a coin. It was that moment I knew I was going to leave him, no matter whether he took me into that bedroom and begged forgiveness on his knees, or whether he raped me. So of the two it was rape − correction, attempted rape − but that wasn't what decided me. It was just before that, when he did what he did to Samantha, and a few moments after when he did what he did to Nat and Tim, that's what confirmed it. He can come down here if he wants ranting his arse off and threatening more violence, or he can offer me all the roses Covent Garden's got selling for a year, and I'll be turning my back on him for real, Dot, no more going back, I can promise you that from here.' She places her hand on her heart. 'Do you believe me?'

'I believe you.'

'I don't even think we need talk about it ever again,' she says, 'never mention his name, even. Now you know everything that's happened. Jessie was a fool for ever staying with him. Perhaps she had her foolish reasons. Thought him a good dad, and the idea of romantic love, despite everything, seemed to prevail, but not any more it doesn't, and now there's no more to discuss. She's down here for good.'

'Stoneham really is to become your home then?' I ask.

'You thought I was joking you?'

'I thought it might've been the heat of the moment.'

'No, Dot, I'm decided.'

'Well, you being here, it'll be the best thing. If for nothing else, we've got Derek to thank for that.'

'If you manage to get it in before you kill him first!' Jessie says laughing.

'OK,' I smile, 'now, let's not think about it any more for today. We'll wake the kids at dinnertime, have some sandwiches, and go for a walk on the beach, how about that? We've to let them forget about last night. The fresh air and the sand is a good way to start. And over the next few days, you and I, we can work out practicalities.'

Jessie nods with enthusiasm, grateful that I am taking over for the time being, putting some order and security back in her life.

'I'm gonna get the house and the salon on the market as soon as possible,' she says, 'so we don't have to be under your feet too long. Though with the property market as it is, I'm worried they won't sell quickly.'

'I don't care how long they take to shift, you are never under my feet, Jess. I like you here, I like the company.'

We get up and go to the kitchen. Jessie sits at the table while I make sandwiches. She insists on helping, but I won't let her, I tell her to relax. I've a loaf of white bread, some tomatoes, a bit of Cheddar, and a few slices of ham. Jessie watches, mesmerised, and saying nothing, as I slice the tomatoes very thin.

'What're you thinking?' I ask.

'I'm thinking, you never told me where you were last night. You weren't at the hospital, I checked. Where were you?'

'I stayed the night at Harold's,' I reply.

'Dot, you didn't!' Her voice is still wobbly, and she's a sort of lisp because she's unable to move her puffball lips as well she might, but nonetheless there's something of the old spirited Jessie I can detect, the Jessie that's always loved gossip, and wanted her Dot to find a fellah. 'You never said.'

'You weren't in any state to hear. I wasn't exactly going to start telling you about my love life the minute you turn up here having escaped your own within an inch of your life! I'm not sure it's appropriate to start talking about it even now.'

'Don't be so ridiculous. Not appropriate, my arse. Whyever not? Tell me.'

So as I'm sat here making the sandwiches, I tell her about everything, from the moment I got back from hers, went straight to the hospital, learned of Stevie's tragic death, and spent the night sitting up with Kelly. I'm telling her everything because, being our Jessie, she's insisting on all the detail. I even tell her that Harold told me he loves me.

'So did you do it with him, then?'

'That's not a very nice way of putting it,' I protest.

'You know what I mean. Well, did you?'

'Yes.'

'You did?' She gives me a hug. 'Oh, Dot, I'm so happy it's all worked out for you.'

'Well, let's not speak too soon, shall we? But the signs are very promising.'

'What was it like? The sex?'

'I can't tell you that, that's private,' I tell her. I suppose when something like this happens to a woman, other women expect her to give even the most intimate details. I of all people should know that. As for me, though in the past week or so I've given away more about myself to my colleagues and Jessie than ever I have before, I can only go so far.

'Aw, come on, Dot.'

'No,' I smile. 'I'm shy about these things. I'd not partaken for thirty-three years, remember, and then it was only the once.'

'It was brilliant, right? Just say that.'

I've finished spreading the marge on the bread so put down the knife. 'Oh, all right, cheeky monkey.'

'So was it?'

'Yes,' I say, beginning to lay the ham on the separate slices.

'Better than you could have possibly hoped for, ever?'

'That's enough now, Jess, enough said.'

'Ah, you're a bore,' she laughs. 'Are you going to move in with him, get married?'

'Give the poor man a chance, it only happened last night.'

'Yeah, but when you're your age, there's no point in hanging about, is there? You grab the moment if you've got any sense.'

'We'll see.'

'Don't tell me you don't think there's any point in getting married at your age.'

'I didn't say any such thing. Oi, pass me the cheese. There's plenty of point in getting married, any age.'

'Good, I'm glad you said that.' Jessie hands me the packet of Cheddar. 'Well, this is a funny turn-up for the books, Dot. Talk about roles reversing. Just as it's my turn to become the nun, you've found you're in love with a lovely man who's in love with you. Funny, innit? We can each carry on where the other's left off.'

'Don't speak too soon.'

'Look, the man loves you, Dot. And he's no Derek, he's not one of Jessie's specials. He's a good and kind and honourable man, got integrity. A woman knows she can trust Harold. She can tell by his face.'

'How can you be so sure?' I ask.

'Aw, come on, you know as well as I do,' she replies.

I nod. 'Yes.'

'And as I was saying earlier,' she adds, 'it's female intuition: bingo, every time. I think it'll be wedding bells before you know it.'

'Hold your horses!'

'Well, certainly if me and the kids are here for too long. You'll be glad of a place down the road to move into to get away from all of us. If it means your moving into his, I'll have no compunction about displacing you from your own home.'

'Thank you very much. You're a laugh, Jess, you know that? Spot of romance in the air, and you're like a teenager all over again.'

'For me, no. For you, yes. Your turn's come, and I want you to be every bit as happy as I was trying to be all these years. You've been rewarded for your waiting.'

'Only I wasn't waiting, far as I was aware.'

'But you'd never given up hope?'

'No, I suppose not, unconsciously, at least, I suspect I never gave up hope.'

'I didn't think so.' Jessie claps her hands together. 'I never thought so.'

'Now, you set to cutting up those sandwiches,' I tell her, reaching for the breadboard. 'And by the way, when you say I've been rewarded for waiting, you're not to think that your upsets with men were a kind of punishment for experimenting. Experimenting was just another way of looking, of waiting, hoping each one as came along might be the right one. There's nothing wrong with that.'

'Didn't do much good, though, did it?' she asks.

'Yes, it did: it taught you the value of what you want now, a bit of time of being by yourself.'

'Took long enough, eh, and a lot of heartbreak along the way. I should've listened to wise old Dot years back.'

'Here, give them over, you're doing a rotten job of cutting them up.' I take the sandwiches off her. 'And look who's now being the hypocrite.'

'You're never a hypocrite, Dot. I think you have to be happy in yourself before you're ready to fall in love, and to have someone fall in love with you.'

'That's the accepted modern theory, I agree. Maybe I'm sticking my neck out a bit here, but I happen to think it's nonsense.'

'You do?'

'Yes,' I tell her. 'I think you can only be truly happy when you love someone who loves you. I don't believe you can be properly happy without. I don't think I was ever properly happy as I'm going to be now I know the man I love loves me. There are those who say it's dangerous to depend on someone else for your happiness because anything might happen to that and then where would you be? Frankly, I say bollocks to that, to coin your phrase. Happiness can be snuffed out any time, or it can last for ever. The chances of survival are equal whether it's coming from inside, or with a little help from someone else. Happiness is happiness no matter where it's coming from, and it's different for all people. I happen to believe it's best with someone else.'

'Oh, that's great, that is, just when I've made this mammoth decision, based on your beliefs I may say, that I want to be alone at last, sort myself out.'

'And there's nothing wrong with that. But, Jess, if I may be honest and say so, you've always been alone. That's not being cruel to say that. That's just to say you've never loved someone who really loves you, you've never been truly with somebody, if you get my meaning.'

'Like you with Harold?'

'I suppose so, if that doesn't sound arrogant of me. After just a few hours, who am I to speak? But you do know when you just know. Hours, days, weeks, months, even years under your belt with that person are immaterial. You can just know, as they say, right away.'

'I've never just known, Dot.'

'I know, my love, so in a sense you've been waiting just the same as me. Only difference is now you've decided to do a different kind of waiting, my kind, unencumbered by men who you know in your heart of hearts are not right, the compromises, the ones who aren't kind enough, or who knock you about. And, yes, you'll be happy to be away from Derek, starting a new life in Stoneham, but I'm not going to pretend to you that's it's going to be easy. You'll miss the excitement of going out with men.'

'No, I won't.'

'OK, maybe not, at first.' I tell her. 'I don't deny it'll be a relief for a time. But being on your own is something you have to grapple with. You may not realise it as you're doing it, but loneliness is something you're fighting off every day, or, rather, keeping it in check. It's tough, hard work.'

'I'll have the kids, and you.'

'Course you will, and we'll always be there. Only remember, you've never not been with a man, practically all your adult life.'

'And I'm not looking either.'

'Not actively any more, no.'

'You're telling me I can't be happy, just me?' she asks.

'No, I'm saying, it won't be all roses by yourself.'

'I know that.'

'And that you'll be happier when you do find the one with whom you just know it's right.'

'Well, I'm not gagging for it.'

'Precisely,' I say, 'and that's what's good, that's what in your favour. You can do without, but you'd be happier with. It's better than can't do without, be happier with a bastard.'

'You're right, Dot.'

'I don't mean to be harsh, Jess. I'm just saying the single life isn't the ball you might be expecting, that's all. Though I'm going to do my best to make sure it's near enough for you.'

Jessie thanks me and smiles. She swears a bit at the pain of moving her disfigured face. 'Oi, ducks,' she then says, 'we'll wake the kids in a minute. First give us one of them sandwiches, they bloody took you long enough, and I'm starving.' Cautiously she bites into one. 'Wow, Dot, that's delicious. I'd watch out if I were you, standards as good as this, we'll be staying put for good.'

As we laugh, she suddenly seems to forget that her whole head is hurting.

Chapter Fifteen

The story of how I left Piccadilly for good is Jessie's favourite. Every time she wants cheering up, or to do a bit of forgetting, she asks me to tell her that story like she's a young girl wanting to hear her favourite fairy tale or something. I must've told it her a thousand times. Now she's doing it again, asking it of me, for her and Harold, and because she doesn't want us dwelling on her troubles I'm happy to oblige.

The day's over and the children are back in bed. They loved our walk on the beach this afternoon, they love this place, seemed to forget their aches and traumas of last night. I'm not saying they're not holding things inside them, but with Jessie's motherly protection and devotion, and a completely fresh start, there's the best possible chance the damage they sustained from the experience can eventually be erased. Jessie and I have just been up to take a peek at them, and they all three are sleeping soundly, thank God, no nightmares. They are beautiful.

One of my colleagues on the team, Dolores, was kind enough to swap shifts with me, so I've tonight off after all, and tomorrow on instead. I thought it was important not to leave Jessie on her own tonight. It was she who insisted I ask Harold round, for my sake, of course, but also partly because, even though she's only met him briefly, she knew he's the type whose very presence is comforting. (The gift he brought us was just that too: comfort food in the form of a box of fondant fancies. 'Bingo,' said Jessie when he produced them; rightly touching it was, like she'd never known a man to get it so spot on.) So it is the three of us are sat here in my wee kitchen, enjoying a light meal of soup and bread, and a few dainty Mrs Topley's cakes fit to lift anyone's spirits.

My kitchen is not much bigger than Harold's. The walls are white brick, the floor cork tiles. There's a blue glass lamp I found in a junk shop hung low over the plain wooden table. It's a table not accustoned to company. I'm usually sat on the settee in my robe and slippers with a tray meal in front of the telly. Occasionally one of my colleagues might come round of an evening for a bite to eat, and even then we tend to eat off our laps next door. It's very rare the table has people at it for a meal. Having Jessie and Harold sat here, though, it feels like the most natural thing in the world. I'm that joyful, them here, I've had to take off my cardy. I may be going on fifty-three, but tonight I'm as hot and glowing as a pregnant woman.

'Dot started a riot,' Jessie's telling him proudly as I'm serving the leek and potato soup. 'Can you believe that?'

'I don't look the type, do I?' I laugh.

'I remember Priscilla saying something about you being a rioter,' Harold says 'and I have to admit I was rather surprised. Impressed, I may say, as well.'

'Go on, Dot, tell us what happened.' Jessie's face, though yellow, blue and purple with bruises and wounds, somehow flushes with anticipation.

I place the saucepan in the sink and sit down to eat and talk. 'It's a long story, Harold,' I warn him, but he isn't deterred. He nods his encouragement.

After the attempted escaped, I tell them, which was over seven years into my time there, Bel and I we were laid low for many months. We were in isolation for three weeks, and on bread and water rations for many more. Bread and water's like a cliché punishment, isn't it, I mean it's the one most parents have been known to threaten their kids with at one point or other. Only they don't on the whole carry it out, because however provoked and angry they might be, it's just too cruel.

Bel and me, we were weakened and we never even spoke about getting out after that, not for a long time. I don't think our resolve left us, I just don't think we had the energy to put it to any good use. I'm not entirely certain what it was eventually changed that, but I have my theories.

If you can imagine, our access to the outside world was limited, to say the least. Visitors were allowed rarely, but there weren't many of us who had folk who could afford, or even wanted to make the trip. Some's didn't have folk at all, their entire family had cut off ties completely for shame. It doesn't seem possible today.

Almost all the families of the girls who'd fallen away wanted nothing more to do with them. Getting pregnant outside wedlock, that's what it was known as at Piccadilly, falling away. It's a lovely phrase I always thought, biblical sounding almost. Falling Away. Pity so often it gave rise to such unchristian consequences, such lack of joy at a new life, such wanting of imagination or understanding, such punishment, such heartlessness. Some families severed contact with their daughters even if they'd done absolutely nothing wrong, like Bel, just existed, only their existence didn't quite conform. These ones were treated with all the due disrespect and cruelty of those who'd actually fallen away, and they were just as much clientele for spurning.

Although we could receive as many letters as came, lots of the girls had no one to write to them. I only had Jessie, really, and Beth spasmodically, as my parents weren't great for putting pen to paper. I don't think they had anything to say. I suppose I got one or two from them all the time I was there. Father's was all about what he'd sold in the shop that week.

Films were all religious, or made in the forties or fifties so hardly constituted a pertinent reflection of our times. There was no television to watch. Even if there had been, we'd only have been permitted to see programmes of a holy nature. As I say, books weren't allowed, and the contraband ones were rubbish, unreadable, so all the reading I've done's been since I left. When I got out I consumed books like I wolfed Mars bars. On Sundays we could read old copies of *People's Friend*. Sounds like a Communist Party pamphlet, but it was rural country magazine, very tame, and even then anything deemed remotely racy was cut out before it got to us. About all's we could get out of it were recipes for hotpot, and the Help page was full of life-threatening agonies like, I can't get hold of this particular type of wool, please can you advise me where I might purchase it?

It's hardly a wonder the sixties passed us by unannounced. But I do remember the new year, 1970. Bel and I had been very subdued for twelve months or so following our escape attempt. We'd stuck together as we always had but I think we'd more or less accepted our fate and were just getting on with what we were made to do. But, as I say, I don't think our resolve ever entirely deserted us.

It's rebirth, I think, might have been partly to do with the dawning of the seventies. A whiff of the feel of the new decade must have passed through to us somehow – an overheard word from some of the outside workers about music or fashions, or what they did with their boyfriends (without incrimination); a letter from a teenage Jessie awakening to hippie values; the unintentional slipping of a film made post-1955 through the strict staff censorship; the sudden appearance in a *People's Friend* of an improbable knitting pattern with a smiley face or a great big flower with floppy petals.

But perhaps more significant was the fact that in the last few months of 1969, maybe even a bit before that, new girls didn't seem to be arriving at Piccadilly any more. Unconsciously, I think we started asking ourselves why that was. Could it be girls weren't being wayward, or not falling away any more these days? Obviously not. Girls have been so-called wayward, and have got pregnant out of marriage since time immemorial, why should the seventies be any different? Perhaps society was becoming more tolerant? We never actually said this out, I don't think any of us could've articulated it as such, it was just a feeling in our bones which seemed to spell good news for us of some sort, we knew not how.

So the atmosphere was ripe for us.

I think, though, the crucial kick-start to Bel's and my dormant resolve, the thing which actually prompted us to take action again was less romantic: the attitude at Piccadilly to bowel movements and menstruation. It was this, I'm afraid, which suddenly got too much for us to bear.

The fact was, the staff had an almost obsessive fascination with the body workings of their inmates. I don't know if it was some sort of vampire-like or scatological fixation they mysteriously shared, but I do know there were two big red books which had to be filled in every day by the matron. In one, detailed descriptions of that morning's bowel movements. I say that morning's because that was the time it was deemed best for us to evacuate them, none other, and if our bowels didn't conform, then they had to be trained to do so. Woe betide anyone who didn't 'go' before morning work began. There was no second chances for twenty-four hours, you'd just have to hold it in till the next morning.

'Tough shit, as they say,' laughs Jessie. 'Unbelievable, innit?'

The other book was called Menstruation. I suppose their theory was that our cycles had constantly to be checked for any irregularities, I mean it was wayward girls they were dealing with here, and they could never be trusted. Quite who they thought we couldn't be trusted with, with barely a man within ten miles of the place, is testimony to the extent to which their earnest imaginations could run away with them.

In keeping with the general attitude to bodily functions, and having them all out in the open, as it were, there was a job known as Sanitary Towel Duty. After the escape, I'd immediately been put on STD. This was the lowest of the low, but whichever girl was in the greatest trouble, she had to stay on this duty till another eclipsed her in terms of sin. There weren't many sins as beat attempted escape. So Bel and I, we alternated doing the STs for many a grim month. I think we broke all records for the longest ever in the history of Piccadilly to be on this gruesome duty. Certainly it felt pretty permanent to me.

Modern times were slow to reach Piccadilly Park, and modern methods of feminine hygiene even slower. Sanitary towels were made of a square sponge literally covered in a piece of (once) white towel, and STD involved washing each one by hand on the washboard. Cleaner – I won't say we ever got rid of the stains of blood, so they were never actually what you could call clean – they were for use by the girls who next started to menstruate. I mean, there weren't even your own with your name on that you alone were responsible for. No, they were shared, and it was the role of whoever was on ST duty to see to it they were all washed. We had lockers in our dormitories, which was an irony, because none of us had a single personal possession between us, it was against the philosophy of the place. We'd not even a bleeding sanitary towel, forgive the pun, to call our very own. Since getting out I've perhaps seen more than my fair share of female blood but, back in my laundry days, even though midwifery was my ambition, there was nothing so disgusting and demeaning as cleaning sanitary towels, soiled by myself or other people. I don't think there's a former Piccadilly girl alive who doesn't bless the invention and availability of the tampon.

At such times as Bel and I could ever snatch to be alone, we discussed our horror of the duty we'd been bound to do for so long. We may have been packed away inside for some long years, for reasons that would forever remain unjust, but this was a task, we felt, out of centuries past, and certainly not fit for the latter part of the twentieth. I don't know why this, of all the practices at Piccadilly, some more inhumane than STD, so goaded us into revolutionary fervour. Looking back I see it as the final assault on our womanhood, something so basic and crude and degrading that it was completely natural it came to the point we could take it no more. We were going to put a stop to our having to carry out this unspeakable task once and for all.

Talk of escape, that is the two of us escaping together again, was useless for obvious reasons. If our luck was to be in a second time, and we managed to get away through the gates, we'd still have nowhere to run to. Bel's Aunt Mary hadn't betrayed us, but hers wasn't the guaranteed safe house we'd last time believed it to be. No, the talk turned to more drastic measures.

Riot. Full-scale riot.

It was the only way possible to overcome the fierce, fifteen-strong staff, and successfully to breach the heavy security in place for those unfortunate 'mental patients' upstairs, as well as for us.

Bel and I knew we needed two things. First, the support of the entire laundry group, with no question of grassers. We knew those upstairs couldn't help us – most of them were probably in strait-jackets, heavily drugged, locked in solitary cells, or all three, but we were definitely doing it for them too. We planned, if we succeeded in gaining our own freedom, to campaign on their behalf. Our second objective was to get our stories to the press so as to cause a public outcry. The signs of the seventies wafting through to us, and our own intuition, as I say, told us the climate outside was changing. It was a subtle thing, I can't entirely put my finger on it. We'd somehow got that the barbaric, Dickensian incarceration of innocent young women was no longer flavour of the month in this newer, more liberal society. If it was society stopping any more women from coming in, then maybe society had turned its leaf to be on our side, it would lobby for freedom on our behalf? But only if we forced an opportunity to remind them there was some of us in here since long ago, ones they'd maybe forgotten about.

I can't say we thought it through as complicated as that. All I can say for sure is we knew we had to stage a riot, and that we'd have to run and run and not stop till we had found some local journalists who could spread the word. That was basis enough for us on which to concoct a plan.

I've got this far and we've finished our meal. I ask Jessie and Harold if they'd like to have a coffee, go next door, sit soft, take a breather. I boil the coffee and put some cups out. Jessie complains the kettle's taking its time, she wants us to settle in the living room without further ado so as to hear the end of her fairy story. I shoo her through, saying it'll only be a minute, be patient, you silly old thing, you're as bad as the kids. Harold lingers near me and the coffee things, and as he picks up the tray to carry it for me, he reassures me he's all ears, he's loving my story.

I thank him.

'Dot,' he whispers, 'I've something to ask you. I don't want Jessie to hear yet in case she's horrified, but you know there's a bed at my house, any time, don't you, if it's too squashed for all of you here?'

'That's very kind,' I say, touched by his generosity, 'but I think it might be rather noisy for you, your house full of children.'

'No, you've misunderstood my meaning,' Harold says, 'though, of course they're all welcome anytime. No, what I meant was, you. You, Dot. I mean, I think you should stay with her for a while, just till she gets less frightened. But when you're both ready, you're very welcome to come and stay with me as long as you like, you know that, don't you?'

'Oh, Harold that's such a kind offer, it'll make me cry.' I'd lifted the kettle to fill the cups, but had to put it down again.

'Oh, no, it's not meant to do that at all.' He puts the tray down too, steps towards me, and puts his arms round me. 'When you're ready, Dot, I know it's so very soon, and it's a lot to think about, but if you wanted to move in with me – for whatever reasons, for Jessie's, or for you own – well. Damn it, Dot, I no longer want to be a man of procrastination. And call it what you will – lack of room here and simple pragmatism, or love, I don't care – would you consider moving in with me? Forgive what you might regard as presumption on my part, and undue haste, but I prefer to think of it as seizing the moment, you see. Too many moments frittered away in the past! After all these years, my love, I'm damned if I'm not going to seize the moment.'

'Oi, you two, that coffee's taking a helluva long time to boil, what're you doing in there? I'm itching for the end of the story.'

It's Jessie, impatient as ever. Harold and I answer her beck and call. He's carrying the tray behind me, but I can feel the glow of his smile on my back, and Jessie can't fail to see the size of mine.

'So what've you both been plotting then?' she asks.

We tell her of our practical plan which just so happens neatly to fit in with that of love. In a few days' time, when Jessie's ready to let me go and not before, I'm going to be moving into Harold's. I've accepted.

She leaps up from the settee and gives me a tight hug in as far as her bruises and injuries will allow. She says that's just wonderful, that is, she's overjoyed for us both. That's typical of our Jessie, that is, her mind's genuinely thinking of our pleasure over and above her convenience. She knows it's not really to do with her. Her circumstances just served as the excuse.

'Permanent, then?' she asks.

'Well,' Harold answers, 'that's the idea. It all might seem to have come about rather fast, but Dot tells me she's no doubts, none at all, and that's exactly the same as me.'

'Ah,' says Jessie, 'that's lovely.'

'Depending on what we all feel's for the best,' Harold continues, 'and what you want, Dot and I might move back here, if she feels she's missing her home. Then, if need be, you and the children can go to mine for as long as you like, or till you find something you like better. I don't mind giving my house up if it means being with this one.' Harold looks over to me.

'Ooh,' says Jessie, 'I've got to sit down, I'm all overcome.'

She has a habit, our Jess, of saying just the right things. Harold and I sit down too.

'OK,' he says, 'I think that's all settled. So now, Dot, my love, do you fancy finishing the story? I think Jessie and I've waited long enough.'

'Happy to,' I say, and so continue.

I think troubling Bel and me more than how on earth we were going to find all these journalists we were depending on, was how we were going to encourage the other girls to side with us to fight our cause. Some of them were so institutionalised it was going to be a job boosting them to action. But Bel and I, we made it our objective. The more institutionalised the girl, the more of a challenge it was to try to convert her to our way of thinking.

It was a systematic form of lobbying we went in for. We assigned ourselves fifteen or so girls each, and gave ourselves a day of working on each one. Remember, there was very little talking allowed, so a day concentrating on one girl wasn't as much as it sounds.

Jesus, with some of them it was nigh on impossible trying to get them round to the plan. Bel's methods of persuasion were more effective than mine. She had more charm on her, that woman, than someone that's learned it off pat at public school. She even had Melanie Chambers working up an enthusiasm by the evening, and Melanie Chambers was so thick with Miss Beveridge, she even got to sit on high table one night and eat special food with the staff. Melanie Chambers had not once in her whole three years at Piccadilly been given a punishment. Unheard of! In that place, even goodie-goodies got punished at times.

To this day, I don't know for sure what Bel can have done to her. When I asked her, she tapped her nose and said, 'If all else fails, Dot, let's face it, blackmail's always a winner.' Bel had a talent for never missing a trick and, because of this resourcefulness, she had masterful weapons which at the perfect moment she could employ to brilliant effect. There was a rumour going round that in secret Melanie used to stroke Miss Salter's breasts (Miss Salter was one of the matrons). I suspect it came from Bel, she'd actually spotted them one evening in the uniform cupboard or something, and it was this would explain Melanie's extraordinary turnabout – Bel threatened to expose them to Miss Beveridge.

Conversion of all thirty girls was a slow process. Some were easily persuadable – unhappiness and frustration are the traditional keys to rebellion, and there was no shortage of either of them. With the majority of girls it was quite easy. Most seemed to convert with anything ranging from mild reluctance and fear, to huge enthusiasm and willingness to do all they could to fight the cause. The latter looked upon Bel and me as like great Scottish heroes in history or something. Joy Macleod, who neither Bel nor I could stand because she was so eager to please and be in with us – aren't damaged young women so unforgiving? – even called Bel Bonnie Princess Charlie. When Bel told me that we put our fingers down our throats and made yuk noises, but at the time Joy said it Bel had had to pretend she was flattered – we both knew the value of support, from wherever it came.

I found only about two or three girls really hard work. Unlike Bel, I had no grounds on which to blackmail them, so I simply threatened them instead. This wasn't very Dot-like behaviour, I know, but needs must for survival, and it's surprising what you'll resort to when you have to. I was strong. I had muscles from years on the callender machine, and lifting them heavy gas irons every day. Weedy Pauline Bishop and Sheena North didn't stand a chance when I told them if they didn't co-operate, I'd put their heads down the toilets and hold them there. Or I'd pin them down and burn their earlobes with matches so if they ever did get out of there they'd never be able to wear pretty earrings again. The first practice was quite common, girls with grudges tended to do that to their enemies on occasion, but I ask myself now, where did the ears one come from? It was so particulary vicious, detailed, female vicious, I can't think now how I could ever have had the mind to think it up. I'd rather not, actually. It reminds me of quite how desperate I must have been.

For better of for worse, anyway, it worked. Within three weeks – some took longer than a day – Bel and I had got the whole damn lot of them to agree, even the hardies Melanie Chambers, Pauline Bishop, Sheena North, and all. Honestly I think that was the hardest part. As long as we could manage to contain the plan, the escape itself would be a doddle in comparison: safety in numbers. It was essential during the lobbying period that none of the newly converted would leak our plan. I'm afraid to say the upkeep of blackmail and threats by ourselves and our more ardent followers like Joy effectively saw to that. Miraculously, nobody grassed. There must have been ever such a *frisson* with Melanie on the occasions she stroked Miss Salter's breasts after she'd been roped into the impending riot, knowing that their thrilling nocturnal comings-together were soon doomed to come to an end. That's a cruel thought I know, but nothing gave Bel and me more pleasure than to think one nice side-effect of our plan was going to be the wrenching apart of this distasteful coupling (not distasteful because they were two women, mind, more because they were two such despicable ones).

There was to be no hanging about. After the very last girl had been canvassed, there was no reason why the riot couldn't take place almost immediately. In fact, it was crucial that it did to reduce the risk of detection to a minimum.

The plan itself was incredibly simple. The night before Bel and I were ready, we would let each girl know of it, and the next morning it would take place at the midday meal. If any of them were to discuss it between themselves, Bel and I would kick them very hard with our clumsy shoes, in the shins. (This had a name for it, it was called shinning.) There was no need for discussion, the rules were completely straightforward. At precisely 12.15 on the chosen afternoon, just when we'd said grace, we'd all rise up and throw our plates of food at the dining-room windows till they broke, and if the crockery wasn't strong enough to do the trick, then we'd use anything that did do the job – chairs, tables, whatever it took to smash them so we could escape.

It may have seemed foolish to stage the riot under the very eyes of the staff, but really we had little choice. The dining-room windows were the only ones in the whole building we had any chance of getting out of – they were the only ones not covered in unyielding wire-mesh. Had we all tried to escape in a riotous throng from the laundry packing-room door, those bitch outside workers would've chased after us, caught us, and brought us straight back again to be skinned alive, or whatever treat was in store for rioters. As it was, the staff who were sat at high table were all in their middle years – around my age now, I suppose, though they seemed ancient, and battleaxes. They weren't fit to run after strong young girls down hill and cross dale. The breasts Melanie Chambers used lovingly to stroke were so huge they'd've made a bolster look like a pincushion, and would've completely obliterated any idea of their owner breaking into a trot, let alone the sprint required to keep up with all of us.

So, anyway, the much-anticipated day arrived, 11 November 1970, and the said hour dawned. We all had bread on our plates with a stinking spread. That was our dinner that day, as most days, and though we never got to eat it that time I'm happy to say, I'll never forget the look of mine. The fish paste was drier than usual, particularly crusty and grey. This is what things were like at the laundry, it may sound exaggerated, but I'm true as my word. I remember feeling so sick with nerves, I thought the rank stench of the paste was actually going to topple me, I was going to throw up on the spot, all over the shop, there and then. Certainly I retched, but I held the vomit back, it's disgusting to say this, but I shoved it back down my throat. Nothing was going to interfere with and scotch our plan, not even the force of nature.

Anyway, once we'd said our truly thankfuls, Bel was as good as her word, and shouted the command. You can't imagine, after the years of silence and whispers, the sheer impact of that, 'Go, go, go!', it was such a sound as would've blasted us all by itself even if we hadn't been intending to act. I can still hear it in my ears, the power of it's not ever left me.

The next bit, perhaps the most important, I'm annoyingly vague about, I'm so sorry. Adrenalin and elation numb the senses in a way any alcoholic drink manufacturer would make millions if he were to pinpoint the formula. They say brides spend the most important day of their life so overcome that, even as soon as their honeymoon, they've nothing but the haziest recollection of the wedding. The riot was every bit as significant a moment in my life for me as a wedding day is for a bride, and of course I can't be specific about it just the same. It was too much to take in. All's I can remember is an overwhelming chaos in that room that day, of noise and movement, and excitement. Excitement's not something you can hear or see like you can noise and movement, but, my God, excitement like that, you can feel it all right, it's so tangible it's like you could pick it up and package it.

You would have thought, strong as we were, we'd have not had the strength to throw tables and chairs at the windows so as to break the panes, but oh yes we did, no worries. Once Bel and I and one or two others started, the rest were quickly incited to follow. Then in whole bunches we scrambled out the vast spaces made in the glass in such a fever we didn't give a fig for cutting our hands and knees. I was the last out, seeing to it all the others made it, and I do remember, standing on the stone sill just before I fled, looking back inside and seeing this scene of rigid mayhem, and the gobsmacked faces of our tormentors who were standing, gaping, immobile and useless with shock.

Running outside into the grounds we were hysterical, hysterics shooting off this way and that, some in groups, some alone, charging wherever our legs would carry us, all directions, our pinafores flapping in the gusts of wind. It was the blowsiest of days, even the trees, bare of leaves, were bending like eager women doing sideways stretches in an aerobics class. Most of us were choking as we ran, not from anything but the sheer shock of fresh air into our stale lungs, first time in years. Honest to God, some of them near enough had the bends.

Even when we got down the hill to the road we kept on running. There were a few buildings not so far away, and unfamiliar-looking cars passing, and people were beginning to gather to watch this dramatic breakout. We were in such an exposed place, I'm sure we could be seen from some distance away. We must have been an extraordinary sight, all these women gone wild across the landscape. Maybe some had come to watch because they'd heard our screams.

It all happened so fast. I lost Bel. When I got through the gates and reached the road, I found I was alone. The girls running nearest me were still a good few yards away. Some going this way, some going that. Cars were slowing down. Some of the girls, Joy was one, were actually flagging them down. There were drivers amongst them that ignored them, others that stopped, wound down their windows but drove on, and one or two let the girls in, then sped away.

Bel and I hadn't worked out the details of what we'd actually do when we did get out. I don't think we knew how we were going to find the journalists we had in mind who were going to spread the word, splash our story on their front pages, and save us. I suppose we'd just hoped one might be walking his dog nearby at the time. Foolish really, but perhaps we knew the solution would have to come to us in the heat of the moment, on our feet as it were, that that was something we couldn't plan till we got out there. It was lucky for us cars were driving by, and people living in places not so far away had somehow been made aware of and come to see the commotion going on up at the park.

Two drivers rejected me. One that stopped to hear my hasty and garbled explanation through his window didn't want to get involved, he said, but wished me good luck all the same. I would've thrown a brick after him had I not thought I might actually kill him if I did so. Such violence in me then, but that's what Piccadilly had done to me, made me into a hooligan.

Just as he sped off, I heard police sirens approaching and saw the arrival of at least four panda cars which started chasing all the girls frantically near to them. One or two screeched to a halt and men in sharper uniforms than ours leapt out and began going crazy to catch us. All the while I was madly hailing a third driver, knowing this was my last chance, and she stopped, bless her, opened a door, hauled me in, and zoomed off faster than I knew speed existed. It turned out she lived close. She recognised our uniform and knew all about our predicament, didn't need any explanations.

This woman was young, maybe thirty or so, and was wearing jeans with colourful embroidered patches, was smoking a cigarette, and playing this amazing singsong music with the words all easygoing and about love.

'Come with me, lass,' she said, and with no prompting from me she drove straight into the centre of Glasgow and to the nearest newspaper office. As she did so, she kept repeating how sorry she was she couldn't have gathered more of us up, only she was scared the police would get her and we'd all be sent back, it was better to save even the one.

I needn't say how surprised I was. I couldn't comprehend it, any of it. I hadn't seen real life for a full nine years. Remember, I hadn't seen anything of what I was seeing now when Bel and I had escaped the time before – we'd travelled to her Aunt Mary's in the back of a windowless van, and on the bus on the way back to Piccadilly the windows had been so steamed up with condensation we might as well have been at the bottom of the deep blue sea. I couldn't comprehend the new world I was seeing in the form of modern shops, and cars, and the dress of the people on the streets. Nor could I quite comprehend that my knight in shining armour should turn out to be a straggly redhead who wore clogs for shoes, and went by the name of Sandra.

Harold is shaking his head. He's saying it's incredible, extraordinary, and that he's panting to hear how it turned out. It's gratifying to have such an interest. It's so long ago now, and most the story so familiar in my mind, I feel pleased that someone – other than Jessie – has sufficient fascination to hear me out.

Well, anyway, Sandra left me on the door of the newspaper office. She didn't want to come in with me, she said, because she was a prostitute and feared the greedy hacks might nobble her for some low-life story about some of her clients. I don't want you to think she was in some way your typical tart-with-a-heart-type thing. I always think that's a patronising view. It implies that someone who's on the game, by the very nature of her profession, must lack sensitivity and compassion, so it's somehow fitting to place any exceptions to that in a neat little pigeonhole with a neat rhyming nickname. Anyway, she wasn't like that. She admitted her act of saving me was in some way a selfish thing, because Piccadilly always loomed in her mind as somewhere she might be sent if she wasn't too careful. I didn't mind, whether for me or her she did it, I was free, that's all that mattered. Before she went her way I asked for her address so I could write and thank her. She said she didn't want thanked, fair enough, but always in my mind she'll be remembered.

I must have looked a right sight in that newspaper office, uniform all askance and burrs sticking all over my socks and skirt, I dunno, wind's legacy still in my hair. I must've been bright pink in the face, I was still out of breath despite the car ride. I'd never seen so many men in all my life, smoking fags like they were all trying to be steam trains. They wore white shirts, with braces and ties, and were making a hell of a racket on their typewriters. The general hum of so many keys going together at once instantly reminded me of the machinery noise in the laundry rooms, only in the newsroom it wasn't the sort to wear me down. There was nothing that day as could have worn me down.

Anyway, that's how the inside story of Piccadilly managed to hit the headlines the next day. All my words came tumbling out, no holds barred. There was no detail I wouldn't tell them, and no detail they wanted me to spare. Just a few hours later, the full horrors as told by me were in black and white covering breakfast tables all over Scotland. And we were right, Bel's and my instincts proved an accurate measure of how society was feeling, at long last, about the antiquated treatment of women. Our unspoken prediction that public opinion might have shifted was partly responsible for our success.

News reached the powers that be just as it reached everyone else in the country. The outcry ensured that within two years Piccadilly Park was completely closed down. The building – a temple to society's shame – was guiltily demolished. The land it once stood on now hosts three windy tower blocks, and the hill we so dramatically ran down has been levelled to accommodate a shopping arcade. They may not constitute the eighth aesthetic wonder of the world, but if they stand as testimony to any small contribution I might have made in history to the betterment of women, then so be it.

Bel's part was no less vital, to be sure, probably more so. To my lifelong regret she was one of the women caught and taken back to the laundry by the police. In fact, only seven out of the thirty or so of us managed to get clean away. I think at the time I would have given my life that one of them had been Bel rather than the undeserving Melanie Chambers – who, incidentally, was last heard of still seeing Miss Salter somewhere in the Highlands, in respectable, but doubtless stroking seclusion.

When I had given my babbling story, I got the journalist to walk me to Glasgow Central station. It was the paper paid for my ticket south to Stoke, and funded the Mars bar which took me two or three sittings to finish and which I've to this day not forgot. The journalist probably couldn't believe his luck, that on a news-thin dreary Tuesday morning a young girl full of such sensation should just wander out the blue up to his desk. He felt a bit of human kindness was my due if it was to help me on the last lap of my escape.

Before the train left, he and I had a coffee together near the platform. I was shaking with fear – the bustle, the people, the very look of the world, it seemed all so strange and intimidating. But I managed to splutter my address at home, and get across that I wasn't going to be there long, I was going to become a midwife far away and live by the sea. I'd send him my new address, I muttered, just as soon as I arrived to start my new life. I made him make me a promise – to investigate whatever happened to Bel, even if it meant forcing his way through that huge wooden door at the park and tying up the staff for the necessary information. If she had been taken back, I said, he was to let Bel know that, wherever I ended up, even if it was Land's End, I would be campaigning on her behalf and that of all the others who never made it, for the closure of Piccadilly. And he was to let me know if there was any way specifically I could help her.

When a week or so later he did write to tell me he'd discovered she was still there, I made it my obsessive business to get her out just as soon as I could. I was sorting my life out, adjusting to the peculiar outside, trying to get away from my parents, and to organise my new life, but all this paled in comparison to the urgency with which I tried to save Bel from the Piccadilly purgatory.

To be honest, it didn't take much more than a little initiative but, even if it had, nothing would've deterred me. On Mother's and Father's newly installed telephone, I rang the London *Times*. It was a long shot, but I got straight through to a woman journalist, I think luck was on my side. And though Glasgow was far away from London, she seemed to know about places such as Piccadilly in other parts of Britain, and Ireland (where they were run by nuns and called Magdalene Laundries), and was surprisingly, gratifyingly, keen to hear what I had to tell her.

'I overheard the whole conversation on the phone,' Jessie tells Harold. 'Dot was amazing, I was so proud of her. We were worried they mightn't decide to use the piece, but two days later, there it was, in the London *Times*, dead on. We couldn't believe it, could we?'

I shake my head. 'Every time I think about it . . .' I can't help but pause to reflect.

'The laundry girls were released within the month,' Jessie tells Harold triumphantly. 'It took longer to get them to let the women upstairs go free, or to places where they could be properly cared for, another couple of years even, but it might've been longer if it hadn't been for Dot's and Bel's tireless efforts. Dot was all the while doing her midwifery training down here, but nothing would've stopped her. Letters to MPs and phone calls and all, whatever it took.'

'What happened to Bel?' Harold asks.

'She got married to the first man that came along,' I tell him. 'On the rare occasions a girl was released from the laundry because the staff felt she'd adequately proved to them her soul had been cleansed, we always used to tell her to find a man quick as she could, get married, have bairns, and then she'd not be stopped in this particular hell-hole again. Piccadilly never took married women, see, even if they went off the rails far more than any of us ever had. It was strictly single girls. I don't think Bel can ever have got that out of her mind. Even though she actually went to the demolition of Piccadilly, so really knew it was no more, I think it existed still very strongly in her mind long after, perhaps more for her than the rest of us, not just because she never left the Glasgow area, but also because she was that sort of imaginative character for whom the past would always pulsate and remain very immediate and real. I suspect the brainwashing we'd subjected each other to, to marry just as soon as we could, with Bel didn't just disintegrate along with the rubble of bricks. Gordon was the first man as came along, and she grabbed him while he was passing. It wasn't the romantic success she'd always been hoping for. Thankfully, after many gruelling years – she really did do her time, that one – she's married again and happier altogether now. And she certainly stuck to the bairns part of the bargain. I think she's had eight in all. We keep writing, so we do – letters and cards at Christmas kind of thing, and birthdays, not much more than that to be honest, because she's a busy woman. But as each birth happened she did always used to write – excuse my French, Harold – "Guess what Dot, it's a girl (or boy), and she's another beautiful fuck–you to the laundry." It was just that spirit of hers as got her in there, and all us lot out. I'll never forget her for that, and because of it will always keep in touch.'

Chapter Sixteen

There is silence between us for a moment or two, then Harold asks after the tiny little thing which had such mammoth consequences on my life.

I am taken aback, and look up at him, wondering how he knows something no one knows, and has hit so accurately upon the one last thing I've yet to tell him. He must have got to know me well very fast. He's come across that one thing in the world which has haunted me these thirty-three years and which I have never, ever talked about, not even with Jessie, not even though she's asked often enough. He's the only other person to have grasped there might be something else bothering me, and the only person other than her to have truly asked, though even if a thousand people had done so, I wouldn't have told them.

'Only if you want to tell me about it, mind,' he adds. 'It's none of my business.'

It is New Year's Day in Harold's house. It's about two in the morning. Jessie and the kids left to go back to the cottage about an hour and a half ago, soon after the six of us together had sung the New Year in. I've stayed behind tonight, for good. Harold and I we've been celebrating this wonderful development with a nightcap in his front room, we're both transported with joy.

Only there's been something niggling in my mind this evening, and it turns out he realised it all along. I thought I was covering it up because it doesn't do to be low on such a happy night as this. But he can read my moods already, and I can't lie to him, I can't.

So a few moments ago I told him I went to see Kelly today with the team's gift of sympathy, and she was being so brave, it was all I could do not to kneel down in front of her and bless her with my humble admiration. She was talking, I told him, about the future, for her and the children, and of how she'd told them they were all going to have to be good, courageous soldiers, and how they were going to be just fine because, although Daddy had gone to Heaven, he was still looking after them.

I admitted to Harold, even at the risk of spoiling our own evening, that just to think about what happened to them, I couldn't help it, it was haunting me, making me smart with anger. I promised him it wasn't often people saw Dot Sheffield like this, but I could get like it at times, about the little things, it was them made me angrier perhaps than anything in the world. I said, you know what I mean by the little things – either everyday inanimate objects, or fleeting incidents you don't even take in at the time, like Stevie misjudging by millimetres the set of a chair, they're almost as unconscious as looking at your watch, but it's these as can wreak such untold misery. Tiny, tiny things I'm talking. They make me mad, so they do. The *injustice*.

It was then he gently asked after the little thing that had so troubled my life.

'My encounter with Alf Whittaker, you mean?' I ask.

'The thing,' he replies, 'that got you sent to the laundry.'

'The pregnancy was what got me sent, of course,' I tell him, 'but it wasn't that that was the tragedy of my life. Far from it, I wouldn't not have had Eliza for all the world, despite the fact I never had her, if you see what I mean. It was the circumstances surrounding the pregnancy that's the tragedy. I've not told a soul in the world about them, Harold, all these years, I've not been able.'

'And you don't have to tell me either.'

'No, I want to, see. I'm longing to. You're the only person I've ever even thought of telling, and I've been wanting to tell you since that drink we had together after we bumped into each other at the clinic. It was when we were talking, I dunno, it just struck me you'd be the type to understand the little thing that's haunted me all these years almost more than any of it.'

He thanks me. We both take a sip of our nightcap – hot chocolate in my case, one small, neat whisky in his – and he offers me an After Eight from a new box I feel he went out and bought specially because he knew I was coming.

'I don't know if you can compare what's happened to poor Kelly with what happened to me when I was roughly her age. I didn't suffer the death of a loved one like her, but I suffered a bereavement of sorts, as the result of one of those small incidents I was just talking about, barely noticeable. The rest of my life I've been trying to remember every second of it to try to draw some significance out of it. I've not managed.'

Harold's hand is still on my knee, it's not shifted, and I don't want it to. I shut my mouth for at least a minute, thinking. He doesn't say anything either. It is not an uneasy silence. It's as easy as if I were alone. I love this man so much. I didn't know Dot Sheffield was capable of it. I didn't know a single individual could have all this love inside her, lying dormant so many years, then suddenly burst forth with such a vengeance as to give a menopausal constitution such as mine the shaking of a lifetime.

'I met Alf Whittaker in the spring of '61 when I'd already started nurse's training but was still coming home for weekends. He was from a village about ten miles away from ours but he moved to ours when he got a job in Stoke, in the Potteries, it was closer for him. I think he saw himself as a bit of a hot-shot round our parts. He was tall with blond hair, and he had a good job. He also got himself in the village cricket team, and the choir, very soon after he moved to Maidenwell. I spotted him first time in church because he had this beautiful voice, and would be singing better than all the other tenors, way better. But he was never concentrating on the song sheets. I think one of the reasons he joined the choir was so he'd have a good view of the village lasses. His eyes'd be swivelling round the congregation. It irritated the hell out of me, I remember. I thought, we can do without your eyeing up, thank you very much.

'My dad admired his voice, and embarrassed Beth and me by asking him to tea one Sunday. Complete stranger. I suppose in a small village in those days it wasn't so odd. My dad liked to vet the newcomers, befriend a potential new customer for his boot polish and plungers. That's maybe unfair, because Father was always genuinely hospitable too. Anyway Alf came. He was all right. Close up he was less irritating than when he was up near the altar posturing in his ruffle for all the girls. He was just your average lad with 1950s good manners and a way of charming his elders and betters. Beth and me, we didn't have much to say to him. We weren't practised in conversation, specially with men. We poured the tea and gave him scones and jam, but Father did all the talking, Lord knows now what about.

'I don't know when it was he decided Alf could be more than a potential customer, that he could be good enough for one of his daughters. After one or two of his three teatime visits, I suspect. Anyway he invited him to join us on our week-long annual holiday to Blackpool, and was accepted. That was one of the moments Father started playing the Wedding March on the piano, so I knew what he had in mind. We were all sat there at the table, eating Mother's blinking cake with little forks, and all I wanted to do was slam the lid down on Father's fingers. I swear to God I could have killed him.'

'What did you do?'

'Nothing. What could I do? Had to sit there and lump it. Just shows how powerless we were in those days. Today's young adults would have stormed out the room telling him where he could shove it!'

Harold chuckles.

'Anyway, it didn't seem to put Alf off. He still came to Blackpool. I don't think I had any feelings either way about his coming. We stayed in the same guest-house we always stayed in, did the same stuff we always did – beach during the day, shows on the pier at night. It was one more face at breakfast, I suppose, one more person to have an opinion on the weather, an extra hand to pass the salt to. Oh, Alf was friendly enough. He bought us all ice-creams in wafers one day, and Jessie dropped hers in the sand, she was only seven or so, the wee poppet. He bought her two more right away. I remember thinking that was a decent thing he did. I liked to see Jessie being treated well and with respect, so I warmed to him for that. But my recollections of him don't come much more than that really.'

I pause. Harold offers me another After Eight and I take one. A thread of the soft mint centre swings from between the dark chocolate and attaches itself to my chin. Harold reaches into his trouser pocket and hands me a clean cotton handkerchief. When I've dabbed away the stickiness, I start to fiddle with the black crinkly envelope the mint came in, folding and unfolding it while I talk.

'I did not fall in love with Alf. His presence wasn't disagreeable, but I never even fancied him. He asked me to accompany him on a walk through the town one night after the evening meal. Even when Father encouraged the idea, and barred Beth from joining us, I thought nothing of it. I thought it'd be nice to see the people out in their finery, to wander amongst them.

'It was a hot night, very hot, close, kind of thing. I was wearing this chintzy cotton dress with cream and dusky pink stripes, I remember, flowers entwined round the cream. Full skirt, tight bodice and a narrow belt to match, no sleeves, and a pale blue cardy knitted by Mother, little fake pearl buttons.' I stop suddenly. 'Goodness, I am giving you all the detail here.'

'I like the detail,' he reassures me. 'So as I can build up a proper picture.'

'Well, we walked the few streets from the guest-house down to the front. There was lots of activity. It was only about ten in the evening but it was dark. We strolled this way and that, hearing a band here, watching a bit of dancing there. Alf asked me to dance, but I said I'd like to walk down by the sea instead. I wanted to kick my shoes off. I didn't have any tights on, and the plastic was making my hot feet swell up. I was wanting a paddle in the water, that's all. I suppose I got my paddle, more than a bleeding paddle . . .' I drift off a moment. I've relived this night so many times, there's not a detail escapes me, and it's important to me to tell Harold them all. I want him to have the whole story. No lies. No omissions or half-truths. I want him to have it all. He doesn't prompt me, but it's a minute or two before I can carry on. I need to take some sharp breaths. This is high-altitude talk for the likes of Dot Sheffield. For thirty-three years she's been party to other people's revelations, especially women's of course, but has always concealed her own.

'We were walking on the sand the few yards towards the tall wooden struts which hold up the pier. Course I didn't know about under the pier at Blackpool. I can't say for sure Alf did either, but he must've known something, I mean nobody, but nobody, could've been as naive as me. There again, how was I to

276

know that that was where Blackpool's complete complement of Love's Young Dream traditionally headed every holiday night, away from parents' eyes, for illicit couplings between the sand and stars, and between each other? It was famous, but no one had told me. I knew about coupling *per se*, course I did, I was doing nurse's training, all the biology was at my fingertips, explained in my textbooks with diagrams and all. Only the actuality of sex was missing. It had never occurred to me folks could do it anywhere other than in bed. So when I heard unfathomable groaning issuing from heaving shadows between the black silhouttes of struts and outsize pebbles, I as likely as not thought I'd happened upon the Walrus and the Carpenter.' I shake my head. 'Unbelievable, really.

'Anyway, as we got closer, I thought it might be members of a gang having a fight, it was very, very dark under there, remember. It wasn't till we were only a few feet away that I realised my mistake, and that before me was any number of biology lessons going on. I swear there must have been twenty or thirty couples under there, maybe even more. Alf and I walked among them, trying to find a space to lie down I suppose, though I hadn't acknowledged that to myself at that point. I was just following him, looking at all the moving silhouettes, white flesh luminous in the blue of the dark. I knew it wasn't proper to look but my eyes were on stalks, and anyway these folk weren't so intent on noticing me to object. Eventually, Alf and I sat down on a space of sand, between a rock and a particularly vigorous biology lesson, unnecessarily noisy in my opinion. The under-the-pier sand was dank from lack of exposure to the daytime sun. I remember the tickling feeling of it as it made a patch through the cotton of my dress to my behind. Alf and I sat there for some minutes not talking or touching. I was thinking it would be more comfortable to be sitting in a nice pub or hotel lounge somewhere, and we could enjoy a lemonade or something then. As we sat there like puddings I became aware of an annoying piece of hair in my mouth. I tried to retrieve it but there was sand on my finger which left a salty grit in and around my teeth and tongue. I always remember this because later, at the laundry, we were made to clean our teeth with salt. Three times a day, then, I was reminded of the very sin which got me there in the first place, and which I was forever supposed to forget. The irony somehow.'

I wonder, briefly, whether to tell Harold the next bit, to continue not to spare him the details. Does he really want to know everything? On the other hand I want to tell him. Jessie once said when you get together with a man you should wipe the slate clean from the very outset, bring out all your skeletons from the cupboard. That way, there's nothing hidden between you, nothing either of you could get upset or angry about later on. That struck me as extravagantly foolish, and I told her so. In fact, I went further: I said I believed that was often the probable cause of many of her disappointed love affairs. No mystery at all. There's got to be honesty, yes, but also there's got to be mystery, surely? I'd tell her you have to strike a sensible balance between the two. But now I realise it's not so easy. I was always preaching, wasn't I, till it happened to me. I mean, if you're in love with someone, or even, as in many of Jessie's cases, you only think you are, there's the urge to tell them secrets, isn't there? I've never had this urge before. It is hellish strong, some's might say unmanageable. Why? I think it's that you want to give them all of you. I could say, I'm very lucky only to have had the urge with one person. After one of her break-ups, I can't remember which now, Jessie told me – in rather too graphic terms I thought, but vivid all the same – that she felt a bit like a road accident. There were pieces of her scattered all over the place, up and down the highways of England, from Stoke to Shepherd's Bush. She said she wished she was like me and had kept herself together so some day she could give the whole of herself to one person.

'I noticed Alf Whittaker was breathing quite rapidly, but I didn't comment on it. All this groaning was still going on around us, and I was still listening agog. We were sat there what must have been ten minutes. Then, just like that, in a sudden burst like a sports car going from nought to sixty, he kissed me – the taste of his tongue was very bland, a mild soft cheese, only milder – undid my zip, had his hand up behind my bra, my knickers down to my knees, and was protruding into my thigh. I had a bit of rock or wood or something else protruding into my shoulder too. I remember thinking what an extraordinary thing it was that a bit of a person could feel as hard as a rock, but that that was Mother Nature for you. His hands were nice and surprisingly soft on my back and arms and neck, in fact his chest and abdomen felt softer than I'd ever felt the softness of someone else's flesh against mine. In Blackpool where at the guest-house there was a bath, I used to lift Jessie out of it sometimes and she'd cling herself round me in a hug and I'd feel her hot little body, but then only through my clothes and her towel. I suppose his body was warm, although the warmth of a man is intimate. I don't really care to remember his warmth. So, anyway, he did the business.

'Alf never raped me that night, Harold. I consented to it. But nor was it a grand and noble passion like something out of poetry or literature. How can I describe the experience? It wasn't horrid, but nor was it ecstatic. I'd compare the pleasure to that when you clean out your ears with a cotton bud. Satisfying enough, but hardly memorable. I only remember the whole episode in such detail because of the amount of times I've forced myself since to go over it in my head. If I hadn't 'fallen away' as they used to say in the laundry, the loss of my virginity would have ever remained hazy in my mind. As it was, this trifling little occurrence got me banged up for nine years, so I've not been allowed to forget it.'

I am coming to the end of my long tale, and already a weight feels as if it's lifting off of me. I'm to have the strength to go the final stretch. I look into Harold's eyes.

'The truth is, Harold, I've often wished it were a rape. If it had been, the violence of that event would have somehow seemed equal to the horror of my incarceration: injustice for injustice. Had I loved the man so that the rages of passion had given me no choice but sensationally to make love to him, I'd have been able better, probably even willingly, to have endured the sacrifice of nine years imprisoned. As it was, I had nearly a decade put away for naught but a sandy but warm grapple under the pier at Blackpool which, under normal circumstances I'd have had no more regard for than a book I'd enjoyed reading well enough but not so much as I'd bother to recommend it to a friend. It's that that's been the cause of so much torment, and the source of all my shame.'

There, I've told it all. There is nothing more to tell. Harold doesn't say a word. What more's there for him to add? Perhaps he's horrified.

My half-finished mug of hot chocolate has grown cold at our feet, and his glass is empty. Jones is asleep. I dread to think the time.

Then Harold leans over and he kisses me. He's far from horrified. My eyes close.

This is one of those moments which has its own consequences, consequences that are far from trifling.